The Malady

Max Simon Nordau

Alpha Editions

This edition published in 2022

ISBN : 9789356715974

Design and Setting By
Alpha Editions
www.alphaedis.com
Email - info@alphaedis.com

As per information held with us this book is in Public Domain.
This book is a reproduction of an important historical work. Alpha Editions uses the best technology to reproduce historical work in the same manner it was first published to preserve its original nature. Any marks or number seen are left intentionally to preserve its true form.

Contents

CHAPTER I. .... - 1 -
   MOUNTAIN AND FOREST. .... - 1 -
CHAPTER II. .... - 24 -
   VANITIES OF VANITIES. .... - 24 -
CHAPTER III. .... - 40 -
   HEROES. .... - 40 -
CHAPTER IV. .... - 60 -
   IT WAS NOT TO BE. .... - 60 -
CHAPTER V. .... - 81 -
   A LAY SERMON. .... - 81 -
CHAPTER VI. .... - 99 -
   AN IDYLL. .... - 99 -
CHAPTER VII. .... - 114 -
   SYMPOSIUM. .... - 114 -
CHAPTER VIII. .... - 129 -
   DARK DAYS. .... - 129 -
CHAPTER IX. .... - 154 -
   RESULTS. .... - 154 -
CHAPTER X. .... - 181 -
   A SEASIDE ROMANCE. .... - 181 -
CHAPTER XI. .... - 204 -
   IN THE HORSELBERG .... - 204 -
CHAPTER XII. .... - 232 -
   TANNHAUSER'S FLIGHT. .... - 232 -
CHAPTER XIII. .... - 257 -
   CONSUMMATION. .... - 257 -

CHAPTER XIV. ....- 277 -
    UDEN HORIZO. ....- 277 -

CHAPTER I.

MOUNTAIN AND FOREST.

"Come, you fellows, that's enough joking. This defection of yours, melancholy Eynhardt, combines obstinacy with wisdom, like Balaam's ass! Well! may you rest in peace. And now let us be off."

The glasses, filled with clear Affenthaler, rang merrily together, the smiling landlord took up his money, and the company rose noisily from the wooden bench, overturning it with a bang. The round table was only proof against a similar accident on account of its structure, which some one with wise forethought had so designed that only the most tremendous shaking could upset its equilibrium. The boisterous group consisted of five or six young men, easily recognized as students by their caps with colored bands, the scars on their faces, and their rather swaggering manner. They slung their knapsacks on, stepped through the open door of the little arbor where they had been sitting, on to the highroad, and gathered round the previous speaker. He was a tall, good-looking young man, with fair hair, laughing blue eyes, and a budding mustache.

"Then you are determined, Eynhardt, that you won't go any further?" asked he, with an accent which betrayed him as a Rhinelander.

"Yes, I am determined," Eynhardt answered.

"A groan for the worthless fellow; but more in sorrow than in anger," said the tall one to the others. They groaned three times loudly, all together, while the Rhinelander gravely beat time. An unpracticed ear would very likely have failed to note the shade of feeling implied in the noise; but he appeared satisfied.

"Well, just as you like. No compulsion. Freedom is the best thing in life—including the freedom to do stupid things."

"Perhaps he knows of some cave where he is going to turn hermit," said one of the group.

"Or he has a little business appointment, and we should be in the way," said another.

They laughed, and the Rhinelander went on:

"Well! moon away here, and we will travel on. But before all things be true to yourself. Don't forget that the whole world is as much a phantom as the brown Black Forest maiden. And now farewell; and think a great deal about us phantom people, who will always keep up the ghost of a friendship for you."

The young man whom he addressed shook him and the others by the hand, and they all lifted their caps with a loud "hurrah," and struck out vigorously on the road. The sentiment of the farewell, and the tender speeches, had been disposed of in the inn, so they now parted gayly, in youth's happy fullness of life and hope for the future, and without any of that secret melancholy which Time the immeasurable distils into every parting. Hardly had they turned their backs on the friend they left behind them when they began to sing, "Im Schwarzen Walfisch zu Askalon," exaggerating the melancholy of the first half of the tune, and the gayety of the second, passing riotously away behind a turn of the road, their song becoming fainter and fainter in the distance.

This little scene, which took place on an August afternoon in the year 1869, had for its theater the highroad leading from Hausach to Triberg, just at the place where a footpath descends into the valley to the little town of Hornberg. The persons represented were young men who had lately graduated at Heidelberg, and who were taking a holiday together in the Black Forest, recovering from the recent terrors of examination in the fragrant air of the pine woods. As far off as Offenburg they had traveled by the railway in the prosaic fashion of commercial travelers, from there they had tramped like Canadian backwoodsmen, and reached Hasslach—twelve miles as the crow flies. After resting for a day they set out at the first cockcrow, and before the noontide heat reached the lovely Kinzigthal, which lies all along the way from Hausach to Hornberg. Over the door of a wayside inn a signboard, festooned with freshly-cut carpenter's shavings, beckoned invitingly to them, and here the young men halted. The view from this place was particularly beautiful. The road made a kind of terrace halfway up the mountain, on one side rising sheer up for a hundred feet to its summit, thickly wooded all the way, on the other side sloping to the wide valley, where the Gutach flowed, at times tumbling over rough stones, or again spreading itself softly like oil, through flat meadow land. Below lay the little town of Hornberg, with its crooked streets and alleys, its stately square, framing an old church, several inns, and prosperous-looking houses and shops. Beyond the valley rose a high, steep hill, with a white path climbing in zigzags through its wooded sides. On the summit a white house with many windows was perched, seeming to hang perpendicularly a thousand feet above the valley. Its whitewashed walls stood out sharply against the background of green pine trees, clearly visible for many miles round. A conspicuous inscription in large black letters showed that this audacious and picturesque house was the Schloss hotel, and a glance at the gray ruined tower which rose behind it gave at once a meaning to the name. Behind the hill, with its outline softened by trees and encircled by the blue sky, were ridges of other hills in parallel lines meeting the horizon, alternately sharp-edged and rounded, stretching from north to south. They seemed like some great sea, with majestic wave-hills and wave-valleys; behind the first appeared a second, then a third, then a fourth, as far as one's eye could see; each one of a distinct tone of color, and of all the shades from the deepest green through blue and violet to vaporous pale gray.

The sight of this picture had decided Wilhelm Eynhardt not to go any further. The others had resolved to push on to Triberg the same day, and above all, not to turn back till they had bathed in the Boden-see. As every persuasion was powerless to alter Eynhardt's decision, they separated, and the travelers started on their walk to Triberg. Eynhardt, however, stayed at Hornberg, meaning to climb to the Schloss hotel again from the other side.

Wilhelm Eynhardt was a young man of twenty-four, tall and slim of figure, with a strikingly handsome face. His eyes were almond-shaped, not large but very dark, with much charm of expression. The finely-marked eyebrows served by their raven blackness to emphasize the whiteness of the forehead, which was crowned by an abundant mass of curling black hair. His fresh complexion had still the bloom of early youth, and would hardly have betrayed his age, if it had not been shaded by a dark brown silky beard, which had never known a razor. It was an entirely uncommon type, recalling in profile, Antinous, and the full face reminding one of the St. Sebastian of Guido Roni in the museum of the Capitol; a face of the noblest manhood, without a single coarse feature. His manner, although quiet, gave the impression of keen enthusiasm, or, more rightly speaking, of unworldly inspiration. All who saw him were powerfully attracted, but half-unconsciously felt a slight doubt whether even so fine a specimen of manhood was quite fitly organized and equipped for the strife of existence. At the university he had been given the nickname of Wilhelmina, on account of a certain gentleness and delicacy of manner, and because he neither drank nor smoked. Such jokes, not ill-natured, were directed against his outward appearance, but had a shade of meaning as regards his character.

As Wilhelm walked into the courtyard of the Schloss hotel he stopped a moment to regain his breath. Before him was the stately new house, whose white-painted walls and many windows had looked down on the high-road; to the left stood the round tower inclosed within a ruined wall, shading an airy lattice-work building, in which on a raised wooden floor stood a table and some benches. Several people, evidently guests at the hotel, sat there drinking wine and beer, and eying the newcomer curiously. The burly landlord, in village dress, emerged from the open door of the cellar in the tower, and wished him "good-day." He had a thick beard and a sunburned face, with good-natured blue eyes. With a searching glance at the young man's cap and knapsack, he waited for Wilhelm to speak.

"Can I have a room looking on to the valley?" asked the latter.

"Not at this moment," the landlord answered, clearing his throat loudly; "there is hardly a room free here, and that only in the top story. But to-morrow, or the day after, many people are leaving, and then I can give you what you want."

Wilhelm's face clouded with disappointment, but only for a moment, then he said: "Very well, I will stay."

"Luggage?" said the landlord, in his short, unceremonious way. "My luggage is at Haslach. It can come up to-morrow."

"Bertha," called the landlord, in such a strident tone that the mountains echoed the sound. The visitors drinking in the kiosk smiled; they were well accustomed to the man. A neat red-cheeked girl appeared in the doorway. "Number 47," shouted the landlord, and went off to his other duties.

Bertha led the new guest up three flights of uncarpeted wooden staircase, down a long passage to a light, clean, but sparely-furnished room. The girl told him the hours of meals, brought some water, and left him alone. He hung his knapsack on a hook on the wall, opened the little window, and gazed long at the view. Underneath was the open space where he had been standing, to the left the tower, and behind, over the ruined walls, he could see the old, neglected castle yard full of weeds and heaps of rubbish—a picture of decay and desolation.

"I have chosen well," thought Wilhelm, for he loved solitude, and promised himself enjoyable hours of wandering in the ruins in company with luxuriant flowers and singing birds.

He barely gave himself time to freshen his face with cold water, and to change his thick walking shoes for lighter ones; immediately hurrying out to make acquaintance with the castle. Before he could get there he had first to find in the tumbledown wall a hole large enough to enable him to get through. He shortly found himself in a fairly large square space, the uneven ground being formed of a mass of rubbish, mounds of earth, and deep holes. Woods protected the greater part of it, most of the trees stunted and choked by undergrowth and shrubs, with occasionally a high, solitary pine tree, and near to the west and south walls half-withered oaks and mighty beeches stood thickly. Here and there from the bushes peeped up bare pieces of crumbling stone and broken pieces of mortar, in whose crevices hung long grasses, and where yellow, white, and red flowers nestled. Climbing, stumbling, and slipping, he worked his way through this wilderness, the length and breath of which he wished to inspect so as to discover a place where he could rest quietly, when he suddenly came to a precipitous fall of the ground, concealed from him by a thick curtain of leaves. Startled and taken by surprise, the ground seemed to him to sink under his feet. He instinctively caught hold of some branches to keep himself from falling, pricking his hands with the thorns, and breaking a slender bough, finally rolling in company with dust and earth, torn-out bushes and stone, down a steep declivity of several feet to a little grass plot at the bottom. He heard a slight scream near him, and a girlish form sprang up and cried in an anxious voice:

"Have you hurt yourself?"

Wilhelm picked himself up as quickly as he could, brushed the earth from his clothes, and taking off his cap said, "Thanks, not much. Only a piece of awkwardness. But I am afraid I have frightened you?" he added.

"A little bit; but that is all right."

They looked at each other for the first time, and the lady laughed, while Wilhelm blushed deeply. She stopped again directly, blushed also, and dropped her eyes. She was a girl in the first bloom of youth, of particularly fine and well-made figure, with a beautiful face; two dimples in her cheeks giving her a roguish expression, and a pair of lively brown eyes. A healthy color was in her cheeks, and in the well-cut, seductive little mouth. Her luxuriant, golden-brown hair, in the fashion of the day, was brushed back in long curls. She had as her only ornament a pale gold band in her hair, and wore a simple dress of light-flowered material, the high waistband fitting close to the girlish figure. Conventionality began to assert its rights over nature, and the girl too felt confused at finding herself in the middle of a conversation with a strange man, suddenly shot down at her very feet. Wilhelm understood and shared her embarrassment, and bowing, he said:

"As no doubt we are at the same house, allow me to introduce myself. My name is Wilhelm Eynhardt. I come from Berlin, and took up my abode an hour ago at the Schloss hotel."

"From Berlin," said the girl quickly; "then we are neighbors. That is very nice. And where do you live in Berlin, if I may ask?"

"In Dorotheenstrasse."

"Of course you do," and a clear laugh deepened the shadow of her dimples.

"Why 'of course?'" asked Wilhelm, rather surprised.

"Why, because that is our Latin quarter, and as a student—you are a student, I suppose?"

"Yes, and no. In the German sense I am no longer a student, for I took my degree a year ago; but the word in English is better and truer, as there 'student' is used where we should say scholar (gelehrter). Scholars we are, not only learners. In the English sense then I am a student, and hope to remain so all my life."

"Ah, you speak English," she said, quickly catching at the word; "that is charming. I am tremendously fond of English, and am quite accustomed to it, as I spent a great part of my time in England when I was very young. I have been told that I have a slight English accent in speaking German. Do you think so?"

"My ear is not expert enough for that," said Wilhelm apologetically.

"My friends," she chattered on, "nearly all speak French; but I think English is much more uncommon. Fluent English in a German is always proof of good education. Don't you think so?"

"Not always," said Wilhem frankly; "it might happen that one had worked as a journeyman in America."

The girl turned up her nose a little at this rather unkind observation, but Wilhelm went on:

"With your leave I would rather keep to our mother-tongue. To speak in a foreign language with a fellow-country-woman without any necessity would be like acting a charade, and a very uncomfortable thing."

"I think a charade is very amusing," she answered; "but just as you like. Opportunities of speaking English are not far to seek. Most of the visitors at the hotel are English. I dare say you have noticed it already. But they are not the best sort. They are common city people, who even drop their h's, but who play at being lords on the Continent. Of course I have learned already to tell a 'gentleman' from a 'snob.'"

Wilhelm smiled at the self-conscious importance with which she spoke. His eyes wandered over her beautiful hair, to the tender curve of her slender neck and beautiful shoulders, while she, feeling perfectly secure again, settled herself comfortably. Her seat was a projecting piece of stone, which had been converted by a soft covering of moss into a delightful resting-place. An overhanging bush shaded it pleasantly. In front lay a corner of the castle; across a smooth piece of turf and through a wide gap in the wall they caught a view of the mountains, as if painted by some artist's brush—a perfect composition which would have put the crowning touch to his fame. The girl had been trying to make a sketch of the view in a well-worn sketchbook which lay near.

"You have given a sufficient excuse for your sketches by your feeling for natural beauty," remarked Wilhelm. "May I look at the page?"

"Oh," she said, somewhat confused, "my will is of the best, but I can do so little," and she hesitatingly gave him her album. He took it and also the pencil, looked alternately at the mountains and on the page of the book, and without asking leave began to improve upon it, strengthening a line here, lightening a shadow and giving greater breadth, and then growing deeply interested in his work, he sat down without ceremony on the mossy bank, took a piece of india-rubber, and erasing here, adding lines there, sometimes laying in a shadow, giving strength to the foreground and lightness to the background, he ended by making a really pretty and artistic sketch.

The girl had watched him wonderingly, and said as he returned the album, "But you are a great artist," and without letting him speak she went on, "and by your appearance I had taken you for a student! But you are not in the least like a student, nor in fact like a German either. I have often met Indian princes in society in London, and I think you are very much like them."

Wilhelm smiled. "There is a grain of truth in what you say, although you overrate it a little. A great artist I certainly am not, nor even a little one, but I have always observed much and painted a good deal myself, and originally I thought of devoting myself to an artist's career; and if I have nothing in common with Indian princes, and am merely a plebeian German, I very likely have a drop of Indian blood in my veins."

"Really," she said, with curiosity.

"Yes, my mother was a Russian German living in Moscow, and whose father, a Thuringian, had married a Russian girl of gypsy descent. Through this grandmother, whom I never knew, I am related by remote genealogical descent to Indians. But you do not look like a German either, with your beautiful dark hair and eyebrows."

She took this personal compliment in good part as she answered quickly:

"There is some reason for that too. Just as you have Indian, I have French blood in my veins. My father's mother was a Colonial, her maiden name was Du Binache."

So they gossiped on like old acquaintances. Young and beautiful as they were, they found the deepest pleasure in one another, and the cold feeling of strangeness melted as by a charm. They were awakened to the consciousness that half an hour earlier neither of them had an idea of the other's existence, by the appearance of a girl in the gap in the wall, who seemed very much surprised at the sight of their evident intimacy. The young lady stood up rather hastily and went a few steps toward the newcomer, a servant-maid, who had brought a cloak for her mistress, and took charge of her album, sunshade, and large straw hat.

"Is it so late already?" she said, with a naive surprise, which left no room for doubt even to Wilhelm's modesty.

"Certainly, fraulein," said the maid, pointing with her hand to the distant mountain, whose peaks were already clothed with the orange hue of twilight; then she looked alternately at her young mistress and the strange gentleman, whose handsome face she inwardly noted.

"Do you think of making any stay here?" asked the young lady of Wilhelm, who followed slowly.

"Yes, certainly," he answered at once.

"Then we may become good friends. My parents will be glad to make your acquaintance. I did not tell you before that my father is Herr Ellrich."

As Wilhelm merely bowed, without seeming to recognize the name, she said rather sharply, and slightly raising her voice:

"I thought as you came from Berlin you would be sure to know my father's name—Councilor Ellrich, Vice-President of the 'Seehandlung.'"

The name and title made very little impression on Wilhelm, but his politeness brought forth an "Ah!" which satisfied Fraulein Ellrich. They left the ruins by an easy path which Wilhelm had not noticed before, and walked together to the entrance of the hotel, where she took leave of him by an inclination of her head. He betook himself to his room in a dream, and while he recalled to his mind the picture of her beautiful face, and the clear ring of her voice, he thought how grateful he was to this chance, that not only had he become acquainted with the girl, but that he had avoided in such a glorious fashion the discomfort of a formal introduction. Also Wilhelm knew himself well, and felt sure that, badly endowed as he was for forming new acquaintances, he could never have become friends with Fraulein Ellrich apart from the accident of his fall in the castle yard.

Dinner was served at separate tables where single guests might take it as they pleased, and Wilhelm was absentminded and dreamy when he sat down. He scarcely glanced at the large, cool dining-room, ornamented with engravings of portraits of the Grand Dukes of Baden and their wives. Six large windows looked into the valley of the Gutach with its little town of Hornberg, and the mountains lying beyond. He hardly noticed the rather silent people at the other tables, in which the English element predominated. He had come in purposely late in the hope of finding Fraulein Ellrich already there. She was not present; but he was not kept long in suspense before a waiter opened the door, and the lovely girl appeared accompanied by a stately gentleman and a stout lady. They seemed to be known to the servants, for as soon as they appeared the headwaiter and his subordinates rushed toward them, and with many bows and scrapes took their wraps from them and ushered them to their places.

Wilhelm, who possessed very little knowledge of society, was somewhat at a loss. Ought he to recognize the young lady? If he followed his inclination, he certainly would do so. But her parents! They seemed to be cold and reserved-looking. Happily all fell out for the best. The Ellrichs walked straight to the table where he was sitting, and in a moment Wilhelm was greeting his lovely acquaintance with a low bow. Her quick eyes had already recognized him from the doorway. She returned his greeting smiling and blushing, and as her father nodded kindly, the ice was broken. Wilhelm introduced himself, and the councilor gave him the tips of his fingers and said: "If you have no objection we will sit at your table." His wife, who gazed at Wilhelm through a gold "pince-nez" with hardly concealed surprise, took her place next to him; on the other side sat her husband, and opposite the daughter's face smiled at him.

The councilor was a well-preserved man of about fifty, of good height, dressed in a well-made gray traveling suit, with a light gray silk tie adorned with a pin of black pearl. His closely-cut hair was very thin, and had almost disappeared from the top of his head. His chin was clean-shaven, but his well-brushed whiskers and closely-cut mustache showed signs of gray. His light blue eyes were cold and rather tired-looking, at the corners of the mouth were evident signs of indolence, and his whole appearance gave an impression of self-consciousness mixed with indifference toward the rest of mankind; his wife, stout, blooming, and tranquil, appeared to be a kindly soul.

The conversation opened trivially on the circumstances of Wilhelm meeting with Fraulein Ellrich, and on the beauty of the neighborhood, which Herr Ellrich glorified as not being overrun.

"I would much rather recommend it for quiet than Switzerland with its crowds," he said.

Wilhelm agreed with him, and related how he was induced by the romantic aspect of the place to give up his original plans, and to anchor himself here. When they questioned him, he gave them some information about Heidelberg and his journey to Hornberg. Frau Ellrich complimented him on his sketch, and while he modestly disclaimed the praise, she asked him why he had not devoted himself to art.

"That is a peculiar result of my development," answered Wilhelm thoughtfully. "While I was still at the gymnasium I sketched and painted hard, and after the final examination I went to the Art Academy for two years; but the further I went into the study of art, and the more attentively I followed in the beaten track of art-studies, the clearer it was to me that he who would secure an abiding success in art must be a blind copyist of nature. Certainly the personal peculiarities of an artist often please his contemporaries. It is the fashion to do him honor if he flatters the prevailing direction of taste. But those of the race who follow after, scorn what those before them have admired, and exactly what those of one time have prized as progressive innovations, they who come after reject as mere aberration. What the artist has himself accomplished, I mean his so-called personal comprehension or his capricious interpretation of nature, passes away; but what he simply and honorably reproduces, as he has truly seen it, lives forever, and the remotest age will gladly recognize in such art-work its old acquaintance, unchanging nature."

Fraulein Ellrich hung on his words in astonishment, while her parents calmly went on eating their fish.

"So," went on Wilhelm, speaking chiefly to his opposite neighbor, "so, I tried when I drew or painted to reproduce nature with the greatest truth; but at a certain point I became conscious of a perception that a hidden meaning in an unintelligible language lay written there. The form of things, and also every so-called accident of form, appeared to me to be the necessary expression of something within, which was hidden from me. The wish arose in me to penetrate behind the visible face of nature, to know why she appears in such a way, and not in another. I wanted to learn the language, the words of which, with no understanding of their sense, I had been slavishly copying; and so I turned to the study of physical science."

"So your two years at the Art School were not wasted," remarked Herr Ellrich.

"Certainly not, for to an observer of natural objects it is most valuable to have a trained eye for form and color."

"Yes, and beside, drawing and painting are such charming accomplishments, and so useful to a young man in society."

"Playing the piano and singing are still more so," put in Frau Ellrich.

"But dancing most of all," cried Fraulein Ellrich. "Do you dance?"

"No," answered Wilhelm shortly.

The words jarred upon him, and a silence ensued.

The councilor broke this with the question:

"Then you are a doctor of physical science?"

"Yes, sir."

"What is your particular department? Zoology, botany?"

"I have principally studied chemistry and physics, and I think of devoting myself to the latter."

"Physics, oh yes. A wide and beautiful sphere. So much is included in it. Electricity, galvanism, magnetism—those are all new faculties very little known; and as regards submarine telegraph the knowledge cannot be too useful."

"These sides of the question have not hitherto interested me. I ask of physics the unlocking of the nature of things. It has not yet given me the key, but it is something to know on what insecure, weak, and limited experiments our vaunted knowledge of the existence of the world of energy, of matter and their properties, depend."

Frau Ellrich looked at him approvingly.

"You speak beautifully, Herr Eynhardt, and it must be a great enjoyment to hear you lecture."

"You will soon have a professorship, I suppose?" remarked Herr Ellrich, turning around to the blushing Wilhelm.

"Oh, no!" said he quickly, "I do not aspire to that; I believe in Faust's verse: 'Ich ziehe... meine Schuler an der Nase herum—Und sehe dass wir nichts wissen konnen;' and I also bilde mir nicht ein, Ich konnte was lehren.' I wonder at and envy the men who teach such things with so much influence and conviction, and I am very grateful to them for initiating me into their methods and power of working properly. But there has never been a likelihood of my venturing to approach young men and saying to them, 'You must work with me for three years earnestly and diligently, and I will lead you to knowledge, so that at last, through the contents of a book, you may get a flying glimpse of the phantom which has so often eluded you.'"

"Your opinions are very interesting," said Herr Ellrich; "but a professorship is still the one practical goal for a man who studies physics. Forgive me if I express my meaning bluntly; there is money to be made in physics through a professorship."

"Happily I am in a position which makes it unnecessary for me to work for my bread."

"That is quite another thing," said the councilor in a friendly way, while his wife cast a quick glance over Wilhelm's clothes, unfashionable and rather worn, but scrupulously clean.

"One can see that this idealist neglects his outward appearance," her good-natured glance, half-apologetic, half-compassionate, seemed to say.

Herr Ellrich changed the conversation to the management of the hotel; discussing for a time the Margrave's wines, the south German cookery, the Black Forest tourists, and a variety of other minor topics. He then asked his daughter:

"Now, Loulou, have you made a programme for to-morrow yet? She is our maitre de plaisir," he explained to Wilhelm.

"A frightfully difficult post," exclaimed Loulou. "Papa and mamma love quiet; I like moving about, and I endeavor to harmonize the two."

Wilhelm thought that the opposing tasks would very soon be harmonized if Loulou subordinated her inclinations to her parents' comfort; but he kept his thoughts to himself.

"I vote that to-morrow morning we go for a little drive. As to the afternoon, we can arrange that later. Perhaps Dr.——" She stopped short, and her mother came to her help and completed the invitation.

"It would be very kind of you to join us."

"I am only afraid that I might be in the way."

"Oh, no; certainly not," said the mother and daughter together, and Herr Ellrich nodded encouragingly.

Wilhelm felt that the invitation was meant cordially, and his fear of obtruding himself overcome, he accepted.

Circumstances at the castle very greatly favored Wilhelm's intercourse with the Ellrich's, or rather with Loulou. In this house on the summit of the hill they met constantly in close companionship. Frau Ellrich enjoyed nothing better than walking on the arm of this handsome young man up and down the wooded slopes, as till now she had been obliged to go without such escort. Herr Ellrich liked to take his holiday in a different way from the ladies. If he felt obliged to take exercise he would borrow the landlord's gun and dogs and shoot. At other times he would lie down anywhere on a plaid on the grass, smoke a cigar, and read foreign papers like the Times from beginning to end. The afternoon was taken up by a nap, and in the evening he would be ready to hear an account of how his family had spent the day—perhaps in a long carriage excursion through the neighboring valleys.

Frau Ellrich was in the habit of appearing at the first table d'hote, and then doing homage to the peaceful custom of afternoon sleep. In the first cool hours of the morning she walked a little in the perfumed air of the pine woods, and the rest of the time she devoted to a voluminous correspondence, which seemed to be her one passion. Thus Loulou was alone nearly always in the morning, and frequently in the afternoon as well, and quite contented to ramble with Wilhelm through the woods, or to sit with him in the ruins, where they learned to know each other, and chattered without ceasing.

The subject of conversation mattered not. They had the story of their short lives to relate to one another. Loulou's was soon told. Her narrative was like the merry warbling of birds, and was from beginning to end the story of a serene dream of spring. She was the only child of her parents, who in spite of outward indifference and apparent coldness adored her, and had never denied her anything. The first fifteen years of her life were spent in her charming nest, in the beautiful house in the Lennestrasse, where she was born. "When we return to Berlin you shall see how pleasant my home is. I will show you my little blue sitting-room, my winter garden, my aviary, my parrots and blackbirds." A heavy trial had befallen her—the only trial that she had yet experienced. She had been sent to England for the completion of her education, and had to suddenly part from all her home surroundings. She stayed there for three years with an aunt who had married an English banker. The visit proved delightful, and she grew to love England enthusiastically. She drove and rode, and even followed the hounds. In winter there was the pantomime at Drury Lane, the flights to St. Leonards, Hastings, Leamington, the mad rides across country through frosted trees behind the hounds in full cry; in summer during the season there were parties, balls, the opera, the park; then in the holidays splendid travels with papa and mamma, once to Belgium, France, and the Rhine, another time to Switzerland and Italy, then to Heligoland and Norway. No, she could never have such good times again. In the following year she went back to Berlin, and had spent a very agreeable winter, a subscription ball, several other balls, innumerable soirees, a box at the opera, lovely acquaintances, with naturally many successes—the envy of false friends, but she did not allow herself to be much disturbed by them.

Wilhelm listened to this chatter with mixed feelings. If she seemed superficial, he reconciled himself by a glance at her beautiful silken hair, at her laughing brown eyes, at her roguish dimples, and instantly he pleaded with his cooler reason for pardon for the lovely girl—he for nineteen years had had other things beside pleasure to think of! These charms seemed enough to work the taming magic of Orpheus over the wild animals of the woods.

"And you were never," he asked timidly as she paused, "a little bit in love?"

"I can look after myself," she answered, with a silvery laugh, and Wilhelm felt as if an iron band had been lifted from his heart, like the trusty Henry's in the story.

"That points to marvelous wisdom in a child of society—seeing so many people—so attractive! You are indifferent then to admiration?"

"I did not say that. My fancy has been often enough touched, but—"

"But your heart has not?"

"No."

"Really not?" continued he, in a tone of voice in which, he himself detected the anxiety.

She shook her head, and looked down thoughtfully. But after a short pause she raised her rosy face and said, "No—better die than speak untruths—I was rather in love with our pastor who confirmed me. He was thin and pale with long hair, much longer than yours. And he spoke very beautifully and powerfully—I felt sentimental when I thought of him. But I soon got to know his wife, who was as pointed and hard as a knitting needle, and his children, whose number I never could count exactly, and my youthful feelings received a severe chill." She laughed, and Wilhelm joined her heartily.

It was now his turn to relate his story. He was as to his birthplace hardly a German, but a Russian, as he first saw the light in Moscow, in the year 1845.

"So you are now twenty-four?"

"Last May. Are you frightened at such an age, fraulein?"

"That is not so old, twenty-four—particularly for a man," she protested with great earnestness.

His father, he went on, was from Konigsberg, had studied philology, and when he left the university had become a tutor in a distinguished Russian family. He was the child of poor parents, and had to take the first opportunity which presented itself of earning his living. So he went to Russia, where he lived for twenty years as a tutor in private families, and then as a teacher in a Moscow gymnasium. He married late in life, an only child of German descent, who helped her middle-aged husband by a calm observance of duty and a mother's love for his children. "My mother was a remarkable woman. She had dark eyes and hair, and an enthusiastic and devoted expression in her face, which made me feel sad, as a child, if I looked at her for long. She spoke little, and then in a curious mixture of German and Russian. Strangely enough, she always called herself a German, and spoke Russian like a foreigner; but later, when we went to Berlin, she discovered that she was really a Russia, and always wished she were back in Moscow, never feeling at home amid her new surroundings. She was a Protestant like her father, but had inherited from her Russian mother a lingering affection for the orthodox faith, and she often used to go to the Golden Church of the Kremlin, whose brown, holy images had a mystical effect on her. She loved to sing gypsy songs in a low voice. She would not teach them to us. She was always very quiet, and preferred being alone with us to any society or entertainment."

When Wilhelm was four years old there came a little sister, a bright, light-haired, blue-eyed creature after her father's heart. She was named Luise, but she was always called Blondchen. She was his only playfellow, as the irritable father in Moscow cared for no acquaintances. His father's one wish was to return to his home, but for a long time the mother would not have it so. At last, in the year 1858, he accomplished his wish. He was then sixty-three years old, and he represented to his wife that after his life of unremitting work, now in its undoubted decline, he had a right to spend the last few years in peace in his native land. He possessed enough for his family to live on; the children would grow and get a better education than in Russia, and above all he wished to keep his Prussian nationality. The mother yielded, and so they came to Berlin, where the father bought a modest house near the Friedrich-Wilhelm gymnasium. This house was now Wilhelm's property. "We children liked Berlin very much. I soon became independent and self-reliant, after school hours wandering in the streets as much as I pleased, and used to make eager explorations in all directions, coming home enraptured when I had found a beautiful neighborhood, a stately house, a statue of some general in bronze or marble. I used to take Blondchen by the hand, and show her my discovery. The Friedrichstadt with its straight streets interested us very much; I had a fancy that the houses were marshaled in battalions, as if by an officer on parade, and that when he gave the word 'March,' they would suddenly walk away in step, like the soldiers on the parade ground. I explained this to my sister, and often when we were in our own street she would call out 'March!' to see if the long row of houses would not begin to move. However, we liked the old part of Berlin better, where the streets, with their capricious and serpent-like windings, reminded us of the crooked alleys of Moscow. The streamlets of the Spree exercised a powerful attraction over us. Blondchen thought they played hide-and-seek with children, who would run through the streets to search for them. They came suddenly into sight where one would least expect to see them, in the yard of a house in the Werderschen Market, behind an apparently innocent archway on the Hausvogtei Platz, at the backs of houses whose fronts betrayed no existence of any water near. My sister so often longed to catch sight of the oily satiny sheen of the river's light in unsuspected places that she would drag me off to note her discoveries. She wanted all the varying sights of the Spree, which showed itself at the ends of alleys, or in courtyards or behind houses, suddenly to appear to her, so that she might have the right to first name her discovery."

He was silent awhile, deep in memories of the past. Then he said: "If I have lingered over these childish reminiscences it is because I have not my Blondchen any longer. On one of our wandering excursions we were caught in a heavy shower of rain, and became wet through. My sister was taken ill with rheumatism, and eight days afterward we buried her in the churchyard."

The mother soon followed Blondchen. Sorrow over the child, and homesickness, combined with weak health, proved too great a strain. Wilhelm remained alone with the dispirited and sorrowful old father, whom he never left except for his three years' military service in the field. Then the father, to shorten the time of separation, accompanied the army (in spite of his seventy years) as an ambulance assistant. The following year he died, and Wilhelm was left alone in the world.

Loulou was not wanting in heart, and she had as much feeling as it is proper for an educated German girl to show. By an involuntary movement, she held out her hand, which Wilhelm caught and kissed. They both grew very red, and she looked wistfully at him with her eyes wet. Had he understood the look, and been of a bold nature, he would have clasped the girl to his breast and kissed her. Her red lips would have made scarcely any resistance. But the confusion of mind passed quickly, the light afternoon sunshine and the sight of the people passing through the breach in the castle wall brought him to full consciousness, and the dangerous step was not taken. Loulou recovered her sprightliness, and going back to his story asked him, "So you have been in a campaign?"

"Certainly."

"Did you become an officer?"

"No, fraulein, only a 'vize-Feldwebel.'"

"Have you fought in a battle?"

"Oh, yes, at Burkersdork, Skalitz, Koniginhof, and Koniggratz."

"That must have been frightfully interesting. And have you ever killed one of the enemy?"

"Happily not. It does not fall to the lot of every soldier to kill a man. He does his duty if he stands up in his place ready to be killed."

"Have you any photographs of yourself in uniform?"

He looked at her surprised and said:

"No, why?"

A roguish smile, which at the last question had curled at the corners of her mouth, broke into a merry laugh.

"I wanted to know whether you marched into battle with your curls, or whether you sacrificed them to the fatherland?"

Wilhelm was not offended, but said simply:

"Dear young lady, appearances give you the right to make fun—"

"Ah, don't be angry, I am ill-mannered."

"No, no, you are quite right; but, believe me, I only wear my hair long so as to save myself the trouble of going to the hairdresser's. If I dared imagine that I should be less insupportable with a tonsure—"

"For heaven's sake, don't think of it, the curls suit you very well." She said this with a frivolity of manner which she immediately perceived to be unsuitable, and to get over her embarrassment, she jumped at another subject of conversation. "So you live quite alone? That strikes me as being very dreary. Still you must have many friends?"

"Yes, so-called friends—comrades from the gymnasium, from the academy, and the university. But I do not count much on these superficial acquaintances—I have really only one friend."

"Who is she"

"He is called Paul Haber, and is Assistant of Chemistry at the Agricultural College."

"A nice man?"

"Oh, yes."

"How old is he?"

"About a year older than I am."

"What is he like?"

Wilhelm smiled.

"I believe he is very good-looking, strong, not very tall, with a fair mustache, otherwise closely shaved, and with short hair, not like me! He thinks a good deal of appearance, and always knows what sort of ties are worn. He dances well, and is very pleased if people take him for an officer in civilian's clothes. But he is a true soul, and has a heart of gold. He is clever too, practical, and would do for me as much as I would do for him with all my heart."

"Hardly one unpleasant word for an absent friend. That is scarcely as my friends speak of me," and she quietly added: "Nor as I speak of my friends. You make me curious about Herr—"

"Haber."

"You must introduce him to us."

"He would be most happy."

Loulou now knew more about Wilhelm than she had hitherto known of any man in the world. Only on one point was she unenlightened, and this she hastened to clear up on the following day, when they were looking for berries in the wood.

"You asked me if my heart had been touched yet. Would it be right if I were to ask you the same question?"

"The question seems very natural to me—I can truthfully assure you I have never been in love, not even with a pastor with long hair."

"And has no one been in love with you?"

Wilhelm looked at the distance, and said dreamily:

"No; yet once—"

She felt a little stab at her heart, and said:

"Quick, tell me about it."

"It is a wonderful story—it happened in Moscow."

"But you were only a child then?"

"Yes, and she who loved me was a child too. She was four years old."

"Ah," said Loulou, with an involuntary sigh of relief.

"When I was about ten years old I was sitting one sunny autumn afternoon in the yard of our house on a little stool, and was deep in a story of pirates. Suddenly a shadow fell on my book. I looked up, and saw a wonderfully beautiful child before me, a long-haired, rosy-cheeked little girl, who looked at me with deep shining eyes, half-timidly, and shyly held her hand before her mouth. I smiled in a friendly way, and called to her to come nearer. She sprang close to me, at once threw her arms joyfully round my neck, kissed me, sat down on my knee, and said, 'Now tell me what your name is. I am a little girl, and my name is Sonia. I am not going away from you. Let me go to sleep for a little.' An old servant who had followed her came up and said in astonishment, 'Well, young sir, you may be proud of yourself, the child is generally so wild and rough, and with you she is as tame as a kitten.' I learned from her that little Sonia lived in the neighborhood, and that her aunt had come to look for her in our house. She would not go away from me, and the old servant had to call her mother, who only persuaded her to return home with great difficulty. She wanted to take me with her, and she was miserable when they told her that my mamma would not allow me. The next morning early she was there again, and called to me from the threshold, 'I am going to stay with you all day, Wilhelm, the whole day.' I had to go to school, however, and I told her so. She wanted to go with me, and cried and sobbed when they prevented her. Then her relations took her home, and I did not see her again. Later I heard that the same afternoon she was taken ill with diphtheria, and in her illness she cried so much for me that her mother came to mine to beg her to send me to her. My mother said nothing to me about it, fearing I might catch the disease. Sonia died the second day, and my name was the last word on her lips. I cried very much when they told me, and since then I have never forgotten my little Sonia."

"A strange story," said Loulou softly; "such a little girl to fall in love so suddenly. Yes," she went on, "if she had grown up—"

She could not say more, as Wilhelm, who had come near her, looked at her with wide-open, far-seeing eyes, and suddenly threw his arms round her. She cried out softly, and sank on his breast. "Loulou," "Wilhelm," was all they said. It had happened so quickly, so unconsciously, that they both felt as if they were awaking from a dream, as Loulou a minute later freed herself from his burning lips and encircling arms, and Wilhelm, confused and hardly master of his senses, stood before her. They turned silently homeward. She trembled all over and did not dare to take his arm. He inwardly reproached himself, yet he felt very happy in spite of it. Then, before they had reached the summit of the castle hill, he gathered all his courage together and said anxiously:

"Can you forgive me, Loulou? I love you so much."

"I love you too, Wilhelm," she answered, and stretched out her hand to him.

"Dare I speak to your mother, my own Loulou?" whispered he into her ear.

"Not here, Wilhelm," she said quickly, "not here. You do not know my parents well enough yet. Wait till we are in Berlin."

"I will do as you like," sighed he, and took leave of her with an eloquent glance, as they reached the hotel.

On this evening a quantity of curious things happened, which Wilhelm so far had not observed in spite of his studies in natural science. He could not touch his dinner, and Herr and Frau Ellrich's voices, against all the laws of acoustics, seemed to come from the far distance, and several minutes elapsed before the sounds reached his ears, although he sat close to the speakers. The waiters and hotel guests looked odd, and seemed to swim in a kind of rosy twilight. In the sky there seemed to be three times as many stars as usual. When the Ellrichs had withdrawn he went toward midnight alone into the fir woods, and heard unknown birds sing, caught strange and magic harmonies in the rustling of the branches, and felt as if he walked on air. He went to bed in the gray of early dawn, after writing from his overflowing heart the following letter to his friend Haber in Berlin:

"MY DEAREST PAUL: I am happy as I never thought of being happy. I love an unspeakably beautiful sweet brown maiden, and I really think she loves me too. Do not ask me to describe her. No words or brush could do it. You will see her and worship her. Oh, Paul, I could shout and jump or cry like a child. It is too foolish, and yet so unspeakably splendid, I can hardly understand how the dull, stupid people in this house can sleep so indifferently while she is under the same roof. If only you were here! I can hardly bear my happiness alone. I write this in great haste. Always your

"WILHELM."

Four days later the post brought this answer from his friend:

"Well, you are done for, that is certain, my dear Wilhelm. Confound it, you have gone in for it with a vengeance! I always thought that when you did catch fire, you would give no end of a blaze. So all your philosophy of abnegation, all your contempt for appearance go for nothing. What is your sweet brown maiden but a charming appearance! Nevertheless you have fallen completely in love with her, for which I wish you happiness with all my heart. I do not doubt that she loves you, because I should have been in love with you long ago if I had been a sweet brown maiden, you shockingly beautiful man. One thing is very like you, you say no word on what would most interest a Philistine like myself, viz., the worldly circumstances of the adored one. I must know her name, her relations, her descent. For all this you have naturally no curiosity. A name is smoke and empty sound. Now don't let your love go too far—sleep, and take care of your appetite, and keep a corner in your perilously full heart for your true

"PAUL"

Wilhelm smiled as he read these lines in the strong symmetrical handwriting of his friend, and hastened to send him the news he desired. In the meanwhile his happiness was continual and increasing, and nothing troubled it but the thought of the coming separation. These two innocent children could hide their love as little as the sun his light. They were always together, their eyes always fixed on one another, their hands as often as possible clasped in each other's. All the people in the hotel noticed it, and were pleased about it, so natural did it seem that this handsome couple should be united by love. The chambermaid, rosy Bertha, saw what was going on with her sly peasant's eye, and by way of making herself agreeable used to whisper to him where he could find the young lady when she happened to meet him on the staircase. Wilhelm good-naturedly forgave the girl her obtrusiveness. Only Herr Ellrich saw nothing. In his foreign newspapers, in the blue smoke from his cigars, in the clouds of powder from his gun, he found nothing which could enlighten him as to the two young people's beautiful secret.

Frau Ellrich certainly had more knowledge than that. In spite of her correspondence and her long afternoon naps, she retained enough observation to see the condition of things pretty clearly. She waited for a confession from Loulou, and as this did not come soon enough for the impatience of her mother's heart, she tried a loving question. After a warm embrace from the girl, a few tears, a great many kisses, the mother and daughter understood each other. Wilhelm had pleased Frau Ellrich very much, and she had no objection to raise, but she could make no answer on her own responsibility, as she knew the views of her husband on the marriage of his only child, and after a few days she made him a cautious communication. Herr Ellrich did not take it badly, but as a practical man of the world he wished to give the feelings of the young people opportunity to bear the trials of separation, and for the present thought a decision useless. The projected visit to Ostend was hastened by some ten days. At dinner he made his decision known, adding, "You have pleased yourselves for three weeks, and now I want you to wait so long to please me." Wilhelm felt bitterly grieved that no one invited him to go to the fashionable watering-place, and Loulou even did not seem particularly miserable. The fact was, that at the bottom of her not very sentimental nature, she did not take the leaving of the Schloss hotel as a matter of great importance, and Ostend with its balls and concerts, its casino and lively society, was not in the least alarming to her. She found the opportunity that evening of consoling Wilhelm, and promised him always to think about him, and to write to him very often, and said she could not be very miserable about their separation, as she felt so happy at the thought of meeting him again in Berlin. The following morning they made a pilgrimage to the castle, the woods, the neighboring valley, to all the places where they had been so happy during the last fortnight. The sky was blue, the pine woods quiet, the air balmy, and the beautiful outline of the mountains unfolded itself far away in the depth of the horizon. Wilhelm drank in the quiet, lovely picture, and felt that a piece of his life was woven into this harmony of nature, and that these surroundings had become part of his innermost "ego," and would be mingled with his dearest feelings now and ever. His love, and these mountains and valleys, and Loulou, the mist and perfume of the pine trees, were forever one, and the pantheistic devotion which he felt in these changing flights of his mind with the soul of nature grew to an almost unspeakable emotion, as he said in a trembling voice to Loulou:

"It is all so wonderful, the mountains and the woods, and the summertime and our love. And in a moment it will be gone. Shall we ever be so happy again? If we could only stay here always, the same people in the midst of the same nature!"

She said nothing, but let him take her answer from her fresh lips.

They left by the Offenberg railway station in the afternoon. Loulou's eyes were wet. Frau Ellrich smiled in a motherly way at Wilhelm, and Herr Ellrich took his hand in a friendly manner and said:

"We shall see you in Berlin at the end of September."

As the train disappeared down the Gutach valley, it seemed to Wilhelm as if all the light of heaven had gone out, and the world had become empty. He stayed a few days longer at the Schloss hotel, and cherished the remembrance of his time there with Loulou, dreaming for hours in the dearly-loved spots. In this tender frame of mind he received another letter from Paul Haber, who wrote thus:

> "DEAREST WILHELM: Your letter of the 13th astonished me so much that it took me several days to recover. Fraulein Loulou Ellrich, and you write so lightly! Don't you know—that Fraulein Ellrich is one of the first 'parties' in Berlin? That the little god of love will make you a present of two million thalers? You have shot your bird, and I am most happy that for once fortune should bring it to the hand of a fellow like yourself. In the hope that as a millionaire you will still be the same to me, I am your heartily congratulatory
>
> "PAUL."

Wilhelm was painfully surprised. What a mercy that the letter had not come sooner. It might have influenced his manner so much as to spoil his relations with Loulou. Now that the Ellrichs were gone, it could for the moment do no harm.

CHAPTER II.

VANITIES OF VANITIES.

A brilliant company filled the Ellrichs' drawing-rooms. These lofty rooms, thrown open to the guests, were more like the reception-rooms in a great castle than those of a bourgeois townhouse in Berlin.

The councilor's drawing-rooms occupied the first floor of the largest house in the Lannestrasse. The carpeted staircase was decorated with plants and candelabra, and the guests were shown into a well-lighted anteroom, and on through folding doors into the large square drawing-room. The walls were covered with gold-framed mirrors reflecting the great marble stove, with its Chinese bronze ornaments; the Venetian glass chandelier, the painting on the ceiling representing Apollo in his sun chariot, while the rows of pretty gilt chairs in red silk, the palm trees in the corner, and the wax candles in the brass sconces on the walls were repeated in endless perspective. On the right was a little room not intended for dancing, thickly carpeted, with old Gobelin tapestry on all the walls and doors; inlaid tables, ebony tables, and silk, satin, and tapestry in every conceivable form. A glass door, half-covered by a portiere, gave a glimpse into a well-lighted winter garden, full of fantastic plants in beds, bushes and pots. On the left of the large drawing-room was the dining-room, with white varnished walls divided into squares by gold beading, and decorated by a number of bright pictures of symbolic female figures representing various kinds of wine. A gigantic porcelain stove filled one end of the room, and a sideboard the other. Through the dining-room was a smoking-room furnished with Smyrna carpets, low divans, chairs in mother-of-pearl, and from the ceiling hung a number of colored glass lanterns. This was intended for old gentlemen who wished to enjoy the latest scandal, and a card table was arranged for them with an open box of cigars.

The decoration of these rooms was handsome without being overloaded, and tasteful without being odd or obtrusive, qualities which one does not often find in Germany, even in princes' palaces. A fine perception would perhaps have felt the want of similarity in style in the numerous rooms, giving them the character of a museum or curiosity shop, rather than that of the harmonious dwelling of educated people of a particular period, and in a certain country. Herr Ellrich was, however, quite innocent of this imperfection. He had not chosen anything himself. Everything had come from Paris, and was the selection of a Parisian decorator, and one of the proudest moments in the councilor's life was on the occasion of the ball he gave on his daughter's return from England, when Count Benedetti, the French ambassador, said to him: "One would imagine oneself in an historical house in the Faubourg St. Germain, c'est tout a fait Parisien, Monsieur, tout a fait Parisien."

The Ellrichs' party was to celebrate the New Tear. Even the richest of the members of the German bourgeoisie is obliged to be educated gradually to the cultured usages of society, and are still far from accomplished in the art of easy familiarity. It finds in its homely culture no hard-and-fast traditions by which it can regulate its conduct, and by a deficiency of observation, or by the want of development of the finer feelings, is only imperfectly helped by foreign or aristocratic manners. Herr Ellrich, who loved splendor and expense, felt that the New Year must be celebrated by rejoicings, and he had therefore invited his whole circle of acquaintances to this New Year's party to rejoice with him.

In the third room the councilor's wife sat near the fireplace in a claret-colored silk dress, ostrich feathers in her hair, and resplendent with diamonds. Nevertheless there was nothing stiff in her demeanor, and she was friendly and good-natured as ever. Grouped around her in armchairs were several ladies, who in their own judgment had passed the age of dancing. Among them were the wives of civil officers, in whose dresses a practiced and capable eye might detect a simplicity and old-fashioned taste, while the wives of certain financiers were gorgeous in then fashionable costumes and the brilliancy of their ornaments. The former felt compensated by the consciousness of their rank and worth for any deficiency in mere outward signs of grandeur, the latter tried by the glitter of their pearls, diamonds, silks, and laces to appear easy and fearlessly familiar. Among the men, the soldiers had everything in their favor. The orders which the civilians wore fastened on the lapels of their dress coats were hopelessly thrown in the shade by the epaulettes of the officers, and the medals decorating their colored uniforms.

Herr Ellrich made a good host, passing quickly but quietly from one group to another. His blight blue eves were cold and tired-looking as ever, and took no part in the rather banal smile which played over his lips, as if the accustomed expression of indifference could never be obliterated. The indolent lines about his mouth were not those of temperament, because if he spoke to a Finance Minister or other notability, although there was no arrogance in his manner, it might be noticed that the instinctive consciousness of his own millions never left him. He had a naturally honorable disposition, which showed itself in every line, and made any cringing an impossibility. The guests praised everything, especially the costly refreshments handed by the servants in faultless liveries.

The dancing-room was a cheerful sight. Girls and young married women flew round over the polished floor on the arms of well-dressed men, mostly officers, spinning and whirling round to Offenbach's dance music, led with bacchanalian fire by a small but distinguished conductor from a red covered platform. It was exciting to watch the rows of couples as they waltzed wildly round, and to the dazzled sight it seemed like a glimpse in a dream into Mohammed's Paradise; as if in his wonderful mirror he had reflected the slim figures of the dancers, with their flashing blue or black eyes, their burning cheeks, their parted lips, their bosoms rising and falling, the scene moving in ever-changing perspective; a sight gay and wonderful as the freakish games of a crowd of elves.

The untiring energy of the dancers was wonderful. During the pauses a girl could hardly sit for a moment to rest, but a strong arm would whirl her away again in the vortex of the dance. A few old gentlemen stood in the recesses of the windows and in the doorways, with the quiet enjoyment of those who look on, and among them was Wilhelm Eynhardt. He stood with his back against a window-frame, almost enveloped in the flowing red silk curtain, so that scarcely any one noticed him. His curls had been shorn, and his thick dark hair only just waved, otherwise nothing was changed in his appearance since the Hornberg days. His black eyes wandered thoughtfully over the changing picture before him. The expression on his face, now slightly melancholy, bore more resemblance to that of a young Christian devotee than to that of the beautiful Antinous, and the intoxication of the gayety around him appealed so little to him, that not once did he beat his foot, nod his head, or move a muscle in time to the satanic music of the Parisian enchanter.

For the first time in his life Wilhelm found himself in fashionable society, and for the first time he wore evening dress. Certainly to look at him no one would have guessed it, for there was no awkwardness in his manner, not a trace of the anxiety and inability to do the right thing, which in most men placed amid new surroundings and in unaccustomed dress would have been so apparent. He wore his evening dress with the same natural self-possession as one of the gray-haired diplomats. The secret of this demeanor was the sense of equality he felt toward the others. It never occurred to him to think, "How do I look? Am I like everyone else?" and so he was as free from constraint in his dress coat as in his student's jacket. He had even the gracefulness which every man has in the flower of his age, if he allows the unconscious impulses of his limbs to assert themselves, and does not spoil the freedom of their play by confusing efforts to improve them. The company did not disconcert him either, in spite of their epaulettes and orders, and titles thick as falling snowflakes. An impression received in his boyhood came back to him, in which he, among strange people in a foreign land, had been accustomed by his father to consider himself as an onlooker. In Moscow he had often met aristocratic people, with as thick epaulettes, and more orders than these, but at the sight of them he had always thought,

"They are only barbarous Russians, and I am a German, although I have no gold lace on my coat." From that time he had always in his mind connected the use of uniforms, as outward signs of bravery, with the conception of an ostentatious and showy barbarism which a civilized European might afford to laugh at. He had gone further; he regarded rank and titles as only a kind of clothing of circumstances, which the State lends to certain persons for useful purposes, just as the wardrobe-keeper at a theater gives out costumes to the supers. He was so convinced on this point that he felt sure it was only the stupid yokel at the back of the gallery who could look with any admiration on a human being merely because he struts about the stage in purple and gold tinsel.

Wilhelm did not give the impression of a man who was enjoying himself. His discontented gaze persistently followed one dark head adorned with a yellow rose.

Loulou, for of course it was she, wore a cream-colored silk crepon dress. Her little feet in pale yellow satin shoes played at hide-and-seek under her skirt. She looked charming, and seemed very happy. She danced with a magic lightness and gracefulness, and she showed an endurance which had elicited applause and acknowledgments from her partners. People were delighted with her, and she hardly allowed herself time to breathe, for as the privileged daughter of the house, she wandered from one partner to another, trying hard to offend as few of her admirers as possible by a refusal. But Wilhelm had no cause for jealousy, as her sparkling eyes continually sought his, and as often as she danced near him she gave him an electrifying glance and a sweet smile, telling him that he might now hold his head high like a conqueror, or humble himself with languishing sentiment, that for her there was only one man in the room, one man in all the mirrors, the handsome youth in the window recess between the red silk curtains. In the short pauses she came over to him and spoke a word or two, always the same sort of thing: "Ah! how So-and-so worries me. What a pity that you don't dance, it would be so lovely. Oh! if only you knew how Fraulein S——admires you, and how angry all the ladies are that you won't be introduced to them." And Wilhelm thanked her with the same quiet smile, took her fingers when he could and pressed them, and stayed in his window corner.

Presently Loulou went toward someone in the room, who looked back at the same time toward Wilhelm. It was his friend Paul Haber, for whom he had obtained an invitation. Paul looked at him proudly and gayly. His short hair was beautifully cut and brushed, his thick blonde mustache curled in the most approved fashion. In his buttonhole he wore the decoration of the 1866 war medal, and when he saw himself in the glass he could say with perfect self-satisfaction, that he looked just as much like an officer as the men in uniform, not even excepting those of the Guard. Since the campaign of 1866, in which Paul had served in the same company as Wilhelm, they had been firm friends, and on this evening he wished to offer his respects before the manifest possessor of her heart, to one of the greatest heiresses in Berlin, also his gratitude for his introduction to this splendid house, and his tender feelings for his comrade. In spite of being occupied with his partners he had time to observe Wilhelm, and the sight of him standing alone in the window recess immediately cooled the nervous excitement wrought by the crowd of strangers. These society gatherings were what he delighted in, and he thought it his duty to try to model his friend in the same way. It was not without a struggle with himself that he let a dance go by and went over to where Wilhelm stood.

"What a great pity it is that you don't dance."

"Fraulein Ellrich has just said the same thing," answered Wilhelm, smiling a little.

"And she is quite right. You are like a thirsty man beside a delicious spring, and are not able to drink. It is pure Tantalus."

"Your analogy does not hold good. What I am looking at does not give me the sensation of a delicious spring, and does not make me thirsty."

Paul looked at him surprised. "Still you are a man of flesh and blood, and the sight of all these charming girls must give you pleasure."

"You know I am engaged to only one girl here, and her I have seen under more favorable circumstances."

"Well! She probably does not always wear such beautiful dresses, and if she were not excited by the music and dancing her eyes might possibly not sparkle so much; that is what I mean about its being a pity that you don't dance."

"That is not it. I have seen this beautiful girl on other occasions engaged in the highest intellectual occupation, and I am sorry to see her sink to this sort of thing."

"Now the difference is defined. I was silly enough till now to think that even in a drawing-room one saw something of the highest form of humanity, and that aristocratic society is the flower of civilization."

"Those are opinions which are spread by clever men of the world to excuse their shallow behavior in their own eyes and in the eyes of others. What these people come here for is to satisfy their lower inclinations—you must see this for yourself; if you do not allow yourself to be influenced by these pretentious, ceremonious forms, at least try to discover the reality that lies beneath them. What you call the height of civilization seems to me the lowest. Do you understand? I feel that cultured people in their drawing-room society are in the condition of savages, and even allied to animals."

"Bravo, Wilhelm! go on; this is most edifying."

"You may jeer, but in spite of you I believe that this is so. Try to discover what is going on in the brains of all these people at this moment. Their highest power of activity of mind, which makes men of them, slumbers. They do not think, they only feel. The old gentlemen enjoy themselves with cigars, ices, the prospect of supper; the young men seek pleasant sensations in dancing with beautiful girls. The ladies seek in their partners and admirers to kindle feelings and desires—vanity, self-seeking, pleasure of the senses, gratification of the palate, in short, all the grosser tastes. All that is not only like savages, but like animals. They are merry and contented at the prospect of a savory meal, and they are fond of playing tricks on each other—both sexes chaff and tease constantly. I believe that the development of our larger brain is the intellectual work of man during hundreds and thousands of years, and it would gratify me to see it raised to a still greater state of activity."

"I am listening to you so quietly that I don't interrupt you—even when you talk absurd nonsense. How can one look doleful and disagreeable if honest, highly constituted men indulge in conversation with each other for a few hours after hard work? I delight in this harmless enjoyment, in which people forget all the cares of the day. Here people shake off the burdens of their vocation and the accidents of their lot. Here am I, a poor devil enjoying the society of the minister's friends, and admiring the same beautiful eyes as he does."

"The harmless enjoyments of which you speak are exactly the signs by which one may recognize the vegetative lives of the savage and the animal. A serene enjoyment is what naturally appertains to the lower forms of life when they are satiated, and in no danger of being tracked for their lives. The oldest drawings on the subject always represent men with a foolish serene smile. So the privilege of development is to rejoice in a satisfied stomach and untroubled security, and all through his life to know no other care or want but comfort of body."

"At last I understand you. The artist's ideal is the 'Penseroso,' and in order to recognize the highly developed man he must be furnished with a proof of his identity, so that the meaning of the creature may not be lost to sight for a moment."

"You may put it in the joking way, but I really mean it. I don't forget how much of the animal is still in us. Of course one wants relaxation. But I don't want to look on while animals feed. Recovery after hard intellectual work means, in your sense, the return for some hours to animal life. Now I prefer the painful ascent of mankind to the comfortable, backward slide into animal nature. If I wished to pose as a statue for you it would have to be 'Penseroso' while eating or drinking, or with a foolish, smiling mask indicating animal contentment."

"Very well. Let us also abolish the public announcement of eating, drinking, dancing and other performances, as the remnants of barbarism or of original animal nature, and let us introduce the universal duty of philosophy. A soiree of Berlin bankers—sub specie oeiernitatis—that would do very well, and you must take out a patent for it."

"Students' jokes, my friend, are not arguments. I am quite in earnest in what I say, and I feel melancholy when I see Loulou and the others playing about like thoughtless animals."

"I am going to speak seriously about the joke now, and show you another side to the question. Is it not in the highest degree foolish of a young man without position, to set against him men who carry the sign of recognition from their king, and the esteem of their fellow-citizens? Cannot the example of the consideration they enjoy spur us to endeavors to attain the same? Cannot your acquaintance with them be made useful?"

Wilhelm shook his head. "No, I prefer all these distinguished men when they are doing their own work. They do not interest me here, because they have laid aside all the characteristics which make distinguished people of them. I think they lower their dignity when I see these statesmen, heroes of campaign, representatives of the people, laughing, joking, and playing together like any little shopkeeper after closing hours."

Paul could not give an immediate answer, and he had not time to think of one; as the music stopped the dance ended, and many people moved toward them, making further conversation impossible. The gentlemen came out of the drawing-room and smoking-rooms and mingled with the dancers. Paul made his way neatly through the crowd toward a fresh, pretty, but otherwise insignificant-looking girl, to whom he had paid a great deal of attention, and with whom he wished to dance again. Wilhelm looked for Loulou, whom he found near her mother. Frau Ellrich spoke to him in a friendly way. "Are you enjoying yourself?" she asked, with a kind, almost tender expression on her melancholy face. Wilhelm would not have grieved her for worlds, so for all answer he took her soft hand and kissed it. To keep himself from speaking the truth he was silent. From the four doors of the room servants now appeared bearing large silver trays covered with glasses of champagne. Loulou stood by the chimney-piece and gave several forced and absent-minded answers to the young man. She followed with her eyes the minute-hand on the clock, and at a slight sign from her little hand a servant came up to her. She took the glass in which the wine sparkled, and at the same moment, the hands of the clock pointing to twelve, she cried loudly like a child, "Health to the New Year! Health to the New Year!" Every guest took a glass, crying joyfully, "Health to the New Year!" and clinked his glass against his neighbor's. Loulou went in search of her father to drink with him; after he had given her a friendly kiss on her rosy cheek, he regarded her with fatherly pride. She went to her mother, taking her in her arms and kissing her on both cheeks. The third person whom she sought was Wilhelm. They could not exchange words, but her eyes sought his and they both flashed a mutual and joyous recognition. Her brown eyes had said to his black ones, "May this be a year of happiness for us," and the black eyes had understood the brown ones in their flight and thanked them. The gay tumult lasted for several minutes, the buzz of talking, the clatter of glasses, and the coming and going of servants. Then suddenly an invisible hand seemed to lay hold of the general disorder, ruling and directing it, dissolving groups who had chanced together, here driving them forward, there arranging them backward. According to some fixed law, without delaying or waiting, an orderly procession was formed into the dining-room. The invisible spirit hand which possessed all this power was thrice-holy etiquette; the law which brought order out of confusion, and gave to everyone his place, was that of precedence. Paul and Wilhelm, these strangers to drawing-room customs, were new to the performance. A smile flitted over Wilhelm's face, over Paul's came a reverent expression. What he saw made a distinct impression of wonderment on him. The constraint ceased immediately the guests had taken their places at the table. The scent of the flowers vied with the perfumes worn by the women and could not overcome them. The crystal glasses sparkled in the light of the wax candles, the jewels, and the bright eyes round the table. The servants poured out the noble Rhine wine, the celebrated Burgundy, the elegant Bordeaux, and the mischievous Champagne, whose colored embodiment was reflected on the white hands of the guests, and carried their imaginations away in its flight from gray reality to the immortal land of rosy dreams.

The meal lasted a long time, then a few of the guests rose; the older ones, who had principally chatted, played, and smoked before midnight, now withdrew, if they had no daughters to chaperon; the young people, however, went back to the dancing-room, the musicians fiddled anew as if they were possessed, and an hour's cotillion was begun, the pretty quick-moving figures being led by a lieutenant of the Guards, who seemed as proud of the honor as if he were commanding on a battlefield. Loulou, who had gone back to the dance, had begged Wilhelm in vain to take part at least in the cotillion, where he need not dance much. She had assured him that he would be more decorated than any other man in the room, and would have more orders, ribbons, and wreaths given him than all the lieutenants put together; but even the prospect of such a triumph could not make him ambitious, and for the first time this evening the beautiful excited girl left him looking out of humor, and glanced at him in a way which was not merely sorrowful but reproachful. Paul, on the other hand, was happy. He kept more than ever near the pretty insignificant girl with whom he had danced so much, and the good-hearted fellow did not feel in the least jealous when, in the long pause of the cotillion, his partner went to speak to his friend who had stood lonely for so long, and had hardly enjoyed himself at all. Paul was sufficiently decorated; he got a sufficient number of glances from girls' bright eyes to be quite contented, he paid a sufficient number of compliments, great and small, for which he was thanked by sweet smiles, and perhaps with tiny sighs, and he had the feeling that he had lived in every fiber of his being, and that his time had been marvelously well employed. He could have stayed for several hours longer, and was quite astonished when toward four o'clock the tireless young people's parents put an end to the evening by their departure.

As Wilhelm came up to Loulou she had ceased to look cross. Near her stood the hero of the cotillion, the lieutenant of the Guards, covered with the little favors the ladies had given him. But that did not prevent her saying in quite a tender voice, "I shall see you soon again, shall I not?" and Wilhelm pressed her little hand warmly.

In the hall Wilhelm and Paul had to distribute gratuities to the waiting servants, a custom (unknown in France and England) which dishonors German hospitality, and a minute later they found themselves outside in the starlit night. It blew icy cold over the Thiergarten; across the darkness the snow-laden trees and the closely-cropped grass looked feebly white. Wilhelm, shivering, wrapped himself in his fur coat. Paul, on the other hand, did not seem to mind the cold; he was still too hot with the excitement of the evening. The waltz rang so clearly in his ears that he could have danced over the snow-covered pavement, and the lights and mirrors of the ballroom shone so clearly before his eyes, and enveloped the dancers with such reality that the desert of the silent, faintly-lit Koniggratzer Strasse was alive as if by ghosts. He recalled to his mind the whole evening, and in the fullness of his heart exclaimed, "Wilhelm, I hope never to forget this New Year's Eve." Wilhelm looked at him astonished. "I do not share in your feelings. How can a glance at such vanity in thinking men give one any feeling except that of pity?"

"I am not hurt at the hardness of your judgment, because you don't understand what I am saying. You know very well I am not frivolous, and that I have learned long ago the seriousness of life. But at the same time I value the entree into the best society of Berlin for what it is worth. Now the opportunity has come, and I shall make it useful."

"Paul, you grieve me. A tuft-hunter talks like that."

"What do you call a tuft-hunter?—if you mean a man who does not want to hide his light under a bushel, I say yes, I am one, and I think that is entirely honorable. I don't want to get on by means of any false pretenses, but by honest work. What is the use of capability if no one notices it? If I can inspire the right people with this conviction, I am in luck. There is no injustice in that."

"I thought you had more pride."

"Dear Wilhelm, don't speak to me of pride. That is all right for you. If my father had left me a house in the Kochstrasse, I would snap my fingers at everyone, and go my own way, as it pleased me best. Or put it the other way round, if you were the middle son in a Brandenburg family of nine, I tell you that you would attribute a certain importance to seeking the favor of influential people. You would become as frivolous as I," added he after a little pause, in which he gave a gentle clap on Wilhelm's shoulder.

"You ought not to throw my father's house in my teeth; you know how I live."

Paul tried to interrupt him.

"Let me finish. A man of your capability can nowadays allow himself the luxury of independence and manly self-reliance, even if he is one of the nine children of a poor farmer; if one has few wants, one is rich whatever one's fortune."

"That is all very well. I know your philosophy of abnegation, and it is a matter of temperament. I am not in favor of starving myself when there is a steaming dish before me. The world is full of good things, and I have a taste for them; why should I not reach out my hand?"

"And so you would dance in the present for what it would win you in the future."

"Why not? It is a very usual way to gain a usual end."

"And the modern society household is the result."

"What would become of a poor fellow without these merciful arrangements for introductions to nice girls? Is one to advertise?"

"So you thought of this in the midst of your poetical soiree?"

"Certainly. You are provided for. Don't think ill of me if I follow your example."

Wilhelm felt the blood flow to his cheeks. He perceived his friend's evident meaning.

"Paul! A fortune-hunter!"

"You may talk. Luck flew to you without your lifting a finger to attract it. Other people must help themselves. Fortune-hunter! That name was invented by hysterical girls whose heads are turned by silly novels. These absurd creatures wish in their childish vanity to be married merely for their beautiful eyes. I should like to ask such a girl whether she would marry a man merely for his beautiful eyes! I have no patience with such nonsense. Suppose a poor man, who is capable and clever, acknowledges in a straightforward way that he is trying to win the hand of a rich woman. He need not upbraid himself about anything, for he gives as much as he receives. What do people want from the world? Happiness. That is the aim of my life, just as it is the aim of the rich woman's. She has money, and for happiness she lacks love; I have love, and for happiness I lack money. We make an equal exchange of what we own. It is the most beautiful supplement to a dual incompleteness."

"It is in this way then that you would offer what you call love to a rich girl! A love cleverly conducted, carefully mapped out—a love which one could control, and on no account offer to a poor girl."

"Rubbish! The love of every man who is in his right mind is carefully planned. Would you be in love with a king's daughter? It is to be hoped not. You could keep out of the way of the king's daughter. Why can I not keep out of the way of the poor girl?"

"That means that the princess' rank is as much a hindrance to love as the poverty of the work-girl."

"I swear to you, Wilhelm, that if I were as rich, or as independent as you, I would not think of a dowry. But I am a poor devil. If I were so unfortunate as to fall in love with a poor girl, I would try to get the better of the feeling. I would say to myself, better endure a short time of unhappiness and disappointment than that she and I should be condemned through life to the keenest want, which, with prosaic certainty, would smother love."

While Paul argued with such ardor and earnestness, he was thinking all the time of Fraulein Malvine Marker, the pretty girl with whom he had danced so often, and he fondled tenderly with his right hand the ribbon and cotillion order hidden under his waistcoat. He did not notice that Wilhelm's expression of face was painfully distorted, nor that his words wounded him deeply. They had come to the Brandenburger Thor, and were walking over the Pariser Platz. Under the lindens they were surrounded at once by noise and bustle. The streets were full of rowdy bands of men who sang and shouted all together, now pushing one another in violent rudeness, now shouting "Health to the New Year," here knocking off an angry Philistine's hat, there surrounding and embracing some honest man who was wearily making his way homeward; insulting the police by imitating their military ways, laying hold of their sticks, talking pompously to the night-watchman, and otherwise playing the fool. After the silence of the Koniggratzer Strasse, the drunken turmoil of this noisy mob was doubly unpleasant, and the two friends hastened to escape into the Schadowstrasse. At Wilhelm's doorstep they took leave of each other; Paul went off humming a snatch of Offenbach up the Friedrichstrasse to his home near the Weidendamme.

Wilhelm was tired, but much too excited to sleep. He lived over again in thought the last few months, and, as often happened lately, he lapsed into painful meditation on his relations to Loulou. After her departure from Hornberg she had not written to him for eight days. Then came a letter from Ostend, in which she called Wilhelm "Sie." She said she was very sorry for this, that it would be painful if she called him "Du" and he did not return it, but it would be safer not to do so, as his answer would certainly be read by her mother, and perhaps by her father also, and they would not wish them to say "Du" to each other. Already this change of tone between them cut Wilhelm to the heart, but almost more still the contents of Loulou's letter. She spoke a little of the sea, whose breakers continually sounded in her soul, and her thoughts, which accompanied them like an orchestra; she seldom mentioned the delightful time in the mountains of the Black Forest, which remembrance he carried always with him; but a great deal about the Promenade, the concerts, the Casino balls, her own charming bathing and society toilettes, and those of extravagant Parisians, who tried by incredible mixtures of colors and style to outstrip each other. She wrote particularly about her acquaintances with celebrated people, and her personal following, and for the rest she hardly missed expressing in any of her letters her regret that he was not with her, and enjoying her varied life. Often in the letter there was a flower, or a piece of wild thyme, which betrayed an undercurrent of feeling beneath the shallowness of the words, and once she sent him her photograph with the words "Loulou to her dearest Wilhelm." So he gathered from her frivolous letters much that was unspoken, and through signs and indications believed that her feeling for him was there and gained strength. His answers were short and rather compressed. The knowledge that they would be seen by her prosaic parents, and that Loulou herself would hardly trouble to read anything in the midst of her whirl of gayety, deprived him of words, stopped the flow of his feelings, and turned his expressions into mere Philistinisms. But, on the other Land, Loulou's mother was delighted to have another correspondent, and so she wrote to him often. These perfumed letters from Ostend refreshed him by the remembrance of the lovable face with the dimples, bringing back again the whole charm of the Hornberg days.

At the end of September came the announcement that the Ellrichs had left Ostend, and were going to pay a visit for a fortnight to friends in England, and toward the middle of October a letter, bearing the Berlin postmark, arrived in Loulou's handwriting. It said:

"DEAREST WILHEM: We came home to-day. I cannot sleep until I have written to you. Come to see me quite soon. Will you not? How glad I am! Are you glad too? A thousand greetings. LOULOU."

He would like to have gone directly to the Lennestrasse, but etiquette stood between him and his fiancee, and showed him in its cold fashion that they were now in the city and not in the forest, that nature had nothing to do with them here, and had handed them over to the laws of society. However, as soon as he dared venture, he went and rang at the door-bell. This first visit was a combination of painful feelings for Wilhelm, for while his heart beat, that now he was near the dearest one on earth, he was conscious that here he was a stranger. A servant dressed in black who opened the door did not seem to expect him, and asked him whom he wanted. When Wilhelm asked for Frau Ellrich, he said shortly that she was not at home. In spite of this Wilhelm took out his card, and holding it out said, "Will you kindly announce me, as I am expected." The man left him in an anteroom, and after a short pause took him into the drawing-room. He soon returned, with a manner entirely changed, and submissively asked Wilhelm to follow him to a little blue boudoir, where Loulou received him with a joyful exclamation, but the first greetings, owing to the servant's presence, were exchanged without an embrace, and when they were alone Wilhelm only found sufficient courage to kiss her hand.

It was quite different now from the old times at the Scloss hotel, and in the woodland paths at Hornberg. Wilhelm had to keep to visiting hours, and was seldom alone with Loulou. He took courage then to say "Du," but it was forbidden before other people. To kiss her in those drawing rooms with their betraying mirrors, and their portieres, and carpets was hardly possible. He was frequently asked to lunch or dinner, and he often went with Frau Ellrich and Loulou to the opera or theater, but all these opportunities were not favorable for young lovers. Loulou wore beautiful frocks, which made her much admired; the people were formal, and tolerated nothing that was not ultra polite and polished, in short, it was impossible to be true and natural as things had been in the forest, where the birds and the happy little squirrels served for playfellows.

Loulou was the first to have pity on Wilhelm's discomfort, and to find means to give their intercourse in Berlin at least a little of the beautiful unconstraint of the old times. Under the pretext that she wished to improve herself in drawing, she obtained many precious hours spent in the blue-room or in the winter garden, where their hands often found opportunities to clasp, and their lips to seek each other's. On the strength of Loulou's English education, which had made her independent and self-reliant, and had freed her from any affectation of shyness, she often walked with Wilhelm to parts of the town which she did not know, or which she had only seen from the windows of a carriage. On one of these voyages of discovery, as she called them, she saw Paul for the first time. He met them in the Konigstrasse, as they stood on the Konigsmauer, Loulou looking half-fearfully down the narrow street. Paul looked very much astonished, and seemed as if he were not going to notice the pair of lovers, but Wilhelm nodded and asked him to join them. So he went home with them, and as soon as he was alone with his friend he fell into rapturous admiration of the lovely girl, as Wilhelm had predicted in his letter from Hornberg. One thing Paul could not understand, and he said so: why had not Wilhelm formally asked for Loulou's hand, why he was not properly engaged to her, and how could an impulsive man bear such a constrained position, which would cease the instant that he was Fraulein Ellrich's declared fiance?

Wilhelm had at first no explanation to give his friend, but he knew very well that he delayed, and that he put off from day to day going to Loulou's parents. His was a sensitive, dreamy nature, and much too thoughtful to allow himself to act from passion. He was accustomed to make his impulses subordinate to his reason, and to ask himself severe questions as to the where, how, and why of things. He was not clear himself as to the condition of things between him and Loulou. Did she love him? There were many answers to that. She seemed pleased when she saw him, and displeased if he appeared to forget her for a day. But what he could not understand was that her head seemed as full as ever of her usual acquaintances, and that she was capable of spending some time in theaters, concerts, and society without looking for him. Full too of talk of her frocks and neighbors, without wishing to interrupt the empty gossip with a look or a kiss to let him know that she was conscious of his presence, and in the middle of her idle talk to say nevertheless that her heart was with him. On the other hand, she showed the tenderest sympathy for him. She longed for a picture of his rooms in the Dorotheenstrasse, where he lived and thought of her. She had been to see his house in the Kochstrasse from the outside. She was apparently proud of him, and repeated to him all the flattering remarks which people made on his appearance and cleverness, with as much satisfaction, as if she spoke of one of her own people. Still all this was only on the surface, and he often had the impression that her feeling for him was weakened at its foundation both by her cold intelligence, and by her pleasure in worldly things.

And he? Did he love her as he should, before he had the right to bind her to him for life? His earnestness and exalted morality looked upon marriage as a rash adventure full of alarming secrets. Was it possible that their two lives should be so blended together that they should withstand every accident of fate? He meant to give himself entirely, to keep nothing back, and to be true in body and soul. Was he sure that he could keep the vow, and that no sinful wishes should come to break it? Already he was thinking that he might not be always happy with her. Certainly her beauty, her wit, the attraction of her fresh, healthy youth charmed him, and when she spoke to him with her sweet voice, he had to shut his eyes and hold himself together, not to fall at her feet and bury his head in her dress. But he feared for himself, for his honor, that a sensual attraction should hardly outlast possession. His innermost being was painfully troubled. Never an elevated word from her! Never a deep and serious thought! Often he reflected that the faults of her upbringing were the inevitable results of her life in the midst of idle people, and that it would be possible to deepen and widen her mind and sensations. If he could only go with her to a desert island, alone with the loneliness of nature, and could live between the heavens and the sea! How soon then could he inspire her thoughts and bring her to his own standpoint. Then the fear would take hold of him that she could not do without theaters, frocks, soirees, and balls, and under the recent impression of the New-Year's party he became despondent, and said to himself, "No. The life of show and appearance has too great a hold on her, and I shall never be able to give her what she wants, and what seems necessary to her happiness." Paul's opinion, which he gave on the way home, struck him sorrowfully. One of the richest "parties" in Berlin! Would not people say he was marrying her for her money? What people said was really nothing to him, and he considered himself free to act as his innermost judgment counseled. But might not Loulou herself believe that her father's money added something to her attractions? He recognized that this feeling indicated a weakness, a want of self-reliance, but the idea that she might be capable of such a thought made him angry. Her money did not attract him! On the contrary, it was an obstacle between them. Why was she not a Moscow gypsy girl? Just as young, and pretty, and charming, but uncultivated, and therefore ready for cultivation and capable of it; poor as a beggar, and therefore free from pretensions, but without knowledge of the world, and therefore without desire for it. How happy they might both be then! Such thoughts ran riot in his brain, and he fell asleep only when the late winter sun shone through the curtains on his tired white face.

    The winter went quickly by under amusements of all kinds. Loulou had never known it so pleasant. The theater season was brilliant, the weather for skating lasted longer than usual, and balls succeeded each other in her father's and friends' houses in rapid succession. Wilhelm only went once or twice, and then he firmly declined any more, to the great astonishment of Frau Ellrich, and the vexation of Loulou, whose pretty face always lit up with pleasure when she saw his dark eyes watching her from the doorways or window recesses while she danced. He said that the sight of social frivolity bored him, and she thought in her naive way, "It is always like that. Men must have some fad." Paul was just the other way. He accepted every invitation, and he had a great many. He had always some new acquaintances to tell Wilhelm of, and often spoke of Fraulein Malvine Marker, who appeared to be Loulou's dearest friend, and no feeling of jealousy prevented him from repeating to Wilhelm that the pretty girl had often inquired about him, always regretting his absence from the Ellrichs' dances.

The beautiful time of the year drew near. Outside the gates of the city, where open places were free to her, the spring triumphed in the budding trees of the Thiergarten. Arrangement of plans for the summer was the chief occupation with most people. The Ellrichs talked of Switzerland, and Wilhelm thought timidly of the charms of the Black Forest. He longed to be back at Hornberg, and he spoke often of being there together in the near future. He did not mention marriage, however, and his formal offer had not yet been made. Loulou thought this very odd, and one day she spoke to her mother about it. Frau Ellrich, however, caressed her pretty child, and kissing her on the forehead said:

"It is nothing but modesty. I think it is very nice of him to leave you in freedom for the whole season."

"I am not free, however."

"I mean before the world, dear child. You are both so young that it would not matter if you did not take the cares of marriage upon you for another year."

And to Loulou that was evident.

CHAPTER III.
HEROES.

All over Germany the corn stood high in the fields, ripe for the sickle. Then suddenly the threatening shadow of war rose in the west like a black thundercloud in the blue summer sky, filling the harvest gatherers with anxious forebodings. For fourteen days the people waited in painful suspense, not knowing whether to take up the sword or the scythe. Then the cry of destiny came crashing through the country, terrifying and relieving at the same time: "The French have declared War!"

That was on July 15, 1870, on a Friday. Late in the afternoon the dismal news was spread in Berlin that the French ambassador at Ems had insulted the king, who had retired to the capital, and that a combat with the arrogant neighbors on the Rhine was inevitable. Before night the street Unter den Linden, from the Brandenburger Thor to the Schlossbrucke, was packed with men overflowing with intense excitement. Without any preconceived arrangement, all the inhabitants decorated their windows with banners and lights, and the streets assumed the festal appearance of rejoicings over a victory. The crowd looked upon this spectacle not as an undecided beginning, but a glorious conclusion. There was no fear in any face, no question as to the future in any eye, but the certainty of triumph in all; as if they had seen the last page turned in the book of fate, with victory and its glorious results written thereon.

Toward nine o'clock a thunderbolt broke over the Brandenburger Thor, and rolled like the breaking of a wave to the other end of the street. The king had left the Potsdam railway station a quarter of an hour ago, and the crowd greeted him with a tremendous shout as his carriage appeared. The people wished by this acclamation, springing from the depths of their hearts, to show their ruler that they were prepared to follow him even to death. But the king was so much absorbed in thought that he scarcely seemed to hear or notice the enthusiasm of the crowd. He saluted and bowed to right and left as a prince is accustomed to do from his childhood, but it was a mechanical action of the body, and his mind had little part in it. His eyes were not looking at the sea of uncovered heads, but seemed fixed, under knitted brows, on the distance, as if they endeavored to decipher there some indistinct, shadowy form. Did the king perceive in this moment the responsibility of one human being to carry such a load? Did he wish in his innermost heart that he might share the weight of the decision with others— the representatives of the people—and not alone be forced to throw the dice deciding the life or death of hundreds and thousands? Who can say? At all events the powerful features of the king's face betrayed no such uneasy doubt—only a deep earnestness and an immovable steadiness of expression. Belief in the divine right of his kingship gave him power over the minds of men, and he took his duties on him in this hour without weakness or failing, grasping with his human hand the obscure spiritual web of man's destiny, and with his limited intelligence trying to unravel the dark threads here and there, on which hung the healing and destruction of millions. In such moments a whole people will become united into one being, swayed by the mastery of a single mind, and await the commands of a single will. It comes, no one knows from whom—all blindly follow. In spite of the superficial differences which men find in one another under similar conditions, the powerful effect of unconscious imitation is surprisingly apparent, and under its operation personal peculiarities disappear.

Wilhelm and Paul that same evening sat at one of the windows of Spargnapani's, looking on the Lindens. The small rooms were filled to overflowing, and the guests were crammed together in the open doorways, or on the stone staircase, where their loud talking mingled with the noise of the people in the street. The king's carriage had hardly passed, when several young men sprang shouting into the room, threw a quantity of printed leaflets, still damp from the press, on the nearest table, and rushed out again. These were the proofs of an address on the war to the king. No one knew who had written it, who had had it printed, who the people were who had distributed it, but everyone crowded excitedly round it, and begged for pens from the counter to add their signatures to it. A few specially enthusiastic souls even put a table with inkstands and pens out on the pavement, and called to the passers-by to sign the paper. Paul was among the first to fulfill this duty of citizenship, and then handed the pen to his friend. But Wilhelm laid it down on the table, took Paul's arm, and drew him out of the crowd into the quiet of the Friedrichstrasse.

"Are you a Prussian?" cried Paul angrily.

"I am as good a Prussian as you are," said Wilhelm quietly, "and ready to do my duty again, as I have done it before, but these silly effusions don't affect me at all."

"Such a manifesto gives the government the moral force for the sternest fulfillment of duty."

"I hope you are not in earnest when you say that, my dear Paul. The government does what it has to do without troubling itself about our manifestoes. It is repugnant to me to have my approval of the war dragged from me without being asked for it. I may not appear to say 'yes' willingly, but at the same time may not have the right to say 'no.'"

Paul followed silently, and Wilhelm went on:

"You deceive yourself as to your duty like all these people, who imagine that they are still separate individuals, and that they can sanction or forbid as they will the declaration of war. I, however, know and feel that I have no longer a voice in the matter. I have only to obey. I am no longer an individual. I am only an evanescent subordinate unit in the organism of the State. A power over which I have no control has taken possession of me, and has made my will of no avail. Is there still a part of your destiny which you have the power to guide as you will? Is there such for me? We shall be forced to join simply in the united destiny of one people. And who decides this? The king, no doubt, thinks that he does; the Emperor Napoleon thinks he does. I say that these two have no more influence over the capabilities of their people than we two have over the capabilities around us. The State commands us, the whole evolution of mankind from its beginning commands them. All of the race which has gone before holds them fast, and compels them as the wheels of the State compel us. The dead sternly point out the way to them, as the living do to us. We all of us know nothing, kings and ministers as little as we, of the real forces at work. What these forces will do, and what they strive to attain to, is hidden from us, and we only see what is nearest to us, without any connection with its causes and final operation. That is why it seems to me better to do what one sees as one's duty at the moment, rather than to give ourselves the absurd appearance of being free in our movements, and certain as to our goal." Paul pressed his hand at parting, and murmured:

"Theoretically you are right, but practically I do not see why the tyrant at the Tuileries need begin with us. He could at least leave us in peace."

The order for mobilization was issued. Wilhelm was surprised to receive his appointment again as second lieutenant, and was nominated to the 61st Pomeranian Regiment. His duties during the next few days took up the whole of his time, and left him hardly a moment to himself. He was free only for a few hours before the march to the frontier, and then he made all the haste he could to say good-by at the Lennestrasse. His heart beat quickly as he hurried along, and now that the time of separation was near, he reproached himself for the irresolution of the last few weeks. He was going to the front without leaving a clear understanding behind him. He tried to convince himself that perhaps it was better so—if he fell she would be free before the world. But at the bottom of his heart this reasoning did not satisfy him, and he lingered over the idea of taking his weeping betrothed to his heart before all the world, and kissing the tears off her cheeks, instead of bidding farewell to her at the station, and holding her to him from a distance by an acknowledged tie. Was not their love alone enough? No, he knew that it was not, and he felt with painful surprise that his contempt for outward appearances, his impulse after reality, were vigorous in him as long as he followed his inmost life alone; but when he came out of himself, and wished to unite another human destiny with his own, these things had become a painful weakness. Through this other life, the world's customs and frivolities began to influence him, and his proud independence must be humbled to the dust, or he must painfully tolerate his own weakness. These reflections brought another with them—it was quite possible that an opportunity might occur at the last moment. He painted the scene in his own imagination; he found Loulou alone, embraced her fervently, asked her if she would be his for life; she said "Yes;" then her mother came in, Loulou threw herself on her neck; he took her hand and asked her in due form if she would accept him as a son-in-law, as he had already gained Loulou's consent. If the councilor was at home, his consent was also given, if not they must wait until he came, and the time could not seem long, even if it lasted an hour. He did not doubt that they would all consent. Things might very likely have happened just as he dreamed of, if he had only come to his determination at the right time, and had not hazarded success on the decision of the last moment, when there was hardly time for a weighty decision.

As he approached the red sandstone house, with its sculptured balconies, and its pretty front garden, he had a disagreeable surprise. At the iron gate two cabs were standing, evidently waiting for visitors at the house. He was shown, not into the little blue-room, but into the large drawing-room near the winter garden, and found several people there in lively conversation. Beside Loulou and Frau Ellrich there were Fraulein Malvine Marker, with her mother, and also Herr von Pechlar, the lieutenant of hussars of cotillion fame.

"Have you come too to say good-by?" cried Loulou, going to meet Wilhelm.

Her face looked troubled, and her voice trembled, and yet Wilhelm felt as if a shower of cold water had drenched his head. The insincerity of their relations, her distant manner before the others, but above all the unfortunate word "too," including him with the lieutenant, put him so much out of tune that all his previous intentions vanished, and he sank at once to the position of an ordinary visitor.

Herr von Pechlar led the conversation, and took no notice of the new guest's presence. He oppressed Wilhelm, and made him feel small by the smartness of his uniform, his rank as first lieutenant, and his eyeglasses. Wilhelm tried hard to fight against the feeling. After all, he was the better man of the two, and if human nature alone had been put in the scale—that is to say, the value both of body and mind—Herr von Pechlar would have flown up light as a feather. But just now they did not stand together as man to man, but as the bourgeois second lieutenant in his plain infantry uniform, against the aristocratic first lieutenant—the smart hussar, and the first place was not to be contested.

In Fraulein Malvine's kind heart there lurked a vague feeling that she must come to Wilhelm's help, and overcoming her natural shyness, she said to him:

"It must be very hard for you to tear yourself away under the circumstances."

She was thinking of his attachment to Loulou, which in her innocence she quite envied.

Oppressed and distracted as his mind was, he found nothing to say but the banal response:

"When duty calls, fraulein." But while he spoke he was conscious of the kindness of her manner, and to show her that he was grateful he went on, "My friend Haber wishes to say good-by to you before he leaves Berlin. He thinks a great deal of you, and is very happy in having made your acquaintance."

Malvine threw him a quick glance from her blue eyes and looked down again.

"What a good thing that I was here when you came," he said softly; "I might certainly not have seen you but for this chance."

"The fact is, gnadiges Fraulein," he stammered, "our duties demand so much of our time."

"Is Herr Haber in your regiment?" she asked.

"No; he has remained with our old Fusilier Guards."

"Ah, what a pity! It would have been so nice for you to be side by side again, as in 1866."

"How much she knows about us," thought Wilhelm, wondering.

"I often think of Uhland's comrades. It must be a great comfort in war to have a friend by one."

"Happily one makes friends quickly there."

"On that point we are better off than the poor reserve forces," remarked Herr von Pechlar, not addressing himself to the speaker, but to Frau and Fraulein Ellrich. "We regular officers pull together like old friends in danger and in death, while the others come among us unknown. I imagine that must be very uncomfortable."

Wilhelm felt that he had no answer to make, and a silence ensued. Loulou broke it by moving her chair near Wilhelm, and began to chatter in a cheerful way over the occurrences of the last few days. How dreadfully sudden all this was! Just in the midst of their preparations to go away. That was put aside now. They must stay behind and do their duty. Mamma had presided at a committee for providing the troops with refreshment at the railway station; she herself and Malvine were also members. There were meetings every day, and then there was running about here, there, and everywhere, to collect money, enlist sympathy, make purchases, and finally to see to the arrangements at the departure of the troops.

"It is hard work," sighed Frau Ellrich; "I have dozens of letters to write every day, and can hardly keep up with the correspondence."

Herr von Pechlar said he regretted that he was obliged to take to the sword; he would much rather have helped the ladies with the pen.

Wilhelm felt that the moral atmosphere was intolerable. He had nothing to say, and yet it was painful to him to be silent. Nobody made any sign of leaving, so at last he rose. Herr von Pechlar did not follow his example, merely giving him a distant bow. Malvine put out her hand quickly, which Wilhelm grasped, feeling it tremble a little in his. Frau Ellrich went with him to the door. She seemed touched, and said with motherly tenderness, while he kissed her hand:

"We shall anxiously expect letters from you, and I promise you that we will write as often as possible."

Loulou went outside the door with Wilhelm, in spite of a glance from her mother. She thought they could bid each other good-by with a kiss, but two servants stood outside, and they had to content themselves with a prolonged clasp of the hand, and a look from Wilhelm's troubled eyes into hers, which were wet. She was the first to speak:

"Farewell, and come back safely, my Wilhelm. I must go back to the drawing-room."

Yes, if she must! and without looking back, he descended the marble staircase, feeling chilled to the bone, in spite of the hot sunlight in the street. He had the feeling that he was leaving nothing belonging to him in Berlin, except his own people's graves.

In the evening he left by one of the numberless roads which at short distances traverse Germany toward the west like the straight lines of a railway. The quiet of the landscape was disturbed by the fifes, rattle of wheels, and clanking of chains, and to all the villages along the road they brought back the consciousness, forgotten till now, that Germany's best blood was to be shed in a stream flowing westward. A time was beginning for Wilhelm of powerful but very painful impressions, not, it is true, to be compared with those which the battlefields of 1866 had made on him when an unformed youth. The war unveiled to him the foundations of human nature ordinarily buried under a covering of culture, and his reason, marveled over the reconciliation of such antitheses. On the one hand one saw the wildest struggle for gain, and love of destruction; on the other hand were the daily examples of the kindest human nature, self-sacrifice for fellow-creatures, and an almost unearthly devotion to heroic conceptions of duty. Now it appeared as if the primitive animal nature in man were let loose, and bellowing for joy that the chains in which he had lain were burst, and now again as if the noblest virtues were proudly blossoming, only wanting favorable circumstances in which to develop themselves. Life was worth nothing, the laws of property very little; whatever the eyes saw which the body desired, the hand was at once stretched out to obtain, and the point of the bayonet decided if anything came between desire and satisfaction. But these same men, who were as indifferent to their own lives, and as keen to destroy the lives of others as savages, performed heroic deeds, helping their comrades in want or danger, sharing their last mouthful with wounded or imprisoned enemies, who returned them no thanks; and after the battle, in the peasant's hut, cradling in their arms the little child, whose roof they had perhaps destroyed, and possibly whose father they might have slain. These impulses, as far apart as the poles, occurred hour after hour before Wilhelm's eyes. He was not a born soldier, and his nature was not given to fighting. But when it was necessary to endure the wearisome fulfillment of duty, to bear privation silently, and to look at menacing danger indifferently, then few were his equals, and none before him. This quiet, passive heroism was noticed by his comrades. The officers of his company found out that he did not smoke, and never drank anything stronger than spring water. They noticed also that dirt was painful to him, even the ordinary dust of the country roads, and that he was dissatisfied if his boots and trousers bore the marks of muddy fields. They thought him a spoiled mother's darling, a "molly-coddle," and their instructive knowledge of human nature found a name for him, the same name his schoolfellows had already given him. They called him the "Fraulein."

But in the day of battle, when Wilhelm with his company stood for the first time in the line of fire, the "Fraulein" was perhaps the firmest of them all. The hissing balls made apparently no more impression on him than a crowd of swarming gnats, and the only moment his courage left him was when he thought he might be thrown into a ditch, which the rains had turned into a complete puddle. He remained standing when all the others lay down, and the captain at last called out to him, "In the devil's name, do you want to be a target for the French?" making him seek shelter behind a little mound, which left him nearly as uncovered as he was before. And after hours of solid exertion, straining nerves and muscles to the utmost, when peace came with night, Wilhelm began a tiring piece of work with sticks and brushwood, out of pity for a weary comrade.

On the strength of these first days before the enemy his position as a soldier was established. A few harmless jokes were made on the march and in the camp on Wilhelm's anxiety as to the removal of mud on his clothes, and on the example he set in going out at night to save the dead and wounded enemy from plunder, but the whole company loved and admired the "Fraulein."

The officers, however, did not entirely share this feeling. This lieutenant was not smart enough. They did full justice to his courage, but thought that he was wanting in alertness and initiative. He lacked the proper campaigning spirit, and they found it chilling that he should be so distant in his manners after so long a time together. Another said that Lieutenant Eynhardt went into action like a sleep-walker, and his calmness had something uncanny about it. The captain was not pleased with him, because he had no knowledge of business; as far as example went he was the worst forager in the whole regiment. If a peasant's wife complained to him, he would leave empty-handed a house whose cellars were stocked with wine, and larders with hams one could smell a hundred yards off. It was all the more provoking as he could speak French perfectly, an accomplishment which no one else in the regiment could, to the same extent, boast of. It came even to a scene between him and the captain, who said angrily to him after a fruitless search in a new and well-to-do village in Champagne: "A good heart is a fine thing to have, but you are an officer now, and not a Sister of Mercy. Our men have a right to eat, and if you want to be compassionate, our poor fellows want food just as much as those French peasants. Deny yourself if you like, but take care that the soldiers have what they need. If ever you get back to Berlin, then in God's name you can please yourself by distributing alms, and buy a place for yourself in heaven."

Wilhelm was obliged to admit that the captain was right, but he could not change his nature. Capturing, destroying, giving pain, were not to his taste. From that time he left other people's property alone, and let the French run if they fell into his hands. He was excellent on outpost and patrol duties, for then his brains and not his hands were at work—then he could think and endure. He could go for twenty-four hours on a bit of bread and a draught of water better than any one, and without a minute's sleep, stand for hours at a stretch holding a position; he was always the first to explore dangerous roads, signing to his companions if he could answer for their safety, and all this with a natural, quiet self-possession as if he were taking a walk in town, or reading a newspaper at Spargnapani's.

Weeks and months went by like a dream, in constant excitement, and the exhausting strain of strength. Christmas passed at the outposts without gifts and with few good wishes, and the thunder of the guns took the place of church bells. January came in with a hard frost, trying the field troops bitterly, and bringing with it hard work for Wilhelm's regiment. The 61st belonged to General Kettler's brigade, which strategically kept the Garibaldi and Pelissier divisions in check. By the middle of January the brigade was in full touch with the enemy. On the 21st the troops broke out from the St. Seine, dashed into the Val Suzon, and after an hour's conflict with the Garibaldians, drove them out and established themselves on the heights of Daix toward two o'clock. Before them were the rugged summits of Talant and Fontaine, the last spurs of the Jura Mountains seen in the blue distances both of them crowned, by old villages, whose outer walls looked down a thousand feet below. The gray walls, the rhomboid towers of the mediaeval churches, brought to one's mind the vision of robber knights rather than the modest homes of peasants. Between these two mountains was a narrow valley, through which one caught a glimpse of Dijon, with its red roofs and numbers of towers, and its high Gothic church above all, St. Benigne, well known later to the German soldiers.

There lay before them the great wealthy town, looking as if one could throw a pebble through one of its windows, so near did it seem in the clear winter air. The smoke went straight up out of its thousand chimneys, exciting appetizing thoughts of warm rooms and boiling pots on kitchen fires. There were the sheltered streets full of shops, friendly cafes, houses with beds and lamps and well-covered tables—but the soldiers stood outside on the cold hillside, chilled to the bone by the north wind, so tired that they could hardly stand, and often sinking down in the snow, where they lay benumbed, without energy to rouse themselves. They had gone for twenty-four hours without food, and had only some black bread remaining for the evening, worth a kingdom in price. Between their misery and the abundance before their eyes lay the enemy's army, and this army they must conquer, if they would sit at those tables and lie in the soft beds. The general wanted to take Dijon in order to remove a danger menacing to South Germany, and to secure the advance of the German army toward Paris and Belfort—the soldiers had the same desire, but their longing for Dijon was for comfort, satisfaction of hunger, and rest.

The German battalion kept on pressing forward. This mistake was hardly the fault of the officers, who on this occasion strove to keep the men back rather than encourage them to advance. The Garibaldian troops had the advantages of superior forces, a greater range of artillery, and sheltered position in the hills, and they pressed with increased courage to the attack. The Germans did not await them quietly but threw themselves on them, so that in many cases it came to a hand-to-hand fight, and serious work was done with bayonets and the butt-ends of rifles. At length the French began to retreat, and the Germans with loud "Hurrahs!" flung themselves after them. But the pursuit was soon abandoned, as they had to withdraw under the fire from the Talant and Fontaine positions, and then, after a short rest, the French again advanced. So the fight lasted for three hours, the snowflakes dispersed by the balls, the men stamping their half-frozen feet on the ground, stained in so many places with blood, but the distance between the German battalion and beckoning, mocking Dijon never diminished. The right wing of the brigade made a strenuous attempt, pressed hard toward Plombieres, forced the Garibaldians back at the point of the bayonet, and took possession of the village, which already had been stormed from house to house. The sight of the slopes before Plombieres covered with the enemy running, sliding, or rolling, acted like strong drink; the whole German line threw itself on the yielding enemy before it had time to regain breath, and amid the thunder of artillery, with the balls from the French reserves on the heights rattling like hailstones, it gained at last a footing on the hill. Some of the troops sank down exhausted in the shelter of the little huts which were strewed over the vineyard, while others followed the division of the enemy which had forced itself between the mountain and the narrow valley behind the French line of defense.

It was now night, and very dark, and to follow up the hard-won victory was not to be thought of, so the German troops halted to rest if possible for an hour. It was a terrible night, and the cold was intense. Campfires were almost useless. The men's clothes were insufficient and nearly worn out. During the last few days, on the march and in the camp, every one had huddled together whatever seemed warmest, and in the pale moon or starlight, figures in strange disguises might be seen. One wore the thick wadded cloak of a peasant woman over woefully torn trousers, another whose toes till now had always been seen out of noisy boots, stalked in enormous wooden shoes, the extra room being filled up with hay and straw. Overcoats from the French and German dead had been taken, and were useful for replenishing outfits—particularly when a German soldier wore red trousers, and the braided fur coat of the fantastic Garbaldian uniform. Many others had bed-clothing and horse-coverings, carpets and curtains, one even went so far as to wear an altar-cloth from some poor village church over his shoulders, and those who still had pocket-handkerchiefs in their possession wore them tied over their ears. Many, however, had nothing but their own torn uniforms, and these tried hard to get warm by rolling themselves close against one another like dogs. The dark masses lay there all among the trodden and half-frozen snow stained with blood, sand, and clay, huddled together one on the top of the other, and if their labored breathing had not been heard, one could hardly have told whether one stood by living men or dead—the dead indeed lay near, many hundreds of them, singly and in groups, scarcely more cramped and huddled together than the sleepers, nor more quiet than they. When the cold, even to the most warmly dressed, became intolerable, they would spring up and stagger about, stumbling over heaps of dead and living men, the latter cursing them loudly.

The dreadful night passed, and at most a third only of the German troops had rested. The gray dawn began to appear in the sky, bugles sounded, and cries of command were heard, but it was hard for the poor soldiers to rouse themselves, to stir their benumbed limbs, which at last were beginning to get a little warm. One after another the ridges of the Jura Mountains became suffused with pink as the sun rose, but the fissures in the hills and the valleys were still dark and filled with thick mist, behind which the enemy's position and the town of Dijon were still invisible. The soldiers soon forced their stiffened limbs into position, the last remaining rations were quickly distributed, and a picked number of the freshest of the men, i.e. those who had had no night duty, went out doggedly against the enemy, with trailing steps and gray, tired-out faces. The crackle of their lively firing aroused the French from sleep, and perhaps from dreams of conquest and fame, put them to confusion, and drove them back toward Dijon. The Germans followed, this time without shouting, and as the fog gradually dispersed, they saw the first skirmishers of the batteries on Talant and Fontaine, apparently far distant against the Porte Guillaume (the old town gate of Dijon, built to imitate a Roman arch of victory), were really quite near them. One more tug and strain and the goal was near. A fresh swing was put into the attack, but the French had found time with the advancing day to gather themselves together, and to be aware of the inferior numbers of the attacking party, and they threw themselves in column formation down the hill, which the German division threatened to attack in the rear. Fresh troops came marching out of Dijon, and the Germans, to avoid being between two fires, drew back again through the valley behind the mountain. The French pressed after them, but were received by the German reserves with such a firm front, that they paused and slowly retreated.

General von Kettler knew that in spite of his momentary success, he could expect no further advance from his half-starved, cold, and weary brigade, and therefore he ordered them half a mile to the rear. The Garibaldian troops, who thought victory could be gained by one strenuous effort, tried to arrest the departing troops, endeavoring to bring them back to another advance. When they were at last distributed in the villages, the exhausted Germans found rest and refreshment for the first time for forty-eight hours. They had lost a tenth part of their powers of endurance in those dreadful two days spent on the hills in sight of Dijon.

The brigade had retreated, as one who jumps goes a step or two backward to obtain more impetus. The next morning, January 23, they ware again on the march to Dijon. This time, however, they chose another way to avoid the batteries of Talant and Fontaine, and approached the town from the north instead of from the west. Following the road and the railway embankment from Langres to Dijon, the German troops pressed forward without halting. The French outposts and breastworks soon fell before the advancing Germans, and made no stand till they got to the Faubourg St. Nicholas, the northeast suburb of Dijon. The greater number of the Germans stationed themselves on the embankment, but the walls of the vineyard, plentifully loopholed, pressed them hard with shot. Toward evening the second battalion of the 61st, to which Wilhelm belonged, received the order to advance. Over pleasure-gardens and vineyards they went, through poor people's deserted houses the four companies of skirmishers worked their way to the entrance of the Rue St. Catherine, a long, narrow street. Just at the end stood a large three-storied factory, whose front, filled with large high windows, looked like a framework of stone and iron. At every window there was a crowd of soldiers; the whole front bristled with death-dealing weapons. Sixteen windows were on each floor, and at every window at least three rows of four soldiers stood. It was therefore easy to reckon the total number at six hundred at the very least.

As the points of the German bayonets came round the corner in sight of this fortress a terrible change took place: in the twinkling of an eye all the openings blazed out at once, and the building seemed to shake from its foundations; forty-eight red tongues of flame blazed out suddenly to right and left, as if so many throats of Vulcan or abysses into hell had been opened, and soon the whole building was wrapped in a thick white smoke, through which the men were invisible. Then a fresh roar and fresh bursts of flame, and fresh puffing out of white smoke, and so it went on, flash after flash, roar after roar came from that awful wall, whose windows were every now and then visible between the volleys of smoke. Hardly one of the soldiers within the line of fire was left standing, numbers were crushed, many more lying dead or wounded-and the furious firing took on a fresh impetus. If the whole battalion was not to be destroyed, it must speedily get under cover. So, running some hundred and fifty yards to the right, they threw themselves into an apparently deep sandpit, and there they lay directly opposite to the factory. During these few minutes the facade, still vomiting fire, bellowed and poured out bullets like hailstones against the sixty men in the sandpit, doing murderous work.

Hardly giving themselves time to take breath, the brave men began to fire steadily at the factory, which up till now appeared, in spite of its nearness, to be very little damaged. The enemy were there completely enveloped from sight, and a lurid red flame through the cloud of smoke was the only guide for the German shot. So the fighting lasted for some time, till an adjutant sprang from over the field behind, which he had reached by a circuitous way, bringing from the commander-in-chief the questions as to what was going on, and why were they there. The major pointed with his sword at the factory, and said

"We must have artillery against this."

"There is none here to have," answered the adjutant.

The major shrugged his shoulders, and gave the command for the Fifth company to storm the factory. While they prepared themselves to leave the sandpit the German firing stopped, and almost at the same time, the French. The enemy could now see what was going on outside, for at this moment the cloud of smoke became less dense. The company broke out of the sandpit, and with the flag of the battalion gallantly waving over them rushed madly toward the door of the factory, while the men who were left behind tried by a furious fire to support their comrades and to confuse the enemy. The strange silence had lasted forty or fifty seconds, probably till the Germans had given some idea of their intentions. This bit of time allowed the storming party to gain, without loss, the middle of the space which separated them from their object, the intoxication of victory began to possess them, and they gave a cheer which rang with the exultant sound of triumph. Again the crashing din began, as terribly as before, it was an uninterrupted sound like the howling of a hurricane, in which no single report or salvo could be distinguished; the whole building seemed to flame at once from the top to the bottom in one red glow, and the bullets flew and whistled in such a confusing mass, that it seemed as if the heavens were opened and it rained balls, a dozen for every four square foot of earth, and the men felt that they must be prepared for repeated attacks of the same description, one after the other without stopping. In but a few seconds half of the company lay on the ground, and the colors had disappeared among the fallen. Those who remained standing seemed for a short time as if stunned. A few, acting on the instinct of self-preservation, fled almost unconsciously. Among the greater part, however, the fighting Prussian instinct prevailed, impelling the soldiers forward and never back, and so with renewed shouts they pressed on. But only for a few minutes. The colors flew upward again, raised by hands wearied to death, only to fall again at once. Three times—four times the flag emerged, sinking again and again, and each flutter meant a new sacrifice, and each fall the death of a hero. Soon there was no one left standing, no man and no standard, nothing but a gray heap of bodies, whose limbs palpitated and moved like some fabulous sea creature, making groaning, ghostly sounds. Ten or twelve poor fellows wounded by stray shots sheltered themselves in the sandpit without weapons, with staring eyes and distorted features. That was all there was left of the Fifth company.

There was deathly silence in the sandpit; the firing had ceased for some minutes. The soldiers looked at one another, and at the mountain of human bodies before them in the evening twilight, and threw doubtful glances at the handful of men just returned, lying exhausted on the ground. Suddenly the major called out:

"The colors!"

"The colors!" murmured several men, while others remained silent.

"We must search for them under the wounded," said the major sadly.

His glance strayed right and left, and seemed to invite volunteers among the twenty or thirty who were nearest to him. The little band cautiously left their shelter, and set diligently to work on the hill of dead bodies. But in spite of the growing darkness they were observed by the French, who began their fire anew, and a few minutes later no living soul was left on the field.

The captain and Wilhelm were now the only remaining officers of the battalion. The former cried: "Who—will volunteer?" and was surrounded by a dozen brave fellows. Wilhelm was not among them. He stood leaning on his sword against the half-frozen side of the pit, observing with sorrowful expression what was going on around him. The captain threw him a strange look, in which contempt and reproach were mingled, then he drew out his watch, as if to note the last moment of his life, and with the cry "Forward!" disappeared in the evening light. He did not reach the spot where the corpses lay thickest. The factory went on spitting fire, and crashing everything down over the heap. The shots, however, came more slowly, and pauses came between them. A shriek was heard, not far distant. Evidently it was one of the wounded who lay on the ground. At the same time a form could be distinguished raising itself up and then sinking again. Heedless of the balls which whistled round his ears, Wilhelm raised his head out of the sandpit and looked over the field. Then he worked himself out on his hands and knees, and to the astonishment of the soldiers in the pit moved away toward the wounded, alone and without hurry or excitement. Over there on the other side they saw him, and although the artillery did not fire on him, he received a brisk volley of single shots without, however, being hit, and he reached the first group of wounded. A hasty glance showed him only stiffened limbs and stony faces. He went on searching, and then he heard close by him a feeble voice saying: "Here!" and a hand was stretched out to him. With one bound he was near the wounded man, and recognized the captain.

"Are you seriously hurt?" he asked, while as quickly as possible he raised the wounded man on his shoulder, who answered almost inaudibly:

"A ball through the chest, and one in my foot. I am in awful pain."

As Wilhelm went slowly back with his burden, he looked so fantastic in the growing darkness, that the French did not know what to make of the strange apparition, and began to fire afresh. "Wilhelm, however, reached the sandpit safely, where friendly arms were stretched out to help him, and relieve him of the captain. He stayed to breathe a moment, and then said:

"If any one will come with me, we might bring in one or two more poor devils who have still life in them."

He was soon surrounded by five or six figures, and he was going with them to search for wounded in the rain of balls which was falling, when with a sudden cry of pain he sank backward. A ball had struck his right leg. His volunteers put him back into the sandpit, and no one thought any more either of the colors or the wounded who lay out there under the fire from the factory. At this moment too an adjutant brought the command to retreat, which the remains of the wearied battalion slowly began, to obey under the command of a sub-officer.

The captain, who could not be moved, was left in a peasant's hut in the village of Messigny, but as Wilhelm's injury was only a flesh wound, and he was merely exhausted from loss of blood, he was sent with the others to Tonnerre, where he arrived the next day, after a journey of great suffering.

The schoolhouse was turned into an infirmary, many of the rooms holding nearly a hundred and twenty beds. Wilhelm was put into a little room, which he shared with one French and two German officers. A Sister of Mercy and a male volunteer nurse attended to the patients in this as well as in the four neighboring rooms. Wilhelm exercised the same influence here as he did everywhere, by the power of his pale thin face, which had not lost all its beauty; by the sympathetic tones of his voice, and above all by the nobility of his quiet, patient nature. His fellow-sufferers were attracted to him as if he were a magnet. Some occupants of the room gave up their cigars when they noticed that he did not smoke. The Frenchman declared immediately that he was le Prussien le plus charmant he had ever seen. The Sister took him to her motherly heart, and the doctor was constantly at his bedside. He was able to give him a great deal of attention without neglecting his duty, as there were few very severe cases under his care, and no new ones came in— Paris had surrendered and a truce was declared.

At first Wilhelm's wound was very bad. It had been carelessly bound up at first, and in the long journey to the infirmary had been neglected, but owing to antiseptic treatment the fever soon abated and then left him entirely. He took such a particular fancy to the doctor that after a few days they were like old friends, and knew everything about each other.

Dr. Schrotter was an unusual type, both in appearance and character. Of middle height, extraordinarily broad-shouldered, and with large strong hands and feet, he gave the impression of having been intended for a giant, whose growth had stopped before reaching its fulfillment. The powerful, nobly-formed he ad was rather bent, as if it bore some heavy burden. His light hair, not very thick, and slightly gray on the temples, grew together in a tuft over the high forehead. The closely-cropped beard left his chin free, and the fine mustache showed a mouth with a rather satirical curve and closely compressed lips A strong aquiline nose and narrow bright blue eyes completed a physiognomy indicating great reserve and a remarkable degree of melancholy. It is no advantage to a man to possess a Sphinx-like head. The pretty faces apparently full of secrets offer easy deceptions, and one expects that the mouth when open will reveal all that the eyes seem to mean. One is half-angry and half-inclined to laugh when one discovers that the face of the Sphinx has quite an everyday meaning, and utters only commonplaces. But with Dr. Schrotter one had no such deception. He spoke quite simply, and when he closed his lips he left in the minds of his listeners a hundred thoughts which his words had conveyed, He was born in Breslau, had studied in Berlin, and had started a practice there when his student day's were over. The Revolution of '48 came, and he at once threw himself head over ears into it. He fought at the barricades, took part in the storming of the Arsenal, became a celebrated platform orator, and relieved a great deal of distress during the reactionary policy which followed, leaving soon afterward, however, to travel abroad. He went to London almost penniless, and at first, through his ignorance of the language, he was barely able to maintain himself, but he soon had the good fortune to obtain an appointment in the East India Company. In the spring of 1850 he went to Calcutta, where he helped to manage the School of Medicine, and some years later was sent to Lahore, where he also established a medical school. After twenty years' service he was discharged with a considerable pension. His return to Europe falling in with the outbreak of the war, he hastened to offer his voluntary services to the army as surgeon. Owing to temperate habits and a strong physique, he had kept in good health, and no one would have dreamed that this strong, fifty-year-old man had passed so many years in an enervating tropical climate. The only signs it had left on his face were the dark, yellowish color of his skin, and the habit of keeping the eyes half-closed. The long years in India had also made a deep impression on his character, and many things about him would have appeared strange and odd in a European. They amounted to sheer contradictions, but their explanation was to be looked for in the environment of his life. Physically he was still young, but his mind seemed very old, and had that appearance of dwelling quietly apart which is the privilege of wise minds who have done with life, and who look on at the close of the comedy free from illusions. His eyes often flashed with enthusiasm, but his speech was always gentle and quiet. In his relations with other men he had the decided manner of one who was accustomed to command, and at the same time the kindness of a patriarch for his children. He was a moderate sceptic, nevertheless he combined with it a mysticism which a superficial judge might have denounced as superstition. He believed, for instance, that many persons had power over wild animals; that they could raise themselves into the air; that they could interrupt the duration of their lives for months, or even for years, and then resume it again; that they could read the thoughts of others, and communicate without help the speech of others over unlimited distances. All these things he averred he had himself seen, and if people asked him how they were possible, he answered simply, "I can no more explain these phenomena than I can explain the law of gravitation, or the transformation of a caterpillar into a moth. The first principles of everything are inexplicable. The difference in our surroundings is only that some things are frequently observed, and others only seldom."

His philosophy, which he had learned from the Brahmins, attracted Wilhelm greatly; it made many things clear to him which he himself had vaguely felt possible ever since he had learned to think. "The phenomenon of things on this earth," said Dr. Schrotter, "is a riddle which we try to read in vain. We are borne away by a flood, whose source and whose mouth are equally hidden from us. It is of no avail when we anxiously cry, 'Whence have we come, and whither are we going?' The wisest course for us is to lie quietly by the banks and let ourselves drift—the blue sky above us, and the breaking of the waves beneath us. From time to time we come to some fragrant lotus-flower, which we may gather." And when Wilhelm complained that the philosophy of the world is so egoistic, Dr. Schrotter answered, "Egoism is a word. It depends on what meaning is attached to it. Every living being strives after something he calls happiness, and all happiness is only a spur goading us on to the search. It belongs to the peculiar organism of a healthy being that he should be moved by sympathy. He cannot be happy if he sees others suffering. The more highly developed a human being is the deeper is this feeling, and the mere idea of the suffering of others precludes happiness. The egoism of mankind is seen in this; he searches for the suffering of others, and tries to alleviate it, and in the combat with pain he insures his own happiness. A Catholic would say of St. Vincent de Paul or St. Charles Borromeo, 'He was a great saint.' I would say, 'He was a great egoist.' Let us render love to those who are swimming with us down the stream of life, and without pricking of conscience take joy in being egoists."

Wilhelm was never tired of talking about the wonderland of the rising sun, of its gentle people and their wisdom, and Dr. Schrotter willingly told him about his manner of life and experience there. So the peaceful days went by in the quiet schoolhouse at Tonnerre, the monotony being pleasantly relieved by visits from comrades, and letters from Paul Haber and the Ellrichs. Paul was going on very well. He was at Versailles, making acquaintances with celebrated people, and had nothing to complain of except that, in spite of the truce, he had no leave of absence to come and see his friend. Frau Ellrich complained of the irregularity of their correspondence during the war. Loulou wrote lively letters full of spirit and feeling. She had been frightened to hear of his wound, but his convalescence had made her happy again. She hoped that it would not leave him with a stiff leg, but even if it did it would not matter so much, as he neither danced nor skated. What a dreary winter they were having in Berlin! No balls, no parties, nothing but lint-picking, and their only dissipation the arrival of the wounded and the prisoners at the railway station. And that was quite spoiled by the abominable newspaper articles on the subject—presuming to criticize ladies because they were rather friendly to the French officers! The French, whom one had known so well in Switzerland, must be of some worth, and it was the woman's part to be kind to the wounded enemy, and to intercede for human beings even in war, while the men defended them by their courage and strength. Some of these Frenchmen were charming, so witty, polite, and chivalrous, that one could almost forgive them had they conquered us. One's friends were suffering so much—one heard such dreadful things. Herr von Pechlar had escaped without a hair being injured, and he already had an Iron Cross of the first class! She hoped that Wilhelm would soon get one too.

Up till now Wilhelm had not been able to answer this question decidedly. One morning, toward the end of February, as he was limping about the room on a stick, the adjutant came in and said:

"I have brought you good news. You have won the Iron Cross." As Wilhelm did not immediately answer he went on: "Your captain has the first class. He is now out of danger. He has naturally surpassed you. I may tell you between ourselves that it did not seem quite the thing, your being so cool about the colors; but the way in which you fetched the captain out was ripping. Don't be offended if I ask you why you exposed yourself for the captain when you refused for the flag?"

"I don't mind telling you at all. The captain is a living man, and the flag only a symbol. A symbol does not seem to me to be worth as much as a man."

The adjutant stared at him, and he repeated confusedly:

"A symbol!"

Wilhelm said nothing in explanation, but went on:

"I regret very much that I was not asked before I was proposed for the Iron Cross. I cannot accept it."

"Not take it? You can't really mean that!"

"Yes, I do. In trying to fulfill my duties as a man and a citizen, I cannot hang a sign of my bravery on me for all passers-by to see."

"You speak like a tragedy, my dear Herr Eynhardt," said the adjutant. "But just as you like. You can have the satisfaction of having done something unique. It is hardly a usual thing to refuse the Iron Cross."

As he went out with a distant bow, Dr. Schrotter came in, and said, smiling:

"What the adjutant said about the tragedy is very true. Decoration appears very theatrical to me, but you might take it quietly and put it in your pocket. I have got quite a collection of such things which I never wear."

"But do you blame the men who despise these outward forms in order to give an example to others?"

"My friend, when one is young one hopes to guide others, as one grows older one grows more modest."

This objection struck Wilhelm, and he grew confused. Dr. Schrotter laid his hand quietly on his shoulder, and said:

"That does not matter. We really mean the same thing. The difference is only that you are twenty-five and I am fifty."

As Wilhelm was silent and thoughtful, Schrotter went on:

"There is a great deal to be said about symbols. Theoretically you are right, but life practically does not permit of your views. Everything which you see and do is a symbol, and where are you to draw the line? The flag is one, but without doubt the battle is one too. I believe, in spite of the historian who is wise after the event, that the so-called decisive battles do not decide anything, and that it is the accidental events which have the permanent influence on the destiny of peoples. Neither Marathon nor Cannae kept the Greeks or Carthaginians from destruction; all the Roman conquests did not prevent the Teutonic race from overrunning the world; all the Crusader conquests of Jerusalem did not maintain Christianity, or Napoleon's victories the first French Empire; nor did the defeats sustained by the Russians in the Crimea influence their development. And finally, I am convinced that Europe to-day would not be materially different, even if all the decisive victories of her people could be changed into defeats, and their defeats into victories. So you see that a battle is a symbol of the momentary capabilities of a people, and a very useless symbol, because it tells nothing of the immediate future, and yet you will sacrifice your life for this symbol, and not for another! It is not logical."

"You are right," said Wilhelm, "and our actions in cases like this are not guided by logic. But one thing I am sure of, if everything else is a symbol, a man's life is not. It is what it appears to be; it signifies just itself."

"Do you think so?" said Schrotter thoughtfully.

"Yes, although I understand the doubt implied in your question. A living man is to me a secret, which I respect with timidity and reverence—who can tell his previous history, what things he does, what truths he believes in, what happiness he is giving to others? Therefore when I see him in danger I willingly risk my life to save his. I know myself, and I estimate my value as a trifling thing."

Schrotter shook his head.

"If that were right, an adult must in all cases give his life to save a child, because he might grow to be a Newton, or a Goethe, and above all, because the child is the future, and that must always taken precedence of the past and the present. But to a mature man that is not practicable. There are no more secrets. Mankind knows that the probable is planted within his own being. Do not seek to find additional reasons for a fact which has already sprung up from unknown forces. It was sympathy which impelled you, the natural feeling for a fellow-creature. And that is right and natural."

Wilhelm looked at Schrotter gratefully as he affectionately grasped his hand.

CHAPTER IV.

IT WAS NOT TO BE.

The sun streamed down on Berlin from a cloudless sky, and all the life of the town gathered in a confused, restless throng in Unter den Linden; but the bustle on this hot summer day, June 16, 1871, had quite a different character from that of eleven months before. And if any one could have listened to it all with closed eyes, he might have distinguished a joyful excitement in the air, in the laughing of children and girls, in the lively gossip of the men; and from all these sounds of joy and chatter he might have detected the signs that overstrained nerves were now relaxed after long hours of weary suspense. What hundreds of thousands had wished and hoped for on that Friday in July had now come to its glorious fulfillment, and Berlin, as the proud capital of a newly-established empire, was giving a welcome home to the army. They had at last found the answer to Arndt's ill-natured question about the German Fatherland, and had set the great Charles' imperial crown on the head of their bold Hohenzollern king.

On one of the raised platforms near the Brandenburger Thor were Wilhelm and Dr. Schrotter. The former had renounced the privilege which belonged to him, as officer in the Reserves, and moreover, as an example, had not claimed his position among those who were wounded in the war, still however wearing his uniform. Had he consulted his own inclinations, he would not have come to see this triumphant entrance, as he took very little pleasure in the noisy enthusiasm of crowds. A great deal of actual vulgarity is always exhibited on these occasions, mingled with some real nobility of feeling. Counter-jumpers and work-girls secure comfortable positions from which to see the processions, groups of calculating shopkeepers with advertisements of pictures and medals of hateful ugliness speculate on the generosity of the crowd, and others push with all the force of their bodily weight to obtain and keep the front places for themselves. Frau Ellrich had sent Wilhelm two tickets, hoping that he would make use of them. Dr. Schrotter wished to see the spectacle, so Wilhelm asked his new friend to go with him.

Near where they sat was the platform for the ladies who were to crown the victors with wreaths. Among them was Loulou. All the emotions and force of character of which she was capable had been brought out by her position. Through the influence of her father, who, in all the difficult and responsible business of the French indemnity had found time to intercede for his little daughter with the burgomasters and magistrates, Loulou's dream was realized; a dream which all the prettiest girls in the best society in Berlin had also shared during the last week. Her enrollment in this troop of beauties was regarded by her less successful friends with envy, but the vexation of disappointed rivals was naturally the sweetest part of her triumph.

The young girls were dressed all alike in mediaeval dresses like the well known pictures of Gretchen in "Faust," with long plaits of hair, puffed and slashed sleeves, and senseless and theatrical-looking little hanging pockets. All were nevertheless conscious of the propriety of their appearance, and felt quite heroic. It really was heroic to sit there hour after hour in the burning sun bareheaded, until all were gathered into one great picture, and a documentary proof could be handed down to their grandchildren in the shape of a large-sized photograph, showing that their grandmothers had been chosen as the official beauties of Berlin in the year 1871. The satisfaction of vanity, involving such a sacrifice, almost deserves admiration.

It was nearly midday when a sudden stir took place in the crowd. Every one on the platforms sprang up and began to wave hats and handkerchiefs. In the windows, on the roofs, in the spaces between the platforms, wherever men could be packed, suddenly all the heads turned to one side, just as a field of corn bends before a breeze. Then uprose a roar of shouts and cheers, deafening and almost stunning in intensity. It was impossible any longer to distinguish tone, but only a tumult, such as a diver in deep water might hear of the surface waves above him. The senses were bemused by the continual succession, of heads set close together like a mosaic, and covering the whole surface of the great street, and by the roar which went up, cheering everything which made its appearance; whether it were the struggling activity of the crowd moving in the center of the street, the sudden fall of foolhardy boys who had climbed into trees or up lampposts, or the short and sharp fights which went on between spectators for the best places, nothing escaped recognition.

Now between the firing of cannons was heard a more distant sound of a warlike fanfare of trumpets, and between the pillars of the central Brandenburg Gateway came the Field-Marshal Wrangel, recognizing all the arrangements with a pleasant smile, and with a radiantly happy expression on his withered face, as the first enthusiasm of the people burst upon him, though he had demanded no part of the triumph for himself. A group of generals followed him in gorgeous uniforms, decorated with shining medals and stars, all bore famous names, attracting the keenest interest and centering the enthusiasm of the crowd. Endless and numberless seemed the ever-changing and richly-colored procession—Moltke, Bismarck, and Roon side by side, all statuesque figures, their eyes with stately indifference glancing at the rejoicing people. They seemed in the midst of this stormy wave of excitement like stern, immovable rocks, standing firm and high above the breaking surf at their feet. Many people had at the sight of them an intuitive feeling that they were not mortal men, but rather mystical embodiments of the power of nature, just as the gods of the sun, the sea, and the storm were the conceptions of the old religions. They passed on, and at a short interval behind them came the Emperor Wilhelm. His supreme importance was emphasized by the space left before and after him. Wreaths covered his purple saddle, flowers drooped over the glossy skin of his high-stepping charger, his helmeted head and his gloved hand saluted and bowed, and on his face shone a mingled expression of gratitude and emotion, which, after the hard, cold bearing of his fellow-workers, was doubly impressive and affecting. Manifestly this conqueror was not like his Roman prototype who had the words, "Think of death," whispered in his ear, while he tolerated the idolization of the people.

The monarch had to hear long speeches from the officials and verses from the trembling lips of the young girls who surrounded him before he could ride further. The train of individual heroes ended with him. The principle of massing together was now the order, in which individuality is no longer recognized.

Battalion after battalion and squadron after squadron in endless lines passed by, until the tired eyes of the spectators could hardly after a time distinguish whether the lines were still moving, or had come to a standstill. The helmets and weapons of the soldiers were garlanded with flowers and foliage, the horses' legs were twined with wreaths, and their feet trod on a mass of trampled flowers and leaves. The strength of the German army seemed to be decked and curled out of it; the lines of marching soldiers had women's faces: here and there a man had a patriotic admirer on his arm, who let it be seen that she had taken possession of his weapon and carried it for him. The officers, as much bedecked as their men, managed nevertheless to preserve their dignity.

The crowd was gradually becoming stupefied by the spectacle, throats were sore with shouting and cheering, and the oppressive heat took the freshness out of the people's enthusiasm. Once more, however, they broke out again, just as when the emperor and his paladins appeared, and this was when the French field-trophies were carried past. Eighty-one standards and flags were there, from the battlefields of Russia, Italy, and Mexico, soaked through with men's blood, gloriously decomposed, torn, blackened with powder, and riddled with bullets. Now the strong arms of German non-commissioned officers carried them in the sultry heat of the midsummer afternoon, these miserable remnants hanging heavy and limp without a flutter, without a spark of trembling life in the silken folds; they looked like imprisoned kings, who with heads bowed down, and despair in their eyes, walked in chains behind the triumphant Roman chariots.

"Look," sad Dr. Schrotter to Wilhelm, when a short pause came in the shouting, and in the rain of wreaths and flowers—"Look what makes the deepest impression on the people, next to the great representative figures. There is the symbol which you despised."

"What does that prove?" answered Wilhelm. "I never doubted that the crowd was roused by appearances, and not by the reason of things. The ideal results of victory one cannot see with one's eyes or applaud with one's hands, but a dismantled banner one can."

"That does not explain everything. Atavism comes into it. The inhabitants of towns in ancient times need to rejoice and cheer in the same way when their victorious troops brought home the tutelary gods of their enemies. It is the same idea, the same superstition, after an interval of three thousand years."

"Yes, it is curious. I was thinking the whole time that one had a picture of ancient civilization before one. The wreaths of flowers, these swaggering figures with their trophies of war, this gay crowd, distributing food and drink, these young girls with their crowns, is it not all exactly the manner in which the people of the Stone Age or the savages of to-day would feast their heroes? Cannot one understand in this that at the beginning of civilization war was the highest object in state and society, an opportunity of enrichment by booty, and a festival for youth? Nowadays we ought to have got far enough to see in war only a weary fulfilling of duty, a barbarous waste of labor, of which we are inwardly ashamed; and we should keep away from this noisy festival as from the execution of a criminal, which may be necessary, but is painful to witness. The progress from barbarism to civilization is frightfully slow."

"It is true; we are still carrying ancient barbarism round our necks, and without a great deal of rubbing you will easily find the primitive savage under the skin of our dear contemporaries who are able to construe Latin beautifully. And these are not the only gloomy thoughts which this spectacle gives me. Look there! over yonder at the other end of the street they are unveiling a monument to Friedrich Wilhelm III., and the festival of victory is spoiled by homage paid to a despot who during twenty-seven years never redeemed his pledge to give the people a constitution. I am forty-eight years old, and yet I have not forgotten my youthful ideas. My generation looked forward to a united as well as to a free Germany, and hoped that unity would not come out of a war, but rather from the freewill of the German people. It is now with us through other means, but I fear not better ones. The aristocracy and the Church will assert themselves again, and the military system will lay its iron hand over the life of the whole nation. People say already that it is the officer and not the schoolmaster who has made Germany great. These changes put my thoughts in a ferment. One has yet to see whether such a society of officers can produce a people, and if its thinkers and teachers could not lead it to a richer cultivation, and its poets to a higher ideal of duty. I am afraid, my friend, that the higher souls in our new empire will not find this an easy time."

"And yet you left your dreaming in India to come home to discomfort," said Wilhelm.

"My longing for Germany never left me all the twenty years I was there. And then I confess that I secretly reproached myself for going away. It is comfortable to turn one's back on the Fatherland, and to find more agreeable conditions in a foreign country. But afterward one tells oneself that only egoists leave their own people fighting against darkness and oppression, and that one has no right to play the traitor to home and belongings, while those left behind are striving bitterly to better their condition."

The procession of troops was still passing, but the young girls had already left their posts; the stands were beginning to empty, and Wilhelm and Dr. Schrotter tried to break through the crowd and go homeward. After a short silence Schrotter again went on:

"Don't misunderstand me," he said; "in spite of thinking this triumphal procession barbaric, and my ideal being different from that of most people, I was deeply moved to-day with sympathy and admiration. This generation has achieved something colossal. My eyes fill with tears when I see these men. For six or seven years they have shed their blood in these wars without a murmur, they have fought in a hundred battles without taking breath, they have neither counted the cost nor spared their labor, and one feels astounded at living amid such heroes, who seem to belong to a fairy tale. This generation has done more than its duty, and if now it is weary and will rest for thirty years in peace, surely no one can reproach it."

Schrotter spoke with emotion, and Wilhelm who would not grieve his friend by a contradiction, repressed a retaliation which rose to his lips, and silently took leave of him.

The life of the community, as of single individuals, went back gradually into its old channels, and so it did with Dr. Schrotter. He had lived hitherto in an old-fashioned quarter of the town, and now, to be as near as possible to Wilhelm, he rented a house in the Mittelstrasse. He established a private hospital in the old Schonhauserstrasse, in the midst of artisans and very poor people, and there he spent daily many hours, treating for charity all those who came to him for help. He soon had a larger attendance than was comfortable, and had to extend the work, without which he could not have lived. He found endless opportunities of relieving misery and distress in this poor quarter of the town, and as he was a rich man, and independent of his own creature comforts, he could put his philosophy of compassion into practice to his heart's content. Wilhelm took up his work again at the Laboratory, and also resumed his visits to the Ellrichs, but it was with an increasing discomfort. The councilor, who had been distinguished for his services in the financial transactions with the French Government, had heard the story of the refusal of the Iron Cross. He thought it very ridiculous, and his early friendship for Wilhelm became markedly cooler. Even Frau Ellrich's motherly feeling for him received a check, and modesty and shyness no longer seemed a sufficient explanation of the unaccountable delay in his love-making. Only Loulou was apparently the same, whenever he came, always lively and friendly, but when he left she was affectionate without any display of emotion, grateful for tender glances, not withholding quiet kisses, but not offering them—her calm manner almost mysterious, as if love were simply something superficial and of small import. Wilhelm could no longer deny that his first love, which had stirred his being to the depths, was a mistake, but he could not bring himself to definitely end the existing conditions. Hundreds of times he was on the point of saying to Loulou that he did not think the tie between them would secure their happiness, and offering her her freedom, but as soon as he began his courage would fail him. If people were present he was confused; if they were alone, her personal appearance had the same charm for him, or rather it awoke in him the remembrance of the delight and enthusiasm he had felt in the past, and prevented him taking a step toward what would do grievous injury to her girlish vanity, if nothing more.

Would this suspense and these fears, which made him so restless and unhappy, always last? He might write a letter to Loulou, as he was unable to say what he wished to in the light of her beautiful brown eyes. Then he threw this idea aside as unworthy of consideration; he could not simply dismiss a girl whom he loved by means of the post. The simple thing to do seemed to wait, until, on the other side, they should grow disgusted with him, and would tell him to go. This agreed with his passive character, which was timidly inclined to draw back before the rushing current of events, and preferred to be carried along by them, just as a willow leaf is borne along on the surface of a stream. Wilhelm could not help noticing that Herr von Pechlar was now a favorite guest at the Ellrichs', that he made himself very fussy about both mother and daughter, and that he had a very impertinent and slightly triumphant air when he met him. He would only have to leave the coast clear for Pechlar and all would be at an end.

Paul Haber, who was in Berlin again, and paying a great deal of attention to Fraulein Marker, was grieved and really angry at the turn his friend's romance had taken. He knew through Fraulein Marker how Herr von Pechlar was trying to supplant Wilhelm, and that he took every opportunity of making abominably false representations about him. There ought to be no more foolish loitering about. It was unpardonable to let the golden bird fly away so easily. Once open the hand, and she might be off. If Fraulein Ellrich was beginning to flirt with Pechlar, it was quite excusable, as Wilhelm's coolness might well drive her to it. But if he stuck to his absurd whim, that she was too superficial for him!—as if every girl were not superficial, and as if a man cannot educate her to whatever level he pleases—then in heaven's name let him make an end of it all, or the affair would become ridiculous and contemptible. But other considerations had weight with Wilhelm.

Through Paul and the officers of his acquaintance he heard very unfavorable things of Pechlar. He was only moderately well off, and had more debts than hairs on his head; perhaps for a son-in-law of Herr Ellrich's that was a venial offense. He was also a common libertine, whose excesses were more like those of a pork-butcher than of a cultivated man. His companions were not disinclined for little amorous adventures—a joke with a pretty seamstress or restaurant waitress were their capital offenses. But the manner in which Pechlar carried on his amours was such as did not commend itself to either the easygoing or cautious among the officers.

Wilhelm clearly saw that Pechlar did not love Loulou—he was probably incapable of loving, and only wanted her dowry. Without a thought of jealousy, and out of compassion for an inexperienced and guileless creature who was dear to him, he thought it his duty to warn her before she sullied herself by becoming bound to such a man. To save Loulou he at last took the step which no respect for his own peace or honor had allowed him to take before.

He went to the Ellrichs' house the next day at the usually early hour of eleven o'clock, and asking for the young lady, he was shown into the little blue boudoir, where he hoped to find Loulou alone. But he was painfully surprised. Herr von Pechlar sat there, and appeared to be in the middle of a conversation with Loulou. She smiled at Wilhelm, and beckoned to him to come and sit near her, without embarrassment. Wilhelm stayed a moment at the door irresolute, then he went forward, and bowing to her without looking at the hussar, said earnestly: "I came in the hope of speaking to you alone, gnadiges Fraulein. Perhaps I may be so fortunate another time."

At these unexpected words Loulou opened her eyes wide. Herr von Pechlar, however, who since Wilhelm's arrival had been tugging angrily at his red mustache, could contain himself no longer, and said in a harsh voice, which trembled with passion:

"That is the coolest thing I have ever heard. May I ask first of all why you cut me on entering the room?"

"I only recognize people whom I esteem," said Wilhelm over his shoulder.

"You are a fool," flashed back Pechlar's answer.

Perfectly master of himself, Wilhelm said to Loulou, "I am extremely sorry that I have been the cause of an outbreak of bad manners in your presence," then he bowed and left the room, while Loulou sat there motionless, and Herr von Pechlar gave him a scornful laugh.

With all his retirement from the world, and his indifference to the usages of society, Wilhelm felt nevertheless a sharp stab of pain, as if he had been struck across the face with a whip. As he walked down the Koniggratzer Strasse it seemed to him as if a bright, fiery wound burned on his face, and the passers-by were staring at this sign of insult. His powerful imagination formed pictures unceasingly of violent deeds of revenge. He saw himself standing with a smoking pistol opposite the offender, who fell to the ground with a wound in his forehead; or he fought with him, and after a long struggle he suddenly pierced the hussar through the breast with his sword. By degrees his blood cooled, and with all the strength of his will he fought against the feelings which he knew formed the brute element in man, and which with his philosophy he believed he had tamed, and he said to himself, "No, no fighting. What good would it do? I should either kill him, or be killed myself. His insulting words really do me no more harm than the yelping of this little dog who is running past me. I will not let a remnant of prejudice be stronger than my judgment."

Although he had come to this resolution, his nerves were still so unstrung that he could not quiet them alone. He felt he must unburden himself to some one, so he hastened toward Dr. Schrotter's. The doctor, however, had not yet returned from his hospital. Wilhelm soon found the inmates of his friend's household, an old Indian man-servant and a housekeeper, also an Indian of about thirty-five, with a yellow face already wrinkled and withered, large dark eyes, and a gold-piece hanging from her nostrils. The old man maintained a respectful attitude toward her, which pointed to a great difference of caste between them. The woman showed by her small hands and feet, and the nobility of her expression, the modest and yet dignified character of a lady, rather than of a person in a subordinate position. Both wore Indian dress, and attracted great attention when they showed themselves in the street. They hardly ever went out, however, and were always busily employed in service for Dr. Schrotter, to whom they were very devoted.

The old man, who spoke a little English, opened the door to him, and told him that Schrotter Sahib would soon be in. The woman also appeared, and beckoned to him to go and wait in the drawing-room, opening the door as she did so. As he went in she crossed her arms on her breast, bowed her head with its golden-colored silk turban, and vanished noiselessly. She only spoke Hindustani, and always greeted Wilhelm in this expressive manner.

The drawing-room, in which Wilhelm walked restlessly up and down, was full of Indian things; oriental carpets on the floor, low divans along the walls covered with gold embroidery and heaped with cushions, rocking-chairs in the corners, punkahs hanging from the ceilings—no heavy European furniture anywhere, but here and there a little toy-like table or stool made of sandalwood or ebony, inlaid with silver or mother-o'-pearl. Everything smelled strangely of sandalwood and camphor and unknown spices, everything seemed to spring and shake under a heavy European foot, everything had such an unaccustomed look, that one felt as if one were in a foreign land, where Western prejudices and standpoints were unknown and inadmissible. These surroundings spoke to Wilhelm dumbly yet intelligibly, and he felt their persuasive power almost immediately. He had recovered his equanimity when, a quarter of an hour later, Schrotter came in.

"What a pleasant surprise!" he cried from the doorway. "Will you stay to lunch with me?"

Wilhelm accepted gratefully, and then related his morning's experiences. Schrotter had made him sit on a divan surrounded by cushions, and listened attentively, while his half-closed eyes, full of fire, rested on his friend's unhappy face. Wilhelm had never mentioned his engagement to Fraulein Ellrich to many of his old friends, but Dr. Schrotter had been told of it in all its circumstances by Paul Haber. Now, however, Wilhelm could not avoid the subject in his mind, and to make his last visit to the Ellrichs, and his behavior with regard to Herr von Pechlar intelligible, he told Dr. Schrotter, in short, concise language, the beginning and subsequent development of his love-affair, and by the confession of his consideration of Loulou's nature, gave a clew to his delay, coolness, and final renunciation.

When Wilhelm had finished, and raised his eyes questioningly to Schrotter, the latter said, after a short silence:

"I congratulate you on the quiet way in which you have told me all this. For a young fellow of twenty-six with deep feelings it is little short of a wonder. But the question is, what do you intend to do?"

"Nothing," answered Wilhelm simply.

"You will not call out Herr von Pechlar?"

"No."

"And if Herr von Pechlar challenges you?"

"He challenge me?"

"Certainly; for although he is the direct offender, we can't overlook the fact, dear Eynhardt, that you first insulted him, which by a nice point of honor would justify him in taking the first steps. The man is evidently bent on a quarrel, so we have to consider the possibility that he may send his second with a challenge."

"In that case I would make it clear that I do not demand satisfaction, but neither will I give it."

There was another pause.

"You are undertaking what may involve serious consequences," remarked Schrotter.

"It appears to me easy enough," said Wilhelm.

"You could not think of an academic career in Germany after it."

"You know I do not aspire to that."

"Beside that, the episode will become an insurmountable barrier in a hundred circumstances of life."

Wilhelm was silent.

"Don't misunderstand me. I have not a word to say in favor of the regulation of duels. I abhor them. It is as stupid and brutal as the offering of human sacrifices to appease angry gods. I myself have never fought in a duel. But I—I am already on the shadowy side of life. I want nothing more from the world. But those still on the sunny side have other things to consider. I think war is a horrible barbarism, still I would not advise any one to hold back from his duty in time of war. Men are often compelled to take part in the foolishness of majorities. I know your heart is in the right place, and that you don't place any exaggerated value on your life. You are content to stand alone in the world, and have no mortgage of obligation on your life. Why will you not fight?"

"Simply because I think as you do about duels. I agree that one must often take part in the folly of the crowd, but I see a difference there. I go and fight in battle because the State compels me. I can struggle against these laws with my feeble forces, and I can exert myself to bring about their alteration; but so long as they exist I must submit to them, or else exile myself or commit suicide. If the duel were a written law, I would fight; but the law as a matter of fact forbids it, and my opinions are in accordance with the law."

"But there are laws of society as well as laws of the State. There are customs which prevail over opinion and prejudices."

"That is not the same thing. If the folly of the majority form itself into laws of the State, the gendarmes see to their enforcement. No judge or jailer compels obedience to the laws of society."

"Something like it, however. It is unspeakably bitter to live without the respect of one's fellow-creatures."

"I am coming to that point. But please do not think me overbearing and conceited. The respect of my fellow-men I hold far more lightly than self-respect. If I despised myself it would be no compensation if every one saluted me, and if I respect myself, it does not trouble me if others hold me lightly. When I am not forcibly compelled I cannot let my own actions be guided by the caprices and fads of other people. So long as it is possible my actions shall be guided by my own judgment. You say you want nothing more of the world—I require nothing more either. The only thing I demand is the freedom of the soul."

"Yes—yes," murmured Schrotter as if to himself, "I know this direction of thought better than you think. It has been brought before me a hundred times by the word and action of Indian fakirs. It seems to me that false freedom of the soul is a chimera. Our most unfettered resolves are called forth by unknown, often by outward conditions, by our own peculiar qualities, by the state of our bodily health, by unknown nervous sources of energy through what we see, hear, read, learn. You make your judgment the sole guide of your actions, but your judgment itself is the result of forces and influences unsuspected by yourself and depending on them. Well! you want to lead the life of a fakir, to unloose the ties binding you to other men, that is one of several ways to secure peace and happiness, which to me also is an object in life. The principal thing is not to be superficial, but to consider both what one requires and what one gives up before turning into a fakir. I respect you in any case."

The drawing-room door opened noiselessly, and the Indian woman appeared, and with a pleasant inclination of her head spoke a word to Dr. Schrotter. He got up and said, "Lunch is ready." They went into the adjoining dining-room, furnished like any ordinary room. On the table was a beautiful silver bowl of Indian work filled with flowers, the sole luxury of this bachelor's table, neither wine nor anything else to drink being visible. Schrotter drank nothing but water, and he knew that Wilhelm's taste was similar. Bhani, as the Indian housekeeper was called, stood close behind her master's chair, never taking her eyes off him. The dishes were brought in by the white-bearded servant, and handed with a deep reverence to Bhani. She placed the dishes before Schrotter, changing them for a fresh course, and poured water into his glass. It was a silent, attentive service, almost giving the impression of adoration. Bhani appeared not to be waiting on a mortal master, but taking part in a sacrifice in a temple, so much devotion was expressed in her noble, warmly-colored face.

A dish of curry spread its oriental scent through the room, and Schrotter continued:

"Tell me, dear Eynhardt, in what way you mean to accomplish your fakir's contempt of the world?"

"Pardon me," interrupted Wilhelm, "the expression does not strike me as quite fair. I don't despise the world, I consider it merely as a phenomenon, valueless to my way of thinking, and in which I fail to find any real actuality."

"I understand quite well; we are not debating on a platform, but chatting over our lunch. I am not troubling either to talk in the correct jargon of school philosophy, and therefore I am at liberty to call your longings after the essence of things, contempt of the world. Now this occurs in two places—either among inexperienced young men of strong, noble natures, instinctively conscious of their own vitality, and intoxicated by their own strength, who feel so overcome by the phenomenon that they undervalue it, and believe that they are able singly to fight against it. Or there are the weak natures, who think that they are capable of changing the phenomenon to suit themselves. As they are not in a position to strive against it they retire sullenly defeated. The story of the fox and the grapes would just express their case, and also an excess of the consciousness of their 'ego.' Those are, I think, the resources from which spring contempt of the world: neither of these cases coincide with yours; you are not young and inexperienced enough for the one, and you are too useful for the other. You are healthy and sound, of average powers and energy, uncommonly well made in body and mind; of the poetical age, comfortably off, and I should like to know how you have come to despise the world?"

"I hardly know. The first impulse came perhaps in Russia in early childhood, where I got into the habit of regarding people around me as barbarous—neither useful nor valuable."

Schrotter shook his head.

"I have lived for twenty years among a subdued and so-called inferior race, but I have learned to love them instead of despising them."

"Very likely I have inherited the feeling from my mother, who was very timid of other people, and given to mysticism."

"Is it not rather your reading? The unhappy Schopenhauer?"

Wilhelm smiled a little.

"I am above all things an admirer of Schopenhauer, although his explanation of the mysteries of the world through the will is a joke. What he has written about the main teachings of Buddhism has influenced me very much."

"I see where you have got to—'Maja Nirvana'"

Wilhelm nodded.

"That is all a fraud," Schrotter broke out, so that Bhani, who never saw him violent, looked up frightened. "I know Indians who have talked endlessly to learned pandits on these questions, and have explained the real ideas of Maja Nirvana to me. It is incomprehensible that people can misuse words on this subject as they do in Europe. Nirvana is not what European Buddhists appear to believe—an absolute negation—a cessation of consciousness and desire; but, on the contrary, it is the highest consciousness, the expansion of individual being into universal existence. Here is the Indian seer's conception: the most limited individuality cares only for his own 'ego.' But in the same measure that he transcends his limitation, the circle of his interest is widened; more actualities and existing phenomena are admitted, and come into sympathy with himself. All things mingle with and extend his own 'ego;' and that can be so widened as to embrace the interests of the whole world, until man can be in as much sympathy with a grain of sand, or the most distant star, and take as much share in the ant, and in the dwellers on Saturn, as in his own stomach and toes. In this way the whole universe becomes a constituent part of his 'ego;' thus his desires cease individually to exist, and are assimilated with the entire phenomenal world, and he longs for nothing beyond this. The 'ego' ceases because nothing is left outside the individual 'ego;' but this Nirvana, this highest step in the perfection of humanity, is, as you can see, not the negation of everything, but the absorption of everything; not something immovable, but rather the wonderful, ceaseless movement of the world's life. Men will not attain to Nirvana through quiet and indifference, but through strenuous labor, not by withdrawing into their 'ego,' but by going outside it. The true Nirvana of the pandits is the exact opposite of your Schopenhauer's Nirvana."

"But how can this conception of the seer's Nirvana coincide with their inactivity and renunciation of the world?"

"People misunderstand the fakir's belief. The Indian wise men think that the work of perfection is performed by the spirit alone, and that the activity of the body disturbs it; therefore the body must rest while the soul accomplishes its full measure of work, while it widens the circle of its interest, and absorbs into itself the phenomenal world. The clumsy understanding of the crowd thereupon comes to the conclusion that to become holy and attain to Nirvana, one must not stir a finger, not even to support oneself."

Wilhelm thought over this new point of view, but Schrotter went on:

"Believe me, true wisdom is neither that of the fakir nor of the man of the world; but as it appears to me, it neither despises the world nor admires it. One must not depend on oneself too much, neither on others. One must always be saying to oneself that one has no lasting importance in the world, but that in this transitory state eternal forces are at work, the same forces which drive the earth round the sun, and which operate on all men and things. Do not let us individualize too much; we are only a piece of the whole, to which we hang by a thousand unknown threads. Let us not either be too arrogant in our bearing toward our fellow-men, in whose company we are the involuntary puppets of unknown laws of development which are leading humanity on to a given epoch."

This conversation had taken Wilhelm's mind off his misfortune, and he had almost forgotten his adventure with Pechlar. He was reminded of it, however, on reaching home about three o'clock, by finding Paul, who always came to see him at that hour.

"What's the news?" cried he, coming cheerfully to meet him.

"I went to-day to see Fraulein Ellrich, to set things right between us."

"Bravo."

"Yes; I went, but I have not done it." And then he related the incident again.

Paul seemed quite stunned while Wilhelm was speaking, and then sprang up in great excitement from the sofa, and cried:

"You will fight the scoundrel, of course!"

"No," said Wilhelm quietly.

"What!" shouted Paul, taking hold of Wilhelm's shoulder and shaking him. "Surely you are not in earnest? You are an officer—you have been a student—you will never let that fool of a fellow place you in a false position!" Wilhelm freed himself, and tried to speak reasonably; but Paul would not listen, and went on, his face red with anger:

"Not only for yourself; you owe it to the girl's honor, if not to your own, to punish the fellow. You won't appear like a coward in a woman's eyes."

"That is an odd kind of logic."

"Do be quiet with your logic and your philosophy, and the lot of them. I am not a logician, but a man, and I feel a mortal offense like a man, and want to settle with the offender."

"Do stop a minute and let me speak a word. I will break off my relations with Fraulein Ellrich, and then I shall not be in a position to fight for her."

"That is very chivalrous!"

"That is silly! Just think of this situation: suppose I wound or kill the offender—come back from the duel, and find the young girl, who is the cause of the quarrel, ready to offer me the prize. I answer: 'Many thanks, fair lady, I do not now wish for it,' and straightway leave her, like the knight in the old ballad."

That seemed to satisfy Paul.

"Very well; then it must not be on her account. But fight you must," and he stopped suddenly, and then burst out: "If you will not fight him, I will."

"Are you mad?"

Paul began to explain that he had the right to do it; he worked himself into a fury, he stuck to his ideas, and it took Wilhelm an hour to bring him to a more reasonable frame of mind. He spared no pains in explaining to him his views of the world's opinion, and that the real cowardice would be to fear the foolish prejudices of society; but it was all in vain, and Paul's angry objections were only silenced when Wilhelm said with great earnestness:

"If nothing that I say convinces you, I can only act in one way with the painful knowledge that our friendship is not equal to such conditions, but only to ordinary occasions."

"Oh! if it comes to giving up our friendship, as far as I am concerned, I must wink at the whole thing; but what I can't stand is your calling the opportunity which allows one to silence a fool, a mere disease."

The crisis was not long in coming. The next morning before Wilhelm went out, a lieutenant of one of the Uhlan regiments stationed at Potsdam called, and said he had come with a challenge from Herr von Pechlar; he declined to sit down, giving his message as shortly as possible, with the least suspicion of contempt in his voice.

Herr von Pechlar had waited the whole afternoon; but as Herr Eynhardt had sent him no message, he could no longer put off demanding satisfaction. The questions as to who was the offender, and what weapons should be used, might now be decided by the seconds. Wilhelm looked calmly into the officer's eyes, and explained that he had nothing further to do with Herr von Pechlar.

"You are an officer in the Reserve?" asked the lieutenant haughtily.

"Yes."

"I hope you understand that we shall bring the case before the notice of the regiment?"

"You are perfectly free to do so."

The lieutenant stuck his eyeglass into his right eye, looked hard at Wilhelm for several seconds, then, with an expression of deep disgust, he spat on the floor, noisily turned round, and without a word or sign, retired, his sword and spurs clanking as he went.

Oh, how hard it was to overcome the instinct of the wild beast! How furiously it tugged at its chain! How it tried to spring after the lieutenant, and clutch his throat in its claws!—but Wilhelm conquered the new cravings of his instinct and stood still. He experienced a great self-contentment at last, and admitted to himself that he would not have been nearly so glad if he had wounded a dozen of the enemy in single combat.

Three days later he received in writing, an order to present himself at eleven o'clock the morning but one following to the Commandant of the 61st Regiment. He took the journey the following evening, and at the appointed hour he was shown into the commandant's private room, where he found also his old captain, raised to the rank of major. He spoke kindly to Wilhelm and held out his hand, while the commandant contented himself with a nod, and a sign to be seated.

"I suppose you know that you have been ordered to come here about the affair with Lieutenant von Pechlar?" he said.

"Certainly, sir."

"Will you relate what occurred?"

Wilhelm answered as he was desired. His recital was followed by a short silence, during which the commandant and the major exchanged glances.

"And you will not fight?" asked the first.

"No, sir."

"Why not?"

"Because my principles do not allow me."

The commandant looked at the major again and then at Wilhelm, and went on

"If I take the trouble to discuss the matter with you quite unofficially, you have to thank the major, who has spoken warmly in your favor."

Wilhelm thanked the major by a bow.

"We know that you are not a coward. You showed great bravery on the battlefield. It is because of that, I feel sorry. You are a faddist, you proved that by your refusal of the Iron Cross, which is the pride of every other German soldier. We are not willing to condemn a mode of procedure, the meaning of which you evidently do not understand, and which all your views of life tend to destroy. I am not speaking now as your superior officer, but as a man—as your father might speak to you. Believe what I say. Fulfill your duty as a man of honor."

"I cannot follow your advice," answered Wilhelm gentle, but firmly.

He was painfully conscious that his answer sounded more roughly and harshly than he intended, but he knew it was impossible to go into a long philosophical discussion, kind and well-meaning as the commandant was.

"We have more than fulfilled our promise, major," said the commandant, and turning to Wilhelm, "Thank you, Herr—"

The major looked out of the window, and Wilhelm had to go without being able to thank him by a look. He felt, however, that this time things had been easier for him to bear, and that the only painful feeling he had experienced during the interview was the vexation he was giving the major.

The Militar Wochenblatt published a short account of his discharge. It made no personal impression on him, but he felt that he was branded in the eyes of others. It, however, seemed to draw Paul Haber nearer to him. He avoided talking on the subject, but every one noticed the quiet way in which he behaved to Wilhelm, his little attentions, his long and frequent visits, as if he were under the impression that he must console his friend in this great misfortune, and stand by him as firmly as possible. Wilhelm knew him as he did himself—how cautious and practically clever he was, and how dangerous it was for him in his own position as Reserve officer to keep up this confidential intercourse with one who had been turned from a hero to a judicially dismissed officer, how perilous for the connection he had with celebrated and influential people, and for the appearance he must keep up in society. Wilhelm valued and appreciated all Paul's heroism in remaining so true and stanch to him, he did not ask for these things, but they were freely given by one who ran the risk of becoming poor, so he was deeply grateful to him.

He considered himself under an obligation to go once more to the Ellrichs', to formally take leave of them; but when he rang at their door he was told that the family had gone away to Heringsdorf. As this had occurred, Paul did not think it necessary to tell his friend what he had heard through Fraulein Marker, namely, that the Ellrichs were very angry about the affair of the duel, and had given orders before they went away that Wilhelm was not to be admitted if he called. Wilhelm now wrote to Loulou (he had avoided doing so earlier), a short, dignified letter, in which he begged her forgiveness for having been so long in finding out the state of his feelings, as the struggle had been hard and painful, but he could now no longer conceal the fact that their characters were not sufficiently in harmony to insure happiness together for a lifetime. He thanked her for the happiest week in his life, and for the deepest and sweetest feelings he had ever experienced, and which would always remain the dearest memory of his life. His photograph was shortly afterward sent back to him, from Ostend; but his letter remained unanswered. He did not learn therefore, that it had made an exceedingly bad impression, and that Frau Ellrich had only been restrained with difficulty by her daughter from writing to tell him how impertinent she thought it of him to appear to take the initiative, when her daughter had first refused to receive him. Herr von Pechlar obtained a long leave, which he spent at Heringsdorf. In September the Kreuzzeitung announced his betrothal to Fraulein Ellrich, which was followed in the winter by their brilliant wedding.

The breaking of Wilhelm's relations with Loulou left a great blank in his life. Up till now he had had in pleasant, hopeful hours, an object to which all the paths in his life led him, to which his thoughts were drawn as a ship steers for a distant yet secure harbor; now the object was gone, and when he looked forward to his future it seemed like the gray surface of the sea at dusk, formless, limitless, without meaning or interest. Even the painful doubt he had been in, his hesitation between the resolve to persevere in the engagement, or to renounce it, the fight between his intelligence and his inclinations, had become familiar to him, and had filled his thoughts by day and his dreams by night. These must now all be renounced. If for the last half-year his love had been only a quiet happiness, or a hardly-defined desire, it was at any rate an occupation for his mind, and he missed the employment very greatly.

He became quieter than ever; his face lost its youthful, healthy color, and he appeared like the typical lover famed in classic story. But his friends did not laugh at him; they bore with him, treated him gently, as if he had been a disappointed girl. Paul, who was filling the place of an invalided professor of agricultural chemistry, and working hard after the college term began, found time to come every day for a long walk in the Thiergarten, and resigned himself to long philosophical discussions which so far had not been at all to his taste. Dr. Schrotter seldom had any spare time during the day; but Wilhelm always took tea with him in the evenings.

Did Bhani know anything of his story?

Had her womanly instinct guessed that his careworn, melancholy expression betrayed an unhappy love story—a subject so sympathetic to women? Anyhow she anticipated every means of serving him, and her glance betrayed an almost shamefaced sympathy.

One November evening they were sitting at the little drum-shaped table in the Indian drawing-room; the teaurn steaming, and Bhani standing near, ready to obey her master's slightest wish. Schrotter touched on the wound in Wilhelm's heart hitherto so tenderly avoided.

"My friend," he said, "it is time that you came to yourself. It is obvious that you are still grieving, instead of fighting against your dreams; you give way to them without a struggle."

Wilhelm hung his head. "You are right. It is foolish; for I see that I do not love the girl deeply enough to spoil my life."

"Come now. You were more in love than you thought; but it is always so; even in pure and passionless natures human nature is very strong, and the first young and pretty girl who comes near enough to you brings out all the dormant feelings, and reason disappears. People often do the maddest things in this period of unrest, which they repent all their after life. I have always mistrusted a first love. One must be quite satisfied that it is for an individual, and not merely the natural inclination for the other sex asserting itself. Your first love, my poor Eynhardt, certainly belongs to this class. Your youthful asceticism has had its revenge; now that your reason has got hold of the reins again, the rebellion of your instinct will soon be subdued."

"I hope so," said Wilhelm.

"I am sure of it. There is no doubt about the end of crises like these, and it really is difficult to take the misery they cause seriously, although it is bad enough while it lasts. It is the most overpowering and yet the least dangerous of diseases. The patient gives himself up for lost, and the doctor can hardly help smiling, because he knows that the malady will only run its course, and will stop like a clock at its appointed time. He can, however, hasten the cure, if he can bring the patient to his own conviction."

He was silent, and seemed sunk in thought. Then he began again suddenly: "I will read you a story about this; nothing is more instructive than a clinical picture."

Bhani sprang to her feet and hastened toward him, but he put her aside with a word, and going into his study he appeared again bearing a folio bound in leather and with the corners fastened with copper.

"This is my diary," he said. "I have had the weakness to keep this since I was sixteen. There are three volumes already, and I began the fourth when I returned to Germany. Listen now, and don't put yourself under any constraint. I will laugh with you."

He opened the folio, and after a short search began to read. It was the romance of his early life, written in the form of a diary, simply told at some length. Quite an ordinary story of an acquaintanceship made with a pretty girl, the daughter of a bookseller, who sat next to him in a theater. Meetings out of doors, then the introduction to her parents' house, and then the betrothal. The Revolution of 1848 broke out, and the many demands on the young doctor turned his thoughts away for the time from plans of marriage. His fiancee greatly admired the fiery orator and fighter at barricades, and told him so, in enthusiastic speeches and letters. The father, however, had no sympathy with reactionaries, and soon conceived a violent antipathy for his future single-minded son-in-law. As long as the democratic party held the upperhand, he kept his feelings in the background, making nevertheless endless pretexts for delaying the marriage. The party of reactionaries broke up, however, and the bookseller declared war; he forbade the young democrat to enter his house, and even denounced him to the police. The young lovers were, of course, dreadfully unhappy, and vowed to be true to one another. He determined to go away, and tried to persuade her to go with him. She was frightened, but he was audacious and insisted. They would go to London, and be married there; he could earn his living, and they would defy the father's curse. All was arranged; but at the last moment her courage failed, and she confessed all to the tyrant, who set the police on the young man's track, and sent the girl away to relations in Brandenburg. The unfortunate lover's letters were unanswered. He left Germany, and heard after some weeks that his betrothed was married to a well-to-do jeweler, apparently without any great coercion.

This story was disentangled from letters, conversations, accounts of opinions in the form of monologues, interviews, visits, and descriptions of sea-voyages; all sufficiently commonplace. But what excitement these daily effusions showed! What boundless happiness about kisses, what cries of anguish when the storm broke! Would it not be better to commit suicide and die together? Was it possible that this quiet man with his apathetic calm could ever have been through these stormy times? It did not seem credible, and Schrotter seemed conscious of the immense difference between the man who had written the book and the man who now read it. His voice had a slightly ironical sound, and he parodied some of the scenes in reading them, by exaggerating the pathos. But this could not last long. The real feeling which sighed and sobbed between the pages made itself felt, and carried him back from the cold present to the storm-heated past; he became interested, then grave, and if he had not suddenly shut the book with a bang when he came to the place where his faithless love was married, who knows—

At all events, Wilhelm had not smiled once; his eyes even showed signs of tears. Schrotter took the book into the other room, and when he came back every trace of emotion in look and manner had vanished.

"So you see," he began, "a sensible boy like I am has behaved like an ass in the past. But I did not shoot myself after all, that was so far good, and I am ashamed to tell you how soon I got over it. I often go past her shop in Unter den Linden, and see her through the window beyond all her brilliants and precious stones. She is still very pretty, and seems happy, much happier no doubt than if she had been with me. She would certainly not recognize me now, and I can look at her and my heart beats no whit the faster. Dwell on my example."

"I am not sure that you are not slandering yourself."

"You can feel easy about that," said Schrotter earnestly. "The disenchantment was quick and complete, and very naturally so. Just get Schopenhauer's 'objectivity' out of your head; I don't believe in Plato's theory of the soul divided into two halves which are forever trying to join again. Every sane man has ten thousand objects which are able to awaken and return his love. All he has to do is not to go out of their way."

"Ought not there to be an individual one?"

"I venture to say no. The story of the pine trees of Ritter Toggenburg, which love the palm trees, is the creation of a sentimental poet. Lawgivers in India to all appearance believe in faithfulness unto death; and the widow or even the betrothed follows her husband to the grave of her own free will. This free-will offering only comes, however, by aid of the sharpest threatening of punishment. I have known fourteen-year-old widows who offered themselves miserably to be burned. If they had known how soon they would be consoled, and new love sprang up, they would have violently resisted such suicide! Bhani there is a living example of this,"

As she heard her name she looked up, and Wilhelm intercepted a look between her and Dr. Schrotter, which all at once made clear to him what he had vaguely suspected before. He turned his head sadly toward the window, and looked out into the foggy autumn evening. He felt almost as if he had committed a crime, in having discovered a secret which had not been freely revealed to him.

CHAPTER V.

A LAY SERMON.

"Es ist eine Lust, in deiser Zeit zu leben!" cried Paul Habor, as he walked with Wilhelm and Dr. Schrotter on the first sunny day the following April. They walked under the lindens full of leaf through the Thiergarten, and home over the Charlottenburger Brucke.

The spirit in which he uttered Hutten's words was at that time dominant and far-reaching. It seemed as though people were all enjoying the honeymoon of the new empire; that they breathed peace and the joy of life with the air, as if the whole nation inhaled the pleasure of living, the joy of youth and brave deeds, and that they stood at the entrance of an incomprehensibly great era, promising to everyone fabulous heights of happiness.

A sort of feverish growth had sprung up in Berlin, an excitement and ferment which filled the villas in the west end, and the poor lodging-houses of the other end of the town: was found too in councilors' drawing-rooms, and in suburban taverns. New streets seemed to spring up during the night. Where the hoe and rake of kitchen-gardens were at work yesterday, to-day was the noise of hammers and saws, and in the middle of the open fields hundreds of houses raised their walls and roofs to the sky. It seemed as if the increasing town expected between to-day and to-morrow a hundred thousand new inhabitants, and were forced to build houses in breathless haste to shelter them.

And as a matter of fact the expected throng arrived. Even in the most distant provinces a curious but powerful attraction drew people to the capital; artisans and cottages, village shopkeepers, and merchants from small towns, all rushed there like the inflowing tide. It made one think of a number of moths blindly fluttering round a candle, or of the magnetic rock of Eastern fairy tales, irresistibly attracting ships to wreck themselves. It recalled to one the stories of California at the time of the gold fever. People's excited imaginations saw a veritable gold-mine in Berlin. The French indemnity flew to people's heads like champagne, and in a kind of drunken frenzy every one imagined himself a millionaire. Some had even seen exhibited a reproduction of the hidden treasure. The great heap of glittering pieces was certainly there, a tempting reality, piled up mountains high, millions on millions, craftily arranged to glitter in the flaring gas-light before their covetous eyes. The real treasure must be at least as substantial as its counterfeit. People began to see gold everywhere; red streaks of gold shone through the window-panes, instead of the warm spring sun; they heard murmuring chinking streams of gold flowing behind the walls of their houses, under the pavements of the streets, and every one hastened to fill their hands, and thirsted for their share in the subterranean gold whose stream was concealed from their eyes. While their lips were being moistened by the stream of gold, they were, as a matter of fact, drinking the transformed flesh and blood of the heroes who had sacrificed themselves on the French battlefields, and in this infamous travesty of the Christian mystery of the Lord's Supper the devil himself took part and possession of them. They followed new customs, new views of life, other ideals. The motto of their noisy and obtrusive life seemed to be, "Get rich as quickly and with as little trouble as possible, and make as much as possible of your riches when you have secured them, even by illegitimate means." So the splendid houses rose up in an overloaded gaudy irregular style of architecture, and the smart carriages with india-rubber tires rolled by, yielding soft and soothing riding to their occupants.

Berlin, the sober economical town, the home of honorable families, extolled for respectability almost to affectation, now learned the disorderly ways of noisy cafes, the luxury of champagne suppers, in over-decorated restaurants, became intimately acquainted with the theaters—gaining doubtful introductions to expensive mistresses. Mere upstarts set the fashion in dress, in extravagance, and all who would be elegant, followed, leading the way to barbaric vices. The old-established inhabitants were many of them weak or silly enough to try to outdo the newcomers, and degraded the quiet dignity of their patriarchal manner of life by speculations on the Stock Exchange. The intelligent middle classes, whose eyes and ears were filled with this bluster of the gold-orgy, found that their former way of living had now grown uncomfortable, their houses were too small, their bread too dry, their beer too common and their views of life began to climb upward in a measure which, whether they were willing or equal in talent to it, forced from them harder work and more dogged perseverance. Political economists and statisticians were drawn into excitement by their knowledge of figures. They extolled the sudden crisis in the money market, the easy returns, the great development of consumption in goods. They quoted triumphantly the amount of importations, the great increase in silk, artistic furniture, glass, jewelry, valuable wines, spices, liqueurs, was called a splendid development of trade; wonderful evidence of the prosperity of all classes, and an elevation of the manner of life of the German people. And if moralists failed to see in these heated desires and idle display, the presence of progress and blessing, they were called limited Philistines, who were too feeble-minded to recognize the signs of the times.

The position of the workingman profited by the new condition of things. Berlin seemed insatiable in her demands for able-bodied workmen. Hundreds and thousands left the fields and the woods, and taking their strong arms to the labor market of the capital, found employment in the factories and the workshops; and the mighty engines still beat, sucking in as it were the stream of people from the country. Berlin itself could not contain this influx. The newcomers were obliged gypsy fashion to put up as best they could in the neighborhood. In holes and caves on the heaths and commons, in huts made of brushwood, they bivouacked for months, and these men who lived like prairie dogs in such apparent misery were merry over their houseless, wild existence. As a matter of fact they experienced no actual want, as there was work for every one who could and would labor. The rewards were splendid, and the proletariat found that its only possession, viz., the strength of its muscles, was worth more than ever before. The workingman talked loudly, and held his head high. Was it the result of having served in one or more campaigns? Had he in the background of his mind a vision of dying men and desolate villages, seen so often on the battlefield? However it was, he became violent and quarrelsome, indifferent alike to wounding and death, and learned to make use of the knife like any cutthroat townsman.

With this return to barbarism (an unfailing result with the soldier after every time of war) went a degree of animal spirits, which made one ask whether the workman had learned something of epicurean philosophy. He had the same excited love of tattling as a thoughtless girl, and the animal love of enjoyment of a sailor after a long voyage. His ordinary life seemed to him so uninteresting, so dull, that he tried to give color and charm to it by taking as many holidays as possible, and making his work more agreeable with gambling and drinking, and going for loafing excursions about the neighborhood. Visits to wine and beer-houses and dancing-rooms were endlessly multiplied, and everything had the golden foundation which the proverb of an age of simplicity hardly attributed to honorable handicraft. Profits were squandered in drink; life was a rush and a riot without end.

But curiously, in the same degree in which the opportunities of work were increased and wages became higher, life everywhere easier, and the ordinary enjoyments greater; just so did the workman grow discontented. Desires increased with their gratification, and envy measured its own prosperity by the side of the luxury of the nouveaux riches.

The hand which never before had held so much money, now learned to clinch itself in hatred against the owner of property, the company promoter; against all in fact who were not of the proletariat. The Social Democrat had sprung up ten years before from the circle of the intelligent political economists and philosophers of the artisan classes. Since the war they numbered thousands and ten of thousands, and now began to grow and widen like a moorland fire, at first hardly perceptible, then betraying through the puff of smoke the fire creeping along the ground; then a thousand tongues of flame leap upward, and suddenly sooner or later the whole heath is in a blaze. Innumerable apostles preaching their turbid doctrines in all the factories and workshops, found hearers who were discontented and easily carried away. The social democracy of the workmen was neither a political nor economical programme which appealed to the intellect, or could be proved or argued about, but rather an instinct in which religious mysticism, good and bad impulses, needs, emotional desires were wonderfully mingled. The men were filled with enmity against those who had a large share of money; the new faith dogmatically explained possession of property as a crime—that it was meritorious to hate the possessor and necessary to destroy him. They were made discontented with their limited destiny by the sight of the world and its treasures; the new faith promised them a future paradise in the shape of an equal division of goods—a paradise in which the hand was permitted to take whatever the eye desired. They were disgusted by the consciousness of their deformity and roughness, which dragged them down to the lowest rank in the midst of school learning if not exactly knowledge; of good manners if not good breeding; the new faith raised them in their own eyes, declaring that they were the salt of the earth, that they alone were useful and important parts of humanity; all others who did not labor with their hands being miserable and contemptible sponges on humanity.

The whole proletariat was soon converted to Social Democracy. Berlin was covered with a network of societies, which became the places of worship of the new faith. Handbills, pamphlets, newspapers, partly polemical, partly literary, in which the mob made their statements and professed their faith stoutly; these, although written very badly, yet by their monotony, their angry reproaches, their invocations, reminded one of litanies and psalms.

Wilhelm felt a certain sympathy with the movement. It was first brought to his notice by a new acquaintance, who had worked with him in the physical laboratory since the beginning of the year. He was a Russian, who had introduced himself to the pupils in the laboratory as Dr. Barinskoi from Charkow. His appearance and, behavior hardly bore this out. His long thin figure was loosely joined to thin weak legs. Light blue eyes looked keenly out of a warm grayish-yellow face; add to these a sharp reddish nose, pale lips, a spare, badly grown mustache and beard of a dirty color, and slight baldness. His demeanor was suave and very submissive, his voice had the faltering persuasiveness which a natural and reasonable man dislikes, because it warns him that the speaker is lying in wait to take him by surprise. Barinskoi, beside, never stood upright when he was speaking to any one. He bent his back, his head hung forward, his eyes shifted their glance from the points of his own boots to other people's, his face was crumpled up into a smiling mask, and working his hands about nervously he crammed so many polite phrases and compliments into his conversation that he was a terrible bore to all his acquaintances. Barinskoi, who was an accomplished spy, intended by his entrance into the laboratory to learn all he could in a circuitous way of persons and conditions.

After a short observation he noticed that Wilhelm seemed isolated in the midst of the others, and was treated coldly by every one except the professor. He learned that this coolness of the atmosphere was on account of the refusal of the duel. After that he tried every possible means to get nearer to him. Wilhelm was working in some important researches, and it was possible that the results would destroy some existing theories.

The professor followed the experiments with great attention, and many times spoke of him as his best pupil in difficult work. That was Barinskoi's excuse for asking Wilhelm if he would initiate him into his work, and explain to him his hypotheses and methods. He added, with his submissive smile and nervous rubbing of the hands, that the Heir Doctor might be quite easy about the priority of his discoveries, as he was quite prepared to write an explanation that he stood in the position of pupil to the Heir Doctor, and had only a share in his discoveries in common with others. Wilhelm contented himself by replying that priority was nothing to him, and that he did not work for fame, but because he was ignorant and sought for knowledge.

Thereupon Barinskoi said he was very happy to have found some one with the same views as himself, he also thought that fame was nonsense, that knowledge was the only essential thing, that it gave power over things and men, that the ideal was to proceed unknown and unnoticed through life, making the others dance without knowing who played on the instrument. That was not what Wilhelm meant, but he let it go without denying it. Barinskoi also tried to claim him for a fellow-countryman, but Wilhelm stopped him, explaining that he was a German, although born beyond the frontier of his fatherland. This slight did not disconcert Barinskoi; he endeavored to produce an impression on Wilhelm, and if one shut one's eyes to his ugliness and fawning ways he was a well-informed man; harshness was not in Wilhelm's nature, so he held out no longer against Barinskoi's importunity—who very soon accompanied him home from the laboratory, visited him uninvited in his rooms, invited him to supper at his restaurant, which Wilhelm twice declined, the third time, however, he had not the courage to refuse. In spite of this Barinskoi would not see that his invitation was only accepted out of politeness. There were many things reserved and unsociable about Barinskoi; for example, he never invited any one to his rooms. He called for his letters at the post office. The address he gave, and under which he was entered at the University office, described him as a newspaper correspondent, which agreed with his daily readings and writings. He frequently disappeared for two or three days, after which he emerged again, as it were, dirtier than before, with reddened, half-closed eyelids, weak voice, and general bloodless appearance. A conjecture as to where he was during this time was suggested by a smell of spirits, beside the fact that students from the laboratory had often seen him late at night at the corner of the Leipziger and Friedrichstrasse in earnest consultation with some unhappy creature of the streets, and that he was often seen haunting remote streets in the eastern districts in the company of women.

Barinskoi declared he was the correspondent of a large St. Petersburg paper, and that he made great efforts to remove the prejudices of Russia against Germany, and to give his readers a respect for their great neighbors. By chance one day Wilhelm read the page of Berlin correspondence, and found that from first to last it was full of poisoned abuse, insult, and calumination of Berlin and its inhabitants. At the next opportunity he put it before Barinskoi's eyes without a word. He started a little, but said directly, quite calmly: Yes, he had read the letter too; naturally it was not by him; the paper had other correspondents, who hated Germans, he could do no more than put a stop to their lies, and find out the reality of their misrepresentations.

Early in this short acquaintance it was clear that Barinskoi was in constant money difficulties. By his own representations the paper paid him very irregularly, and the most curious accidents constantly occurred to prevent the arrival of the expected payments. Once the money was sent by mistake to the Constantinople correspondent, and it was six weeks before the oversight was cleared up. Another time a fellow-writer who was traveling to Berlin undertook to bring the money with him. On the way he lost the money out of his pocket-book, and Barinskoi had to wait until he went back to St. Petersburg, to inquire into the case. By such fool's stories was Wilhelm's friendship put to the proof. Barinskoi did not stop at borrowing money occasionally, with sighs and groans, but every few days, often at a few hours' interval, a new and larger loan would frequently follow.

All this was a dubious method of consolation, and yet Dr. Schrotter, or rather Paul Haber, decided that though further contact with Barinskoi must be avoided, he was an object of increasing interest to Wilhelm. Barinskoi had many ideas in sympathy with his, which he did not find in others, and their views of society and practical maxims of life were so much in common that Wilhelm was often puzzled by this question: "How is it possible that people can draw such completely different conclusions from the same suppositions by the same logical arguments? Where is the fatal point where one's ideas separate—ideas which have so far traveled together?"

Barinskoi thought as Wilhelm did, that the world and its machinery were mere outward phenomena, a deception of the senses, whose influence acted as in a delirium. All existing forms of the common life of humanity, all ordinances of the State or society appeared to him as foolish or criminal, and at any rate objectionable. He considered that the object of the spiritual and moral development of the individual was the deliverance from the restraint, and the complete contempt of all outward authority.

So far his opinions agreed with Wilhelm's, and then he disclosed the laws of morality which he had evolved from them.

"The whole world is only an outward phenomenon, and the only reality is my own consciousness," said Barinskoi; "therefore I see in the would only myself, live only for myself, and try only to please myself, I am an extreme individualist. My morality allows me to gratify my senses by pleasant impressions, to convey to my consciousness pleasant representations, so as to enjoy as much as possible. Enjoyment is the only object of my existence, and to destroy all those who come in the way of it is my right."

Wilhelm wondered whether this frightful code could possibly belong to the same views of life which, in despising the enjoyment of the senses, denied desires, demanded the sacrifice of individuality for the sake of others, and found happiness in the enjoyment of love for one's neighbors, and in the struggle for human reason over animal instinct?

Barinskoi understood Wilhelm's character and saw that he could quite safely trust to his forbearance and his single-mindedness, so he made no further secret of the fact that he was a Nihilist and an Anarchist. When Wilhelm asked him if he imagined what the realization of his theories meant, he had the answer ready.

"We demand unconditional freedom. Our will shall not be confined by the will of others, or by oppressive laws. The Parliament is our enemy as well as the monarch, the tyranny of the autocrat as well as that of the majority, the coercion of laws of the State, as well as those of society. We will gather together groups according to their free choice and inclination out of the fragments of annihilated society, that is, if we can manage to procure our enjoyment as well in groups as alone. These groups will unite into larger groups if the happiness of all demands a larger undertaking than a single group can secure, such as a great railway, a submarine tunnel, and the like. In some cases it may be necessary that a whole people, or even the whole of humanity, should be in one group, but only up to a certain point, and only until this point is reached. Naturally no individual is bound to a group, nor one group to another; binding and loosing go on perpetually, and with the same facility as molecules in living organisms unite and separate."

Barinskoi occupied himself particularly with the labor questions. Not that the distress and want of the very poor, the economical insecurity, the general misery, troubled him at all. He was cynically conscious that he was as indifferent to the laborer as to the capitalist; the laborer's inevitable brutalization, his hunger, his bad health, and short term of life touched him as little as the gout of the rich gourmand, or the nerves of fine ladies. He saw, however, in the proletariat a powerful army against prevailing conditions. He could trace among the discontented masses the possession of the crude vigor which the Nihilists wanted, to crush the old edifices of the State and society, and it was this which interested him in the movement and its literature. He knew the last accurately, and initiated Wilhelm into it, and so the latter learned all about socialism, its opinions of the philosophy of production, its theories and promises. He learned also that sects had already been formed within this new faith, which the revelations of the socialistic prophets explained differently; and that they furiously hated each other, and were as much at enmity as if they were a State Church with a privileged priesthood, benefices, property and power.

The complaints of the proletariat appeared to Wilhelm of doubtful value. In every age there were economic fevers, which were not caused by misery, but by discontent and wastefulness, and if he saw a workman staggering through the streets, his legs tottering beneath him, he guessed that his weakness was not caused by hunger, but by beer or spirits. He understood that mankind believed in an unbroken work of development within nature, and in their own self-cultivation. The theory of socialistic teaching, namely, the conditions of production and distribution, could be constantly remodeled just as other human institutions, i.e. the customs of governments and societies, the laws, ideas of beauty and morality, knowledge of nature, and views of society. His sympathies went out to those who were convinced that the present economical organization had lived out its time, and were endeavoring to remove it.

Wilhelm's friends interested themselves warmly in this new sphere of thought. Paul was a member of the National Liberal Election Society, and was enthusiastic about Bennigsen and Lasker, who possessed enough statesmanlike wisdom to surrender fearlessly to the opposition, and determine to go with the government. To these present experiences Dr. Schrotter joined the half-forgotten training of '48, and agreed to belong to a society of the district; he had soon an official appointment, and placed his experience and knowledge at the disposal of the sick and poor of the town. He did not interest himself at first in political strife. He was very uneasy about the turn things were taking, and considered that it was not right to rebel against the existing conditions of things, which to the majority of people were agreeable enough.

"You have fought and bled for the new empire," he said; "I left it while I was in India to get on as best it could; if the others think themselves well off, I don't see why they should not have the satisfaction of the results of their work, just because of the sulky temper of criticism."

Wilhelm had often taken one or other of them to his society, but without their being much interested in the meetings. One day he asked his friend whether he would not go with him to a social democratic meeting. Schrotter was quite prepared, as he saw that Wilhelm was really in earnest, and was trying to come in contact with the realities of life. Paul abominated the social democrats, but he sacrificed himself to spend an hour there with Wilhelm.

The meeting they were to attend was at the Tivoli. It was a disagreeable evening in April, with gusts of wind and frequent showers. The sky was full of clouds chasing each other in endless succession, the flames of gas flickered and flared, and the streets were covered with mud which splashed up under the horses' feet. The three friends went in spite of bad weather to the Tivoli on foot. In the Belle Alliance Strasse they came upon groups of workmen going in the same direction as themselves, and as they reached the place in the Lichterfelder Strasse, they were accompanied by a long stream of people. At the entrance to the club they found themselves in the midst of a crowd, and could only advance very slowly unless, like the others, they pushed and elbowed their way. Mounting a few steps they reached an enormous garden, lighted by the fitful beams of the moon as she emerged from the clouds, and a few gaslamps. On the right was a Gothic building, which would have been sufficiently handsome if built in stone, but with barbarous taste had been executed in wood. At the end of the garden some more steps led to a broad, four-cornered courtyard, on the right of which the iron spire of the National Memorial was dimly visible, while to the left was a large building of red and yellow brick with a four-square tower at either end, a pavilion projecting from the center, and a number of large windows. Over the entrance in the center of the building was the inscription in gold letters on a blue ground:

"Gemesst im edeln Geistensaft
Des Wemes Geist, des Brodes Kraft"

In the little anteroom a few sharp-looking, rather conceited young men were standing, either the instigators or organizers of the meeting. They eyed the people who came in with a quick look of assurance, offering a pamphlet, which nearly every one bought. Through this anteroom was the hall, large enough to hold a thousand people comfortably. Several tables for beer stood between red-covered pillars which supported the ceiling, and on the right was a platform for the speakers. Wilhelm, Schrotter, and Paul Haber found places not far from this, although the hall was soon filled up after they came in.

Wilhelm's first impression was not favorable. He had bought a pamphlet at the door, and in it he read foolish jokes, clumsy tirades against capitalists, and drearily silly verses. If the party possessed quick and cultivated writers, they had certainly not been employed on this leaflet. His finer senses were as shocked at the meeting as his taste was at the pamphlet. Mingled odors of tobacco-smoke, beer, human breath, and damp clothes filled the air; the people at the tables had an indescribably common stamp, unlovely manners, harsh, loud voices, and unattractive faces. They gossiped and laughed noisily, and coarse expressions were frequent. The earnest moral tone, the almost gloomy melancholy which Wilhelm had found so attractive in socialistic writings, was absent, and it seemed to him as if the new doctrine in its removal from the enthusiast's study to the beer-tables of the crowd had lost all nobility, and had sunk to degradation.

Paul took no trouble to conceal the disgust which "this dirty rabble" gave him. He gazed contemptuously about him, and every time that one of his neighbors' elbows came near his coat he brushed the place angrily, and muttered half-aloud:

"Well, if I were the government I would jolly soon stop your meetings."

Dr. Schrotter, on the other hand, found the sight of the crowd rekindle in him all the feeling of sentiment he had had for the old democrats; he felt his heart overflow with pity and tenderness. With his physician's eyes he pierced through the brutal physiognomies, and observed them with kindness and sympathy, making his friends attentive too.

"One of the martyrs of work," he said gently, indicating a haggard man sitting at the next table who had lost one eye.

"How do you know that?"

"He must be a worker in metal, and has had a splinter in one of his eyes. He had the injured eye removed to save the other."

Here was a baker with pale face and inflamed eyelids, coughing badly—consumptive, in consequence of the dust from the flour—his eyes affected by the heat of the oven. Here was a man who had lost a finger of his left hand—the victim of a cloth loom; and here a pallid-looking man, showing when he spoke or laughed slate-colored gums—a case of lead-poisoning, with a painful death as the inevitable result. And it seemed as if over all these cripples and sickly people the Genius of Work hovered as the black angel of Eastern stories, tracing on their foreheads with his brush—on this one mutilation, on this one an early death. Schrotter's observations and explanations placed the whole meeting in a different light to Wilhelm. The coarseness of the men, even the dirt on their hands and faces, touched him like a reproach, and in their jokes and laughter he seemed to hear a bitter cry.

A reproach, a complaint against whom? Against the capitalists, or against inexorable fate? Wilhelm asked himself whether the conditions of labor were attributable to men, or were not the result of cruel necessity? Could the capitalist be responsible for the accidents of machines, the dust from flour, the splitting of iron? If these workmen had not been one-eyed or consumptive could they have performed their work for the commonweal? Was it not true that if mankind would not renounce its claims to bread and other necessities, it must pay for the satisfaction of wants with the tribute of health and life? that every comfort, every pleasure added to existence was paid for by human sacrifice? that the masks of tragedy worn at this meeting were merely the corporate expressions of a law which united development and progress with pain and destruction? In this case the whole socialist programme was manifestly wrong, and the sum of the workman's grievances was not the result of the economical arrangements of society, but of the eternal conditions of civilization, that the theory of the methods of labor and their amelioration was not the expectation of an equal division of property, but rather of the contrivances of the inventor.

While Wilhelm was absorbed in these reflections the first speaker of the evening appeared on the platform, a little dapper man, restless as quicksilver, with long hair, large mouth, and a shrill voice. He opened the meeting with an extraordinary volubility, in a whirl of pantomimic gesture and excitement, violently denouncing the capitalists; "infamous bloodsuckers" as he called them. He painted hopelessly confused pictures, with constant faults of grammar—of the hard fate of the workingman, and the black treachery of the property-owning classes. They were slaveowners who paid them their daily wages by shearing the wool off their backs, and enjoyed riotous luxury themselves while the poor destitute ones were engulfed in a chasm of misery. The workman must possess the fruit of his labor himself, like the bird in the air, or the fish in the water. He who produced nothing was a parasite, and deserved to be extirpated; he was only a drag, consequently a poison for the rest of mankind. The Commune in Paris was the first signal of warning for the thieves of society. Soon the great flood would burst forth which would carry away all thieves and tyrants, usurers and bloodsuckers, and the workingmen must be united and get their weapons ready. Unity was strength, and to allow themselves to be fleeced by these hyenas of capitalism was an insult to any free, thoughtful man.

He went on in this style for about half an hour, during which time the words came out in a constant stream without a moment's pause. Schrotter's expression became sad, while Paul banged the table with his mug and cried "Bravo" at every grammatical mistake, or every false analogy. Angry glances were cast at him from neighboring tables, as in his applause was recognized contempt for the speaker whom they admired so much. No one laughed or joked, all were silent to the end; at every violent expression of the long-haired Saxon, eyes flashed, heads nodded approval, and feet stamped excitedly. So eagerly did the meeting drink in this excited orator's words that they quite forgot to drink their beer, and the waiter, bringing in a fresh supply, had to go out again with an exclamation of surprise.

When the speaker had finished and resumed his seat, Schrotter and Paul, to their immense surprise, saw Wilhelm spring to his feet in the midst of all the stamping and applause and go to the platform. What was that for? He went up and began to speak in an undertone to the organizers of the meeting. They put their heads together, looking at the card Wilhelm had given them; then one of them rose, and coming to the front of the platform, shouted so as to be heard above the clamor:

"True to our principles of listening to opponents, we are going to allow a guest to speak: it is not part of the programme, but no citizen shall have cause to complain that his mouth has been stopped."

Any one could understand what this meant, as Wilhelm stood alone in the middle of the platform and waited with folded arms for silence and attention. His dark eyes looked straight at his audience, and he began in his clear, quiet voice: "What you all feel in this meeting is discontent with your fate, and a wish to improve it. I do not believe, however, that the honored speaker before me has shown you a way which will bring you any nearer to your desires. You wish that the State shall nurse you in sickness, and provide for you in old age. What is the State? It is yourselves. The State has nothing but what you give it. If it provides for you in sickness and old age, it takes the money out of your own pockets. You do not want the State for that. In days of health and strength you could yourselves lay aside spare money for bad times without the services of gendarmes, or assistance of executors. The last speaker spoke of hatred for the owners of property, hatred of profit. Hatred is a painful feeling. It adds to the pain of existence another, and very likely a greater one. A soul in which the poison of hate is at work is heavy and sad, and can never feel happiness. If you would not burden your lives with hatred it might be possible that you would become happy."

A murmur arose in the meeting, and a voice in opposition called out loudly. "The fellow is a Jesuit." "Parson's talk," cried another from the corner of the room. Wilhelm took no notice of the interruption, but went on.

"Why do you object to the owners of property? On account of their idleness? That is not just. Many of them work much harder than all of you, and bear a weight of responsibility which would kill most of you. But suppose we grant that many rich people waste their lives doing nothing. Instead of envying these unhappy people, I pity them from the bottom of my heart. I would prefer death a thousand times to life without duty and work."

The murmur grew stronger and more threatening.

"I wish," cried Wilhelm, raising his voice, "I wish I were rich and powerful. Then I would invite those who scorn my words now, to live quite idly for a year or six months. I would take care that no employment was possible for them, that their days and weeks should be quite empty. Then they would see how soon they would raise imploring hands to those who had condemned them to idleness. Neither guards nor walls would keep them to the softly-cushioned golden-caged prison of indolence, they would fly as if for their lives, and go back to the place where their work was, which they had previously thought like hell."

"Let us see if we would," cried some with contemptuous laughter.

"In what has the rich man the advantage of you? He lives better, you say. He can procure more enjoyments for himself. Are you sure that these so-called enjoyments bring happiness? Your healthy hunger makes your bread and cheese taste better than the rich dishes at noblemen's tables, and the suffering which fills every life is more bitter in the western villa than in the workingman's back room, because there they have more leisure to endure it in, and every fiber of the soul has its own torture."

"What do you get for defending the rich man?" called a voice from the hall.

"I am telling you the penalty of property. You must be just in everything. Granted that the rich man is a criminal; granted his idleness is an offense to your activity; granted that his roast meat and wine make your potatoes taste insipid; it is in the order of things that you should envy him. But what comes out of this envy? Let us admit that you could carry through anything you undertook. The rich man would be plundered and even killed, and his treasures divided between you. We forget that the rich man is human; we deny him the mercy which the poor man claims from his fellowmen; we take up the position that to reduce a rich man to beggary is not the same injustice as to profit by the work of a poor man; we enjoy the idea of the rich man, hungry and shivering, when at the same time the hungry shivering poor man has become our pretext for robbing the other. Do you believe that you would then have improved your lot in life? Do you think that you would be any happier? Just think it over for a moment. The rich people are exterminated, their goods are divided among you; you are already making a discovery, viz., that the wealthy people are in a very small minority, hardly one in two hundred, and that the division of their whole property amounts to very little for each of you. But suppose, for the sake of argument, that you all become rich. What then? You throw away your working clothes and dress yourselves in silk; you deck yourselves with silver and gold ornaments, and you sit on soft-cushioned sofas. Think how long these luxuries would last—

a month perhaps, at the most a year. Then the rich man's wine is all drunk, and his larder empty, the silk clothes are worn out, and the sofas torn; you cannot eat precious stones and gold, and if you do not mean to starve you must begin working again, and after the extermination of the rich man and the division of his property you are exactly in the position you were in before."

He paused a moment or two, in which there was silence for the first time, and then went on:

"This all means that your bondage is not laid on you by man, but by Nature herself. Life is hard and wearisome, and no laws or orders of State or society can make it otherwise. The simple minds of men understood this a thousand years ago, and they did not rest until they had found out a reason for everything, so they sought through the authors of the Jewish Bible for a reasonable explanation of our mournful destiny on this earth, and comforted themselves with the assertion that mankind was atoning for the sins of its forefathers. You, the sons of the nineteenth century, do not believe in this any longer, but see in the system of profits and the injustice of our social conditions the causes of your misery. Your explanation is, however, fully as much a fabrication as the Biblical one. Pain and death are the conditions of our existence, and for that reason cannot be done away with. If a miracle could happen, and you could all be happy in the way you wish, namely, living your life without work, without suffering, and with a great deal of enjoyment, what would happen then? The race would increase so fast that after one or two generations there would hardly be elbow-room, and bread would be as scarce as it is now. It is the difficulty of providing for children which limits the population, and this difficulty fixes the limit. Understand this too, do what you will, you can only procure momentary relief, and every relief procured means an increase of population. Whatever your methods of labor are, however the fruits of it are distributed, you will never produce up to the satisfaction of your wants; and the sweat of your brow will always be in vain if you set yourself against the hostile forces of nature."

Wilhelm paused a moment in the deep stillness which now reigned in the hall, and then went on:

"I do not deny that your lives are troublesome and hard, but I believe that you make your pain unnecessarily difficult to bear, and add to it by imagination. You feel your lot to be hard because you see rich people, who in the distance appear to you to be happy. I have already told you that the rich are an exception, and that the world cannot guarantee the existence of a millionaire of to-day for long. At most you can make the few rich men poor, but you cannot make all the poor men rich. But why compare yourselves with such people? Why not with those who have gone before us? Look back, and you will find that your lives are not only easier but very much richer than the generations who have gone before you. The poorest among you live better, quieter, and pleasanter lives than a well-to-do man a thousand years ago, or than a prince of primitive times. You complain that your labor is hard and unhealthy? You live longer, in better health, and freer from anxiety than the huntsman, fisherman, or warrior of the barbarous ages. What you most suffer from is your hatred, not your need, your ambitions, your envy. Men can live healthily and happily on water, but you will have beer and brandy. You earn enough to buy meat and vegetables, but you will have tobacco for yourselves and finery for your wives, and that cannot go on. Your daily bread might taste well enough, but it becomes bitter in your mouths when you think of the millionaire's roast meat. Struggle then against this envy which spoils the smallest enjoyments for you, and which in point of fact rules your lives, and do not try to find happiness in the satisfaction of requirements artificially created. Do not live for the satisfaction of your palates, but rather for the improvement of intellect and feeling. There is enough pain and misery in the world, do not add hatred to it. Have the same mercy for other creatures which you expect for yourself. Trouble and danger are common to all. Things are only bearable if all combine to pull together, if the strong join hands with the weak and the hopeful with the timid. You will not be healed by envy and hatred, or by the goading on of your desires, but by love, by forbearance, by self-sacrifice, and renunciation."

This closing sentence was not to his hearers' taste. Disapprobation and ominous sounds greeted him as he came down from the platform. "Amen," said one scornfully; "A Psalm," said another; "Get thee to a nunnery, Ophelia," cried a wit; while loud cries of "Turn him out," were heard. "Pearls before swine," muttered Paul; while Schrotter pressed his hand and said: "You are right."

The noise grew louder, and then a new speaker appeared on the platform, this time evidently a cultivated, thoughtful man and an adroit speaker. The organizers of the evening were unwilling to allow the meeting to retain the impression of Wilhelm's speech, and had placed a clever opponent to follow him, who said clearly and concisely that the speaker before him might be a friend of mankind, but he was certainly an enemy of culture, because the progress of civilization was always the result of new requirements and the seeking of their fulfillment, and if men limited their wants or denied them altogether, mankind would be brought back to the condition of savages or wild beasts. The progress of culture depended on the awakening of requirements and their satisfaction, and not in limiting or renouncing them. The love of mankind might be a very beautiful thing, but the speaker ought not to come and preach to the poor, who held together and helped each other without his advice. Let him go and preach to the rich, for whom he seemed to feel so much pity and tenderness. Why should the minority attract to itself the existing means of life, and leave the majority to starve, as the capitalists did now? why should the provisions not be divided between all, so that the whole community should have a part?

Paul had wished to leave when Wilhelm had finished, but the latter waited out of politeness to hear his opponent speak, and when the speaker had ended in a storm of applause, the three friends left the meeting. When they were outside, Dr. Schrotter said to Wilhelm:

"Do you know that you are a first-rate speaker? You have everything that is necessary for moving a crowd in the highest degree."

"Hardly that, I think."

"Certainly, I mean it: a noble appearance, a voice which goes to the heart, remarkable calmness and assurance, uncommon command of language, and an idealistic earnestness which would move all the better spirits among your audience. You have shown us to-night the road you ought to take. You must devote your gift to speaking in public, you must endeavor to become a deputy. If you fail in this, you will sin against our people."

"Bravo! I had already thought of that," cried Paul.

"A deputy—never," said Wilhelm. "If I spoke well to-day it was because I was sorry for the poor, ignorant men who listened to the silly talk of a fool as if it were a revelation from Mount Sinai, but I could never presume to have any influence in Parliament or in the fate of governments."

"And so you call what is every citizen's duty 'presumption,'"

"Forgive me, doctor, if I say I do not believe that. Only those who are acquainted with the laws and their development should have anything to do with the nation's destiny. But only a few isolated individuals know these laws, and I am not one of them."

"Do you think that the government know them?"

"Oh, no."

"And yet the government does not hesitate to rule the people's destiny according to their intelligence."

"It reminds me of the poet's expression, 'Du glaubst zu schieben und du wirst geschoben.'"

"What is the movement that you mean?"

"An unknown inner organic force which defines all the expressions of life, of single individuals and united societies alike. It develops as a tree grows.

No single individual can add anything to it or take away from it, no single individual can hasten or retard the development or give it any direction."

"In one word—the philosophy of the Unknown."

"That is so."

"Very good, and if a government oppresses a people, robs them of their freedom, perpetually finds fault with them and ill-treats them, they must bear it quietly, and comfort themselves by the thought that the government is controlled by the infallible, all-powerful Unknown."

"Rob them of their freedom? No government can rob me of my spiritual freedom. Freedom rules continually in my mind, and no tyrant has the power of subduing my thoughts."

"You make a great mistake there," said Dr. Schrotter gravely. "From you, Dr. Wilhelm Eyuhardt, no gendarme certainly can take away your freedom, because you are mature, and your opinions of things are settled. But a tyrannical government can hinder your children from succeeding to your freedom of mind. It can teach lies and superstitions in the schools, and compel you to send your children there. It can set an example of public morality which can demoralize a whole people. It can draw up manifest examples of miserable intentions and conduct of life, through whose imitation a people voluntarily mutilates itself or commits suicide. No, no; it does not do to limit oneself to oneself, and to struggle upward for one's individual spiritual freedom. One must go out of oneself. What does it matter if one makes mistakes? It is true, as you say, that no single individual knows the whole of truth; but every individual possesss a fragment of it, and altogether we have the whole. Look at India, there you have existing what we should become if we all followed your philosophy, they live in their own spiritual world, and are indifferent to any other, they endure first the despotism of their own government, then a foreign conqueror, and finally lose not only freedom and independence, but civilization, and become not exactly slaves, but ignorant, superstitious barbarians."

"The German people will not get to that," said Wilhelm, smiling.

"Thank the men for that," cried Schrotter, "the men who think it their duty to take part in the welfare of their country, and to exert themselves for the spiritual freedom of others. An energetic sympathy with public affairs is a form of love for one's neighbor. Say that constantly to yourself, without letting yourself be deceived by the hypocrite who handles politics as others do the Stock Exchange, merely to make profit out of them."

While they talked they had arrived at Schrotter's house door. It was nearly midnight, and had stopped raining, and all the houses except

Schrotter's were dark. Light shone from the two windows of his Indian drawing room, and one of the curtains was drawn aside a little, leaving a face clearly visible. It was Bhani, who was waiting patiently for Schrotter's return, and gazing eagerly down the street. As the three friends stopped at the door the head disappeared, and the curtain fell back again into its place.

CHAPTER VI.

AN IDYLL.

The feverish pulse of a city is not felt in the same degree in all parts of it. There are places from which all circulation seems shut out, and where the rapid stream of life hardly shows a ripple. Quiet houses are there, only separated from the noisy street by the thickness of a wall. They seem to be many miles from the heated movement of life, and their inhabitants complacently gaze from their windows with the same unconcern as they would look at a picture on their own walls—a view perhaps of violence or excitement, a storm at sea, or a battle.

The Markers' house in the Lutzowstrasse was just such a peaceful island in the tossing sea of the city. It was only a few steps from the Magdeburger Platz—the first story in a stately house with a round arch over the door. Three generations of women—grandmother, mother, and daughter—lived there, without a single man to take care of them, attended only by an old widowed cook and her daughter, who had grown up into the position of a waiting maid. A dreamy, monotonous life they lived here, like that of the sleepers in the palace of the Sleeping Beauty behind their hundred-year-old hedge of thorns.

The grandmother was the head of the house—Frau Brohl, a lady of over sixty years, and a widow for the last twenty. She was a small thin woman, her figure very much bent, with snow-white hair, a narrow, pale face, and pretty brown eyes. She moved slowly and with great exertion, spoke softly and with shortness of breath, and seemed weary and sad. She looked as if she had some hidden sickness, and as if her feeble lamp of life might soon flicker out. As a matter of fact she had never had a day's illness; her appearance gave the impression of weakness, and increasing age made her neither better nor worse. Even now she was the first to rise in the morning and the last to go to bed; had the best appetite at table; and, in her occasional walks, was the least tired.

Her late husband—Herr F. A. Brohl, of the firm of Brohl, Son & Co.—had been one of the largest ship-brokers in Stettin. They had lived together for a quarter of a century in peace and happiness, and her eyes filled with tears when she remembered that part of her life. It was a beautiful time, much too good for a sinful human being. They had a house to themselves, with large high rooms, and every day she received visits from the richest women of the town, and visited them in return. There was never a betrothal, marriage, or christening in a well-known family to which she was not invited;

every child in the street knew her and smiled at her; and the suppers in her hospitable house were renowned as far as Russia and Sweden.

The marriage was blessed by one daughter, who grew up to be a rather pretty, well-mannered, and well-grown girl. Her horizon stretched from the storeroom to the linen-press, and from the flatiron to her book of songs. She felt a high esteem for her father—just as everyone does for a rich man—and for her mother, if hardly love, at least a boundless respect. She regarded her as almost more than human, and the care with which she listened to her mother's instructions into the secrets of the kitchen, the market, and the linen-room, was almost unnatural. She was afraid she would never attain to the fluctuations of price in the fish market in different seasons of the year, the starching of muslins, the time it took to cook a pudding, and how much sugar went to a pot of preserved fruit; and her mother destroyed the last remnant of self-confidence when half-pityingly, half-contemptuously she told her that she was not sufficiently developed to understand such things. When Fraulein Brohl was old enough, her parents married her to Herr Marker. It was hardly a love match, but in Brohl, Son & Company's house such folly as love was not considered. Herr Marker was the son of a wholesale coffee-merchant, and was neither handsome nor distinguished-looking; he was small, thin, bandy-legged, with an unwholesome complexion, a peevish expression, and almost bald-headed.

Herr F.A. Brohl soon found that he had made a mistake, and been in too great a hurry. The old Marker lost his fortune in an unlucky speculation during the Crimean War, and was only saved by Brohl from the shame of bankruptcy. He died soon afterward of grief, and left his son nothing but debts. The young Marker showed no special genius for the coffee business, but an uncomfortable ambition for speculation in stocks. He opened an exchange office, and entered into transactions with the Exchanges of Berlin, Frankfort, and Amsterdam, and after a short time the last penny of his wife's dowry disappeared. His father-in-law dipped into his pockets and renewed the dowry, but stipulated that Marker in the future should ask his advice before any undertaking. This Marker felt as a deep humiliation, and rather than submit to Brohl's tyranny, preferred to loaf all day with his hands in his pockets at the Exchange, and shortened the evenings by going to the club, and boring people with endless stories of the meanness and thick-headedness of his cad of a father-in-law, who in his old-fashioned, narrow-minded Philistinism had not the least capacity for any great undertakings.

Brohl died soon after, and Marker experienced a new and painful sensation. His wife did not inherit a penny by her father's will, his whole property under limited conditions going to the widow. This was specially arranged for by Brohl to prevent Marker from laying his hands on more capital. He shook his fist at the opening of the will, and broke out into unseemly abuse; he went all over Stettin, and cried out that he was robbed, that the old rascal had plundered him. To his wife and mother-in-law he also talked day after day and night after night, saying how shamefully he had been treated, and that it was his mother-in-law's duty to make good the mistake. Frau Marker could not endure this perpetual grumbling and badgering, and Frau Brohl became weak with not only her son-in-law but her daughter constantly at her ear. She consented to give him a large sum to put him into a new business, which he described as having a brilliant and unfailing future, and after a great deal of begging and worrying she at length brought herself to the far greater sacrifice of a removal to Berlin, that Marker might have a greater sphere for his energies. So the stately house in the Frauenstrasse with its lofty rooms was abandoned, and exchanged for the small flat in Berlin.

The departure from Stettin was a miserable one. It was desperate work packing the thousand things which had gathered together during the quarter of a century in careless profusion. It was heart-breaking to be obliged to leave behind the stores of wood, coal, and potatoes in the cellar, the cranberry jam in the storeroom, which the Markers, in their grandeur of ideas, did not think worth the trouble of taking with them! And the farewell visits to the rich friends, in whose family festivals she would never more take part; and the last visit to the Jacobkirche, where she would never more go on Sundays and meet her intimate friends, for whose benefit she wore the family ornaments, and the stiff silk dress. There were many tears and sobs, but the cup was drained like the others; and Marker began his new life in the Lutzowstrasse with his wife, his mother-in-law, and the little Malvine, who was the only child of their marriage.

At first things went on pretty well. Frau Brohl often had tears in her eyes when looking at the familiar furniture in her room, which had been designed for a house three times as large, and she would rather have sacrificed one of her hands than one of her old sofas or tables. But Marker was gay as he had never been before, and full of wonderful stories of the future importance of his firm, astounding both the women, and even making them respect him, which feeling had never before influenced them. He had an office in the Burgstrasse, near the Exchange, shared by other young men, and came home every day with new reports of the wonderful business he was doing.

A day came, however, when he had no news to tell them, when his complexion was as yellow as ever, his eyes avoided the questioning glances of his mother-in-law, and after playing at concealment for a whole week, he was at last forced to tell them that he had again lost all his money. He hastened to add, however, that every thing could be saved if the mother would once more set him on his feet; in every new undertaking one had to pay something for learning; he had hardly understood his position so far, but now he knew what he was about, he must be contented with modest profits. Frau Brohl made a fresh sacrifice, giving Marker his position in business again after six months. He had hardly the courage to come home with new plans, but used to steal in quietly like a shadow on the wall, sit down at table with a heart-breaking sigh, sulked with the women, and often was heard talking to himself in this fashion: "This is no sort of life. If women hold the cards, stupidity is trumps. The woman in the kitchen, the man in business," and so on. Finally the thing happened which Frau Brohl had foreseen with anxiety—Marker came with a new project, for which he wanted fifty thousand thalers. It was an entirely new idea, unheard of before; it couldn't miscarry, it must bring in a hundred thousand; with one stroke all the former losses would be retrieved. Then he stopped talking, and showed yards of figures, read aloud letters of advice, and went on reading and talking and crackling papers for an hour to Frau Brohl, following her from the drawing-room into the kitchen, from the kitchen back to the drawing-room; and when she took refuge in her bedroom, he read to her through the door. However, it was no good, and Frau Brohl stood firm. Then Marker tried a new method. He was argumentative before, now he became tragic; he threatened to throw himself out of the window, to become dangerously ill, to go away and never be heard of again. He left half-finished letters on his writing-table, in which he announced his death to his acquaintances, laying the blame on his wife and mother-in-law; in short, poor Frau Brohl, whose existence had become a veritable hell, with a heavy heart put her hand once more into her pocket, and gave Marker what he wanted.

Everything now went on as smoothly and merrily as before. After a few weeks Marker again lost everything, and seemed so upset that he stayed away all day without coming home. At last he appeared again, and hesitatingly, with a timid expression, begged for forgiveness. "Very well," said Frau Brohl, "only I hope you will not begin all over again." Her hopes were not realized. The spirit of speculation had too strong a hold over Marker to be kept back. After he had remained quiet for about a year, he actually had the effrontery to ask his mother-in-law for more capital. But this time she was like a rock. "Not a penny," said Frau Brohl, and kept her word. Marker wept, and she let him weep; he talked of suicide, and she advised him to use a rope, as he did not understand the use of firearms. He had run through half her money, and the other half she meant to defend like a lioness. The specter of poverty rose up before her, she reflected that rich people would cast her out of their society, and look upon her as a weak woman without any self-respect, conquered by Marker's tenacity.

There were no more storms after this, and peace reigned in the tightly-crammed flat in the Lutzowstrasse, but it was peace which concealed a great deal of grumbling and sulkiness. Marker very seldom spoke, and his obstinate silence was made easy for him, for the women at last hardly ever spoke to him. Every week he had a certain sum given him for pocket-money; Frau Brohl paid his tailor's and bootmaker's bills, and he was treated in fact as if he had done with this world. His business was to take the little Malvine to school and fetch her home again, and on the way he grumbled incessantly to the child about her mother and grandmother. The former he called "she," and the latter "the old lady." He never mentioned their names. Malvine had noticed that at home they never spoke to her father; in her childish way she imitated this contemptuous silence. The only bright spot in his existence was a visit to some old business friends, where he unburdened his overflowing heart, and complained by the hour together of the tyrants in his house, who trod him under-foot, and ill-treated him now that he was unfortunate. He was the victim of two silly women, but he would show them one day of what he was capable. "She" and "the old lady" were too stupid to understand him, but he hoped he would not die until he had seen them on their knees before him. In this way he ceaselessly kept up the smouldering rage within him; his face became more and more yellow, he grew thinner, he lost his appetite, he looked as if he were suffering from some dreadful malady. He said nothing, however, about his health, but seemed to find a comforting satisfaction in the reflection that "she" and "the old lady" would one day be surprised to see him lying there, and that would be his revenge. And so it came to pass—one morning he was too weak to leave his bed. At luncheon Frau Brohl and Frau Marker noticed his absence, and went to look for him; as they had taken no notice of him for so long, they were not aware how shriveled and emaciated he had grown, and were now shocked and astonished to see how miserable and frail he was. They sent for a doctor; Frau Brohl made some elder tea; Frau Marker sat up all night by the sick-bed, but nothing could be done. A few days later he died, with a look of hatred at his mother-in-law, and a movement of aversion from his wife.

Nothing was changed in the household; there was another place at table and a room at liberty, which was soon filled with the things overflowing from the drawing-room. Frau Brohl still had a passion for preserving and pickling, which had descended to her daughter and her granddaughter, and also a passion for needle-work. Year in and year out the three sat at the window of their drawing-room over embroidery, lace-making, and such like, working as if they had to earn their daily bread. They were mistresses of all kinds of fancy work, and invented many more.

Frau Brohl was unequaled in her inventions of new kinds of work. Such things as book-markers and slippers, paper-baskets, bed-quilts and tablecloths, card-baskets, and chair-cushions were all too simple—the mere a b c of the art. Wonders like embroidered pictures for the walls, various kinds of fringes for the legs of pianos, fireplace hangings, gold nets for window-curtains, mottoes for the canary's cage, silk covers for books, were the order of the day. When any one came in he was first struck with surprise, which quickly changed to bewilderment. Wherever he looked his eye fell on some piece of work, with no repose or unadorned space. Here a row of family portraits, in plush and gold frames, all looking stiff and uninteresting—on inspecting them at close quarters, they were seen to be not painted but embroidered in colored silks. There hung a melon, the outside of the fruit represented by yellow, green, and brown satin, the stalk by gold thread, the little cracks and roughnesses by gray silk applique, the whole thing fearful and absurd in its exuberance. And wherever one went or stood, sat down or laid one's hand, there wandered a huge wreath of flowers in Berlin wool, or the profile of a warrior in cross-stitch sneered at one, or a piece of hanging tapestry of pompous pattern and learned inscriptions flapped at one, and everything was rich and tedious and terrifying and shocking in taste; and when one's tired eyes looked out of the triply be-curtained windows into the street, one fell convinced that little angels would come down out of the sky clad in what was left over of the rococo furniture draperies, bordered with gold.

This unsightly museum of useless things was the occupation of Frau Brohl and Frau Marker's lives, and here Malvine grew up to be the pretty girl to whom we have been introduced at the Ellrichs'. Her mother was a sort of elder sister to her, and the only authority in the house was the grandmother. She ordered the servants, and her daughter paid her the same timid reverence as in the time of her short frocks. Frau Marker seldom opened her lips except to eat, or to answer her mother in a parrot-like sort of echo. Frau Brohl's energetic spirit stirred even in these narrow boundaries. She did not feel at home in Berlin; she met no one she knew in the streets, and in fact knew no one, and this feeling of being among strangers, as if at some out-of-the-way fair, made her so uneasy that she hardly ever went out. Often since Marker's death she had thought of returning to Stettin, but when she reflected how dreadful it would be to pack up and unpack again all the thousand pieces of work, her courage failed her. All the same she lived with her heart and soul in Stettin. A local paper from Stettin was her only reading. She kept up a regular correspondence with all her old acquaintances, who gave her news of all the engagements, marriages, births, and deaths of the rich people she had known. If Stettin people of good standing came to Berlin she called on them and invited them to dinner, when her former celebrated triumphs in cookery were repeated. If she found out that any wealthy inhabitants of Stettin had been in Berlin without informing her of the fact, she took it so much to heart that she had to go to bed for a week. A few Stettin families, who in the course of the year emigrated to the capital, constituted her circle of visiting acquaintances, enlarged later by Malvine's school friends, and introductions at their houses. The connection with the Ellrichs was through the Stettin circle. Frau Brohl gave a large soiree twice in the course of the winter, when the invitations they had received were returned. Since Malvine was grown up there had been dancing, although the small size of the drawing-room, and the displacement of all Frau Brohl's needlework, set everything in great confusion.

This kind of life and its surroundings naturally could not develop Malvine's mind and character in any high degree. She missed any stimulus from her mother or from her grandmother; she only learned to respect rich people, to fathom the mysteries of the kitchen, and to cultivate a taste for peculiar and original fancy work; she was, however, a good-tempered, rather slow-witted girl, of well-balanced mind, without a trace of capriciousness or the nervous temperament so common to city life; within her limited view of things she had a good, honest intelligence, and with her plump figure and her round, rosy face, which bore witness to her grandmother's kitchen, she was very comely in men's eyes.

Paul Haber had already become acquainted with the flat in the Lutzowstrasse during the winter before the war, and he liked the quiet he found in the corners of the little rooms, and in the muffled voices of these three women. The friendship was continued during the war by means of frequent letters, and on his home-coming Paul renewed his visits with pleasure. By cautious inquiries he had gathered that Malvine had sixty thousand thalers in cash as her dowry, and would inherit double that sum. Her modest, quiet, amiable disposition made him drift into a strong attachment; her appearance was sufficiently womanly and charming, and her steady, practical views on things, utterly unromantic an unenthusiastic, harmonized entirely with his own. It was refreshing for him to hear her chatter about people and things with the calm good sense of a Philistine, especially in a society where the bombastic and exaggerated talk of original, poetically minded young ladies had repelled and bored him. At his first meeting with Malvine Marker he had thought that she was the wife for him, and since he had become friendly with her and her circle, he said to himself, "This one and no other."

The three ladies liked him immensely. Frau Brohl took him at once to her heart, and that was the chief consideration. His appearance made a good impression on her. He was strongly built, not too thin, in fact, showing signs of a respectable probable stoutness in later life; his face was full, and his complexion healthy, his mustache carefully trimmed, and his hair closely cropped; he certainly dressed well. The young men of her former rich acquaintances were of the same type, so also was the late F.A. Brohl when she first met him. He was gentlemanly, without a doubt, and he must be well off to employ such a good tailor and friseur. She also noticed, with an immense satisfaction, that he had a due appreciation of fancy work. He did not, like some superficial people, regard these housewifely creations as merely pretty or useful things, but appreciated them as works of art, and wondered at the difficulty of these marvelous fabrications. Complicated lacework, or embroidered pictures, filled him with amazement, even if applique had no effect on him. When Frau Brohl noticed these marks of distinction in him, she did not hesitate to invite him to dinner on Sunday—at first occasionally, and afterward regularly, and with increasing pleasure she noticed that in other ways he also reached the ideal she had imagined in him. He had a good appetite, and it was not necessary for him to say in words how much he enjoyed the dishes set before him, every look and gesture showed it plainly. He evinced a warm sympathy for family events, even when they did not concern him in any way, and he had the same genuine esteem for rich people, which had been handed down for three generations in the Brohl-Marker families. She thought that he showed no disinclination to be her granddaughter's husband, only at first she pondered over his calling in life. She knew perfectly well that the highest professorship could only earn in a year what an ordinary ship-broker made in a month. At the same time she reflected that even a merchant made a bad job of it sometimes, as her son-in-law's example had shown her only too plainly; that the title "Professor" sounded very well, and if he did not make very much money at most, at least he could not lose it, and she came to the conclusion that in the circumstances a professor could make his wife very happy. Frau Marker had nothing to say about the matter, and was quite prepared to accept a son-in-law from her mother's hand, as she had formerly accepted a husband, so the fact that Paul had not made a very favorable impression on her did not matter very much.

There remained only Malvine—but just there lay the difficulty. The girl was always kind and friendly to Paul, she took his homage without any coquetry or apparent disinclination; when they went out walking she took his arm quite unaffectedly; when they were invited to meet in society, by a tacit agreement he took her in to dinner, had the privilege of the greater part of the dances, and was her partner for the cotillion. But whether they were alone or in company, whether they danced or talked, whether he came or went, she showed a perfect unconcern and freedom of manner to which he longed to put an end. She was much too cold and collected even for his unsentimental nature. He would have forgiven some agitation, some confusion, a few blushes now and then, perhaps a sigh, but these signs of the heart's flutterings were nowhere forthcoming. As they were out one day alone together, something happened which filled Paul with doubt and trouble. Malvine had been attracted to Wilhelm when first she saw him, and since then she had incessantly thought and talked of him. He was so handsome, he spoke so charmingly! She thought it astonishing that any one should not love him, just because his admiration was mingled with so much shyness. She herself was much too insignificant a person to think of loving him, and beside, he was not free, and it would have been a sin to think of the man who was engaged to her friend. This enthusiasm for Wilhelm naturally did not escape Paul's notice, but it did not disquiet him, because he took into account Malvine's nature. "It is a harmless fancy," he said to himself, "the sort of fancy girls take sometimes for princes whose photographs they see in shop-windows, or for actors whom they have admired as Don Carlos or Romeo; later on they laugh over their childish folly, and these fancies never prevent the pretty enthusiast from marrying and being happy."

Nevertheless, things became suspiciously different after the breach between Wilhelm and Loulou. In Malvine's somewhat narrow but well-regulated mind a brave romance had been mistakenly built up. Now Wilhelm was free: now she need have no feeling of duty on account of that superficial, pleasure-seeking Loulou, who had never been worthy of him. Was it impossible that he might notice her? would be grateful for her sympathy? and perhaps—who knows—later—he might seek consolation from her—who was so ready to give it? The concluding chapter of this girlish romance remained her own secret, but the beginning she boldly declared. She explained to her grandmother, as well as to Paul, that now Dr. Eynhardt was in need of being comforted, it was the duty of his friends to try to overcome his sorrow. She proposed that Paul should bring him as often as possible, and she obtained from Frau Brohl the unwonted permission of inviting him to the Sunday luncheon. Wilhelm had little pleasure in going into ordinary society, especially to strangers, but this invitation was so warm and pressing that he could not bring himself to refuse it.

When Wilhelm was there Paul was put completely in the background. Malvine had no words or glances for any one but Wilhelm, and if she spoke to Paul it was only to thank him for having brought Dr. Eynhardt to the Lutzowstrasse. If Paul came alone he was mortified to see a shadow pass over Malvine's face, and he was forced to listen to a string of inquiries after his friend. He had been conscious for a long time that he must try to reconcile himself to this condition of things, and if he felt himself rebelling, he reminded himself he must have patience and wait, trying to console himself with the thought that Malvine's enthusiasm was only on her side—Wilhelm's demeanor seemed to show that he did not guess what was going on in the girl's mind. His manner was courteous and friendly, but there was really no difference between his demeanor toward Frau Brohl and toward the young girl. While Malvine blushed and became confused when he entered the room, Wilhelm, on his side, spoke to the grandmother, mother, and daughter with exactly the same pleasant smile, and his hand rested not a moment longer in Malvine's than in that of her grandmother. On his side there was evidently nothing to dread. He felt he had a defender and support in Frau Brohl. The old lady kept a sharp lookout on her little world with her dim-sighted eyes. She noticed that Malvine was unable to withstand the charm which Wilhelm exercised over her, and she could not bring herself to be angry with the girl. She herself liked the young man extremely, admired his handsome face, his fine voice, his modest, unassuming manners, but she felt instinctively that he belonged to quite a different world from herself, and that in a sense they would always be strangers. When he spoke she could not follow his thoughts, although she felt that they were very profound; when she spoke he listened with the greatest politeness, but nothing more came of it. He tried to be attentive to her stories about engagements and separations, he was entirely uninterested in rich people, he did not praise the best dishes at table, and he even went so far as not to conceal his aversion for the design of the horrible knight in cross-stitch. Beside all this, his clothes were bad, and although he had a house of his own, it was only a little one. No, Wilhelm as a relation was not to be thought of. He was not of their own flesh and blood, like that good, delightful Paul Haber.

It was not in Paul's nature to wait patiently in suspense, and he determined to put an end to his uncertainty. Malvine seemed to him as desirable as ever, and he had built up in his mind a future, of which Malvine and her sixty thousand thalers were the foundation. He must know whether she were for him or not; in the one case to transform his castle in the air into reality without loss of time, and in the other case not to waste the best years of his life in aimless disappointment; not to let other opportunities slip by. He was not quite clear, however, on one point, To whom should he make his proposal? To Frau Brohl? That would be the most practicable way, no doubt, as the bent, pale old lady, with the soft, sighing voice, ruled everything in the house, and if she promised the hand of her grand-daughter, she would certainly keep her word. But it went against the grain to put any constraint on the girl, and he felt that he would be ashamed to answer "No," if Frau Brohl were to ask him if he had already spoken to Malvine. Then if he were to go in a straightforward way to Malvine, and say, "I can no longer hide from you that I love you, and that I want you to be my wife, will you consent?" there was a great deal of risk in that, for if she misjudged her own feelings, and said that she loved some one else, and so could not listen to him, the rupture between them would be accomplished, and it would be no use to him if later she found out that she had been mistaken in her feelings. There could be no secure step for him, on that he was quite decided.

If he could approach neither Frau Brohl nor Malvine, there was one way clearly open to him, and he took it without further delay.

One sunny afternoon in May, a few weeks after the Labor meeting at the Tivoli, Paul came to see Wilhelm, and asked him to go for a walk with him in the Thiergarten. Wilhelm was soon ready, and while they were walking

Paul was astonishingly quiet, and seemed sunk in deep thought. He suddenly broke the silence, and when they were under the trees, without any beating about the bush, asked his friend:

"Wilhelm, do you love Malvine?"

Wilhelm stood still, as if rooted to the ground, and in boundless astonishment he said:

"Are you off your head, Paul?"

"I implore you, Wilhelm," said he in an anxious way, "just answer 'yes' or 'no,' because the happiness of my life depends on your answer."

"But I never thought of it," cried Wilhelm, grasping Paul's hand. "What put such an idea into your head?"

"Then you are not in love with Malvine?" asked Paul obstinately.

"No, I am not in love with Malvine, if you will have the answer in that precise form."

"I thought as much, but I wished to have the answer from your own lips;" and as they walked, he continued, "Do you see, Wilhelm, if you had loved Malvine, I would have got out of your way; I would have submitted to fate without any struggle or opposition."

"Have I been injudicious? Perhaps too intimate? Forgive me, Paul, if it is so. It happened quite unintentionally. I only thought of her as my friend's fiancee, and believed her also to be a friend of mine."

"I don't mean that, Wilhelm; you have always behaved awfully well—with great tact, and all that. But you have not seen how it has been with Malvine; she is quite mad about you, especially since you have been free."

"You imagine these things."

"Be quiet, you impatient baby, and hear what I have to say. I believe it is not love Malvine has for you, but it only wants a word or a look from you to turn it into love. If she were convinced that you feel only as a friend for her, she would be contented to admire you from a distance, and begin to care a little more for an inferior specimen of mankind like myself."

"I feel quite in despair about it. How could I be so blind, so stupid?"

"Never mind; it is not all over yet. I know Malvine. She is a simple-minded girl, without a bit of sentiment in her, mentally and morally healthy. If she knew she had nothing to expect from you, I am perfectly certain that nothing would stand in the way of my happiness."

"I will do whatever you wish—and first of all, I must put a stop to my visits there."

"I must ask more from you than that, my poor Wilhelm. Merely staying away is too passive. You must act. I want you to talk to Malvine, and somehow explain to her that you don't love her."

"How can I possibly do that?" cried Wilhelm, really startled. "I should have no right! If she laughed in my face and called me a fool and a lout, I should feel I deserved it."

"You ought to know that she would not do that. I know I am asking a very unusual thing, and a very difficult thing, but I feel I can ask such a sacrifice from your friendship."

As Wilhelm did not immediately answer, Paul said, seizing his hand:

"Once more, Wilhelm, if you have any thought of Malvine, I will not stand in your way."

"But, Paul—"

"And perhaps I ought to wish it for you; Malvine is a good, dear girl, and will make the man who marries her happy all his life."

"Don't say any more; I have already told you that she is sacred to me as your fiancee, and beside, I should have no claim on her, even if I did not know how you stand with regard to her."

"Well, then, you must help me to reclaim her from her mistake. You alone can do it, and I am sure that later—very soon, in fact, she will be grateful to you."

Wilhelm was silent, looking at Paul in anxious suspense. At last, with a deep sigh, he said:

"Well, if I must—"

"You are a brick," cried Paul, and embraced him before the passers-by, who turned round to look at them with astonishment.

On the next day, at twelve o'clock, Wilhelm rang at the Markers' flat in the Lutzowstrasse. Through the little peephole he caught a glimpse of some one, then the door flew open, a maid ushered him into the drawing-room, and without waiting for him to speak, said:

"Frau Brohl is in the kitchen; I will fetch her."

"Thank you," said Wilhelm, rather feebly; "there is no hurry. Is—is—the Fraulein at home?"

The girl was already at the door, and turning round, stared at Wilhelm with astonished eyes.

"Yes; shall I say that you would like to speak to her?"

Wilhelm nodded, and the girl went out. After a short pause Malvine stood before him, offering him her white hand, with its short fingers, while her face flushed to the roots of her hair.

"Might I speak to you, Fraulein?" he said, in a low, constrained voice.

Malvine went very white, all the blood seemed to leave her heart, and she almost gasped for breath. After a short silence she whispered, "Certainly, Herr Doctor," and took him into the little room next the drawing-room, which contained a modest bookcase, a writing table, and chairs in red damask. She sat down, and Wilhelm took a chair near; they were silent for a minute or two, while she, with eyes downcast, went alternately red and white, and could scarcely breathe. There was no pretense this time about her agitation. It seemed as if suddenly a flash of lightning had illuminated his mind, showing him a picture of this trembling, pretty girl clashed to his heart, and he with his arms round her. It only lasted for a second, but it struck him like an electric shock, and left in his mind a mingled feeling of trouble, shame, remorse and vexation. He had a consciousness of danger, and he felt that he must make a great effort to become master of the situation and of himself.

"Gnadiges Fraulein," he began, "what I want to say to you will seem odd, and perhaps audacious, but I beg you in spite of that to hear me to the end."

Malvine sat motionless, breathing quickly.

"I do not know," he went on, "in what position you and my friend Haber are with regard to each other, but you must have noticed, without any explanation, that he loves you."

At the mention of Paul's name, Malvine for the first time raised her eyes, and looked at Wilhelm with such a troubled expression that he felt still further alarmed. He had broken the ice, however, and he made a courageous effort to regain his asssurance.

"Dear Fraulein," he said impressively, "I am afraid there has been some misunderstanding between us, which it is my duty toward you, toward my friend, and toward myself, to explain. My behavior has perhaps aroused an impression which it should not have done. There is no doubt that I ought not to have shown you how warm my friendship is for you—for you, a good and beautiful girl, who have inspired my best friend with such a love; but really I considered that so long as the engagement between you and Paul was not clearly arranged, that you would understand my position. If I seemed happy to be near you, it was because I told myself how happy my friend would be when he could call you his own; if you seemed to read warmth and tenderness when I looked at you, it was because I was and am so grateful to you for so happily influencing Paul."

While he was speaking Malvine had sunk back in her corner, and had closed her eyes with a deep sigh. A few large tears began to roll down her cheeks. Wilhelm touched her hand, which was cold as ice. She made a feeble effort to draw it away, but he held it fast and went on:

"Dearest, best Malvine, do not bear me any grudge for this abominable half-hour, and believe me that it is only out of consideration for your life's happiness. I quite understand how it has all happened. Your kind heart was filled with pity for me, and in your innocence you gave the pity another name. It was quite natural that you should be uncertain of yourself, while you thought you were loved by two men, and that the confusion prevented you seeing clearly with your own heart. Now you know that Paul loves you, and that the day on which he dares call you his will be the first happy one I have had for a year. You will be able to come to a determination more easily, as it concerns your own happiness equally with Paul's. Paul is a good fellow, and worthy of the woman who will bear his name."

He bent over her hand and pressed his lips to it. Malvine sobbed aloud, and putting her arms on his shoulders kissed his hair, then sprang away and flew to her room. Wilhelm hurried away in great confusion, thankful that he had been spared meeting either Frau Brohl or Frau Marker. He only breathed freely when he found himself in the street.

Paul was informed the same afternoon of the conversation which had taken place, Wilhelm delicately passing over Malvine's outburst of feeling, and he hurried at once to the Lutzowstrasse to take by storm the fortress in which his friend had already made a breach. He was received by Frau Brohl, who nodded in mysterious manner, and took him into her bedroom, at the back of the flat, through the dining-room. In her soft, feeble voice she mildly reproached him for not having more confidence and coming to speak to her sooner. She then related to him what had happened. She had heard with great surprise that Dr. Eynhardt had come and gone away again, without saying good-day to her. As she was going to ask what the visit meant, Malvine came and embraced her grandmother, crying bitterly, to the old lady's great distress. With many tears she had given a confused and broken account of the interview with Wilhelm, begging Frau Brohl to comfort her and foretell that it should end well. Frau Brohl explained that Malvine was now in her room, meaning that Paul must not try to see her just at present. Such a silly, inexperienced creature must have time given her to learn to be reasonable, beside, she (Frau Brohl) would take care of everything, and Herr Haber could call her grandmamma now if he liked. He kissed her hand, deeply moved and grateful, and her eyes filled with tears. She then explained the situation to Frau Marker, who, after looking very much surprised, also embraced her son-in-law. It was a dignified scene, tender, and, as befitted an honorable family, without any over display of feeling; if all the wealthy people of Stettin had been assembled there, they could have expressed nothing but admiration.

On the next day Frau Brohl spoke to her grand-daughter. She made her understand that there were no real objections to be made, that she was silly and was acting against her own happiness. Paul was much the better match of the two, was more chic and practical than Wilhelm, had better prospects in life, and was really better-looking than his friend. Above all she liked Paul, and did not like Wilhelm, and that ought to be taken into account. Malvine was not inaccessible to such arguments, as Paul was really sympathetic to her. Soon her tears ceased to flow, and her sighs became fainter and fainter. In two days' time she regained her appetite, signs which Frau Brohl noticed, and quickly imparted to Paul. At their first meeting he showed a little anxiety, and she, a good deal of constraint, but that soon passed off, and as they were constantly together, she found a great deal of pleasure in his manly good looks and honorable qualities. Beside, it was spring! the sun shone, the sky was blue, her room was full of the fragrance of flowers, which Paul brought every day with the regularity of a postman, and fourteen days later they were engaged, and his first kiss was given in the presence of her grandmother, mother, and Paul's parents. Her heart felt very warmly toward him, and she would have felt dreadfully confused had not Wilhelm, with characteristic good feeling, declined the invitation to be present.

Frau Brohl arranged for the wedding to take place after Whitsuntide. At the Zwolf-Apostelkirche she wore her heavy silk dress and all the family ornaments, as on the Sundays at church at Stettin. Her bent figure was straighter than usual, and a smile of proud satisfaction lighted up her pale, melancholy face. Several rich friends from Stettin had come over to Berlin for the wedding. She leaned on the arm of the bridegroom's father, Herr Haber, a dignified old gentleman with a long beard. Paul wore his uniform and a Japanese order, which had been conferred on him by a Japanese pupil at his lectures on agricultural chemistry. Several officers in uniform were in the church, and a large number of professors, councilors, etc. Paul's round face beamed with happiness, his blond mustache looked triumphant, his hair was mathematically cut, and a field-marshal might have sworn that he was a regular officer. The bride was rosy, and looked happy. Her veil and wreath were made by the family, and her satin dress covered with their embroidery. Wilhelm was one of Paul's witnesses. When he went to congratulate the happy pair after the ceremony, Malvine looked at him; a gentle glance, with perhaps a mild reproach in it. Paul, however, grasped his hand, and whispered into his ear:

"Your friend for life, Wilhelm, for life."

CHAPTER VII.

SYMPOSIUM.

Paul had hardly returned from his wedding trip to Paris when he surprised his friends by a series of quite unexpected business engagements. He gave up his post as lecturer, in spite of the fact that the appointment as professor for the next six months depended on it; he left his young wife for three weeks, during which nothing was heard of him, except an occasional letter bearing the postmarks of Hamburg, Altona, or Harburg, then he appeared again, and told Malvine that they were to remove from Berlin, to spend in future a portion of the year in Hamburg, but to live chiefly on some property near Harburg. He had decided to leave his academic profession and become a practical landowner, and accordingly had taken a large leasehold estate. He gave Wilhelm and Schrotter further particulars of his plans. The place he had bought was hardly to be called an estate, but a wild desert bit of moorland called "Friesenmoor," growing only a kind of marsh grass. This piece of land, from which nothing but peat could be obtained, was worthless, and he had bought it for a few thalers. After many years of study on the subject, and without saying a word to any living soul, Paul had come to the conclusion that this arid moor could be made into rich arable land by proper cultivation, and seeing money was to be made out of this possession, he decided without loss of time to put his theories into practice. There was always the risk that he might lose his money, but he had great confidence in his science, and "nothing venture, nothing have." He considered it quite unnecessary to explain everything about his speculation to Malvine and the old lady. He knew, too, that merely the word "speculation" would frighten them to death.

The separation from Malvine dissolved her grandmother and mother into sighs and tears, but during the short time that they had known Paul, his quiet, determined character had made such an impression on the two women that they submitted without a word to whatever he arranged. Frau Brohl packed up several boxes for her granddaughter, filled with the work of her hands, gave her various recipes for preserving fruits and for fish sauces, and let her go. She withstood bravely the temptation to fill up the empty room with the overflow furniture from the drawing-room, and spoke on the contrary of leaving the room free, so that the young couple might make it their headquarters when they came to Berlin. Paul hypocritically invited Frau Brohl and Frau Marker to come and live on his estate—he did not even fear two mothers-in-law. Grandmother and mother, though pleased with his attachment for them, declined with thanks. The cunning dog had reckoned on that refusal. He would have been in a terrible dilemma had they accepted.

He would then have had to reveal the whole truth, and tell them that his so-called "property" was a mere swamp, where there was no place for one's feet to tread unless clad in waterproof boots; hardly a fit place for townspeople, accustomed to comfort. Before the changes on the Friesenmoor could be brought about one fell into pools, one's feet got fast in boggy earth, and the only inhabitants at present were waterfowl, frogs and toads. He did not even take Malvine to his property but lived in Hamburg, going to Harburg every morning and returning in the evening.

In a short time the neighborhood between the Seeve and the Suderelbe wore a different appearance. Hundreds of laborers were to be seen on the moor, which hitherto had reflected only the sky in its silent pools. Dams were thrown up, trenches dug, a dwelling house was raised on piles, numbers of business offices, and quite a village for workmen, all mounted and secure on piles of wood, stakes, and stone foundations. Flatboats floated on the pools, the houses were roofed in, windmills flapped their sails, and Paul, who had ordered and built everything, came every day to see how the workmen were getting on. In the autumn he took Malvine for the first time to Harburg, and leaving the carriage at the office brought her by boat to the border of the Friesenmoor, to show her the picture all at once. The men stood on each side of the new house with their shovels and pickaxes, and greeted the young wife with such a hearty cheer that her eyes filled with tears. The broad flat surface of the marsh was now arranged in regular lines where the water was being drawn off, all so well superintended and orderly, that Malvine could not help thinking of a chessboard. The windmill moved its long restless arms, as if to welcome her as mistress here; the one-storied dwelling house, raised on stone steps, lay there hospitably built on a raised terrace, with its number of large well-lighted rooms opening a vista of peace and happiness to Malvine, and she thought it all so delightful that she would have liked to send for her furniture from Hamburg and stay there. Paul, however, reflected what danger there might be to her in her condition to stay through the winter in a house not yet dry, and so she gave in to his wishes.

At the end of March a telegram from Hamburg announced the birth of a fine boy, to whom Wilhelm was to stand godfather. He was to be named Paul Wilhelm, and to be known by the latter name. When the warm weather came, Paul and his family were to go to the moor, and during the removal Malvine went with her mother and grandmother, who had both nursed her tenderly, to Berlin for a visit. Paul went through a great deal of worry and anxiety this summer. He had everything at stake in waiting for the results of his undertaking. All his money was in the buildings, the earth-works, and waterworks; if the barren swamp did not yield twice the sum intrusted to it he was a ruined man. But as July drew near, and Paul looked at the thick standing ears of barley and wheat, he felt the weight of his anxiety lifted, and in August he proclaimed in letters to his friends that the battle was won, the harvest more abundant than he had dared to hope for, and the remaining half-year would complete the transformation of the worthless moorland into a veritable Australian gold mine. He regarded his property now with a parental tenderness, as if it were some living being whom he had trained and educated. The first harvest had given him experience, and opportunity for new work, and he stayed through the autumn and winter in his house in the midst of his workmen, whom he felt inclined to canonize. The men now formed a little colony with their wives and children, and Paul was as happy as possible within the limited boundary of his horizon, between the Suderelbe and the Seeve.

These two years had been outwardly uneventful for Wilhelm. In the mornings he worked in the Physical Institute, in the afternoons he worked at home, in the evenings he gossiped with Schrotter—a journey to Hamburg and a fortnight's visit to the house on the Friesenmoor had given him change. Paul came pretty often to Berlin, and found in the society of his old friends the enjoyment of his early years renewed, and Wilhelm with his girlish face, his enthusiastic eyes, and his unworldly manner did not seem a year older. The professor of physics, who had frequently been invited to go abroad to direct the teaching in other European and foreign schools, asked Wilhelm to go with him to Turkey, Japan, and Chili—as professor. He had the highest opinion of Wilhelm, and deeply regretted that his misadventure with Herr von Pechlar made an appointment in Germany impossible. Wilhelm, however, declined, on the ground that he did not feel an aptitude for teaching, only for learning.

He had scarcely any intercourse now with Barinskoi, whose immoral views at last became unbearable; he rarely saw him except when he came to borrow money. Of late a new acquaintance had come into his limited social circle. This was a man of about thirty-five, called Dorfling, an overgrown thin creature, with long, straight gray hair, and deep intellectual eyes in his thin face. He came from the Rhine, and was the son of a rich merchant, into whose business he should have gone. However, when he was twenty-six he boldly told his father that the world outside was of deeper and wider interest to him than account books. The father died, and Dorfling hastened to put the business into liquidation, and devote himself to philosophical studies. For a year he drifted from one school to another, sitting at the feet of the most celebrated teachers and plunging himself into their systems. In the autumn of 1872 he appeared suddenly in Berlin, and renewed his old acquaintance with Wilhelm. Since then he had become a frequent guest at Dr. Schrotter's dinner table, and a companion to Wilhelm, in his afternoon walks.

Dorfling was the most wonderful listener that any one could wish to have, though he himself was rather silent. If the talk turned on great questions of knowledge, morality, the object of life, Dorfling's share in the conversation consisted in the following half-audible remark: "Yes, it is a powerful and interesting subject. I have just been working at it, and you will find my opinions in my book." If he were asked to give his opinions now, or at least to indicate them, he shook his head and gently said, "I am not good at extempore speaking. My thoughts only come out clearly when I have a pen in my hand." Not a day passed by without an allusion to "the book," to which he devoted his nights, and of which he always spoke, with emotion in his voice, as the work of his life.

It was impossible to get more information out of him, either about its title, scope, or contents. It was a philosophic work, no doubt, as he always said on speaking of such subjects, "I have mentioned that in my book." But that was all that could be got out of him. Schrotter and Wilhelm were too good to tease him much about it, though the former, with a suspicion of a smile, would say that he hoped this and that would have a place in the book, so that one might at least know his opinion on it. Paul, who always saw him when he came to Berlin, used to ask whether the book was not yet ready. Dorfling gave no answer, but his pale face grew paler, and an expression of pain came to his eyes.

Barinskoi, who now sponged on Dorfling just as he had previously done on Wilhelm, giving them in fact turn and turn about, had the bad taste to make jokes continually about the book, at one time calling it the Holy Grail, another time comparing it to the diamond country of Sindbad's tale, and in a hundred ways making vulgar and sceptical jokes. On one of his outbreaks of dissipation he had disappeared far longer than usual, and on his return he looked more miserable than ever. Dorfling made some kindly inquiries, and learned that he was recovering from an attack of inflammation of the lungs, and Barinskoi, by way of showing gratitude, remarked, "The doctors gave me up, but I held out, as I do not mean to die until I have read your book." Dorfling, with a contemptuous look, turned his back on him.

One day, soon after the Easter of 1874, Dorfling brought his friends a great piece of news. The book was ready, it was even in the press, and would be published in a few days by a large firm, but he wanted to present them with copies before the book appeared at the shops. He therefore invited them to a little festival to celebrate the occasion. He had been thinking over the book for seventeen years, had been eight years in writing it, and as it had taken such an important place in his life, he must be pardoned a little vanity about it now. Paul had a written invitation sent him, and he thought the occasion was sufficiently important to come to Berlin on purpose.

On the appointed evening they all met at eight o'clock at Borchardt's in the Franzbsischen Strasse. A dignified waiter, who in appearance and manner looked more like an ambassador, received the guests, and took them into a private room on the left side of the large room above the ground floor. This little room was all lined with red like a jewel case, thick red portieres were over the doors, and the amount of gas with which it was lighted made it rather warmer than was comfortable. A large table with divans on three sides of it nearly filled the room; it was beautifully decorated and covered with flowers. Numerous wineglasses were placed before each guest, and champagne was cooling in an ice-bucket near the door.

Dorfling was there, and received his guests as the waiter lifted the heavy portiere. He was in evening dress, and his slightly flushed face beamed with pleasure. His friends regretted keenly that they had come in ordinary morning clothes, and expressed their apologies. He interrupted them, saying they must overlook one of his little whims and not say anything more about it.

Then they sat down to table, impressed by his charming manner. Dorfling put Schrotter on his right hand, and Wilhelm and Paul on his left; near Schrotter was Barinskoi and a friend of Dorfling's, named Mayboorn. This man was, like Dorfling, a Rhinelander, he combined a successful career as a writer of comic verses with a confirmed pessimism. When he had written one of his merriest couplets, he would stop his work and sigh with Dorfling over the tragedy of life. The papers treated his farces as rubbish, but the public adored them. The earnest critic would hardly touch his name with a pair of tongs, but the theatre managers fought for possession of his work. He had a beautiful wife who worshiped him, two wonderful children, and the appearance and bearing of Timon of Athens.

At Dorfling's summons two waiters came in; one of them put a large dish of oysters on the table, while the other placed a thick octavo volume before each guest.

"The last of the season," cried Barinskoi gayly, and helped himself to oysters.

"The book! Bravo!" said Paul, and held out his hand to Dorfling.

There was a short silence, while they all, even the cynical Barinskoi, contemplated the book before them, On the pearl-gray cover they read;

"The Philosophy of Deliverance, by X. Rheinthaler."

"What an expressive title," said Wilhelm, breaking the silence first.

"Admirably adapted for a comic song," remarked Mayboom, with a melancholy air. Barinskoi laughed loudly, while Dorfling looked blandly at him. The comic poet sighed deeply and began to eat.

"But why Rheinthaler?" asked Paul.

"I at first wanted the book to appear anonymously; but the public is accustomed now to see a proper name on the title page. If it does not find one, its curiosity is excited, and what I particularly wished to avoid comes to pass, namely, the diversion of attention from the essential to the unessential."

"That does not explain why you have not put your own name to it," said Paul.

"My own name? What for? What is a name? What is an individuality, which a name symbolizes? The thoughts which I have put down in this book are not from me, the transient accident called Dorfling, but from the absolute everlasting thing which thinks in my brain. I am merely the carrier of the truth, appointed by it. What would you say if a postman put his name on all the letters he delivers?"

"I should not be capable of such self-effacement," said Paul. "If I had devoted the best years of my life to any work I should be unable to renounce the recognition I had earned."

"Recognition, Herr Haber. What sort of word is that? One does what one does, not because one wills, but because one must; not on account of an operation aimed at, but because of a compelling cause. He who reckons on any kind of reward for his works is on the same footing as a silly woman who claims men's approbation because she is pretty or an unreasoning child, who wants to be praised and petted because he has eaten his dinner. A mature perception arrives at this idea of the duty which one must fulfill, and in no hope of the gratification of individual vanity or self-seeking. Recognition! Does the wind hope for recognition from the ships it helps to sail? Is it blamed if it dashes the ship to pieces? It blows, as it must, and is perfectly indifferent about what men say, and as to its effect on trees, and chimney-pots, and ships. My brain is now thinking just as the wind blows. There is no difference between my organism and what goes on in the atmosphere. Both obey the laws of nature, and I merely fulfill these when I write a book."

"I quite agree with you," said Wilhelm.

The oysters had been eaten, and some wonderful Markobrunner drunk. The waiter now brought some Printaniere soup. The conversation halted, as everyone had involuntarily opened his copy of the book, some of them perhaps really curious to read, the others out of sympathy for the writer.

"Please don't read it now," said Dorfling, "the book will be just the same to-morrow, but the soup will be cold."

"That is the remark of a philosopher," said Barinskoi, and poked his pointed red nose in the savory steam from his soup.

"It is difficult to tear oneself away," said Schrotter; "it would be very friendly of you to give an idea of the thoughts at the foundation of your thesis."

"How could I explain a whole system intelligibly in a few words?" said Dorfling.

"You could leave out all the proofs and the development, we can read those presently in your book. You need only just give us the main ideas of your 'Philosophy of Deliverance.'"

All the guests joined in Schrotter's request, Paul the most eagerly, for the idea of having to read through that thick, dry book had frightened him, and now he saw the possibility of knowing its contents in an agreeable and comfortable way.

Dorfling objected at first, but as his friends insisted he began.

"The phenomenal world, in my opinion, is the foundation of a single spiritual principle which you can call what you like—strength, final cause, will, consciousness, God. This eternal principle separates part of itself from its own being—and this is the soul of mankind. Every soul perceives clearly that it is a part of an eternal whole; it feels itself unhappy and uneasy in its fragmentary existence, and yearns to go back again to the whole from whence it came. Individual life means removal from that all-embracing whole; individual death is the complete union of finite parts with the infinite whole. Thus, although life is a necessity, it is a continual pain, and ceaseless yearning; death is the freedom from pain and the fulfillment of that yearning. The only aim of life is death at the end of it, and death is the goal toward which every activity of the living organism eagerly strives."

Paul looked at Wilhelm and Schrotter, but as they were silent he said nothing. Schrotter after consideration, said:

"Why do you separate a part of the eternal principle from itself?"

"To make its unity manifold through divisibility, to arrive at the consciousness of the 'ego,' through the creation of an absolute negation."

"Your eternal principle then," said Schrotter, "appears to you like some lord or master, who is lonely because he is by himself in the world, and wishes to have the society of others."

"Over this, however, is placed the creation of the negation arriving at the consciousness of its own 'ego,' in addition to the knowledge of the object it has in view; thus consciousness precedes the rest," said Wilhelm.

Dorfling shook his head.

"These objections are close reasoning. You will find them answered in the book."

"You are right," said Schrotter, "it is unfair to criticize before we have read the book. I only want to make one remark, not in the sense of criticism, but rather to confirm a fact. Your "Philosophy of Deliverance" is no other than a form of Christianity which looks upon the earth as a vale of tears, on life as a banishment, and on death as going home to the Father's house. The theology of the Vatican would not find a hitch in your system."

"Forgive me, doctor," answered Dorfling. "I see a great difference between my system and Christianity. Both of them hold that life is a misery, and death is the deliverance. But Christianity does not explain why God creates men, and sends them to the misery of earth, instead of leaving them in peace in heaven. I, on the contrary, claim that I explain the creation of living and conscious beings."

"Your assertion then means that the eternal principle of phenomena creates organisms, with the object of arriving at the consciousness of itself?"

"Exactly."

"Now, we have already answered you as to that," said Schrotter, "and I will not keep back my objection any longer. Let me get away for a moment from your system, and say that between metaphysics and theology I do not see the least difference. A metaphysical system and a religious dogma are both attempts to explain the incomprehensible secret to human reason. The negro solves the riddle of the musical-box, believing that a spirit is inside it, which gives forth musical sounds at the white man's command; and that is precisely what priests and philosophers do when they explain the great workings of the universe by a God, or a principle, or whatever they call their fetich. Human nature always wants to know the why and wherefore of things. When we are not sure of our ground, we help ourselves by conjectures, or even by imagination. These conjectures are senseless or reasonable, according to whether our knowledge is insufficient or comprehensive. Men are satisfied in their childhood with stories as explanations of the world's mysteries, in their maturity they advance to plausible hypotheses: the stories yield to theology, hypotheses to philosophy. Religion presents a fictitious solution to the riddle in a concrete form, and metaphysics in an abstract form; the one relates and asserts, the other argues and avoids the improbable. It is only a difference of degree, not of character."

"That is just so," cried Wilhelm. "Metaphysics are as incapable as religion of disclosing what lies behind the phenomenal world, and I cannot conceive (forgive me, Dorfling, if I say straight out what I mean), I cannot conceive how a philosopher can really take his own system in earnest. He must know that his explanation is only a conjecture, a possibility at the best, and he actually has the temerity to preach it as a fixed truth. No, my friend, I do not expect anything from metaphysics. It only interests me as a means for studying psychology. The history of philosophical systems is a history of the development of the mind of humanity. The systems are only valuable as testimonials to the endless extent and possibility of human thought. All the systems put together do not contain a spark of objective truth."

"That is upon the whole the difference between natural science and metaphysics," said Schrotter. "Science regulates the boundary between what is known and what is not known, and declares when the limit is reached. Our knowledge has attained to a certain point, and beyond that we know and understand nothing, absolutely nothing. Metaphysics will not stop at that limit. It confuses knowledge and dreams together, and manufactures out of the two something quite worthless. It explains things which it does not understand, and which cannot be understood, and offers us detailed descriptions of countries into which it has never traveled, and where mankind probably never will travel."

"May I say a word in defence of your metaphysics?" said Dorfling, with a slight smile.

"Yes, go on," cried Barinskoi. He had drunk more than all the rest put together, and the serious conversation seemed to afford him great amusement.

"Look here, Eynhardt. I cannot possibly uphold your statement that metaphysics do not contain a spark of objective truth. To be certain of that, one must also be certain what objective truth is. But you are not certain, as you very well know, and so logically you must admit the possibility that metaphysics can hold a spark of objective truth. I am of an entirely different opinion on this point. I believe that the science of the actual content of things, the foundation of all appearances, the laws of the universe, in short, everything which you call objective truth, is the property peculiar to the atoms, of which the world formerly existed. Absolute science, I say, is inherent matter, like motion and gravitation. Matter does not learn of them, it possesses them. A cell has not studied chemistry, but with unfailing accuracy it executes its wonderful chemical operations. Water knows nothing of physics and mathematics, but it flows from the spring, just as high as the laws of hydraulic pressure command."

"Bravo," interrupted Mayboom, "that explains at last something I never understood; and that is, why a flower pot should fall off a window straight on the heads of people in the street, with unfailing accuracy."

"Please, Mayboom, no bad jokes to-day," said Dorfling gently.

The comic song writer sighed and again sank into deep thought, and the philosopher went on:

"The science of truth, to which every atom adheres, dwells in men. We must not forget that man is a collection of countless millions of atoms; the collected consciousness of mankind can know just as much of what each atom knows, as a whole people can understand of Greek or Sanscrit because one or other of its members can read those languages. Only through intercommunication can the knowledge of the few become the knowledge of the many. The development of the living being I regard in this way, that the atoms at first only hang loosely, gradually becoming more closely knit together, until they make a substantial organism. The single atoms in the course of this process of development step over the boundary toward consciousness. At first it is a trembling, insecure foreboding, like the sensation of light to one nearly blind, then the outlines of truth become clearer, and all at once grow sharp and clearly defined. The different attempts at explanation of the secrets of the world are the expression of these forebodings of truth. So every one of the religious and philosophical systems is to my mind a grain of the truth, and the whole of it will be found in the great unity which we shall reach in a higher development."

"As charming as a pretty story," said Schrotter, "but—it is only a story after all. You conjecture that the thing is so situated, but you are not in a condition to prove it; and if I deny it, you have no means of compelling me to believe, as I can compel you to believe that twice two makes four. No, no; nothing can come of these metaphysical speculations. The whole philosophy is not worth psychological treatment. We are no further to-day than the old Greeks, whose knowledge led to the formula, 'Know thyself.' We can hope to know ourselves some day, to know what goes on in our brains. I hardly believe, however, that science will ever arrive at it."

"The study of natural science has brought me to the same conclusion," said Wilhelm. "We know nothing to-day of the nature of phenomena—we knew nothing yesterday, and we shall know nothing to-morrow. The great advance in thought has only brought us to the point of no more self-deception, and exactly knowing what we do know, whereas yesterday men deceived themselves, and imagined that the fables of religion and metaphysics were positive knowledge. The history of physical science is in this respect very interesting. It teaches that every step forward does not consist of a new explanation, but rather goes to prove, that the earlier explanations were untrustworthy. The sphere of the exact sciences does not grow wider, but narrower. It would be very instructive to study the history of natural science at the point it has reached."

"Why do you not write such a history?" asked Schrotter.

"Why? It would be foolish to add another book to the millions of books already written. All that one can say about it is soon said. Anything really new is written once in a thousand years, all the rest is repetition, dilution, compilation. If everyone who writes on a subject were to read first everything which has been written on that subject, he would very soon throw his pen out of the window."

"I must again differ from you," said Dorfling. "I think it is best, that we so seldom know all that has been thought and written on a subject. It is best that we write new books without wearying to read the millions of others. I grant that most books are only repetitions of earlier ones. But it is unconscious repetition, and it is exactly that which gives it a wonderfully new meaning. It proves unity of mind, identity of science. Thousands of men daily discover gunpowder. Many of them laugh, because gunpowder was first discovered two hundred years ago. I do not laugh. I see in it the manifestation of the eternal unity of phenomenal principle. So many men could not arrive at the same thought if they were not fragments of a whole; now you know why I have written a book, and also, why I have not put my individual name on the title-page."

From the next room they heard a woman laugh in a wild, excited way, glasses chinked together, and a man's voice was just distinguished in conversation. Barinskoi pricked up his ears and winked at Paul; the others paid no attention.

"Do not misunderstand me," said Wilhelm, answering Dorfling's last remark. "I do not mean to say that your book is superfluous. You had every right to it, having made it the object of your life."

"Not the object of my life," interrupted Dorfling. "The only object I have in life is death, which I call deliverance."

"Very good; I will say then, when you conceived it your duty to write it."

"'Duty' yes, I will allow that word to pass. Let us rather say impulse, or instinct. If one has a perception one also feels an impulse, which one calls a feeling of duty to share it with others."

Wilhelm smiled.

"You believe even in perception. That proves above all what you mean by your duty. I know, to my regret, that I have no perceptions to share with others, and the duty of my life is only toward my own moral education and greatest possible perfection."

"That is not enough," Paul broke in, "this self-culture in one's own study does no one any good. For that reason I do not mind if I appear unphilosophical. One has duties toward one's fellowmen. One must be useful to the State, as a good citizen. One must make money, to add to the national wealth."

"Bravo, Herr Haber," said Mayboom gravely. "You speak like a town-crier," and after a short pause he added, "That is a great compliment from me."

"We express the same meaning in different forms," answered Wilhelm. "How can you add to the national wealth? By making yourself a rich man. And I try to be useful to the community by educating myself in the greatest possible morality, and the highest ideal of a citizen. No one can work outside of himself when every individual strives to be good and true, then the whole people will be good and noble."

"Now you are disputing as to your life's duty," cried Baninskoi, whose eyes glowed, and whole face was red with the alcohol he had imbibed. "Prove first that it is a duty. I deny without exception every duty to others. Why should I trouble myself about the world? What are my fellow-creatures to me? Dinner is trumps, and long live wine!" and he drank a glassful.

"It is an instinct born with us," said Wilhelm, without any vexation, "to care for one's fellow-creatures, and to feel a duty in sympathy for others."

"But suppose I have not got this instinct?" answered Barinskoi.

"Then you are an unhealthy exception."

"Prove it."

"The best proof is the continuance of mankind. If the instinct of sympathy with others were to fail among men, humanity would long ago have ceased to exist."

Barinskoi laughed.

"That is a convenient arrangement. Instinct then is the only foundation for your duty, and the continuance of humanity is the only sanction of your instinct. I will leave you to listen to your instinct, and sympathize as much as you like, but for my part I joyfully renounce this duty; the only punishment I should be afraid of is the destruction of mankind, and that is not likely to happen in my lifetime."

"There is another punishment," said Mayboom solemnly, "that I take this bottle of champagne away from you on account of—your bad behavior."

While he spoke he took away the bottle, and Barinskoi tried to get it back again; a little struggle ensued. Dorfling put an end to it by an emphatic "Please don't do that." Turning to Wilhelm he went on:

"I do not believe in your idea of duty; you place instinct at the foundation. I use another word. I call your instinct the foreboding that each has of its being, and its outflow toward the eternal phenomenon of principle. At all events, that seems to suffice for a foundation. But I conceive duty to be quite a different thing. You limit your view to self-culture, and have love for your fellow-creatures, but no desire to instruct them. Now, I think that culture should begin with oneself, but end with others. That is my idea of love for humanity. One need hardly go out of oneself to do this. One can influence things remote without disturbing oneself. Just think of the magnet; it is an immense source of influence, called example. It sets an astonishing example without moving out of itself—an example which cannot be overlooked, and powerfully affects the imagination."

"One illustration for another," said Schrotter, who had shown his interest in the conversation by nodding his head now and then. "You wish man to play the part of a magnet; that is not enough, I want him to play the part of a cogwheel. He must catch hold of his surroundings while he moves, he must also move all those round him. Everyone cannot be a magnet; we are not all made of the same stuff. But one can make a cogged wheel out of whatever one will—and beside, a magnet only influences certain substances. It will draw iron, but cannot attract copper, wood, or stone; but the cogwheel takes hold of anything near it, of whatever material it is made. I will not work the illustration to death. You can see by this what I mean. I think a far-reaching activity is the first business of mankind. Our nerves are not so much those of sensation as of movement; we do not only take in impressions from the outside, we are provided with organs which give out impressions received from within. Every sensation of movement which nature sends through us is a summons to be answered by an action, not only self-culture, not example, not passive good-will toward others, but by the intention an object of activity toward the world and humanity. The Middle Ages summoned up the business of life in the words, 'Ora et Labora.' They are beautiful words, and after this lapse of time we take the meaning out for ourselves, in other words, 'Think and Act.'"

The woman's laughter from the next room became louder, and then they heard chairs pushed back, and the noise of departure. The rustling of a silk dress, with the clinking of spurs and sword, passed the door, became fainter, and then ceased. It was near midnight, and Schrotter rose to go. He was thinking of Bhani, who was sitting up for him at home. The dinner must have been paid for beforehand, for the guests were spared the sight of a money transaction to chill the end of their pleasant evening. The cool night air felt refreshing after the heat of the small room. Dorfling declined the offers his friends made to accompany him home. They all wished him "Farewell."

"Die well, would be a better wish," replied Dorfling, and with these strange words in their ears they left him.

Schrotter and Wilhelm went a part of the way with Paul, who had the furthest to go. For a little while he was silent, then he broke out:

"I declare this is beyond my comprehension. The whole time I was there I felt as if I were in a vault with a lot of ghosts. You, Herr Doctor, were the only living being among them; I breathed again when I heard you talking. If I had not head the sounds from next door, and had not had the realities of our dinner before me, I should have thought I was dreaming."

"What has put you out so, my dear Paul?" said Wilhelm.

"What! Are you men of flesh and blood? Are you really alive? There we sat for four mortal hours, and the talk was wearisome to a degree, never one sensible word."

"Now! now!" protested Schrotter.

"Herr Doctor, forgive me, but I must repeat it, never one sensible word. Do you call Dorfling's 'Philosophy of Deliverance' sensible? or, Wilhelm, your philosophy of self-culture, which, with all deference to you, I call philosophical onanism? Only six men, two of them under thirty-five, and the whole blessed evening not one word about either pleasure or love."

They had come to the place where Friedrichstrasse and Leipzigerstrasse cross each other; and Schrotter signed to them to look toward the left corner. There under a gas lamp they saw Barinskoi in earnest conversation with a woman.

"Yes, look at him! That brute is still the most reasonable among all your philosophics. He has his method of sponging, and enjoys himself according to the category of Aristotle. But your metaphysics—"

"What do you really want, Paul?"

"Well, I want you all to have to do for once with practical life, with two hundred workmen to pay and ten thousand acres of land to see after; and artificial manures and the price of corn to worry you; then perhaps you would take a little less interest as to whether the soul was a phenomenon or an india-rubber ball, or whether men were magnets or cogwheels."

Wilhelm only smiled. He had long ago given up trying to bring his practical friend to ideal views. At the corner of the Kochstrasse they separated, and Paul continued his way to the Lutzowstrasse, while Wilhelm and Schrotter turned back.

Twenty minutes later, as Wilhelm entered his bedroom, his eyes fell on a letter for him in Dorfling's handwriting. He opened it, greatly surprised, and read as follows:

"DEAR FRIEND: When you read this I shall be free from all trouble and all doubt. I have accomplished what I set myself to do, and I am going back to eternity from this limited sphere. May you be as happy as I shall be in a few hours! Keep a friendly thought for me as long as you stay in this world of misery, and believe that he who writes this had the warmest friendship for you."

"L. DORFLING."

Wilhelm stood as if thunderstruck. Was it by any chance a dreadful joke? No; Dorfling was incapable of that. It must be a grim reality. He ran quickly out of the house to seek Schrotter. The old Indian servant opened the door, and in his broken English informed him that Schrotter Sahib had found a letter when he reached home and had immediately gone out again.

Wilhelm could now doubt no longer, and running swiftly, he reached the street where Dorfling lived, waited in agonizing suspense for the door to be opened, flew up the stairs, and through the open door to his friend's bedroom. There he found Schrotter; Mayboom was also there sobbing, and a tearful old servant. In an arm chair near the bed was Dorfling, still in his dress coat and tie, his head sunk on his breast, his face hardly whiter than in life, his arms hanging down, and in the middle of the white shirt-front a great red stain. On the floor lay a revolver.

Wilhelm, horrified, took his friend's hand. It was still quite warm. His agonizing look sought Schrotter's, who answered in a hushed voice, "He is dead."

Then his tears broke out, and his trembling fingers had hardly strength to close the lids over his friend's eyes, those eyes which looked so strangely quiet and peaceful as if they now knew the answer to the Great Secret.

CHAPTER VIII.

DARK DAYS.

Dorfling's suicide made a profound impression on Wilhelm, and for months he was haunted by the vision of that motionless form with its white face and blood-stained breast. It had a weird fascination for him, causing him to revert constantly to that tragical May night that had begun with a cheerful dinner, and ended in a fatal pistol shot. Paul's comment on the occurrence was short and concise. "The poor chap was mad," he said, and there the matter ended as far as he was concerned. Mayboom revered his friend's memory as he would a saint, and erected a kind of chapel to him in his house, in which Dorfling's portrait, his book, and various objects belonging to him, thrown up in relief against draperies and surrounded by a variety of symbolical accessories, were set forth for the pious delectation of the master of the house and his visitors. Schrotter held aloof from this cult. He appreciated Dorfling's character, his consistency, his strength of will and highmindedness as they deserved, but he was never tired of preaching and demonstrating to Wilhelm that all these admirable qualities had been turned out of their proper course by a disturbing morbid influence. It was monstrous, he contended, that a system of philosophy should arm you for suicide. What if the premises should prove false? Then your voluntary death would be a frightful mistake which nothing could retrieve. One has no right to risk making such a mistake. He believed in development, in the progress of the organic world from a lower to a higher stage. Progress and development, however, were conditional upon life, and he who has recourse to self-destruction sets an example of unseemly revolt against one of the most beautiful and comforting of all the laws of nature. Moreover, suicide was a waste of force on which it was simply heartrending to have to look. There were so many great deeds to be done which called for the laying down of life. In a thousand different ways one might benefit mankind by Winkelried-like actions. If one was determined to die, one should at least render thereby to those left behind one of those sublime services which demand the sacrifice of a life.

In their frequent conversations upon this subject, he was so earnest, so eloquent, so markedly intentional, that Wilhelm finally gave him the smiling assurance that he was preaching to a convert. It was true, he had the highest respect for a man who did not hesitate to cast life from him when his whole mind and thought led him to the conviction that death was preferable to life; and unprincipled as suicide might be from an objective point of view, subjectively considered, there surely was an ideal fitness in making one's actions agree to the uttermost point with one's opinions? Nevertheless, he himself did not approve of Dorfling's deed, and would certainly never imitate it, for one could never know what intentions the unknown powers might not have with regard to the individual; by committing suicide he maybe threw up some possible mission, or by his premature departure disturbed the action of the great machine in which he—as some small screw or wheel—doubtless had his modest place and function.

As if to prove to Schrotter that he was no disciple of the "Philosophy of Deliverance," he turned his attention, more than he had ever done before, to the realities of life. Dorfling left a remarkable will. He bequeathed his fortune—most advantageously invested in a house in Dusseldorf and in public funds—yielding a yearly income of about thirty-five thousand marks, to his two friends, Dr Schrotter and Dr Eynhardt, with the sole charge that out of it they should provide a sufficient competency for his old servant, dating from his father's time, who had attended him literally from the cradle to the grave. The fortune was to be theirs conjointly and indivisibly, and should one of them die, to devolve to the survivor, who in his turn was to make such arrangements as he thought best to insure its being applied, after his death, in accordance with the testator's views. He expressed the hope that his two heirs would use the income derived from the property in alleviating the misery inseparable from human existence, of which throughout life they must be witnesses. Dorfling's only near relative was herself very wealthy and generous-minded, and did not dispute the will, it was accordingly proved.

Wilhelm declared from the first that he understood nothing of the management of a fortune, of business papers, and so forth, and wanted to hand over the administration of the whole to Schrotter. Schrotter, however, would not hear of it, and after vying with one another in generous self-disparagement and mutual confidence, they finally agreed that Schrotter, being a practical man, and conversant with the ways of business and the world, should take the management of the fortune upon himself, but that Wilhelm should receive a monthly sum of fifteen hundred marks out of the income to apply as he thought best to the relief of the needy. The other half of the income was at Schrotter's disposal, who put it, of course, to the same use. In his capacity as member of the deputation for the poor, and also as parish doctor, he came in contact with much poverty and misery, and was able to direct Wilhelm's charity into the right channels. It became Wilhelm's regular afternoon employment to visit the homes of those mentioned to him as in need of relief, that he might the better judge for himself of the true state of the case, make personal inquiries about the people, and step in where help was necessary and deserved.

Only now did he learn what life really was, and what he saw neither increased his pleasure in being alive nor made him proud to be a man among men. Needless to say, it was not long before the news reached the circles of the professional beggars that there was a gentleman in the Dorotheenstrasse who had a considerable yearly sum of money to give away. The result was that his modest apartment was so besieged by petitioners that his old landlady, Frau Muller, the widow of a post-office official, with whom he had boarded and lodged for seven years, was goaded to desperation, and declared that if the disgraceful rabble was encouraged she would be obliged to part from Wilhelm, though it would be her death, she being so fond of him and so used to his ways. Wilhelm was wise enough to admit the justice of her complaint, and empowered Frau Muller to turn away ruthlessly all such visitors whose names were unknown to her, or who came without recommendation, which orders she carried out with such virulence and relentlessness, that the worshipful company of professional beggars rapidly came to the conclusion that it was useless trying to gain admittance to Dr. Eynhardt as long as he was guarded by the tall, bony old lady who opened the door but would not leave hold of it. So the unceasing tramp of dirty boots on the echoing stair was hushed, and Wilhelm saw no more of the crape-clad widows of eminent officials who required a sewing machine or a piano to save them from starvation; the gentlemen who would be forced to put a bullet through their brains if they did not procure the money to pay a debt of honor; or the unemployed clerks who had eaten nothing for days, and who all had a sick wife and from six to twelve children (all small) at home crying for bread; or the foreigners who could find no work in Berlin, and would return to their native countries if he would give them a few thalers to pay their fourth-class railway fare; and similar interesting persons, the endless diversity of whose life-histories had kept him in a chronic state of surprise for months. In place of the visitors he now received letters, as many as if he had been a cabinet minister. It was the same old story, only less affecting, because generally deficient in style, and faulty as to spelling, and no longer illustrated by tearful, vigorously mopped eyes, abysmal sighs, and hands wrung till they cracked. For a time Wilhelm went to every address given in these letters, in order to see and hear for himself, but after awhile his powers of discrimination were sharpened, and he learned to distinguish between the impositions of swindlers and professional beggars, and the real distress which has a claim to sympathy.

By degrees, it is true, he became convinced, even in the chill dwellings of real poverty, that this was hardly ever entirely unmerited. Where it had not been brought about by laziness, frivolity, or drink, its source was to be found in ignorance or incapacity, in other words, in an inefficient equipment for the battle of life. He judged all these circumstances, however, to be the outward and visible signs of obscure natural laws, and that to interfere with rash and ignorant hands in their workings was as useless as it was unreasonable. He therefore pondered seriously whether, by denying to a portion of mankind the qualities indispensable to success in the struggle for existence, Nature herself did not predestine them to misery and destruction; whether the irredeemable poor—those who after each help upward invariably fell back in the former state—were not the offscourings of humanity, the preservation of whom was a fruitless task, and altogether against the design of Nature?

Fortunately, he did not allow his deeds of brotherly love to be darkened by the shadow of these and kindred thoughts. He brought forward reasons which always ended by triumphing over his cold doubts. Misery was possibly the outcome of inexorable natural laws, but then was not compassion the same? The poor were poor under the pressure of some irresistible force, but did not the charitable act under the same pressure? Moreover, was Wilhelm so sure that he himself was better equipped for the race of life than those unfortunates who went under because they chose a trade for which they were neither mentally nor physically competent, or because, from laziness or obstinacy, they insisted on remaining in Berlin, where nobody wanted them, when a few miles off they might have found all the conditions conducive to their prosperity? How could he know whether he would have been capable of earning his living if his father had not left him a plentifully-spread table? In the rooms that contained so little furniture and so many emaciated human beings, into which his charitable zeal led him every day, he pictured himself, pale and thin, without food, without books; and although he had the harmless vanity to believe that privation and penury would affect him less deeply than the poor devils he visited, the idea that he saw his own face before him, as it might have been had he not had the good luck to be his father's heir opened his hand still wider, and added to the money words of sympathy and comfort, which afforded the recipients—unless they were utterly hardened—as much pleasure as the donation itself.

Beside his almsgiving, he now had another occupation which took up all his surplus time. Schrotter had not let the suggestion drop which he made at Dorfling's dinner-party, and had persuaded Wilhelm so long that he finally rouse himself to attempt an account of the ways and means by which the human mind has freed itself of its grossest errors. It was to be entitled "A History of Human Ignorance," and promised to be a most original work. He would endeavor to show what idea people had had of the universe at various periods, how they explained the phenomena of nature, their connection, their causes and effects. He would begin with the childish superstitions of the savages, and continuing through the so-called learned systems of the ancients and of the Middle Ages, would bring his history up to the theories of contemporary scientists. He would demonstrate the psychological causes of the fact that man, at a certain stage of intellectual development, must necessarily fall into certain errors, and by the aid of what experiments, experiences, and conclusions he had come gradually to recognize them as such. How the fresh interpretation of a single phenomenon would overturn, at one blow, a number of other phenomena hitherto considered entirely satisfactory, how prevailing scientific theories, instead of assisting the fearless observer or discoverer, invariably hindered him and turned him from the right path, in proof of which assertion he brought forward such striking examples as Aristotle's convulsive endeavors to make each of the senses correspond to one of the four elements in which they believed in his day, and Kepler with his fantastic efforts to prove the supremacy of the Pythagorean seven in the solar system. The object of the book was to show that the history of human knowledge is a history of false inferences and the erroneous interpretations of correctly observed phenomena, that the increase of knowledge always means the destruction of existing opinions, that of all the scientific systems up to the present day, only those retained their position which proved the futility of earlier theories—never those which built up new structures on the foundations of the old house of cards that had been blown down. In a word, that progress means not the acquisition of fresh knowledge, but an ever-extended consciousness of the futility of the knowledge we thought to possess.

Wilhem spared himself no pains with this work. He brought all the thoroughness and industry of his honest nature to bear upon it, would accept no statement at second-hand, but went for every information to the fountain head. It would cost an immense amount of time, but after all he had that at his disposal. There was no need for him to hurry, seeing that he did not write from ambition or for any material advantage, but simply for his own gratification. He began by rubbing up his school Greek sufficiently to enable him to read the ancient philosophers with ease, which he achieved in a few months, and then set to work to learn Arabic, that being the chief language of science in the Middle Ages. Schrotter was seriously alarmed at these extensive preparations, and hastened to procure, through his pandit friends, some English extracts from the scientific literature of India, lest Wilhelm might think fit to study Sanscrit, and decades would pass before he came to write the first word of his book.

Thus four years went by, years full of work, though they left no visible traces. Meanwhile the aspect of things in the new Empire had become very different. Men breathed the oppressive air with laboring breasts; the bright dawn which promised so glorious a day had, been followed by sullen mists, and the blue sky had disappeared behind heavy, leaden-gray clouds, through which no comforting ray of sunshine pierced. Where was all the glowing enthusiasm, the rapture of hope and joy that, in the first years after the great war, had flushed every German cheek and lit up every eye? Throughout the length and breath of the land the opposing factions confronted one another like armed antagonists preparing for a duel to the death. Town and village rang with execration and satire, with howls of rage or satisfied revenge vented by German against German. The Roman Catholic shook his clinched fist at the Protestant, the liberal at the conservative, the protectionist at the free-trader, the partisan of absolute government at the defender of the people's rights. Everywhere hatred and malice, everywhere a mad desire to gag, to maltreat, to tear limb from limb; this unfettering of the basest human passions giving meanwhile such an impetus to bribery, corruption, and unprincipled advancement for party purposes as to resemble the loathsome luxuriant growth of mildew in the damp corners of some neglected storeroom.

The high tide of the foreign millions had ebbed away, showing itself to have been no fructifying Nile but a destructive lava stream, leaving the country charred and desolate after its passage. The gold that only yesterday had poured through greedy fingers, had turned to-day to ashes and withered leaves like the goblin gold of a fairy tales. Diminished inclination for work, an insanely increased demand for the luxuries of life, the accepted ideas of morality shaken to their foundations by scandalous examples of triumphant vice and villainy—these were the blessings that remained after the so-called impetus following on the "Downfall." Work was scarcer, wages lower, but the flood of country people seeking work continued to roll toward the capital, overcoming with irresistible force the backward wave of unfortunates who could find no employment in the building yards, the factories or the workshops, trampling blindly over the bodies of the fallen, like a herd of buffaloes which marches ever straight ahead, which nothing can turn out of its course, and when it arrives at a precipice over which the leaders fall, presses onward till the last one is swallowed up in the depths. The misery and privation became heartrending to witness. Each morning you might see in the working quarters of the town and suburbs hundreds of strong men, their hands—perforce idle—buried in their torn and empty pockets, going from factory to factory asking for work, while the overseers would wave them off from afar to avoid a useless interchange of words. If, in the years of the French milliards, the workingman had turned socialist out of sheer envy and wantonness, he became so now under the sting of adversity, and in all the length and breadth of Berlin there was hardly one of the proletariat who was not a fanatical disciple of the new doctrine, with its slashing denunciations against all that was, and its intoxicating promises of all that was to be. Wilhelm had many opportunities of intercourse with the unemployed. He gave help as far as his fifty marks a day would reach, and kept the wolf from many a door. But the miraculous loaves and fishes of the gospel would have been necessary to successfully alleviate even the distress which he saw with his own eyes, and although much of the preaching of the social democrats still seemed to him mere phrase-making and altogether mistaken, he yet came gradually to the conclusion that somewhere—he did not precisely know where—in the construction of the social machine there must be a flaw, seeing that there were so many people who could and would work, and yet were doomed to despair and ruin for lack of employment. The spring of 1878 came round, and brought with it two attempts on the life of the emperor within three weeks. Scarcely had the people recovered from the horror caused by Hodel's crime when it was shaken to its depths by Nobiling's murderous shot.

On that terrible Sunday, June the 2d, Wilhelm had dined with Schrotter, and about three o'clock they started for a walk. In the few steps that separate the Mittelstrasse from the Linden they saw what was going on in the town. In Unter den Linden, however, they were received by the yells of the newspaper men calling out the first special editions, and found themselves in the stream of people pouring toward the Palace or to No. 18, where they pointed out the window on the second floor from which the too-well-aimed shot had fallen.

From the special editions, from the confused remarks and exclamations of the crowd in which the two friends found themselves, and the information they obtained from the grim-looking policemen, rougher and less communicative than ever, they learned all that was necessary of the bloody deed which had taken place an hour ago. Wilhelm could scarcely control his horror, and even Schrotter, though calmer, was deeply moved and downcast. All pleasure in their walk was gone, and they decided to return to Schrotter's house.

"It is simply hideous," said Wilhelm, as they turned into the Friedrichstrasse, "that we have such brutes living among us! We know, of course, that there is a great deal of distress, but a man who can revenge his own trouble on the person of the emperor must be lower than the beasts of the field. And men who at this time of day have such ideas on State organization are electors!"

"Good heavens!" cried Schrotter, with unconscious vehemence, "you are surely not going to make the popular mistake of drawing sweeping conclusions from these outrages? Such occurrences have no outside importance. They are the acts of madmen. Their following so closely upon one another is the very surest proof of that. There are in Germany thousands—perhaps tens of thousands—of unhappy creatures whose minds are more or less unhinged, though their inexperienced surroundings do not know it. Some exceptional event will suddenly put the entire population in a state of ferment, the imagination of the already morbidly inclined will be particularly strongly affected thereby; they picture the occurrence to themselves till it takes hold of them, and drives out every other thought from their minds, becomes a nightmare, a possession, and finally an irresistible impulse to do the same. After every event of the kind, you hear that a whole number of people have gone mad, and that their insanity is somehow connected with it. No such thing. They were mad before, and the insanity which had lain dormant in them only waited for a chance shock to give it definite form and character."

They had reached Schrotter's door by this time, and were on the point of entering, when a policeman stepped up to them, and touching Wilhelm's arm, said:

"Gentlemen, you will have to come with me."

"Why, what do you mean?" they exclaimed, very much taken aback.

"Better make no fuss, but come quietly with me," answered the policeman, "This gentleman accuses you of making insulting remarks against his majesty."

Only now did they become aware of a man standing behind the policeman and glaring at them in fury.

"Are you mad?" Schrotter burst out angrily. "That is for the magistrate to decide," exclaimed the man, in a voice trembling with rage; "and you, policeman, do your duty."

Passers-by began to gather round the group, so, to bring a disagreeable scene to a close, Schrotter said to Wilhelm:

"We had better go with the policeman; I suppose we shall be enlightened presently."

A short walk brought them to the police office in the Neue Wilhelms Strasse, where they were taken before the lieutenant of police. The policeman deposed in a few words that he had been standing at the corner of the Friedrich and Mittelstrasse, the two gentlemen passed him in loud conversation; the third gentleman, who was following them, then came up to him, and told him to arrest them because they had spoken insultingly of his majesty, and here they were. He had neither seen nor heard anything further.

The lieutenant of police began by asking their names. When they told him—"Dr. Schrotter, M. D. one of the members for Berlin and Professor Emeritus," and "Dr. Eynhardt, Doctor of Philosophy, householder," he offered them chairs. The informer introduced himself as "non-commissioned officer Patke, retired, member of a military association, and candidate for the private constabulary."

"What have you to bring forward against the gentlemen?"

"I walked behind the two gentlemen from the Linden to the Mittelstrasse. They were conversing loudly about the attempted assassination, and I naturally listened."

"It does not appear to me so very natural," commented the lieutenant dryly.

The informer was a trifle disconcerted, but he soon recovered himself, and proceeded in a declamatory manner:

"The younger gentleman—the dark one—expressed himself in very unbecoming terms with regard to his majesty the emperor, and said among other things, that the outrage was of no real importance. I am a patriot, I have served his august majesty; if his majesty—"

"That will do," the lieutenant broke in, ruthlessly interrupting the retired non-commissioned officer's flow of language, which he accompanied with a dramatic waving of the right arm. "Can you repeat the 'unbecoming terms' of which, according to your account, this gentleman made use?"

"I cannot remember the exact words. I was too excited. So much, however, I remember distinctly—he declared the attempt upon his majesty's life to be an occurrence of no importance."

Wilhelm now broke in.

"Not a word of that is true," he said quietly. "Neither of us said one word which could justify this inconceivable charge."

"The remark which this informer seems to have taken hold of," Schrotter observed, "was not made by my friend, Dr. Eynhardt, but by me. I did not say either that the occurrence was unimportant, but that it had no general significance—that it was not a proof of the prevailing feeling at large."

"It comes to the same thing whether you say it has no importance or no significance," interrupted the informer. "That gentleman may have made the remark, but I certainly heard it, and as a loyal servant of his majesty—"

"That is quite enough," said the lieutenant of police authoritatively. Then turning to the two friends—"I am very sorry, but as things stand at present, I must let the law take its course. Do you persist in your charge?" he asked the informer.

"Yes, Herr Lieutenant; my duty to my sovereign—"

"Silence. Gentlemen, I shall be obliged to notify the matter to the proper authorities. I expect you will be called upon to clear yourselves before the magistrate, which I have no doubt you will be able to do successfully. I need not detain you any longer."

Wilhelm and Schrotter bowed courteously and withdrew, without vouchsafing a glance at the informer. The latter lingered, as if he would have liked to continue the conversation with the lieutenant of police, but an emphatic "You may go!" sent him rapidly over the threshold of the office.

Five days afterward, on a Friday, Schrotter and Wilhelm were summoned to appear in the Stadtvogtei [Footnote: A certain prison in Berlin.] before the magistrate, a disagreeable person with a bilious complexion, venomous eyes behind his spectacles, and the unpleasing habit of continually scooping out his ear with the little finger of his left hand. The two friends, the informer, and the policeman were present. The magistrate could not have received them differently if they had been accused of robbing and murdering their parents. To be sure, he behaved no better to the informer. His expression of unmitigated disgust was perhaps a freak of nature, and no indication of the true state of his feelings.

He had a bundle of papers before him, in which he searched for some time before opening his mouth.

"You are accused of having made use of offensive expressions regarding his majesty," he said to Schrotter.

"On a preposterously unfounded charge," he retorted.

"And you too," he turned to Wilhelm.

"I can only repeat Dr. Schrotter's answer."

"Give your evidence," he ordered the policeman.

The man did so.

"Could you understand what the gentleman said?"

"No."

"How far was Patke behind them?"

"A few steps."

"You must be more exact."

"I can't say more exactly than that, for I paid no attention to the gentlemen till I was told to arrest them."

"Is it your opinion that Herr Patke could have heard distinctly what the gentlemen were saying to one another?"

"I dare say he might have understood if they spoke very loud, but I can't say for certain."

"Herr Patke, what have you to say?"

The former non-commissioned officer, who had donned his 1870 medal for the occasion, hereupon assumed a strictly military bearing, fixed his eye firmly on the magistrate, and began in a sing-song voice:

"I happened to be in the street last Sunday when the infamous wretch lifted his murderous hand against the sacred person of our august monarch. My heart bled; I was beside myself; I could have torn everybody and everything to pieces. As I walked along I noticed these two gentlemen, who looked to me suspicious from the first—"

"Why?" asked the magistrate.

"Well—the one with his black hair, and the other with his hooked nose—I said to myself, 'Those are Jews!'"

The magistrate suddenly bent over his papers, and gave a kind of grunt. Even the policeman, in spite of his wooden official air, could not repress a smile. Patke continued:

"Then I heard the younger gentleman say, 'It serves his majesty the emperor quite right.'"

"Did he actually say, his majesty the emperor?" interrupted the magistrate.

"No," answered Patke eagerly, "I say that."

"You are only to repeat the gentleman's actual words."

"He actually did say that it served the emperor right."

"This is beyond a joke," Schrotter burst out. "Why, man, I wonder the lie does not stick in your throat and choke you!"

"I must beg you not to address the witness," said the magistrate brusquely. Then to Patke severely—"That is not what you said in your first charge."

"I was confused then; I did not recollect distinctly. But later on it came back to me."

"That is very improbable. What have you to answer, Dr. Eynhardt?"

"Simply, that the man's statement is absolutely untrue. I never uttered or thought words bearing the remotest resemblance to those he quotes."

"What my friend does not say is," broke in Schrotter, "that, on the contrary, he expressed the deepest and most painful emotion at the crime."

The magistrate shot a venomous glance from under his spectacles at Schrotter, but quailed before those flaming half-closed blue eyes fixed so sternly upon him.

"Well, and what have you to bring forward against the other gentleman?"

"That gentleman said the outrage was of no great importance."

"In your first account you said the outrage had no real significance, and that Dr. Eynhardt made the remark."

"Whether he said 'no importance' or 'no significance,' it is all the same thing, and one cannot so easily distinguish the speaker when one is walking behind. I may have been mistaken on that point."

"You do not repudiate the remark?" asked the magistrate of Schrotter in his most biting tones.

"Your expression is not very happily chosen. By repudiating I understand the declaring of a fact to be false when we know it to be true. I am not in the habit of doing that, nor should I suppose it of you, Herr Staatsanwalt."

"I need no instruction from you," the other returned angrily.

"It would seem so, however" Schrotter calmly rejoined.

The magistrate grunted several times and then asked, after a pause, during which he was particularly busy with his ear:

"You admit the statement, then?"

"Not altogether. It is true that I said the attempt on the emperor's life had no general significance, but I meant by that and the rest of what I said, that if the political parties should make this isolated crime (committed by an undoubtedly insane person) the excuse for adopting measures inimical to the liberty of the public in general, they would be doing something both unjustifiable and reprehensible."

"Can he have said that?" asked the magistrate, turning to Patke.

"I don't know. I only know what I said just now."

Renewed grunting, renewed digging in the ear and turning over of papers. "Hm—hm," he muttered to himself testily, "that is not enough. It is too indefinite, in spite of strong grounds for suspicion." Then he looked up, and in a tone which was meant to convey as much scorn as possible, he asked Schrotter—"You played a part in the political events of 1848?"

"Yes, and the recollection of it is the pride of my life."

"I did not ask you about that. And you are at present the chairman of a district society of progressive opinions?"

"I have that honor."

"There is nothing further against you. And you, Dr. Eynhardt, you refused the Iron Cross in the late campaign?"

"Yes."

"You were discharged from the army without comment?"

"Yes."

"For declining a duel," observed Schrotter.

"Dr. Eynhardt is of age, and can answer for himself. You have attended Socialist meetings?"

"Only once."

"And made speeches?"

"One speech?"

"And that was directed against Socialism," said Schrotter again.

The magistrate grew lobster-red in the face.

"It is really scandalous," he cried, quivering with rage, "that I am repeatedly obliged to remind a man of your position that he is only to answer when spoken to. Why didn't you say yourself, Dr. Eynhardt, that you had spoken against the Socialists?"

"Because you did not ask me," answered Wilhelm, with a gentle smile.

After a slight pause the magistrate resumed—"You are on friendly terms with a Russian named Dr. Barinskoi?"

"You can hardly call it that. I did know him, though not exactly in a friendly way, but for two years I have quite lost sight of him."

"Did you know that Dr. Barinskoi was a Nihilist?"

"Yes."

"And you did not let that make any difference to you?"

"I was not afraid of infection," said Wilhelm, and smiled again.

"Perhaps not, but of being compromised," growled the magistrate.

"That idea has not troubled me as yet."

"You inherited from a friend who committed suicide a large fortune, which you use chiefly for the benefit of Socialist workmen?"

"I use it for the benefit of the poor, and those I certainly find more frequently among the Socialist workmen than among factory owners and householders."

"I'll thank you to remember that this is not the place for making bad jokes!" roared the magistrate.

"You are quite right," Wilhelm answered serenely. "I know nothing more unpleasant than bad jokes."

Schrotter looked as if he were going to embrace his friend. He had never seen him from this side.

"Did it never occur to you to put yourself in communication with the clergymen of your district, these gentlemen having far greater facilities for finding out deserving objects of charity than a private person?"

"I will answer that question when you have had the goodness to explain to me what connection it has with this man's denunciation."

The magistrate glared at him in a manner calculated to wither him on the spot, but only met a quiet, smiling face which he was incapable of intimidating.

"May I request you now," said Schrotter in his turn, "to ask the witness Patke if for the last few weeks he has not been a candidate for a post as detective on the political police staff?" Schrotter too had made a variety of inquiries since last Sunday, and had learned this fact.

"That is so," stammered Patke, turning very red. "In these terrible times, when the Socialists and the enemies of the country—"

"Silence, Herr Patke," interrupted the magistrate angrily; "that has nothing to do with the business on hand." He reflected for awhile, and then said with the most deeply grudging manner—"The statement of the one witness—seeing too that it is indefinite in some important points—is not sufficient to warrant me in passing a sentence, in spite of many good grounds for suspicion afforded by your past history and known opinions. I will therefore dismiss the charge, if only to avoid the public scandal of a Member being accused of lese majeste."

Schrotter was boiling with rage, and had the greatest difficulty in restraining his naturally passionate temper. "Many thanks for your kindness," he said in a choking voice, "and for this scoundrel you have no reprimand?"

"Sir," screamed the magistrate, springing out of his chair with fury, "leave this room instantly; and you, Herr Patke, if you wish to bring an action for libel against the gentleman you may call upon me as a witness."

Patke was too modest to avail himself of this friendly offer. Wilhelm dragged Schrotter out of the office as fast as he could, and even outside they still heard the magistrate's grunts of wrath.

Dark days followed, in which Schrotter seemed to live over again the worst horns of the "wild year." A moral pestilence—the craze for denunciation—spread itself over the whole of Germany, sparing neither the palace nor the hut. No one was safe, either in the bosom of the family, at the club table, in the lecture room, or in the street, from the low spy who, from fanaticism or stupidity, from personal spite or desire to make himself conspicuous, took hold of some hasty or imprudent word, turned it round, mangled it, and brought it redhot to the magistrates, who seldom had the courage to kick the informer downstairs. Such unspeakable depths of human baseness came to light, so full of corruption and pestilence, that the eye turned in horror from the incredible spectacle. The newspapers brought daily reports of denunciations for "lese majeste," and when Schrotter read them he clasped his hands in horrified dismay and exclaimed, "Are we in Germany? are these my fellow-countrymen?" He became at last so disgusted that he gave up reading the German papers, and derived his knowledge of what was going on in the world from the two London papers which, from the habit of a quarter of a century, he still took in. He wished to hear no more about denunciations by which, with the aid of police and magistrates, every kind of cowardice and vileness, social envy and religious hatred, rivalry, spite, and inborn malevolence, sought a riskless gratification, and usually found it in full measure. But it took away all pleasure in social intercourse. One learned to be cautious and suspicious. One grew accustomed to see an enemy in every stranger, and to be upon one's guard before a neighbor as before some lurking traitor. Hypocrisy became an instinct of self-preservation; every one carefully avoided speaking of those things of which the heart was full, and Berlin afforded an insight into the mental condition of the people of Spain during the most flourishing period of the Inquisition, or of Venice in the days when anonymous denunciations poured into the yawning jaws of the Lions of St. Mark's square.

The Reichstag was dissolved, the people of Germany must choose new representatives, and the chief, if not the sole question to be decided by the election was, Are the Socialists to be dealt with under a special act, or to come under the common law? Schrotter now felt it justifiable, nay, that it was his duty, to throw off the reserve he had maintained since his return to the Fatherland, and come forward as a candidate for the Reichstag, though for a suburban district, as the city district to whose poor he had been an untiring benefactor as physician and friend, with help, counsel, and money, was not available.

At a meeting of his constituents he laid down his confession of faith. A special act, he explained, was in no way justified, would indeed be ineffectual, and lead away from the object they had in view. The government would be guilty of libel if it made the Socialists answerable for a crime committed by two half or wholly insane persons; it was the duty of the government to prove that these attacks were the work of the Socialists: that proof, however, it had been unable to discover. Moreover, no special act in the world could hinder people of unsound mind from committing insane deeds—the crimes of a Hodel or a Nobiling could not be predicted, but neither could they be prevented by any kind of precautionary measure. The sole result of a special act would be to make the Socialists practically outlaws in their own country. That would constitute not only a terrible severity against a large class of their fellow-citizens, but a frightful danger to the State. In hundreds and thousands of hearts it would destroy the sense of fellowship with the community in which they lived; they would look upon themselves as outcasts, and become the enemies of their pursuers. It would be exactly as if some thousands of Frenchmen were set down in the midst of the German population—in the army, in the cities, the factories, the arsenals and railways, where they would only wait for a favorable opportunity to revenge themselves on their conquerors. That would be the inevitable result if the Socialists were deprived of the security of the common law. He considered the Socialist doctrines false and mischievous, and their aims senseless and—fortunately—unattainable, and for that very reason he did not fear them. But deprive the Socialists of the possibility of expressing themselves freely in word and print, and their grievances, which now found vent in harmless speechifying, would assume the form of practical violence.

His speech made an impression, but that of a rival candidate a still greater, for he succeeded in rousing the deepest and most powerful emotions of his hearers, by the plain statement that whoever refused the government the right of adopting such measures as it thought necessary for the safety of the public, simply delivered the life of their aged and beloved sovereign into the hands of assassins. At the election, Schrotter had on his side only a small number of independent-minded voters, who were able to remain unmoved by sentimental arguments. The workingmen would not vote for him, knowing him to be an opponent of Socialism. The rival candidate was returned by a large majority.

The Reichstag assembled, the Socialist Act was passed, Berlin declared to be in a state of semi-siege, and a great number of workmen dismissed from the city. It was November, and winter had set in with unusual severity. On a dark and bitterly cold afternoon, old Stubbe, who had been agent in the Eynhardts' house for twenty years, entered Wilhelm's room.

"What is the news, Father Stubbe?" cried Wilhelm, as he came in.

"No good news, Herr Doctor. Wander the locksmith—you know the man who rents the second floor of the house in our court—has been turned out by the police. It seems he's a very dangerous customer; I must say I have never noticed it. He was always very decent; the children were a bother, certainly—always running about the court and getting between your feet. Well, we all have our faults; and then, too, he didn't pay his rent in October."

Wilhelm, who was well acquainted with Father Stubbe's flow of language, and did not greatly admire it, interrupted him at this point.

"Well, and what is the matter?"

"What's the matter, Herr Doctor? Why, the wife is there now with the five children, and there's no earning anything, and yesterday she took away a cupboard to turn it into money somewhere—not that she can have got much for it, it was all tumbling to pieces. The rest of the furniture will take legs to itself soon, I dare say, for six mouths must be fed, and where is food to come from? There will be no removal expenses anyhow, for there will soon be nothing but the bare walls. There's no question of paying the rent, and never will be, as far as I can see; so I thought I had better ask what was to be done with the poor things."

"What can we do?"

"We could seize the bits of sticks they still have, though that would not cover the rent that is owing. The best thing, perhaps, would be to tell Frau Wander just to take her things and clear out; then at least we could relet the rooms."

"Frau Wander does not work?"

"How can she?—five children, and the youngest still at the breast."

"I will see to it myself, and let you know what is to be done."

"Very good, Herr Doctor," said Stubbe, much relieved. He had a kind heart and it was only his strict sense of duty that led him to mention the case of the Wanders, and particularly the unpermissible selling of the furniture, to the owner of the house.

Stubbe had barely reached home before Wilhelm appeared in the Kochstrasse. His house lay between the Charlotten and Markgrafenstrasse, and was an old and unpretentious structure, looking, among the stately houses of a later period which surrounded it on all sides, like a poor relation at a rich and distinguished family gathering. During the "milliard years," building speculators had offered him considerable sums for the ground, but he was not to be prevailed upon to sell the house left him by his father. It was only seven windows wide, and had consisted originally of one story only, but a low second story had been added, recognizable instantly as a piece of patchwork. A great key hanging over the entrance announced the fact that there was a locksmith's workshop inside. The courtyard was very low and narrow, and roughly paved with cobblestones, between which the grass sprouted luxuriantly. At the further end of this court stood the "Hinterhaus," likewise two-storied, on the ground floor of which the locksmith carried on his resounding trade.

Accompanied by Stubbe, Wilhelm mounted the worn wooden staircase leading to the second floor. The flat consisted of a kitchen and a room with one window. Even when the sun was most lavish of his rays, it was none too light there; now, in the early-falling dusk of a dull late autumn day, Wilhelm found himself in a dim half-light as he opened the door. There was no fire in the stove, no lamp upon the table. In the cold and darkness he could just distinguish among the sparse furniture a slim, wretched-looking woman sitting on a chair by the table, nursing a baby wrapped in an old blanket; a tall, large-boned man in workman's clothes, with a bushy beard and gloomy eyes, leaning against the wall beside the window, and some fair-haired children, unnaturally silent and motionless for their age, crouching side by side on the bed, only swinging their legs a little from time to time.

At Wilhelm's entrance with a friendly "Good-evening," the woman rose from her seat and gazed at the intruder with hostile eyes, the children ceased swinging their legs, and the workman shrank away from the window into the deeper shadow of the corner.

"The landlord," Stubbe announced solemnly.

Frau Wander threw up her head. "Now then, what do you want now?" she said hurriedly, her bitter tone beginning on the ordinary pitch, but rising rapidly to a shrewish scream. "It's the rent, I suppose; and I suppose we're to have notice to quit? It's all one to me. I've got no money and so I tell you; but what's here you can keep, and you can have the skin off my back too, and I'll throw in the children beside. They can drag a milk-cart as well as dogs. Why don't you cut my throat at once and have done with it?"

"But, my good woman," cried Stubbe, horror-stricken, "what are you thinking of? The Herr Doctor only means well by you."

Wilhelm had come quite close to the poor thing, who had worked herself up into such a state of excitement that she was trembling from head to foot, and said in that gentle voice of his that always found its way to the heart:

"You are worrying yourself unnecessarily, Frau Wander. I have not come about the rent, and nobody is going to turn you out of your home. Herr Stubbe here has been telling me about your troubles, and I came to see if we could not give you a little assistance."

She stared at him speechless, with wide-open eyes. The children on the bed began to whisper to one another. Wilhelm took advantage of the pause to say a few words in Father Stubbe's ear, whereupon the old man vanished.

"Why don't you offer the gentleman a chair?" said the workman, coming out of his dark corner.

The woman slowly drew forward a chair, round the torn seat of which the straw stood up raggedly on all sides. Wilhelm thanked her with a wave of the hand.

"Do not be afraid of me, dear Frau Wander," he went on. "Tell me something of your circumstances."

"What was there to tell?" answered the woman, still somewhat ruffled. He could see for himself how things stood with her. Her husband had been turned out of Berlin; but much the police cared if she and her five children starved or froze to death. It would have come to that already if some of her husband's fellow-workmen had not given them a little help in their distress, like her present visitor, the iron-worker, Groll. But what could they do? They had not anything themselves, and the police were always after them like the devil after a poor soul. What did they want of them after all? Her husband had held with the Socialists certainly, but he had done nobody any harm by that. Ever since Wander had gone over to the Socialists he had left off drinking—not a drop—only coffee, and sometimes a little beer; and he was always good to his wife and children, and he had no debts as long as he had been able to earn anything. The locksmith downstairs had discharged him after the second attack on the emperor, although he was a clever workman; but the master was afraid of the police, and none of the others would risk taking him on. That was bad enough, but it was not so hard to bear in the summer, and the Socialists held faithfully together, and now and then there was a penny to be earned. But now—now that he had to go away, and winter was at the door— She could keep up no longer, and burst into tears.

Wilhelm seated himself cautiously on the broken chair, and asked, "Where is your husband now? and what does he think of doing?"

"He is trying to get through to the Rhine, and get work at Dortmund, or somewhere in that neighborhood," she answered, while the tight sobs caught her breath, and she wiped away the tears with the back of her hand. "If he can't get any work he will go to France, or Belgium, or even America, if he must. But that takes a lot of money, and where is one to get it without stealing? We are to come to him when he has found work, and can send us the money for the journey. Till then—"

With the free arm that was not holding the child she made a hopeless gesture.

At that moment the door opened and Father Stubbe came in, carrying in one hand a lighted candle, and in the other a great, fresh-smelling loaf of bread. He placed both upon the bare table, and then discreetly withdrew.

"Bread! bread!" cried the children, awakened to sudden life, and jumping off the bed they gathered round the table with greedy eyes, clapping their hands. There were four of them—the youngest a mite of two or three, who only babbled with the others; the eldest, a pale little girl of seven or eight years.

"Children! Just let me catch you!" scolded the mother; but her voice shook with nervous excitement.

"Please, Frau Wander, won't you cut the children some bread first? We can talk afterward."

In a twinkling the eldest girl had fetched a knife from the kitchen, the children continuing to clap their hands delightedly, and Frau Wander cut them large slices, and while she was so engaged, "We have never had anything given us, Herr Doctor," she said; "we have always earned our living with honest work. It is hard to have to come to this; but what can you do when the police put a rope round your neck?"

"You must not worry any longer, dear Frau Wander," said Wilhelm, "but you must not speak like that of the police. You do yourself no good by it, and perhaps a great deal of harm. We will do what we can for you. Never mind about the rent. You will stay on quietly here, and allow me to assist you with this trifle." He pressed two twenty-mark pieces into the half-reluctant hand so unused to accepting alms. "And Herr Stubbe will give you the same sum every month till you are able to join your husband."

He held out his hand, which she grasped in silence, incapable of finding suitable words to thank him, and he hurried to the door. The mechanic hastily snatched up the candle from the table, ran after him and lighted him downstairs, murmuring with real emotion:

"Thank you a thousand times, Herr Doctor, and may God bless you!"

And all the way downstairs Wilhelm was followed by the children's jubilant song of "Bread! bread!"

One morning a few days later—it was December the 2d—as Wilhelm was sitting at his writing-table engaged in making notes from a thick English book of travels on the Australian savage's ideas on nature, he heard a sound of quarreling going on in the hall. He could distinguish Frau Muller's irate tones, and then a man's voice mentioning his name. He gave no further heed to the dispute, thinking it was doubtless some importune person in whom worthy Frau Muller had detected the professional beggar, and was therefore driving away. But it did not leave off, and grew louder and louder, Frau Muller's voice rising at last to an exasperated scream—there even seemed to be something like a hand-to-hand fight going on—till Wilhelm thought it behooved him to see what was happening, and, if need be, come to the rescue of his faithful house-dragon. He opened the door quickly and received Frau Muller in his arms. If he had not caught her, she would have fallen backward into the room, for she had leaned—a living bulwark—against the door, defending the entrance with her body against two men, one of whom was trying to push her away, while the other, standing further back, was restraining his companion from grasping Frau Muller all too roughly. In the daring man who did not shrink from laying sacrilegious hands upon the furious and snorting landlady, Wilhelm instantly recognized the mechanic whom he had seen at Frau Wander's. At sight of him the man raised his hat politely, and before the gasping Frau Muller, who was simply choking with excitement, could find her tongue, he said:

"Beg pardon, I am sure, Herr Doctor, for disturbing you; but we really must speak to you. I knew from Herr Stubbe that you are always at home at this hour, so I would not let the lady send us away."

"The lady indeed!" Frau Muller managed at last to exclaim. "Now he talks about ladies, and a minute ago he had the impudence—"

"You must excuse us, madam," said the workman with the utmost civility; "we meant no harm, and we simply must speak to the Herr Doctor."

"Come in," said Wilhelm curtly, and not overwarmly, while he pressed the still angrily glaring Frau Muller's hand gratefully.

The second visitor now mentioned his name—it was that of one of the most prominent leaders of the Social Democrats in Germany. Wilhelm signed to the two men to be seated, and asked what he could do for them.

"I heard through the mechanic Groll here," answered the stranger, pointing to the other man, "what you did for Frau Wander. That encouraged us to come to you with a request."

At a sign from Wilhelm he continued:

"You have seen one of our cases for yourself, and that not by any means the worst. We have dozens of such cases, and there will probably be hundreds more. Our union does what it can. Every member gives up part of his week's wages for the unfortunate victims, and thereby we perhaps save the government from the crime of having condemned innocent women and children to death by starvation. But our people are poor, and have to fight against want themselves. We cannot expect any great sacrifice from them. What we want is a considerable lump sum to enable us to send on the families of the exiled workmen to join their respective bread-winners. So we go round knocking at the doors of our wealthy associates, who, though in consideration of the times they do not care to declare themselves openly for us, nevertheless have a feeling heart for the workingman's distress."

All the time he was speaking he looked Wilhelm straight in the eyes. Wilhelm bore his gaze quietly, and answered:

"If you think I share your opinions you are much mistaken. I consider that you are pursuing a false course, that you make assertions to the workingman which you cannot prove, and promise him things you cannot fulfill, and I frankly confess that I do not envy you the responsibility you have taken upon your own shoulders."

The leader stroked his short beard with a nervous movement, and the mechanic twisted his hat awkwardly between his hands. Wilhelm went on after a short pause:

"But that does not prevent me from sympathizing with the distress of women and children, and I shall be very glad to do what I can if you will give me a detailed account of the state of affairs."

In a few plain words the visitor gave a sketch of the circumstances, all the more heartbreaking for its very unpretentiousness. So many men dismissed, so many wives, so many children, so many parents and near relatives unable to support themselves. Of these so many were sick, so many women lately confined, so many cripples. So many had prospects of better circumstances if they could get away from Berlin. For that purpose such and such a sum was necessary. So much was already in hand. He stated the amount of certain large donations, and added—"I will not mention the names of the subscribers, as it might happen that it would be to your advantage not to know them."

Wilhelm had listened in silence. He now opened a drawer of his writing-table, took out a yellow envelope in which Schrotter was in the habit of giving him, on the first of every month, fifteen hundred marks out of the Dorfling bequest, and handed the sum which he had received the day before, and was still unbroken, to the workingmen's leader. The man turned over the three five-hundred-mark notes, and then looked up startled. Wilhelm only nodded his head slightly.

The leader rose. "It would be inadvisable to give you a receipt. You have no doubt, I think, that your noble gift will be used for its proper object. Thank you a thousand times, and if you should ever stand in need of faithful and determined men, then think of us."

A week later, to the very day, early in the morning a police officer brought Wilhelm an official document summoning him to appear that afternoon before the head police authorities in the Stadtvogtei. He presented himself at the appointed hour in the office, and handed the document to an official, who, after glancing at it, asked:

"You are Dr. Wilhelm Eynhardt?

"Yes."

He took up a paper lying ready at hand, and said dryly: "I have to inform you that, in accordance with the Socialist Act, you are ordered out of Berlin and its purlieus, and must be out of the city by to-morrow at midnight at the latest."

"Ordered out of Berlin!" cried Wilhelm, utterly taken, aback. "And may I ask what I have done?"

"You must know that better than I," answered the official sternly. "However, I have no further information to give you, and can only advise you to address yourself to the Committee of Police, in case you require a day or two more to regulate your affairs."

At the same time he handed him the paper, which proved to be the written order of banishment, and dismissed him with a slight bend of the head.

Wilhelm went without a word. Naturally he turned his steps almost unconsciously to Schrotter, to whom he held out the police paper in silence. Schrotter read it, and struck his hands together.

"Is it possible?" he murmured. "Is it possible?" He paced the room with long strides, then suddenly stood still before his friend, and laying his hands on Wilhelm's shoulder, he said in tones of profound emotion: "I never thought I should live to see such things in my own country. I am nearly sixty, and it is late in the day for me to begin a new life. But really I find it difficult to breathe this air any longer. Where shall you go?"

"I do not know yet myself. I must collect my thoughts a little first."

"Whatever you decide upon, I have a very good mind to go with you. There is nothing left for me to do in my old age but emigrate again."

"You will not do that!" answered Wilhelm hurriedly. "Men like you are more badly needed here than ever. You must stay. I implore you to do so. Remember how you reproached yourself for twenty years, because you were not there when the people were struggling against the Manteuffel reaction. And then—your patients, your poor, the hundreds who have need of you."

Schrotter did not answer, and seated himself on the divan. His massive face was gloomy as midnight, and the fiery blue eyes almost closed. After awhile he growled: "But why—why?"

"Oh, I suppose because of the fifteen hundred marks for the families of the dismissed workmen."

"Of course!" cried Schrotter, clapping his hand to his forehead.

"Dorfling's gold does not come from the Rhine for nothing," Wilhelm smiled sadly. "Like the Nibleungen treasure, it is doomed to bring disaster on all who possess it."

As Schrotter did not answer, Wilhelm resumed: "And as we are on the subject, we may as well settle that matter at once. Of course you will use the whole income now for your poor?"

"Not at all!" cried Schrotter. "Why should things not remain as they are? Wherever you may take up your abode, the poor you have always with you."

Wilhelm shook his head. "I may possibly go abroad, and you see, Herr Doctor, I am prejudiced in favor of my own country. I think we shall carry our Dorfling's intentions best by using his money for the relief of German necessity."

Schrotter made no further objection. That Wilhelm would not, under any circumstances, use a penny of the money for himself he knew perfectly well, and in the end it was all the same whether the poor received it from his hand or Wilhelm's. He merely wrote down some addresses which Wilhelm gave him of people to whom he gave regular assistance, and whom he recommended to Schrotter to that end.

When toward evening Wilhelm returned home, and, as was inevitable, told Frau Muller the news, she nearly fainted, and had to sit down. She was struck dumb for some time, and then only found strength to utter low groans. Her lodger turned out of Berlin like a vagrant. A householder too! Such a respectable, fine young gentleman, whom she had watched over like the apple of her eye for seven years—dreadful—dreadful. But it was all the fault of the low wretches who had forced their way in last week. She had thought as much at the time. If she had only called in the police at once! The police—oh yes, she had all due respect for the police, she was the widow of a government official, and she loved her good old king certainly—but that they should have banished the Herr Doctor—that was not right—that could not possibly be right! Frau Muller could not reconcile herself to the thought of parting. She would go to her friend and patron the "Geheimer Oberpostrath," and he would use his influence in the matter; and at last, seeing that Wilhem only smiled or spoke a few soothing words to her, she burst into tears and sobbed out: "I am so used to you, Herr Doctor, I don't know how I am going to live without you." She only composed herself a little when Wilhelm told her that, for the present at any rate, he was going to leave his books and other goods and chattels where they were, for he might perhaps be allowed to return after a time, and meanwhile a young man, whom she knew, and who was studying at Wilhelm's at Schrotter's expense, should board and lodge with her, and she would receive the same sum as Wilhelm had always paid.

With night came counsel. Wilhelm decided to go first to Hamburg, where Paul lived during the winter, wait there till the spring, and then arrange further plans. He visited the grave of his father and mother, gave Stubbe orders as to the management of the house, took leave of a few friends, visited one or two poor people whom he was in the habit of looking after, and then had nothing further to keep him in Berlin. The rest of the day he passed with Schrotter, who found the parting very hard to bear. Bhani, whom they had acquainted with the matter, had tears in her beautiful dark eyes—the last remnant of youth in the withered face. And as he left the dear familiar house in the Mittelstrasse she begged him—translating the Indian words plainly enough by looks and gestures—to accept an amulet of cold green jade as a remembrance of her.

That night at eleven o'clock a slow train bore Wilhelm away from Berlin.

At the station he caught sight of the face of his old friend Patke, whom he had come across more than once during that day. The former non-commissioned officer had apparently reached the goal of his ambitions and become a private detective.

Schrotter had stood on the step of the carriage till the very last moment, holding his friend's hand. Now Wilhelm leaned back in his corner and closed his eyes, and while the train rattled along over the snow-covered plain, he asked himself for the first time whether after all Dorfling had been quite such a fool as most of them considered him to have been?

CHAPTER IX.

RESULTS.

On alighting next morning at the station in Hamburg, Wilhelm found himself clasped in a pair of strong arms and pressed to a magnificent fur coat. Inside this warm garment there beat a still warmer heart, that of Paul Haber, who had received a letter from Wilhelm the day before, telling him of his dismissal from Berlin, and that he was leaving for Hamburg by the last train before midnight, and whom neither the cold and darkness nor the extreme earliness of the hour could restrain from meeting his friend at the station.

Their greeting was short and affectionate.

"A hearty welcome to you!" cried Paul. "We will do our best to make a new home for you here."

"You see, I thought of you at once when I had to look about me for some resting-place in the wide world."

"I should have expected no less of you. Keep your ears stiff, and don't let the horrid business worry you."

Wilhelm's bag was handed to an attendant servant, and the two friends walked off arm in arm toward an elegant brougham lined with light blue, with a conspicuously handsome long-limbed chestnut and a stout, bearded coachman, which stood waiting for them.

Wilhelm mentioned the name of the hotel where he intended to stay, but Paul cut him short. "Not a bit of it! Home, Hans, and look sharp about it!" And before Wilhelm could offer any remonstrance, he found himself pushed into the carriage, Paul at his side. The door banged, the footman sprang on to the box, and off they went as fast as the long legs of the chestnut would carry them.

For the last two years Paul had owned a villa on the Uhlenhorst, in the Carlstrasse, and there the fast trotter drew up. Wilhelm had said but little during the drive, and Paul had confined the expression of his feeling of delight to clapping his friend on the shoulder from time to time, and pressing his hand. Rather less than half an hour's drive brought them to their destination. Paul would not hear of Wilhelm making any alteration in his dress, but drew him as he was into the smoking room on the ground floor, where Malvine came to meet him, and received him in her hearty but quiet and uneffusive manner. She was the picture of health, but had grown perhaps a little too stout for her age. She wore a morning wrap of red velvet and gold lace, and looked, in that costly attire, like a princess or a banker's wife.

"You must be very cold and tired," she said; "the coffee is ready, come at once to breakfast—that will put some warmth into you—you can dress afterward." She hurried before them into the next room, where they found an amply spread table over which hovered the fragrant smell of several steaming dishes. It was a lavish breakfast in the English style; beside tea and coffee there were eggs, soles, ham, cold turkey, lobster salad, and several excellent wines. A servant in the livery of a "Jager" waited at table.

Wilhelm shook his head at the sight of all this splendor. "But, my dear lady, so much trouble on my behalf!"

"You are quite mistaken," Paul answered for Malvine, and not without a smile of satisfied pride; "it is our usual breakfast—we have it so every day."

Wilhelm looked at him surprised, and then remarked after a short pause: "I would never have written to you, if I had dreamed that you would get up before daybreak, and upset your whole household in order to fetch me from the station."

"Why, what nonsense! We are quite used to getting up early. At Friesenmoor we have to be still earlier."

"But that is in the summer."

"So it is, but then our broken rest is not made up to us by the sight of a friend."

While they devoured the good things, and Paul, who despised tea and coffee, sipped his slightly warmed claret, he remarked, between two mouthfuls, "I was struck all of a heap by your letter. You turned out! the most harmless, law-abiding citizen I ever heard of! What in the world did you do? You need not mind telling me."

"I cannot say that I am aware of having committed any crime, Paul."

"Come now, something must have happened, for the police does not take a step of that kind without some provocation—it's only your beggarly Progressives who think that, but nobody who knows the fundamental principles of our government and its officials would believe it."

"You seem to have become a warm admirer of the government."

"Always was! But, upon my word, when I see the way the opposition parties go on I am more so than ever—positively fanatical."

"Then I have no doubt that you will consider that I did commit a crime."

"Ah! so there was something after all?"

"Yes, I contributed fifteen hundred marks to a collection for the distressed families of the Social Democrats who had been dismissed from Berlin."

"You did?" cried Paul, dropping his knife and fork, and staring at Wilhelm in amazement.

"And that seems so criminal to you?"

"Look here, Wilhelm, you know I'm awfully fond of you, but I must say you have only got what you deserve. How could you take part in a revolutionary demonstration of the kind?"

"I did not, nor do I now see anything political in it. It was a question of women and children deprived of their bread-winners, and whom one cannot allow to starve or freeze to death."

"Oh, go along with your Progressionist phrases! Nobody need starve or freeze in Berlin. The really poor are thoroughly well looked after by the proper authorities. The supposed distress of these women and children is a mere trumped-up story on the part of the Revolutionists—a means of agitation, a weapon against the government. The beggars simply speculate on the tears of sentimental idiots. They get up a sort of penny-dreadful, whereon the one side you have a picture of injured innocence in the shape of pale despairing mothers and clamoring children, and on the other, villainy triumphant in the form of a police constable or a government official. And to think that you should have been taken in by such a swindle!"

"I suppose you do not see how heartless it appears to speak so lightly of other people's hunger, sitting oneself at such a table as this?"

"Bravo, Wilhelm! Now you are throwing my prosperity in my teeth like any advocate of division of property. I trust you have not turned Socialist yourself? you who used not to have a good word to say for the lot."

"Never fear—I am not a Socialist. Their doctrines have not been able to convince me yet. But for years I have seen the distress of the working people with my own eyes, and I know that every human being with a heart in his body is in duty bound to help them."

"And who says anything against that? Don't we all do our duty? Poverty has always existed and always will to the end of time. But, on the other hand, that is what charity is there for. We have hospitals for the sick, workhouses and parish relief for the aged and incapable, for lazy vagabonds who won't work, it is true, only the treadmill."

"That is all very fine, but what are you going to do with the honest men who want to work but can find none?"

"Wilhelm, I have always had the highest respect for you, your wisdom, your intellect, but forgive me if I say that, in this case, you are talking of things you do not understand. Everybody who wants work finds it. I hope you will be at my place next summer. Then you'll see how I positively sweat blood in harvest-time trying to get the necessary number of laborers together, and what I have to put up with from the rascals only to keep them in good humor. Don't try on any of these windy arguments with a landowner—people that want work and can't find it indeed! Let me tell you, my son, neither I nor any one of my country neighbors can scrape together as many people as we need."

"But everybody cannot work in the fields."

"There, at last, you have hit the bull's eye—that is where the shoe pinches. Agriculture offers a certain means of livelihood to all who can and will work properly. But that does not suit the lazy beggars. The work is too hard, and, more particularly, the discipline on an estate is too strict for their fancy. They would rather be in the town, rather starve in a workshop, or ruin their lungs in a factory, because there they have more freedom—that is, they can go on the spree all night and shirk their work all day, if they like—they can play the gentleman, and think themselves as good as any general or minister. Under these circumstances, it is no wonder that they soon come to want, and instead of admitting that it is entirely the fault of their own pigheadedness and perversity, they go and turn unruly against the government. They should be turned out neck and crop, the whole pack of them."

"Don't excite yourself so, Paul," warned Malvine gently, as her husband grew crimson in the face and ceased to eat.

Wilhelm remained unruffled. "So you think the Socialist Act was quite justified?"

"Justified! Why, my only objection to it is that it is much too mild. A State has a right to use every means it can—even the sharpest—to defend itself against its deadly enemies. To deal mildly with the enemies of society is to be unjust to us, the orderly and industrious members of the community, who work hard to get on, and who don't want to be for ever trembling for their well-earned possessions, because thieves and vagabonds—as is the way of all robbers—would like to enjoy the good things of this life without working for them."

"My good Paul, that is the language of fanaticism, and, of course, it is useless to try to reason against that. Only let me tell you this. I do not believe that the Socialists want to rob anybody; I do not believe that they are enemies to the State and to society. They too desire a State and a society, but different from the existing ones; they too have an ideal of justice, but it is not the one that has become traditional with us. Under the new order of things, as they have arranged it in their minds, there should be room for every individual, every opinion, all sorts and conditions of men. What the ruling classes say against them to-day has been said against the adherents of all new ideas since the beginning of time. Whoever tried to make the slightest alteration in the existing order of things was always considered, by those who derived advantages therefrom, to be a foe to the State and to society in general-a robber and a revolutionist. The early Christians enjoyed exactly the same reputation as the Socialists to-day. They were looked upon as enemies of the whole human race, and were torn to pieces by wild beasts, though—doubtless to your regret—it has not come to that with, the Socialists. And nevertheless, though lions and tigers are a good deal worse than police officers, the principles of Christianity have triumphed, and there is nothing to prove that the principles of Socialism will not triumph in their turn."

"Prophet of evil omen!" cried Paul.

"Not necessarily so. Where would be the misfortune? I am firmly persuaded that a Socialist State would not differ in any important point from the accepted forms of government of the day. The administrative power would merely be transferred from the hands of the military and the landed aristocracy to another class. To those who do not want a share in the governing power, it is all the same who wields it. You see, human nature remains the same, and its organization alters only very gradually, almost imperceptibly, though it sometimes changes its name. Christianity promised to be the beginning of the thousand years' reign, but in the main, everything has gone on just as it was before. A Socialist State would not be able to make the sun rise in the west, or do away with death any more than we can. They would have ministers, custom-house officers, policemen, virtue, vice and ambition, self-interest, oppression and brotherly love just as we do, and if the Socialists come into power, they will soon pass special acts and prosecute the followers of other opinions just as they are being prosecuted to-day. That is all upon the surface, and does not touch the root of things. Why excite yourself about a mere shadowplay?"

"In practical matters," answered Paul, laughing, "I consider I am the better man, but you certainly beat me at metaphysics. Prophecy decidedly comes under the heading of metaphysics, so I strike my colors before you."

"The sooner the better," said Malvine; "especially as it is quite unpardonable of you to start off on a long discussion when our poor friend must be so tired and sleepy."

It was eight o'clock by this time, and Wilhelm really felt the want of rest. But before going to his room he asked after his godson, little Willy.

Malvine was evidently expecting this, she ran to the door and called into the next room: "Come here, Willy—come quick—Uncle Eynhardt is here and wants to see you." Whereupon the boy came bounding in, and threw himself with a shout of delight upon Wilhelm's neck. Willy was still his mother's only child. He was nearly six years old, not very tall for his age, but a fine, handsome, thoroughly healthy child, with firm legs, a blooming complexion, the dark eyes of his grandmother, and long fair curls. He was charmingly dressed in a sailor suit with a broad turned-back collar over a blue-and-white striped jersey, long black stockings, and pretty little patent leather shoes with silk ties. Wilhelm lifted up this young prince, kissing him, and asked, "Well, Willy, do you remember me?" He had not seen, him for eighteen months.

"Of course, I do, uncle, we talk about you every day," cried the child in his clear voice. "Are you going to stay with us now?"

"Yes, that he is!" his father answered for the friend.

"How jolly! how jolly!" cried Willy, clapping his hands with glee. "And you will teach me to ride, won't you, uncle? Papa has no time."

"But I don't know how to ride myself," returned Wilhelm with a smile.

Willy looked up disappointed. "What can you do then?"

"Be a good boy now," Malvine broke in, "and leave uncle in peace and go back to the nursery. You shall have him again later on."

After more kisses and caresses Willy ran off, and Paul led his guest to the room prepared for him, where at last he left him to himself.

Wilhelm had visited Paul on his estate during the preceeding summer, but since then had only seen him in Berlin. The house on the Uhlenhorst was new to him, and he marveled at the solid sumptuousness that met the eye at every turn. The visitor's room was not less splendidly furnished than the smoking and breakfast rooms he had already seen, and when he looked about him at the great carved bedstead with its ample draperies, the silk damask-covered chairs, the thick rugs, the marble washstand, and the toilet table with its array of bottles and dishes of china, cut glass, and silver, he could not help feeling almost abashed. His friend Paul had become a very great gentleman apparently!

And so in point of fact he had. The Friesenmoor had proved itself a very gold mine, and in the district round about they calculated that it yielded a clear return of a hundred or a hundred and twenty thousand marks a year. Paul had long ago been in a position to make use of his right of purchase on the estate, and had acquired about two thousand acres of adjoining marsh lands beside, though at a considerably higher price, and was now the owner of a well-rounded estate of twelve thousand acres, the admiration and pride of the whole neighborhood. He had converted the cultivation of the marshland, which six years ago had been but a bold theory, into an established scientific fact, and his methods, the excellence of which was amply proved by his almost tropically luxuriant harvests and uninterruptedly increasing wealth, were assiduously imitated on all sides. Paul Haber was acknowledged far and wide to be the first authority on the management of marsh land. The government had long since taken note of his success and kept an eye upon his doings, and was furnished by the Landrath with regular accounts of his agricultural progress. Young men of the best county families contended for the privilege of being under him for a year's practical farming. Foreign governments sent professors, lecturers, and practical agriculturists to him, partly to inspect his arrangements, partly to study his methods under his personal supervision, in order to adopt them in their own countries. Paul was more than a landed proprietor, he was a kind of professor holding his unpretentious lecture in the open air or in the appropriately decorated smoking-room of the Priesenmoor house, always surrounded by a troop of eager and admiring listeners of various nationalities, and mostly of high rank.

Of course, under these circumstances there was no lack of outward marks of distinction. Two years before he had been promoted to a first lieutenancy of the Landwehr. A row of foreign decorations adorned his breast, and last year, when he was visited by the Minister for Agriculture, accompanied by the Landrath, the Kronen Order of the fourth class was added to the rest. Paul was on the District Committee and County Council, and if he was not deputy of the Landtag and member of the Reichstag, it was only because he considered all parliamentary work a barren expenditure of time and strength. He stood in high repute in the county, which was proved by his election to be the president of the Society for the Cultivation of Moors and Marshes, a society founded by his followers and admirers, and which counted among its members some of the most important landowners of the whole of Northern Germany.

These circumstances could not fail to react on Paul's character. He no longer tried to look as much as possible like a smart officer, but rather like a country gentleman of ancient lineage. The thick fair mustache had abandoned its enterprising upward curl, and now hung down straight and long. The model parting of the hair was in any case out of the question, a distinguished baldness having taken the place of the old luxuriance, and his figure had fulfilled all the promises of his youth. In his dress Paul still cultivated extreme elegance, only that it partook more of the bucolic now in style than of the drawing-room as in former days. He wore high patent leather boots with small silver spurs, well-fitting riding breeches, a gray coat with green facings and large buckhorn buttons, a blue-and-white spotted silk necktie tied in a loose knot with fluttering ends, an artistically crushed soft felt hat, and in his dog-skin gloved hand a small riding-whip with a chased gold head. With all its dandyism it was a model of good taste, and in no single detail smacked of the parvenu, and that for the very good reason that Paul was no parvenu, but a man who was conscious of having attained to a position which was his by nature and by right. He had never suffered from undue diffidence, and his success had naturally increased his sense of his own value, which, however, he did not display in any bumptious or aggressive manner as one who would force reluctant acknowledgment of his merits, but quietly and naturally, seeing that he received full and voluntary recognition from all sides. He believed in himself, and was quite right to do so, for everybody else believed in him too. He spoke with authority, for there was no one about him who did not hang upon his lips with respect, and mostly with admiration. He made assertions and gave his opinion with the assurance of superior knowledge, but he had a right to do so, for it always referred only to matters about which he knew, or was fully persuaded that he knew, more than most people. Even his wealth did not go to his head, but acted on him like a moderate amount of drink upon a man who can stand a great deal. He enjoyed to the full the comforts and amenities of life which his large income enabled him to procure, but he did it for his own pleasure, not for the sake of what others would think; for his own comfort, and not for show. He liked to keep good horses and dogs, an admirably appointed table and cellar, and a large staff of well-drilled servants. On the other hand, he avoided anything approaching to display, was never seen at races, went to no fashionable baths, gave no grand entertainments, nor had a box at either theatre or operahouse, belonged to no club, and never played high. His wife wore perhaps rather more jewelry and followed the newest Paris fashions a trifle more closely than was absolutely necessary at Friesenmoor or even the Uhlenhorst, but as she remained as simple and unaffected as before, nobody could think any the worse of her for this small inherited weakness.

Toward his own family Paul had behaved in a most exemplary manner, affording thereby the strongest proof that though he had risen he was no upstart. The numerous members of his family and the men who had married into it nearly all had to thank him for their advancement or actual support. Some were employed on his estate, others he had trained in his particular branch of agriculture, after which, and with his recommendation, they had found no difficulty in obtaining brilliant positions as stewards or leaseholders of estates, and two of his brothers had appointments on royal domains. He had, therefore, every right to self-congratulation, as having fulfilled all the duties of a model man and citizen far beyond what necessity demanded.

For Wilhelm, Paul still retained the affection and friendship of his early days, only that, unconsciously to himself, it had taken on a certain fatherly tone; although there was a difference of but one year between them, there was a touch of protecting consideration and pity about it, such as strong men feel toward a weaker and less perfectly developed creature.

The first day Paul left his friend to have a thorough rest, but the next morning early he knocked at his door and asked if he might come in.

"Certainly," was the answer, and opening the door at the same moment, Wilhelm appeared fully dressed and ready for inspection.

"You have kept up your old habit of early rising—that is right," said Paul, and clapped him on the shoulder.

"So have you," returned Wilhelm with a smile.

"I—oh, that's different. I am a farmer, and you know the proverb—'The master's eye makes the cattle fat.' But your books don't require to be fed and watered at break of day. As you are ready, come down now, and we can have a chat over breakfast."

Malvine met him downstairs with a friendly smile and shake of the hand. This morning she wore a long blue morning gown with gay colored embroidery at the throat and wrists and a little lace cap with blue ribbons. The breakfast was as elaborate as on the day before.

"I want to take you over to my place to-day, Wilhelm. We have a shooting party, the weather is lovely, and it will be a nice change for you."

"Thanks, Paul, but I would much rather you left me here. I am no sportsman, as you know very well."

"We'll soon make you into one. Nobody is born a sportsman, or rather we are all born sportsmen, but forget it in our wretched town life, and afterward have to set to work and learn laboriously the art that came so naturally to our forefathers. Not, however, that you need fire a single shot, it is more for the healthy out-of-door exercise, and to show you Friesenmoor in its winter dress, and for the society which will interest you. They are neighbors of mine—nearly every one of them a character—old Baron Huning, who fought in the Crimea as an English officer, Count Chamberlain von Swerte, crammed with curious court stories, Graf Olderode, who, in spite of his gout, will jump for joy when I introduce you as the best friend I have in the world, and add that you have just been banished from Berlin under the Socialist Act. And then there are my pupils—I've got a Russian prince among them, and a very near neighbor, a young nobleman from the Marches, an officer in the Red Hussars. Now don't be a slow coach, come along."

"You are very kind, but I should be very sorry to make your gouty Graf jump, even for joy."

"Dr. Enyhardt is quite right," Malvine now joined in. "What an idea too to carry him off from me before he has had time to settle comfortably. You stay with me. Herr Doctor; this is my day, and you shall make the acquaintance of some charmingly pretty girls this afternoon. That will interest you more than Paul's old Chamberlains."

"All right," laughed Paul; "but you had better look out, Wilhelm, I smell a rat. Malvine has designs upon you, she wants to get you married. If you came with me you would be the hunter, but if you stay here you will find yourself in the position of the game."

"And if he is," retorted Malvine, "it is surely the better part to let yourself be caught by a pretty girl than to go and shoot poor hares and wild ducks."

Paul did not press his invitation, and drove off a minute or two later, not to return till the following day. Malvine, however, put her threat into practice, and persuaded Wilhelm with gentle insistence to join her afternoon coffee party, and be introduced to all her lady visitors and take part in the conversations. The introduction caused Malvine a little embarrassment. Only now did she fully realize the fact that her guest was nobody in particular. She was painfully conscious of the baldness of his name and his simple title of Dr., and the absence of any sort of distinguishing mark by the addition of which she might recommend him to the special notice of her circle of friends. He was not a landed proprietor, nor a professor, not even a master. Nor could she conscientiously say, "the celebrated Dr. Eynhardt." He had no military title, and to introduce him as "the handsome Dr. Eynhardt" would hardly do. Fortunately she had no need to mention the latter adjective. The ladies observed without further assistance how remarkably handsome this gentleman was with his girlish complexion, silky, raven-black hair and beard, and lustrous dark eyes. Charming lips drew him constantly into the conversation, which, cultivated and many-sided, ranged from the weather to the recently-closed Paris Exhibition, from Sarasate to Vischer's last novel. Wilhelm had not a word to say on these important subjects, and so spoke in monosyllables, or not at all, till the ladies, who were most of them very animated, came to the conclusion that he was as stupid as he was handsome, "as is usually the case, my dear."

At supper Malvine was indefatigable in asking Wilhelm how he liked this dark girl, and what he had said to that fair one, and what impression the piquante little one with the boyish curly head had made upon him? When he frankly confessed that he had paid very little attention to any of the young ladies, and could scarcely remember one from another, she was very much discouraged. It was decidedly no easy task to help this clumsy person along. All three girls of whom she had spoken were heiresses, and beautiful and well-educated beside—what more did he want?

Alas! he did not want anything at all, but to be left in peace, and that was the aggravating part of it. Malvine had set her heart on marrying him, and marrying him well. Her sentiment for him had long since given place to other and less agitating feelings, as beseemed a model wife, mother, and landed proprietress. She was grateful to him for having recognized and set right the mistaken impression of her girlish heart. She was seized with discomfort at the thought of what might have been. Where would she be now if she had become Frau Dr. Eynhardt? A woman without fortune, of no position or importance, and at the present moment even homeless and a wanderer. As things had turned out she was wealthy and distinguished, the best people in Hamburg and the whole of Luneburg came to her house, and she ruled like a small queen over a large settlement of dependents. And all this she owed to her dear Paul, who, during the seven years of their married life, had never given her one moment's pain, never cost her eyes a single tear. Out of her grateful acknowledgment that Wilhelm had materially assisted in the founding of her agreeable destiny, and the unconscious lingering remains of her former attachment, there had sprung up a very tender friendship for him, the unusual warmth of which would have at once betrayed its hidden origin to the experienced analyst of the heart. She wanted to see him happy, she considered earnestly what was lacking to him to make him so, and was sure that it could only be a rich and pretty wife. This happiness then she determined to procure for him, an easy enough task, as her set contained a large selection of "goldfish."

If he would only meet them halfway! The young ladies, obviously very well disposed toward him, could not make the first advances. And yet on the following Thursday he sat there in the midst of the gay chatter just as quiet and wooden as on the first occasion, made no advances to any of the girls, singled out no one from the rest. After that Malvine was obliged to make a pause in her well-intentioned maneuvres, for the third Thursday was Christmas Eve, and her time was taken up in preparations for the Christmas-tree.

For this festive occasion Frau Brohl and Frau Marker came over from Berlin, as had been their custom ever since Paul had taken the house on the Uhlenhorst. Frau Marker had grown very stout, and her hair showed the first silvery threads, otherwise she was blooming and as silent as ever. Old Frau Brohl was simply astounding. She had not changed in the smallest degree, time had no power over her, she was just as doubled up and colorless, and her movements just as slow as ever, her brown eyes had the same tired droop, and her low, complaining voice the old tone of suffering. But her appetite had grown, if anything, rather larger, and, apart from one or two colds in the winter, she had not known an hour's illness during the whole time.

Needless to say, the grandmother did not come empty-handed. She brought two cases with her, one of which contained a large quantity of excellent bottled fruit, which Malvine still preferred to any her own highly-paid cook could prepare, while the other was filled with a choice collection of fancy work. On these treasures being unpacked, it was discovered that the inventive genius of the old lady of seventy was still undiminished. For the master of the house there was a game-bag made of interwoven strips of blue and red leather, somewhat in the Indian manner, very curious, and of course, impracticable Malvine received a silklace veil, the pattern in large marshmallows—a graceful play upon her name.

Frau Brohl had worked at this masterpiece for a year and a half. For little Willy, in consideration of the aristocratic propensities one might expect, or at any late encourage, in the heir to a large estate, there was a Flobert rifle, the strap of which was ornamented after an entirely new method by cutting out thin layers of the leather and inserting gilt arabesques and figures. For the house in general there were some ingenious arrangements in fir cones and small shells.

The Christmas-tree was set up in the great drawing-room on the ground floor and reached almost to the ceiling. It was a beautiful young fir, so fresh and fragrant of pine that the breath of the woods seemed to cling to it still. A large party had gathered for the lighting-up. Beside the relatives of the aristocratic pupils, who had come over from the estate, there were some neighbors from the Uhlenhorst, with five or six little children, and the Chamberlain von Swerte with his high-born wife. The couple were childless, and not wishing to spend their Christmas alone, had accepted Paul's invitation, and come all the way from their little castle near Ronneburg to the Ulhenhorst.

The chamberlain was the lion of the evening. Paul took an opportunity of whispering to Wilhelm, "Herr von Swerte is of the House of Hellebrand— one of the first families in the county—tremendously ancient lot!" Old Frau Brohl had observed the little gold tab on his coat tail—the chamberlain's sign of office, and manuevered skillfully in order that she might frequently obtain a back view, and so gaze upon the proud badge in silent awe and admiration. The children had no eye for such matters, but rushed shrieking with delight round the tree, whose branches shed such gorgeous presents on them. Willy got a hussar uniform, with sword, knot, boots and spurs all complete, and would not rest till he had been taken to his room and dressed in it, and then appeared before the company in this martial attire. His mother's eye grew dim with pride and joy when Herr von Swerte lifted up the little warrior to kiss him, and said heartily: "Well, my dear Herr Haber, he will make a smart cavalry officer some day!"

At dinner Wilhelm found himself beside Frau Brohl. The old lady was still fond of him, and never forgot how well he had behaved at a critical moment, and with what modest self-perception he had acknowledged that he was not the husband for her granddaughter.

Searching about for something agreeable to say to him, or for a subject that would be sure to interest him, she suddenly remembered one, and said, between the fish and the roast, "Have you heard the story about your old flame, Frau Von Pechlar?"

Wilhelm started and changed color.

Frau Brohl never noticed, and continued in her soft complaining voice: "Your guardian angel saved you there, Herr Doctor. You would have come off nicely if you had married Fraulein Ellrich. There have been all sorts of rumors for years, but now it has come to an open scandal. She has left Herr von Pechlar and gone off with a count, who has been hanging about her for some time. They say she has gone to Italy with him."

Wilhelm made no reply, but he was surprised himself to feel how deeply the information affected him, so that he could not breathe freely all the evening, and although it was late before he got to bed, he could not sleep for hours, thinking of the girl he had once loved, who was now rushing blindly down the path of dishonor. Why should the thought pain him so much? Do heart wounds heal so slowly and imperfectly that a rough touch can make the scar burn and throb after long years? Or was it regret at the besmirching of a picture which till now had shone so purely and been so sweetly framed in his memory? He did not know, but for days it depressed him to the verge of melancholy.

In return for the hospitality he had received New Year's Eve was spent at Herr von Swerte's. The whole Haber family, with Frau Brohl and Frau Marker—the white grandmamma and the brown grandmamma, as Willy called them, to distinguish them from one another—drove over in the afternoon to Ronneburg by way of Harburg, but Wilhelm could not be prevailed upon to accompany them. Paul took him severely to task; Malvine represented to him, with an eloquence unusual to her, the horrors of a lonely New-Year's Eve; Frau Brohl pointed out the advantages of celebrating the festive occasion in a company composed entirely of rich people; and even Willy entreated, "Do come, Onkelchen, you can take care of me on the road." All their persuasion proving fruitless, they finally left him to his fate, and he remained behind alone.

Night found him at the writing-table in Paul's study, his head in his hand, lost in thought. At last he shook himself out of his deep brooding and wrote the following letter to Schrotter:

"My Revered Friend, I will not now break the habit of eight years, but will spend my New Years' Eve with you, the person who stands nearest to me in all the world. I am alone in this grand villa, the servants seem to be enjoying themselves downstairs over their roast goose and punch, Paul has taken his family and gone into the country to the castle of a neighboring estate owner by whom he is evidently very much impressed, and I can chat with you undisturbed.

"I wish you could live for a time in close contact with Paul, as I am doing, you would be surprised and pleased. His development has been wonderfully logical, and he now affords the spectacle, so intensely interesting to the observant eye, of a person whose every capacity, under the influence of the most favorable combination of circumstances imaginable, has attained to the utmost limit of growth which is possible to it. Paul has become the ideal type of our North German landed proprietor. He is ultra conservative, and considers the Socialist Act too mild. He loathes parliamentarianism, but would wish that the Landrath had not the power to appoint even a police constable without the consent of the estate owners of the district, and raves about local police prerogative. His only newspaper, beside the little local one, is the Kreuzzentung, he is learned in the Army List, and the writing-table at which I am sitting is strewed with volumes of the Almanac de Gotha. He looks after his subjects—for I think he calls his workmen his subjects—in a truly fatherly or feudal manner, but I do not doubt that he would drive the best of them off the estate with dogs, if, even in the depth of winter, they did not stand hat in hand the whole time they were talking to him. The sole problem of the universe which has any sort of interest for him is the outlook of the weather for the harvest. The course of human or superhuman events arouses his wonder, his doubts, or his anxiety only in proportion as it affects the price of corn. He cannot grasp that one should have any other aim in life than to become a successful agriculturist. He finds full satisfaction in his work, and what between a charming wife and an adored child he would afford an example of what the fables and proverbs tell us does not exist—a perfectly happy man, if one thing were not lacking, the little word 'von' in front of his name. I trust he may not die without obtaining it, and then the world will have contained one mortal who has known absolutely boundless happiness.

"But in writing to you in this strain my conscience pricks me. Is it not unkind toward Paul, whose attachment to me is positively touching? Is it not churlish to exercise such cold crticism upon a friend whose faithful affection has never for one moment wavered? He surrounds me with endless proofs of his affection, and is always on the lookout for something which may give me pleasure. He is a passionate sportsman—his only passion as far as I can see—and worries me twice a week to join him on his shooting expeditions. He is a masterly 'skat player, and is most anxious to enrich my existence by the joys which, according to him, this intellectual game affords to its adepts. When I venture timidly to propose that I should leave him and live by myself, he looks so honestly hurt and grieved that I have not the courage to insist further. And Frau Haber, kind soul, who is so set upon getting me married and thereby insuring my happiness! I and marrying! What have I to offer a woman? Love? I am too poor in illusions. Amusements—society—the theater? All that is a horror to me. And moreover, I question if I have a right to bring a being into the world, over whose destiny I have no control, and whose existence would most certainly be richer in pain, and misery than in happiness; and I know unquestionably that I have no right to teach a light-hearted girl to think, and force her to exchange the artless gayety of a playful little animal for my own fruitless speculations and never-to-be-satisfied yearnings.

"In face of all this, serious doubts arise in my mind. Is it for me to speak with superciliousness and superiority of Paul, or to look down upon him? I ask you, as I have been asking myself every day these three weeks—is he not the wise man and I the fool? He the useful member of society, and I the mere hanger-on? His life the real, mine the shadow? That he is happy I have already said; that I am not, I know. His system therefore leads to peace and contentment, mine does not. He has set a child into the world, and though, of course, he does not know what its ultimate fate will be, he sees for the present, as do I and everybody else who is not blind, that it fills his home with sunshine and warmth. He provides hundreds with their daily bread. That is, I know, of no moment to the universe; it is of very little importance whether a few more obstruse human creatures walk the face of the earth or not. But meanwhile, the creatures in question enjoy more agreeable sensations, if, thanks to Paul's exertions, they have a comfortably spread table every day. I cannot boast of any such achievements. The only good I ever did my fellow-men did not proceed from me but from our friend Dorfling, who simply used my hand as an instrument for carrying out his charitable designs. My personal compassion, my love for my companions in ignorance and suffering bears no fruit, benefits no one, and it frequently seems to me that, if the truth were known, I am an egoist of the deepest dye.

"If I could at least act consistently with the philosophy which directs nay views of life! But I am not even capable of that. Systematically, I concede no importance to outward forms. Maja does not count me among her devotees. What are houses? What are the phantoms who inhabit them? A transient semblance, a delusion of the senses! And yet, I am conscious that I miss just those houses which happen to stand, in Berlin and that I feel an unspeakable longing for the phantom called Dr. Schrotter. Once again it has been proved to me that I am an unconscious plaything in the hands of unknown powers, for again, as more than once in my life, and always at decisive moments, some outside agency has interfered in my fate, and disposed of me contrary to my own intentions, by sending me out of Berlin and away from you. But, nevertheless, my appreciation of this fact does not give me the strength to accept the inevitable in silence and without repining.

"Enough—I will not pain you. Only this much I should like to add that life is really harder to bear than I had thought for.

"Farewell, dear and honored friend; remember me affectionately to Bhani, who, I trust, does not suffer too severely from this hard winter, and always believe in the faithful friendship and devotion of your

"WILHELM EYNHARDT."

Three days later Wilhelm received the following answer from Schrotter:

"DEAREST FRIEND: Your long and welcome New Year's letter troubled me much on account of the state of mind I see revealed in it. I think, however, that it is explained by the fact of your being rooted up out of your accustomed surroundings that you are oppressed by Haber's hospitality, and that you have as yet made no plans for the future, and I trust that your spirits will improve when these three circumstances are altered.

"I have always considered Haber, with all his good qualities of heart and character, a thoroughly commonplace man, and your observations verify my opinion to the full. And yet I quite understand that the sight of his prosperity and self-satisfaction should give you food for thought, and raise the question in your mind whether his philosophy—if I may use the word—or yours, is the right one. That is a great question, and I do not presume to answer it, either in general or for your particular case; and all the more, for the very good reason that your life is only really beginning now. You are not yet thirty-four, you may yet do something great, something pre-eminent, and who knows if those very qualities which have made your life unproductive hitherto, may not enable you later on to do things beside which the achievements of a Paul Haber shrink into insignificance? On the other hand, I am persuaded—quite apart from your respective ways of life—that you have chosen the better and higher part.

"Human nature is like a tower with many stories; some people inhabit the lower, others the higher ones. The inhabitants of the cellars and ground floor may, in their way, be good, decent, praiseworthy people, but they can never enjoy the same amount of light, the same pure air and wide view as those who live on the upper stories. Now you, my dear young friend, live several floors higher up than our good Paul Haber, whom, however, I value and am very fond of. But there are people living over our heads too. I have known Indian sages who looked down upon all we strive after and with which we occupy ourselves with the same pitying wonder as you do on Haber's passion for sport and 'skat,' and his longing for a title;

who have difficulty in understanding that we should earn money, be ambitious, entertain passions, conform to outward rules of custom, and, under the pretext of education, laboriously study rows of empty phrases. These Brahmins have still higher interests and a yet wider view than the noblest-minded and wisest of us, and the knowledge that such pure and all-embracing spirits do exist ought to teach us to be humble, and not despise those who may still cling to some vain show that we have overcome, and attach importance to matters which no longer possess any in our eyes.

"One thing I have in my heart to wish for you, my dear friend—that you could take life with a little of the unreflecting simplicity of those who accept—what the moment offers without troubling themselves as to the why and the wherefore. You bow to those high powers who, for instance, have caused you to be banished from Berlin; then submit yourself to those still higher ones, who let you live and feel and think. Do not fight against the natural instincts which lead you to cling to life and love. Your fears that you have nothing to offer a wife are groundless. There are women who do not seek their happiness in the vanities which you very properly detest. Do all you can to find such a woman. Bestow life as you have received it, and leave your offspring cheerfully to the care of those powers who rule over your own life and destiny. For my part, I should be very sorry to see your race die out.

"And why reproach yourself that you provide no one with daily bread? Man does not live by bread alone; and by simply being what you are, you supply many people—myself for instance—with a pleasure in life and a belief in your future career that is worth more than daily bread.

"Bhani thanks you for your kind message. She incloses two verses for you, of her own composition. Here you have them in prose translation—'My beloved master and his humble handmaid miss the dear friend with the soft eyes and gentle voice. We live as in a bungalow in the season of rains—clouds and ever clouds, and no sun. When will the sky be blue, and the sunshine come again? and when wilt thou eat rice once more at the table of my lord?' In the original it certainly sounds much prettier.

"Let me know soon what you think of doing, and be assured of the hearty affection of your old

"SCHROTTER.

"POSTSCRIPT: Just read the enclosed extract from my to-day's Times. That man's development was as logical as Haber's."

In the letter Wilhelm found, beside Bhani's poem, written in delicate Sanscrit characters on yellow paper, a cutting from an English newspaper, in which he read that a Nihilist of the name of Barinskoi, in St. Petersburg, had for some time excited the suspicions of his confederates by his luxurious and showy style of living. In order to discover the source from which he drew the money for it, they appointed one of their female members to be his mistress. She had shared in his extravagances, and soon obtained proofs that he was in the service of the police, and sold his fellow Nihilists. A secret court condemned him to death, and a few days ago he had been found dead in his rooms, his throat cut, and his body literally hacked to pieces.

In January Wilhelm received an unusual visitor. It was a leader of the workingmen of Altona, who told him, without further circumlocution, that the Socialists had kept their eye upon him, had found out where he was living, and now sent him, the Altona man, to see if anything could be made of him.

"What do you mean by that?" asked Wilhelm in astonishment.

"I mean," returned the visitor, who had introduced himself as Stonemason Hessel, "whether you could not be persuaded to join us openly."

As Wilhelm did not answer at once, Hessel resumed—"Our party needs men like you, who are independent and bold, have a university education, and speak well. You are all that, as we know. By banishing you from Berlin they have, in point of fact, made you one of us. So go a step further, Herr Doctor; defend yourself, take up the fight the government has forced upon you. You have a million of determined workmen at your back, who will gladly accept you as their leader."

"Excuse my frankness," said Wilhelm at last, "but I really cannot think you are serious in your proposal."

"It is a very serious matter to us," cried Hessel. "I speak in the name of the heads of the party, and have means of convincing you of the reality of my proposal if you have any doubts about it."

"But how do you come to know about me?"

"That is very simple. You are not, perhaps, aware how well organized we are, and how we follow up everything that may be of use to us afterward. We know what you did for our party in Berlin, and that you are suffering for it now. We know your circumstances, and that you have a considerable sum of money at your disposal, and, I repeat, we want educated men. Most of us have not had the means to get much schooling. The struggle for our daily bread uses up all our time, and all the brains we have. Look at me, Herr Doctor, for years I never had more than five hours' sleep, and always used half the night to learn the little I know. There are plenty of people among us who—more's the pity—are distrustful of the better educated—call them upstarts, and won't have anything to do with them. Their idea is that the proletariat should be led by proletariars. But that is nonsense. No oppressed class has ever yet been emancipated by its own members. It was always by high-minded men of wider views out of the upper classes. Catilina was an aristocrat, and put himself at the head of the populace. Mirabeau belonged to the Court, and overthrew the monarchy. Wilberforce, the defender of the negro, was not black himself."

Wilhelm now for the first time looked more attentively at this stonemason, who talked so glibly of Catalina, Mirabeau and Wilberforce, and the thought passed through his mind that, at any rate, there was one good thing about Social Democracy—it brought education into circles to which it otherwise would never have penetrated.

"And so," Hessel wound up, "we workmen too must be led to victory by educated men."

"You overlook one point, however," remarked Wilhelm. "To be your leader, one must before all things share your convictions."

"It is quite impossible that an educated and thoughtful man should not see the injustice of the present social system. The government, which oppresses us, sees it as clearly as we do ourselves. It is not fighting for a conviction, but for the supremacy of a certain class."

"'It is impossible,' is no argument. In point of fact, I do not hold with your doctrines. I know that the working-classes suffer, but I do not know why, and I do not believe your theorists when they say it is all because the workingman is ground down by the capitalist. Furthermore, you speak of leading—where am I to lead you to?"

"To victory against the plundering feudalism of the State."

"That is a mere phrase. I know of no plan which will sweep poverty and distress from the face of the earth. Even if you raise a revolution and it succeeds, even if you destroy the feudal State and build up a workingman's State upon the ruins, you will thereby only have improved the condition of a select few, not of the whole—not even of the many. I would not like to be in the shoes of your present leaders, preachers and prophets, when you have conquered, and your followers demand to see the results of your victory. How little they will then be able to fulfill of the promises they have made to-day."

"So it is your opinion that there is nothing to be done for us, and that we ought calmly to be left in want, and slavery, and ignorance?" Hessel asked angrily.

"I think," returned Wilhelm, "that it is the bounden duty of every man to love his neighbor, and help him where and when he can."

"Oh yes," said Hessel with a sneer, "that is the standpoint of the Church—the standpoint of the Middle Ages. You would give us alms. No, thank you, we accept no presents. We demand our rights, not charity."

Wilhelm thought to himself that he had not always found the Socialists so proud, but kept the thought to himself, not wishing to hurt Hessel's feelings, who seemed to be an honest fanatic.

"Do not let that be your last word," Hessel went on. "You are probably but slightly acquainted with our doctrines and writings. Come nearer to us. Come to our meetings—talk to our workmen. You will find that many of us have very clear heads, and know exactly what we want, although the majority do still cling a good deal to phrases. You will assuredly soon begin to interest yourself in the emancipation of the proletariat. And what a future to look forward to! You might be another Lassalle, famous powerful, adored by thousands, received as a savior wherever you show yourself—make a triumphal progress through all Germany, perhaps through the world. And over and above, the consciousness of having rendered such mighty service to your fellow-men."

Wilhelm rose.

"I seem to myself to be playing a rather ridiculous part in this scene," he said; "it is a parody of the Gospel story of the Temptation. Unfortunately, I have not the smallest particle of ambition, and have no desire to be either famous or mighty, or to make triumphal progresses. If I could really do anything for you, believe me, I would do it gladly. But I assure you I possess neither the philosopher's stone, nor a prescription for a universal panacea. I do not believe either that the remedies they recommend so highly to you are very effectual, so I am much obliged to you for your confidence in me, and beg you to leave me in my obscurity."

Hessel gave him a dark look, stood up, turned slowly away, and left him without one word, or even offering him his hand.

Wilhelm had sent to Berlin for a box of books, and tried to go on with his work, but found no real pleasure in it. A deep despondency had come upon him, and the idea that his life was wholly purposeless took more and more hold upon him. Often, after studying earnestly for a day or two, and making extracts for his book, he would ask himself, "Why take all this trouble? Who is going to be made wiser or happier by this rigmarole?" and his pleasure in the work was gone again for days. The consciousness of exile, instead of being blunted by time, weighed ever more heavily upon him. He never realized till now what an absolute necessity it was to his nature to lean upon a kindred spirit, for he had never before been without one. Since the death of his father he had first had Paul, and then Dr. Schrotter, whom he had seen daily, and thus had always had some one to share his mental life. Now he was separated from Schrotter by distance, and from Paul by the great change in their views, and found no sufficient support when left to himself. If at times the sight of Paul's perfect self-content and happiness roused in him the wish to follow his example, it was quickly overruled by the conviction that neither Paul's commonplace, practical occupations, nor his worldly success, would afford him, Wilhelm, the smallest satisfaction.

He passed his days and weeks in self-communings and spiritual loneliness, in spite of Paul's and Malvine's endeavors to interest him in men and things. He allowed himself to be drawn into Malvine's afternoon receptions, and the two or three parties they gave during the winter; but refused to accompany them to other people's balls and dinners. He was happiest of all with Willy, who was very fond of Uncle Eynhardt. He took him for walks, told him stories, was never tired of answering his endless questions, amused him with little chemical experiments, and in default of the riding lessons let him ride upon his knee. And as he passed his fingers through the child's long curls, he often thought, in spite of all his philosophic doubts, how wonderfully pleasant it must be after all, to bring forth some such sweet golden-haired mystery that would cling to its parent and break away from him—a continuation and yet a wholly new departure that had its roots in the past, and yet struck out boldly into the future, and whose bright gaze would be trying to penetrate the riddle of the universe when he himself had long since sunk into oblivion. Had Malvine been something more than good-natured and commonplace, had she possessed a little more tact and insight into the human heart, she would have seen that in Wilhelm were now combined all the conditions necessary for predisposing him for marriage— the sense of a spiritual void, the longing for love and companionship, a consciousness of being alone in the midst of a cheerful, peaceful family circle, and the desire to see his own life renewed in that of a child. What he needed was that some one should frankly make the first advances, and overcome his natural shyness and diffidence by a bold and saucy attack. With a little tact and diplomacy, a clever woman would have had no difficulty in putting up a bright girl to attempt so easy a fight and victory. But Malvine never thought of such a thing. Social etiquette withheld the various young ladies on whom the Habers' quiet guest had made no small impression from taking those first steps, which are considered unwomanly and humiliating, although in most cases they invariably bring about the desired results, and so Wilhelm continued to sit in his corner, and the group of pretty heiresses in theirs; the winter passed, and Malvine's darling wish was still unfulfilled.

Easter came round, and with it the migration of the family to Friesenmoor House. Wilhelm would have liked to seize this opportunity for withdrawing himself from a hospitality which weighed heavily on him, but Paul put down his timid revolt with a high hand.

"None of that now. You are coming with us, and can see what country life is like for a whole summer," he declared, and there the matter rested.

The estate and its surroundings possessed no picturesque charms. The land stretched in uniform flatness from the sluggish Suderelbe to the equally sleepy Seeve, and the Fuchsberg at Ronneburg, with its height of two hundred feet, was a giant of the Alps or Cordilleras, compared to the floor-like evenness of the country round about. From the platform of the tower which Paul had built on to his house, giving it quite a baronial appearance, one could see for miles across country, almost to Hamburg, the spires of which were plainly visible on a clear day. But far and near one saw nothing but cornfields and meadows, that had the regularity of a carpet pattern, intersected by clay-colored dikes, straight ditches full of stagnant brown water, here and there a busy windmill, and in the distance the smooth-flowing watercourses which bounded the landscape. The picture was laid on from a meager palette; a few browns and greens, slightly relieved and enlivened by the vigorous tones of the whitewashed walls of the laborers' cottages, some standing apart, some collected together like a little village.

And yet, though the view from the tower might not seem very attractive, a walk through the country revealed many a peculiar charm to the observant and divining eye. Here one stood upon ground where man had wrestled with Nature and subdued her. At every step one encountered the marks of that struggle and victory, reminding one of Jacob's mysterious encounter with the angel. The waters of the marsh were now forced within the prescribed limits of a system of drains and canals. Luxuriant crops triumphed over reeds and rushes, which were now only permitted to fringe the edges of the ditches. Sleek, mild-eyed cows grazed and ruminated where formerly the wildfowl built her nest. Chaos was vanquished, and had to own man for her lord and master.

Here, upon the scene of his labors, Paul's figure assumed a certain epic dignity. As a stern lord with a handful of armed followers keeps down a subjugated people, so Paul, at the head of a few hundred workmen, held sway over the unruly forces of Nature always more or less ready to revolt. There were always dikes to be repaired, ditches to be deepened, drain-pipes to be laid or improved, or artificial manure to be carted, and Paul was active from break of day till nightfall, either on foot or on horseback, hurrying from one end of the estate to the other, everywhere ordering or giving a helping hand, and always leading his troops himself to fresh onslaughts against the resisting elements. He did it all quietly, without any fuss or attempt to reflect credit on himself, and left it to others—to strangers, poetically inclined pupils or students on their travels—to say that his conquest of the Friesenmoor was a Faust-like achievement.

He had built a whole village for his laborers, to right and left of the highroad leading to Friesenmoor House. The cheerful, clean, whitewashed cottages, with their green-painted window-frames, were thatched with rushes and surrounded by gardens in which young fruit trees, not yet sufficiently strong to forego the support of poles, already gave promise of their first harvest of apples and pears. The village hall and the school-house were distinguished by superior size and green-glazed tile roofs; nor was a church, with a pointed belfry and weathercock, missing. For Paul was a model landowner, who took ample thought for the welfare of his dependents, and as soon as his means permitted it, had hastened to build a church and appoint a pastor, providing thereby, at the same time, for one of his numerous relatives. In his ardent loyalty to his king, he had expressed the wish to call his village Kaiser-Wilhelm's Dorf, and had received the desired permission.

In Kaiser-Wilhelm's Dorf, it was evident, content and comparative prosperity reigned supreme. Behind every house was a pigsty, behind nearly every one a cowshed. The men looked strong and hearty; the women, carrying dinner to their husbands in the fields, or sitting knitting on the benches in front of their doors, all presented bright and cheerful faces, and the school would hardly contain the crowd of flaxen-haired, blue-eyed children, whose rounded cheeks gave evidence of a never-failing and amply spread dinner-table.

In the beginning, all this made a vast impression on Wilhelm. As the struggle with nature is man's real and normal task, he instinctively feels an emotion almost amounting to joy wherever he comes upon evidences of victory. But, as usual with Wilhelm, this first instinctive emotion was followed by the usual fatal speculations, and he said to himself, "Paul has converted swamps into cornfields, has enriched himself thereby, and supports some hundreds of families. Good! but what further? This great achievement has as its primary result, that people are fed who otherwise perhaps would not eat so much or so well, or merely would not feed on this spot at all. But is the filling of one's own and other people's stomachs the first and highest aim of life?"

Paul tried hard to interest him in the details of farming. He took him about, showed and explained everything to him, and finally brought out his pet scheme—that he should sell the house in Berlin, and buy instead some marshland near by, which was to be had for a moderate sum; he would give him a helping hand at first, and as property of that kind could very well afford a steward, he could easily get him a first-rate one. They would be neighbors, Wilhelm would have a larger income and fewer wants, and live in peace and comfort. Wilhelm was profoundly touched by the affection which was manifest in Paul's every word and thought, but the prospects he opened up before him offered him no attractions.

In July, when the harvest was ripening for the sickle, and man had nothing to do but leave the sun to its work of brooding on the fields, Paul went one day to a committee meeting in the town. When he came home he remarked to Wilhelm at supper:

"What do you think? They have discovered that I am harboring a dangerous Social Democrat. The Landrath actually remonstrated with me on the subject in a discreet and well-meaning way. I can't tell you how the man amused me," and he laughed again as he recalled the conversation. But all his amusement vanished when Wilhelm answered:

"The Landrath was quite right. A political outlaw is very doubtful company for a man in your position, and I cannot think how I came to overlook the fact myself."

In vain did Paul endeavor to turn the matter into a joke; in vain that he showed himself inconsolable at his stupidity in having told the story. Wilhelm declared firmly that he must leave his friend, and bringing his whole force of will to bear upon it, carried his intention through.

The next day Paul's carriage took him to Harburg. The parting was trying to all of them. Paul's leave-taking was prolonged, and he made his friend promise he would return next year for some weeks at least to Friesenmoor House. Malvine had tears in her eyes as she said, "No one will care for you so much as we do." Even little Willy was downcast, and gazed with a reproachful look at the friend who could find it in his heart to desert him. As the train moved off he called out to Wilhelm, in his ringing, childish voice, "Come back soon, Onkelchen, and bring me something nice."

CHAPTER X.

A SEASIDE ROMANCE.

Wilhelm's immediate destination was Ostend. He hardly knew himself how he came to fix on that particular place. Since those days, long past, when his thoughts had hovered for weeks round the Belgian watering-place, the name had remained in his mind, and now, with his desire to spend some months in company with the sea, Ostend was the first place that occurred to him.

It was the middle of July, and watering places not very full as yet, nor were there many people staying at the Ocean Hotel where he stopped. Two Americans, who had begun a summer tour on the Continent by a short stay at Ostend, made friends with him on the first day after his arrival, when they found he could speak English. They invited him to join them on their walks, and made him give them information about Germany, and especially about Berlin, which they intended visiting; in return they told him all about the north coast of France, with its watering-places, big and little, which they had "done" last year from Cherbourg to Dunkirk.

Strolling the next afternoon with his new acquaintances along the Digue, a few steps in front of them he saw a lady, plainly and darkly but most elegantly dressed leaning on the arm of a tall man. They walked slowly, and were evidently lost in contemplation of the softly rolling sea. At first he paid but little attention to the couple, and would not have noticed them at all had not the Digue been very empty of visitors just then. But, strange to say, his gaze kept wandering from the oily surface of the sea, and the steamers and fishing-smacks plowing their way through it, to the slender figure of the lady, who looked small beside her tall companion; and there gradually dawned upon him a dim idea that that slight figure reminded him of somebody—that he had seen those delicate contours, those graceful proportions, that light and gliding gait before. Without hastening his steps he soon overtook them, and recognized at the first glance that it was Loulou. She too turned her head involuntarily to look at the passing trio. As she caught sight of Wilhelm a sudden pallor overspread her face, and with an unconscious movement of terror she dropped her companion's arm. Both stood stockstill, as if suddenly deprived of the power of motion, and gazed at one another wide-eyed. The silent encounter only lasted a few seconds, but the play on both sides was so marked that it could not fail to excite the attention of the lookers-on. Loulou's attendant cavalier looked in surprise from her to him, and evidently thought the proceedings most extraordinary. But before he had time to ask for an explanation, Wilhelm had turned on his heel and was walking rapidly back to the hotel. The two Americans followed him in silence. Nothing in the scene had escaped them, but as true Anglo-Saxons they had too much native reserve to ask for a confidence which was not offered them.

Wilhelm was most painfully affected by the encounter, and not for worlds would he risk the possibility of meeting again with the unfortunate woman and the man to whom she now was bound in sinful union. That same day he took leave of his Americans, and left Ostend early the next morning; at once fearful and relieved, as though fleeing successfully from the scene of a dark deed of his own committing.

After a long and tiresome journey, not made pleasanter by having to change four or five times, he arrived late in the evening at Eu, where he spent the night. The next morning, an hour's drive in a hotel omnibus brought him to Ault, a small market-town in the department of Somme, which the Americans had recommended to him as the quietest, cheapest, most unpretending, and at the same time picturesquely situated of any of the seaside places on the north coast of France, at least as far as Dieppe.

Wilhelm found Ault to be all it had been described. The little place presented a well-to-do, self-respecting appearance. The High Street, at right angles with the shore, and rising gently toward the higher, billowy country beyond, was wide and straight as a dart, and scrupulously clean; the roadway was macadamized, and a flagged pavement ran along the two rows of houses. At its upper end, broad and defiant, was a wonderful mediaeval church in the earliest Gothic style, with high pointed windows, a severely beautiful west door, and a mighty square tower. The church blocked the way, and forced the street to make a bend in order to pass round it. This building, which would have adorned a capital, stood there haughty and arrogant like a gigantic knight in full tilting armor in the midst of the common people, and seemed to wave the simple, unpretentious provincial houses to right and left with a lordly gesture so that nothing might intercept his view of the sea. Beside the High Street there were a few little side alleys, mostly inhabited by locksmiths, who worked with untiring industry from morning till night, keeping up a cheerful but far from unpleasing din which, mingled with the roar of the breakers below, reached the ear as a soft musical ring of metal. The only prominently ugly features in the charming picture were the few villas on the neighboring heights, built by retired Paris grocers and haberdashers; liliputian, pretentious, with blatant, highly-colored facades, ludicrous imitations of baronial fortresses, Venetian palaces, or Renaissance chateaux.

The inhabitants of Ault were a peaceable, sober-minded people. No one was ever drunk, nor was the sound of quarreling ever to be heard. There were few public-houses; several places, however, dignified by the name of cafes. The natives were so far accustomed to summer visitors that they did not take much notice of them, but happily not so much as to direct their whole thought and energy to fleecing them. It seemed as if the people of Ault had merely arranged a bathing place for the purpose of deriving a little amusement out of the strangers, not in order to make a living out of them, that being quite unnecessary, as their comfortable figures, good clothes, and well-filled shops could testify.

Wilhelm took up his quarters in the Hotel de France, situated just where the High Street swept round the side of the church. As the house was separated from the sea by the whole opposite row of houses, one only caught a glimpse of it as a narrow, glittering streak across the intervening roofs from the second-floor windows. The view from the front windows was the more remarkable. They looked out upon the churchyard which lay behind the Gothic cathedral. Not that there was anything depressing in the sight; it made, on the contrary, a cheerful impression, with its carefully tended flower beds and magnificent old trees, which almost hid the modest headstones they overshadowed, and in whose branches count less singing birds had built their nests, while noisy troops of children played under them at all hours of the day.

Wilhelm directed his steps at once to this churchyard, where, beside the modern iron crosses, there were marble headstones showing dates that went back to the seventeenth century. In the oldest as well as the newest inscriptions the same name occurred over and over again, speaking well for the settled habits of the population. And, according to the inscriptions, most of those buried here had lived to be eighty or ninety years of age. Had Ault been a professedly fashionable bathing place, one might have been tempted to think that this churchyard, with its cheering records in stone and iron of the longevity of the natives, had been set down in the very center of the town to encourage the visitors.

The Hotel de France recommended itself by extreme cleanliness, but otherwise it was very simple. The rooms contained only such furniture as was absolutely necessary, the dining-room was bare of decoration, and therefore happily free of those gruesome colored prints which the commercial traveller delights to sow broadcast over the unsuspecting country towns. Only the so-called salon boasted the luxury of a cottage piano, a polished table, a few cane chairs, and a looking-glass over the chimneypiece, on which lay a box of dominoes and a backgammon board, eloquently suggestive of mine host's ideas as to the most suitable occupation for his guests.

The hotel proprietors were as simple and homely as their house. The man wore a seaman's cap and a blue coat with brass anchor buttons, and was more than delighted if you took him for a seafaring man. He had, in fact, been to sea once, as ship's cook, or steward, or something of the sort. Now he sat most of the time in the cafe of the hotel, supplied the neighbors with little drams of cognac, and told the visitors endless stories of the buying and selling of property in the little town. His wife was the soul of the establishment. She possessed the gift of omnipresence. At one and the same moment you might see her in the kitchen and in the outhouses, in the hotel and in the cafe. The servants, of whom there was a considerable number, answered to a look, a bock of her finger. You could hear her clear voice from morning till night in the courtyard or on the stairs. Everywhere she lent a helping hand, and her busy fingers accomplished as much as all the men and maids put together. With it all she was never out of temper, always had a word or a smile for every passer-by, took a personal interest in each of her guests, took instant notice of a diminished appetite or a pale cheek, and always sent up lime-flower tea to anybody who happened to come rather later than usual to breakfast.

The hotel was pretty full when Wilhelm arrived, but he made no attempt to mix with the company he met twice a day at the table d'hote. His French had grown somewhat rusty for want of practice, and he did not trust himself to join in the exceedingly lively and general conversation till he had regained something of his old fluency in long daily talks with the landlord. Beside which, he did not feel greatly drawn toward his fellowguests. Their high-sounding and pompously-expressed platitudes bored him, their absurd views on politics, their parrot-like and yet self-satisfied remarks on literature and art filled him with compassion. One guest in particular, who sat at the head of the table, and generally led the conversation in the loudest tones, succeeded in making him very impatient, in spite of the mildness with which Wilhelm usually judged his fellows. He did business in sewing machines in Paris, but here gave himself out as an "ingenieur constructeur," and belonged to that class of persons who cannot endure not to be the center of observation wherever they happen to be. It has been said of a man of that stamp, that if he were at a wedding he would wish to be the bridegroom, and if at a funeral to be in the place of the corpse. At the dinner table of the Hotel de France he reigned supreme. His strong point lay in the perpetration of the most ghastly puns, which he would discharge first to the right and then to the left, and finally, with a roar of laughter, over the whole table. In his outward appearance, too, he sought to create a sensation. He was not dressed, he was costumed. He wore long stockings, knickerbockers and a tight-fitting jacket, and when he stood up, tried to produce effects with his calves, spread his legs wide apart as if, like the Colossus of Rhodes, ships were to pass beneath, and affected sporting and athletic attitudes generally. He was accompanied by a lady who had at first roused the horrified disgust of the others by her appetite, which surpassed every known human limit, and then proceeded to make herself still more hateful by a frequent change of costume.

Wilhelm's immediate neighbor was a lady of somewhat exuberant outline, but extremely plainly dressed, and without a single ornament, of whom at first he took no more notice than of the rest of the company. She returned his silent bow at coming and going, and acknowledged the little attentions of the dinner table—the handing of salt or entrees, of bread or cider (the table beverage)—with a low "Merci, monsieur," accompanied by a pleasant smile and an inclination of the head. The acquaintance began with a look. It was after a more than usually exasperating pun from the man in the knickerbockers, and involuntarily their eyes met, after which they exchanged glances each time he came out with a particularly blatant piece of idiocy. They could not long remain in doubt that their opinion on the prevailing conversation was identical, and the unanimity of their tastes was still further demonstrated by the fact that the lady was as silent during the meals as Wilhelm.

The interchange of looks was presently followed by words. It was the lady who broke the ice by alluding to a somewhat peculiar incident. It happened to be market day, and Wilhelm had been watching with interest the cheerful bustle in the High Street, and the new type of country people: the men with their carts bringing in calves, pigs, and grain, fine-looking fellows, with tall sturdy figures, and shrewd, clean-shaven faces above the blue cotton white-embroidered blouses and severely stiff snow-white shirt collars; and the women in round dark-brown cloaks reaching to their feet; the drum-beating, yelling tooth-drawers and patent medicine venders praising their remedies against tapeworm and ague with incredible volubility, and the couple of majestic gendarmes in their imposing uniforms, with yellow leather belts and cocked hats, who found no occasion to exhibit their stern official side to the noisy, laughing, but well-behaved crowd. After strolling for awhile among the carts and people, Wilhelm had caught sight of a large and handsome donkey, gone up to him and stroked him, and said a variety of friendly things to him.

At dinner, noting that his neighbor was looking about in search of something, he asked politely:

"Madame is in want of something?"

"The water, if you please," said she.

He handed her the carafe, which was out of her reach; she thanked him, and, not to let the conversation drop, added with a pleasant smile:

"Monsieur seems fond of donkeys?"

"Indeed!" He answered, surprised.

"I saw you this morning patting and stroking a splendid donkey."

He had not thought of it again.

"Yes, now I remember," he answered, "it was a charming beast, with wonderfully wise, thoughtful eyes."

"Do you think so too?" she cried, delighted. "You must know, I have a special weakness for donkeys, and consider that, next to dogs they are by far the most intelligent of our domestic animals. They have such a look of profound wisdom, such stoical philosophy and resignation, that I feel they are quite a lesson to me."

Wilhelm could not repress a smile at her lively tone.

"I should like to think," he said, "that our agreeing in a good opinion of the donkey is a sign that the ungrateful world has at last come to a proper appreciation of this ugly fellow-laborer."

"Ugly?" she exclaimed. "I don't think so at all! Look at his delicate hoofs, his elegantly-tufted tail, the soft, silvery gray of his coat with the velvety, black markings, and his ears are very becoming to him. It is such an injustice always to compare him with the horse. He is altogether a different type, but quite as handsome in his way."

"Then you would whitewash Titania in 'Midsummer Night's Dream?'"

She laughed "Well, Titania might have done worse. But how is it that the donkey has come to be the symbol of stupidity?"

"Perhaps because of his want of spirit, and his perversity."

"No, I believe it is something else. People found a great, strong animal that could, if it liked, be just as difficult to manage, and resist just as well as a horse, and yet was quite content with the worst of food, required neither stable nor grooming, worked till it dropped, and never bit or kicked. So they said, an animal that is strong enough to hurt us, and yet puts up with any kind of treatment, must necessarily be deadly stupid. That is how it was. People cannot believe that one may be good-tempered and uncomplaining and yet have any brains. With them to be wicked and violent and pretentious is to be clever. If the donkey would refuse to eat anything but oats and barley, and turned and rent anybody who annoyed him in the slightest degree, you would see how people would immediately have the highest respect for his intellect."

"You seem to have a low opinion of your fellow-creatures, madame?"

"It is their own fault then," she replied, gazing through the window into the courtyard.

After this conversation Wilhelm looked for the first time more attentively at his neighbor. He had a general impression of her being tall and stout, with a remarkably clear, bright complexion. Now he took in the details. In spite of the fullness of her figure she was slender about the waist, and her small slim hands, with their tapering fingers and pink nails, retained the purity of their outline, and had by no means degenerated into mere cushions of fat. The proudly-poised head was crowned by a wealth of heavy, pale brown hair with dull gold reflections in it, waving in soft, downy locks round her forehead. The cheeks were very full but firm, and the well shaped, boldly modeled nose stood in exactly the right proportion to the rather large face. The light brown eyes with their remarkably small pupils were conspicuously lively, and flashed and sparkled incessantly on all sides. Their expression was extremely intelligent and generally mocking, and if you looked long at them you gained the somewhat uncomfortable impression that that cold clear glance could, on occasion, stab a heart as cruelly as would a dagger. But her most striking feature was her mouth—a sudden dash of violent coral-red in the opalescent white of her face. This brutal effect of color exercised a peculiar fascination and riveted the attention. The eye lingered upon those lips—so voluptuously, so sinfully full, so burning, blood-red that in the chastest mind, even a woman's, they must suggest the image of vampire-like kisses. Take her for all in all, she was a magnificent creature, this woman of thirty, overflowing with health and life, in all her triumphant display of full-blown womanly beauty. Not a man in the hotel but had looked at her in undisguised admiration, and if they had not yet ventured to make advances to her, it was because she intimidated them by her cold hauteur, or by the mocking twinkle of her eye.

Only for Wilhelm, now that she had really taken notice of him, did those eyes begin to grow soft and gentle, and when they met his turned meek and harmless, and, in their apparent innocence, seemed to plead to him for notice, confidence, instruction. He did not remain impervious to their influence. It afforded him distinct pleasure to sit at table beside this beautiful woman and show her small attentions. On his long walks he caught himself thinking deeply about her, while the blood coursed with unwonted heat through his veins. He marked her entrance into the dining room or salon by his heart stopping suddenly and then racing on in wild, irregular beats, and if he looked at her the indecorous thought came to him that it would be a joy to stroke those firm, round cheeks, to pass one's fingers gently over those swelling lips, but more especially to bury one's hands in that flood of silken hair. These various discoveries rather took him aback, and resulted in increasing his reserve almost to the point of rudeness. He still only met her at the table d'hote, and never attempted to approach at any other time, although she had asked him repeatedly if he did not take walks or make excursions into the country.

One morning, soon after the conversation about the donkey, he went down to the beach, where, it being the bathing hour, the whole visiting population of Ault was assembled. The coast met the sea at this point as a perpendicular wall of rock a hundred and fifty feet high, stretching away to the west in an endless line, but on the east side, sloping gradually down, till about two miles further on, it lost itself in the flat line of the shore. Where the sweep of the bare, gray cliff made a slight backward curve, the sea had washed the shingle together to form a little beach covered with pebbles from the largest to the smallest size. Here two rows of modest wooden cabins were erected, which served as bathing houses, and beside these, a great wooden structure on wheels, not unlike the enormous house-caravans in which the owners of shows and menageries and such-like wandering folk travel about from fair to fair. The French flag fluttering from a pole on the top of the caravan drew attention to it, and on closer inspection one read above the entrance—which was approached by a movable wooden staircase—the proud legend "Casino d'Ault." Yes, Ault actually boasted a casino, with an entrance fee of ten centimes a head, and in the single room, which occupied the whole structure, you found a jeu de course, and other games of hazard, exactly as they had them in the most renowned and elegant dens of thieves of the fashionable watering places.

Here, however, nobody went to the dogs. Life on the shore was prim and patriarchal. Whole families sat or lay about on camp stools or on traveling rugs, the wives in morning wraps, the husbands smoking in linen suits; the former occupied with needlework, the latter reading the newspapers or novels. The young people ran about barefoot and in bathing costume, or lay at the edge of the water fishing for shrimps, which they rarely or never caught. There were merry, noisy groups of bathers in the shallow water near the shore, splashing one another, shrieking at the approach of the larger waves, bobbing up and down, and shouting encouragement to the newcomers, who only ventured timidly and by degrees into the chilly waters. As very few of the bathers could swim, this all took place in the close vicinity.

At first Wilhelm had been rather shocked to see the two sexes bathing together, and that the girls and married women—coming out of the sea with their legs and arms bare, and their clinging, wet bathing dresses revealing the outline of their forms with embarrassing distinctness—should calmly stroll back to the bathing houses under the open gaze of the men. For that reason he even refrained from going to the shore at the bathing hour, or bathing there himself. By degrees, however, he grew accustomed to it, seeing that nobody thought anything of it, and that the almost nude figures disported themselves among their equally unconcerned parents, relatives, and friends with the naive unconsciousness of South Sea Islanders.

As he made his way, not too easily, over the rolling shingle between the chattering, lazy groups, he saw his neighbor of the table d'hote sitting, a little apart, on a camp stool under a large dark sunshade, an open book on her lap, and her eyes fixed on the smooth, bright surface of the ocean. She noticed Wilhelm, and smiled and nodded pleasantly, almost before he could bow to her. There was something of invitation in her nod, which, however, he did not follow, he could not have said exactly why. Confused, and a prey to all sorts of undefined emotions, he continued his walk till he reached the point where the waves, breaking at the very foot of the cliff, prevented his going any further. As he turned, ho remembered that he would have to pass her again, and considered if he could not avoid it by keeping close to the cliff and so get behind her. But why go out of his way to avoid her? That was driving shyness to the verge of churlishness. She was friendly toward him, why repay her kindness by such foolish and uncalled-for reserve? And ashamed, almost indignant at himself, he came to a sudden determination, and directed his steps straight toward the lady. She had watched him all the time, and now smiled to him from afar, as she saw him making for her.

When he got up to her he stood still and raised his hat. She saved him the embarrassment of making a beginning by saying at once in the most natural tone in the world:

"How nice of you to come and keep me company for a little while! Won't you sit down on this plaid?"

He thanked her, and did as he was bid, seating himself on the thick, soft rug. His head was shaded by the great parasol, the sun warmed his knees.

"Are you a great admirer of the sea?" asked the lady.

"I hardly know myself yet. I must make its nearer acquaintance first," answered Wilhelin.

"I confess that it leaves me quite unmoved. No, not that exactly, for I am rather vexed at it for giving so many idiots an excuse for ranting and absurd sentimentality. Now just look at all these people on the beach. In reality they are bored to extinction, and enjoy the Boulevards infinitely more than this expanse of water, which is quite meaningless to them. And yet you have only to mention the word—the sea—and they will instantly turn up their eyes and start off repeating the lesson they have learned by rote about their rapture and enthusiasm, just like a musical box which grinds out a tune when you press a button at the top. The sea was invented by a few romantically inclined poets. But I deny that there is any truth in then rhapsodies; the sea is hopelessly monotonous, and monotony excludes the possibility of beauty or charm. One has at most the same feeling for it as for a mirror in which one sees oneself reflected. The sea is a blank page, which each one fills up with whatever he happens to have in his own mind, or, if you like it better, a frame into which one puts pictures of one's own imagining. I grant that you can dream by the side of the sea, for it does nothing to disturb your dreams or give them any particular bent or coloring. But can it give the impulse to thought and emotion like the eve-changing outlines of mountain and forest? Never! People with unsophisticated minds know that well enough. The population of the coast always builds its houses with their backs to the sea.

"As a defence against the storms," Wilhelm interposed.

"That may be. But that is not the only reason. It is because the sight of that eternal waste of waters, without a boundary line, without the variety or movement of life upon it, bores them, and they prefer to look out upon the country with all its expressive and varying outlines."

"But the expression which you see in a landscape—you put that into it yourself, by an effort of your own imagination. Forests and mountains are in themselves as inanimate as the sea."

"Quite so; but the landscape has features which remind us of something else, which play, as it were, upon the keyboard of our associations, and it thus calls up the pictures with which we proceed to enliven it. The sea does nothing of this, and the best proof of that is, that no painter has ever yet used the sea by itself for his model. Did you ever know of an artist who painted nothing but the sea?" "Yes, Aiwasowky."

"Who is he?"

"A Russian who paints extraordinary sea pieces."

"What! Only water—without shore, or people, or ships?"

"I remember a picture with absolutely nothing but water, only a spar, or a mast floating on it."

"There, you see!" she cried in triumph. "That broken mast is a trick of the artist. There lies the story. You instantly think of a wrecked ship; you see men, catastrophes, weeping widows and sweethearts; the spar becomes the central point of the picture, and you forget all about the sea. Moreover, the ancients, who surely had an eye for all that is grand and beautiful, they did not know either what to do with the sea. They were a magnificent race, healthy-minded realists—and kept strictly to the evidences of their senses without adding anything transcendental. The sea only appealed to their ear. Homer's adjectives for the sea are only expressive of sound—the resounding, the jubilant, the loud-rushing; hardly more than once does he allude to the gloomy or the wine-colored sea."

"You have your classics at your fingers' ends, like any philologist."

"That need not surprise you. With regard to the really beautiful, I have neither pride nor prejudice. Even the fact that the common herd of the reading public has made a point of praising him for a hundred years does not prevent me from enjoying a true poet."

"But if you dislike the sea so much why do you come here?"

"Oh," laughed the handsome lady, "that is the fault of my doctors. They sent me to the sea to thin me down, and by their orders I was to choose a very dull, very remote bathing place, where I should be sure not to meet any acquaintances. For directly I have friends about me, I enjoy myself, laugh, talk, and then I get stout again. Now to-day, for instance, I have acted contrary to my medical orders—I have had a very pleasant chat with you."

"You are too kind. You have given everything and received nothing in return."

"That is exactly what I like—always to give, never to receive."

"That is not woman's way usually. But you are very exceptional. Pardon a possibly indiscreet question—do you write?"

"Good gracious! Do I look like a blue-stocking?"

"I never made a distinct picture of that type."

"You need not be afraid, I am not an authoress. The most I have ever done in that way was to give a novelist, or a comedy-writer of my acquaintance, a little help now and then. When they want a lady's letter, they like me to write it. But you—I suppose you are an author?"

"No, madame; I study natural science."

"A professor then?"

"No, only an amateur."

"Ah! And you are French?"

"I am German."

"Impossible!" exclaimed the lady.

"Why impossible?" asked Wilhelm, smiling.

"You have no accent, and you look—"

"You probably think that every German has light blue eyes, flaxen hair, and a long pipe?"

"That is certainly pretty much how we picture Germans to ourselves in Spain."

It was his turn to be surprised. "You a Spaniard?"

"And how had you pictured a Spanish lady? Of course with jet black eyes and hair, and a mantilla?"

Wilhelm nodded.

"There are fair Spaniards, however, as you see. In fact, it is very common in our best families—an inheritance perhaps from our Gothic ancestors."

"I suppose, like all Latins, you despise the Germans?"

"I beg, monsieur, that you will not class me with the mass. I wish to be regarded as an individual. Whatever the prejudices of the Latins may be, I have my own opinion. Your nationality in a matter of indifference to me. I only consider the man," and she gave him a look that sent the blood flaming to his cheek.

The hotel meals were always announced by a bell which could be heard quite well on the shore. In the heat of their conversation, however, they did not notice the signal. A lady's maid whom Wilhelm had often seen at the hotel—a middle-aged, female dragoon with a mustache and a very stiff and dignified deportment—now came up to the lady and said:

"Madame la Comtesse did not hear the dinner bell?"

She rose and took Wilhelm's arm without further ado. The maid followed with the rug and the camp stool. The beach was quite deserted, everybody having gone to dinner. The tide was rising, and had nearly covered the strip of beach. The thunder of the waves, mingled with the rattle of the pebbles which they sucked after them as they receded, followed the couple as they slowly made their way back to the hotel.

On the road home they passed the post office. The maid, whose gentle name of Anne hardly matched her martial appearance, had hurried on in front to fetch her mistress' letters and newspapers. She handed them to the lady, who smilingly tore off the wrapper from her Figaro and gave it to Wilhelm, saying: "You do not know my name yet?" Wilhelm read, on the slip of paper: "Madame la Comtesse Pilar de Pozaldez—nee de Henares." "My father," she added in explanation, "was Major-General Marquis de Henares."

"And here is my very plebeian name," returned Wilhelm, pulling out his card and handing it to her.

"There are no such things as plebeian names—only plebeian hearts," said the countess, as she glanced at the card, and then put it away in her own elegant tortoise-shell case, which bore her monogram and crest in gold and colored enamel.

The acquaintance was now fully established, and after dinner the countess invited Wilhelm, in the most natural manner possible, to accompany her on a walk into the country.

The surroundings of Ault were very pretty. Emerald-green meadows alternately with a few cornfields decked the gentle billowy uplands, which sloped away abruptly toward the sea. Trees stood separately or in groups reaching to the edge of the cliff, over which many of them bent their storm-disheveled heads and gazed into the waves below. Here and there were small inclosed woods, and it was at the edge of one of these, about a quarter of a mile walk from the town, that the countess seated herself on a mossy bank in the shade. Wilhelm sat down beside her on the gnarled root of a tree; Anne was sent home, to return in two hours' time, but Fido was allowed to remain. He was a silvery-white sheepdog with a sharp muzzle, stiff little pointed ears, and a bushy tail curling tightly over his back. He had attached himself to Wilhelm from the first moment, and gave vent to his delight when caressed by having a severe attack of asthmatic coughing, puffing and blowing.

"You live in Paris, do you not?" asked the countess after they had exchanged remarks on the scenery.

"No," returned Wilhelm, "up till now I have lived in Berlin, but I had to leave for political reasons, and now I am a sort of vagrant without any actual home."

"Ah—a political refugee!" cried the countess. "How charming! Of course you will take up your abode in Paris now—that is the sacred tradition with all political exiles. Yes, yes—you must; beside, how horrid it would have been to part after a few weeks and go our separate ways—you to the right, I to the left—and with only the consoling prospect of meeting again some day beyond the stars! So you will come to Paris, and if you have any intention of getting up a revolution in Germany, I beg that you will count me among your confederates. You need not laugh—Paris is swarming with Spanish refugees of all parties, and I have had plenty of opportunity of gaining experience in the planning of conspiracies."

"I have no such ambition," answered Wilhelm, smiling, "and am, in any case, no politician, although I enjoy the distinction of being an exile."

"Shall you take up any profession in Paris? I have connections—"

"You are very good, Madame la Comtesse. You will perhaps think less of me, but I have no actual profession."

"Think less of you. On the contrary, to have no profession is to be free—to be one's own master. Any one who is forced to earn his living must, of course, have a profession. But it is never anything but a necessary evil. It is only pedantic people who look upon it as an object of life. At most, it is a means to an end."

"And what do you consider to be the real object of life?"

"Can you ask? Why, happiness of course!"

"Happiness—certainly. But then each one of us has a different conception of happiness. To one it is knowledge, to another the fulfilling of duty, to lower natures wealth and worldly honors. Therefore, it is possible to imagine that some one may find happiness in pursuing a profession."

"Oh, no, my dear Herr Eynhardt, those are the mistaken views of gloomy and limited natures who are incapable of recognizing the true object of life. There are no two ideals of happiness—there is but one."

"And that is?"

"To wish for something very, very much—and get it."

"Even if it is something foolish?"

"Even then."

"And even if one should lose if afterward?"

She gazed for a while into the distance in silence and then said firmly—"Yes, even then." And after a pause she added—"You have, at least, had a moment of absolute happiness—when you found your wish fulfilled. And what more do you want? One only lives to experience such moments."

"Unfortunately, your theory of happiness does not fit every case. Where is the happiness to come from for one who has no wishes at all, or who wishes for something unattainable—perfect understanding, for instance?"

"A human being without a wish—is there such a thing?"

"Yes, Madame la Comtesse, there is."

"You perhaps?" she asked quickly.

"Perhaps," Wilhelm returned.

"Then you are not in love?" she said, and let her brilliant eyes rest upon his melancholy face.

He shook his head gently without looking at her, as if ashamed of the want of gallantry in such a confession.

"But at least you were once?" she persisted eagerly.

"Have I ever really been in love? Perhaps—Or no, I do not know myself."

"Thankless creature! You hesitate—you are not sure! How shameful of you to deny the gods you have once worshiped! But that is the way with you men. If you cease to love, you will not admit that you ever had loved. Tell me, was there ever a moment in your life when you could have answered my question—'Are you in love?'—with an unqualified Yes?"

"Yes, I have known such a moment. But, looking back upon it now—"

"No, no, you were quite right then and you are wrong now. That is just your great mistake. You imagine that one can only love once, and that love, to be real, must last forever. My poor friend, nothing lasts forever, and the truest love is sometimes as perishable as the loveliest rose—the most exquisite dream. But it is not to say that because it is over we are to deny that it ever existed. You may not feel anything now, but that is no reason for declaring that you did not feel it then. You thought you were in love, and therefore you were. It is sophistry to try to persuade oneself of the contrary in after days."

"You are a brilliant advocate of your views, Madame la Comtesse, but nevertheless may one take a momentary delusion—"

"Delusion' And who shall say, my German philosopher, if our whole existence may not be a delusion?"

"Ah, there you drive my philosophy very hard," murmured Wilhelm.

"Never been in love?" exclaimed the countess, and her lustrous hazel eyes flashed, "why you would be a monster. I suppose you are nearly thirty!"

"Nearly thirty-five."

"I congratulate you, Herr Eynhardt, I should have taken you for at least five years less But whether thirty or thirty-four, it would be culpable to have reached that age without having been in love. For you surely are not—a disciple of Abelard."

At this point-blank question Wilhelm reddened and cast down his eyes like the boy he really was in some respects. She observed his embarrassment, not without secret amusement.

"But seriously," she went on, "your little bit of love is the best there is about you men. No, it is the only good thing, the only thing that makes your bluntness, your selfishness, your want of sentiment bearable."

"Yes, so the women say. They see nothing in the whole world or in life but love. They judge men solely according to their capacity for, or their zeal in, loving. And yet it takes more strength and manliness to resist love than to give way to it. They only care for men who are slaves to that passion. I admire those chaste and saintly men who have been able to cast off the bonds of the flesh. The highest point of the human mind is only reached by him who has never suffered himself to be dragged down by his senses. Christ taught the denial of the flesh both in precept and example. Newton never knew a woman."

"I know nothing about Newton," she retorted, "but Christ had a feeling heart for the Magdalen and the adulteress. Beside, Christ was a God, and I am speaking of ordinary mortals, and it is only through woman, through your love of woman, that you become heroes and demigods."

"No," Wilhelm answered bluntly, "it is woman who drags man down to the level of the beasts. We have a German fairy tale in which a bear becomes human as soon as he embraces a woman. In real life it is just the opposite. The knowledge of woman, the lust of the flesh, transforms man into a beast. You know the classics so well and are so fond of them—there is no apter allegory than the story of Semele, who desired once to see her lover, Jupiter, without the weaknesses and infirmities of the flesh—as the Lord of High Heaven—and perished at the sight."

"Very well," said she softly, "you may despise me and say I am like Semele. I prefer a warm-hearted, loving beast to an icy-cold and proud philosopher. Anyhow, I am very fond of animals," and, lost in dreamy thought, she stroked Fido, who began to gasp and choke with delight, and eagerly licked the caressing hand. After a pause she resumed slowly—"I should never have thought you were such a desperate woman-hater. You have heaped insult on my sex and consequently on me. I expect you to make reparation for that by—being very nice to me."

She looked him deep in the eyes and stretched out her hand, which he seized in confusion and pressed. Suddenly he let it drop. The countess looked up in surprise, and following Wilhelm's gaze, she caught sight of the hotel wit and his lady coming along the deep pathway that ran round the foot of the wooded hill, on the slope of which they were sitting.

"Oh,—what do these common people matter?" exclaimed the countess in a tone of vexation. "And what is the harm, if they do see us? They will only boast, when they get back to their shop in Paris, that they saw a great lady in Ault."

But for all that, the dangerously sweet spell of the moment was broken, and did not return before Anne arrived, whom Fido ran sneezing and wriggling to meet.

For the rest of the day Wilhelm was silent and thoughtful, seeming to awake from a dream each time the countess spoke to him at dinner. She was perfectly aware of what was going on in him, and sought by looks, words, and manner to increase the effects of the afternoon's conversation. When the meal was over she took Wilhelm's arm again and asked—totally unconcerned that the rest of the company exchanged glances—"What are you going to do this evening?"

"I thought of taking a little walk on the shore," he stammered shyly.

"Oh, selfish creature!—and leave me all alone, though I might be bored to death? No, come up to my room. You have never paid me a visit yet. Anne will get us some tea, and we can talk."

The countess had two rooms on the first floor, most plainly furnished, without a carpet or a single decoration on the walls. One of the rooms served as bedroom, the other as salon. At least it contained no bed, but a chaise longue instead, a rocking chair, and a table with a jute cover. The countess was inwardly much amused at Wilhelm's timorous hesitation in crossing her threshold. She relieved him of his hat and gave it to Anne, who hung it on a nail with the utmost gravity, but could not refrain from casting a curious glance at Wilhelm from time to time.

When the tea was on the table, and Anne had discreetly retired into the bedroom, closing the door behind her, the countess began: "As we are to become friends—no, we are friends already; tell me, you are my friend, are you not?"—she held out her hand, which he pressed warmly and retained in his—"you ought to know who I am and how I live. I will tell you the whole truth—I never lie, it is so vulgar and cowardly. The worst that can be said of me, you shall hear out of my own mouth. And still I hope that, after you have heard all, you will not feel less kindly disposed toward me than before."

She moistened her blood-red lips in the tea without leaving hold of his hand.

"I am married. My husband, Count Pozaldez, is Governor of the Philippine Islands. I have lived for years in Paris. The count had the post given to him in order to put a few thousand miles between him and me. We have no divorce in Spain, and that was the only way of insuring to me a little peace and freedom." She took another little sip. "From this you will understand," she went on, "that I am not happily married. You must know that I am an only child. My father, the Marquis de Henares, idolized me. He was a soldier through and through, very stern and reserved toward everybody, even my mother, who never really understood his rare nature. Only to me he showed his heart of gold, his high and noble character, his deep feeling—a prickly pear, outside rough and inside honey-sweet. He brought me up as if I was to be a cabinet minister, and treated me like a beloved comrade from the time I was twelve, so that my mother was often jealous of me. When I grew up, he would sometimes say, 'Whoever wants to marry my Pilar will have to fight with me first.' And he meant it. You probably know that we develop early in Spain. At sixteen I was not very different from what I am now. Count Pozaldez was a young lieutenant of cavalry, and my father's adjutant. Of course we saw a good deal of one another, and he soon began to behave as if he were madly in love with me. I was not averse to him, for he was young, handsome, and aristocratic. And what else does a girl of sixteen look for? I naturally had no difficulty in understanding his glances and his sighs, but it went on for months without his making me a formal proposal. One day he wrote me a letter eight pages long, in which he informed me that, as he possessed nothing in the world but his sword, he dared not venture to lift his eyes to the heiress of the richest landowner in Old Castile; beside that, he was not worthy of me, only a king could be that—the wretch! But I will come back to that later on. On the other hand, however, he could not live without me, and if I did not return his love he was resolved to put a bullet through his brain. Of course I instantly saw him with a bullet-hole in his forehead, and shed tears for the poor young man. I did not want anybody to die for my sake. I pictured to myself how beautiful it would be to make a young man, without fortune or position, with nothing but his love for me, happy, rich, and great by the gift of my hand. I showed the letter to my mother, and asked her what was to be done. She at once took up the young man's cause. My soul would most assuredly fall a prey to the devil if I let poor Pozaldez kill himself. He was of good family, and would soon make his way as the son-in-law of the Marquis de Henares. I must unquestionably do something to raise his spirits. My mother's advice coincided with my own feelings. I allowed the count a secret interview, and he had permission to ask my father for my hand. He did so in fear and trembling. He was dismissed with scorn and contumely. My mother and I then used all our influence to turn my father, and—I was married to Count Pozaldez before I was seventeen."

She was silent for a little while, and then went on: "I will make my story short. One year afterward, when I was in bed with my first child, he brought his mistresses to the house. I was determined to leave him on the spot. My mother brought about a reconciliation. Soon after that he began to ill-treat me. I suffered that in silence too, to avoid a public scandal, and more particularly for my father's sake. He would have killed him if he had known. Later—later—I must tell it you, so that you may grasp the whole situation—the villain did all he could to direct King Amadeo's attention to me—he had just come to Madrid. When I noticed his base schemes—as I could not fail to do—that put the finishing touches. I gave him the choice between a scandalous lawsuit, which would have deprived him of my fortune, and voluntary banishment by accepting some government post across the sea with half my income. He finally chose exile and the money, and I was free. I left Madrid and settled in Paris. You can imagine the circumstances—a young woman of twenty-three—alone, whose life could not possibly be filled by the care of two little children."

"Two children?" asked Wilhelm.

"Yes," she answered, and hung her head.

"There is cowardice of which even a courageous woman will be guilty when, out of consideration for public opinion, she continues to live under one roof with the father of her first child. And then—you must take me as I am, with all my imperfections, for which some good qualities may perhaps make up."

She looked at him humbly, with the eyes of an imploring child, and continued in a low voice:

"The Spanish colony in Paris received me with open arms. There was no end to the entertainments, soirees and theaters. But can that satisfy a young and embittered woman thirsting for happiness? Of course I received a great deal of attention. An attache of our embassy succeeded in attracting me. I swear to you that I struggled long with him and myself, but his passion was stronger than my powers of resistance."

Wilhelm would have drawn away his hand, but she held it fast, and went on hurriedly.

"I have finished. For four years I shared his life, and then discovered that I had deceived myself a second time, and put an end to a connection which had lost the excuse of sincerity For two years now I have been free—for two years my heart has been at rest. Tell me, can you condemn me now that you know all?"

"It is not for me to judge you," said Wilhelm sadly. "All I think is that you have had a great deal of misfortune in your life."

"Yes, have I not?" cried the countess eagerly.

"Do not misunderstand me. You had the misfortune to make a mistake in thinking you loved Count Pozaldez."

"How should a sixteen-year-old child know? The first passably good-looking, well-bred man who flatters her wins her heart."

"That is only too true. But if a young girl throws away her heart so lightly, she has no right to complain if she has to repent of it for the rest of her life."

"But that is a terrible theory!" exclaimed the countess, and dropped his hand "What? One wakes to a knowledge of the world and of life—one is wretched, one sees that there is such a thing as happiness, and how it may be obtained, and one is not to stretch out a hand to grasp it? You would really be so cruel as to say to a woman—young, and in need of love—in childish ignorance and folly you were guilty of a mistake, all is over for you, abandon all claims to love and hope, sunshine and life, pass your years in mourning, and bury yourself alive, you have no further right to share in the joys of life?"

Wilhelm left her string of passionate questions unanswered, and continued the thread of his former discourse:

"But most certainly an older and more sensible woman, who should have learned wisdom from a first error, has no right to be guilty of a second one."

"Oh, how hard you are!" murmured the countess.

"What would you have?" said Wilhelm. Then with a sudden inspiration: "A woman has every right to love; but then you have loved—twice."

"No, no, not even once. I thought so perhaps, but—"

"But, according to your own assertion this afternoon, one has been in love really if only one seriously believes one is. And it is thankless to deny one's love later on. Do not contradict yourself."

"And you, monsieur le philosophe," she returned, raising her head, and her burning gaze encompassed him as with a circle of fire, "do you not contradict yourself too? A little while ago you were demonstrating to me that you were a part of nature, and that unknown natural forces were at work within you, directing all you did, and to-day you extol the mortification of the flesh, which certainly has nothing to do with your unknown natural forces."

He was going to reply, but she laid her soft hand upon his mouth.

"Oh, please, monsieur le philosophe, do not prove to me that I am wrong. Be indulgent to my inconsistencies, as well as to everything else, I know I am full of contradictions. I am no German philosopher. But nature too is full of contradictions—first day, then night—now summer, now winter. But in spite of it all I can be very consistent and true to myself in a question of real importance."

Wilhelm drew away from the hand that caressed his lips and cheek, and said, averting his eyes:

"You are a beautiful woman, and have a most exceptional mind, and it must be happiness indeed to be loved by you, but in order that that happiness might be full, one would have to love you in return, and there are men—I do not know whether to call them too proud or too fastidious—who can only love with their whole heart or not at all, and who cannot endure that the woman they love should treasure another image or other memories in her life."

"Stop, my friend, stop!" cried the countess. "You do not realize what you are saying. That comes of your pride and vanity. You always want to be the first—to write your names at the head of a blank sheet. Why? Is the conquest of a silly, ignorant girl more flattering than that of a woman of sense, who can compare and judge? Is not your triumph a thousand times greater when a disappointed, deeply-skeptical woman lays her heart at your feet, and says—'You I will trust, you will bring me healing and happiness'—than when a young girl gives you her love because you happen to be the first man who asks for it? Other images!—other memories! Do you know so little of a woman's heart? Do you imagine that the past exists for us when real true love comes upon us? We see nothing in the whole world but the one man, we cannot believe that our heart has not always beat for him, and we are firmly persuaded that we have always known and always loved him and him alone."

The eyes that gazed at him glowed with maenad-like desire, and bending suddenly she covered his hand with lingering, burning kisses.

Wilhelm passed his hand soothingly over the masses of her silky hair, and it flashed across him how much he had once wished to be able to do so, and now his wish was fulfilled. Was fulfilled desire really happiness, as this beautiful woman asserted? His heart beat loud and fast; he was conscious of emotions long unfelt, and—yes, these emotions were pleasant ones.

He moved as if to rise, but she clung to his arm to hold him back. He pointed to the door of the room from which Anne might appear at any moment.

"Do have a little more pride of spirit," said the countess; "one does what one likes, without caring what the servants think."

"Let me go," he entreated, and stroked her beautiful hair.

"Why?"

"It is late, and the air in here is close. I should like to take a turn by the sea. Please—"

She looked at him, and a mysterious smile played about her full lips; she dropped his arm.

He hastened away toward the shore, where the waves were rolling in, rattling the pebbles and striking the cliff with dull, heavy thuds. The August night was mild and full of stars, and there was scarcely a breath of wind. The tide was rising, wave after wave rolled in, fell over, and swept up the beach in a thin white sheet of foam. Further out the sea was calm and deserted, only in the extreme distance the lights of some passing steamer crept over the smooth dark waters like tiny glowworms.

Wilhelm's mind was in a tumult. This woman—what a strange, terrifying creature. Why was she throwing herself at his head? And who knows if only at his? And then—what need to tell him her story? Perhaps it was a wild, insane flare of passion; but how could he have roused it? There was nothing in him to account for it. And she did not know him—knew nothing about his life or his character. She was beautiful certainly—beautiful and alluring, and clever and original—a most exceptional woman. She might well be able to disarm a man of his self-control, and paralyze his will. But after that—what then? How would it end? Better not begin—not begin. That would be the wisest ending.

He left the shore and returned to the hotel. The view before him was remarkable. At the further end of the street rose the church, its Gothic flourishes outlined sharply against the lighter background of the sky. Just behind it stood the full moon, tracing—as if for its amusement—the silhouette of the roof of the church tower upon the ground. Where the shadow of the church ended, the moon poured its silvery light in a broad flood over the street, and further off painted, with, a bold stroke of the brush, a glittering streak of white light across the sea, away to the semi-transparent mists on the horizon.

Passing first through the shimmering light, and then through the black shadow of the church, Wilhelm reached the hotel, where the lights were already extinguished. Without lighting the candle, which he found ready for him at the foot of the stairs, he mounted to his room. He was surprised, on reaching the door, to find Fido lying in front of it, his nose resting on his outstretched paws.

"I suppose they have shut you out, and you want a night's lodging with me," said Wilhelm; "very well, I won't refuse you my hospitality—come in."

He opened the door and let the dog pass in before him, then followed, pushed the bolt, and put the candlestick down on the table. Suddenly two cool, bare arms were laid about his neck, and his startled cry was smothered by the pressure of two burning lips upon his own.

CHAPTER XI.

IN THE HORSELBERG

The good landlady of the Hotel de France was not a little surprised next morning when Wilhelm came down to the kitchen and informed her that he must leave that forenoon. And when very soon afterward Anne appeared, and announced in her stiffest, most impenetrable manner that Madame la Comtesse desired two places, for herself and her maid, in the hotel omnibus which went to the station at Eu, the landlady remarked, "Indeed!" and there was a liberal interchange of meaning glances in the kitchen.

At no price would Wilhelm remain at Ault. The countess, who liked the place well enough, begged, entreated, and pouted in vain. He was not to be persuaded. He protested that he knew himself too well to think that he would be capable of keeping up the appearance of reserve toward her which decency demanded. And he need not, she declared; she considered herself free to do as she pleased, and so was he; their love did not interfere with their duty toward anybody, and so it was immaterial if people found it out and talked about it.

Her utter disregard for the trammels of convention, her cool contempt for the opinion of others, filled him with horror.

"No, no, I could not look one of them in the face again."

"But do you suppose that these people are any better? You surely don't imagine that the man with the calves and his ravening wolf are married?"

"How can you say such things!"

"Why, you big baby, one can see that at a glance. He is far too nice to her for her to be his legitimate."

"That may be. At all events he has had so much consideration for outward appearance as to pass the person off as his wife. But we made our acquaintance here, under their very eye."

"Wilhelm!"—from her lips the name sounded more like Gwillem—"I should not know you for the same person. Why, where is your boasted philosophy and stoicism to which you were going to convert me? Is that your indifference to the world and its hypocritical ways, its prejudices and its sneers?"

She was quite right. He was untrue to his principles, but he could not do otherwise. He had had the courage to decline the duel with Herr von

Pechlar, but he had not the boldness to let the foolish gossips of the table d'hote be witnesses of his new love-making. Why? For the very simple reason that, in his heart of hearts, he disapproved of his liaison with Pilar.

As he would not give in, the countess resigned herself to what she called his "schoolgirl crotchet," and they traveled together to St. Valery-en-Caux, another little seaside place several hours' journey from Ault.

Here they took rooms together at a hotel, and wrote themselves down as man and wife. The countess' letters were forwarded by the postmistress at Ault under cover to Anne. The only thing that disturbed Wilhelm's peace of mind was the presence of Anne. Her manner was just as impassive, her face as solemn as before, and she never showed that she noticed any change in her mistress way of life. But it was just this cold-blooded acceptance of facts which must at the very least excite her remark that upset him so much, and every time Anne came into the room and found him with Pilar, he was as much ashamed as if she had surprised him in some cowardly and wicked deed. Did he happen to be sitting beside her on the sofa, he started as if to jump up; if he had hold of her hand, he dropped it on the spot. Pilar noticed it, of course, and thought it an excellent joke. She was herself perfectly unconcerned before Anne, and put no constraint on herself whatever in her presence. On the contrary, she thought it great fun to throw her arms round Wilhelm when the maid came and he attempted to move away, or she would tutoyer him and kiss him to her face, and was intensely amused at his embarrassed and miserable air as he suffered her caresses, though not without a stolen gesture of objection. His shyness was not unobserved by Anne's quick though furtive eyes, and she owed him a grudge for wishing to exclude her from his secret.

But with the exception of the discomfort caused him by this silent witness, his happiness was unalloyed. He lived in a constant rapture of the senses, and Pilar took good care that he should not awake from it. She never left him to himself, except during the two hours in the morning which she devoted to her toilette. It was her peculiar habit to steal away in the early morning while Wilhelm was still asleep, and repair noiselessly to the dressing-room, where Anne was already waiting, and where she gave herself up into the skilled hands of the maid, who kneaded her, washed and rubbed her, and treated her hands, feet, and hair with consummate art, and the aid of an army of curious instruments and an exhaustive collection of cosmetics. She would then appear to wake Wilhelm with a kiss. On opening his eyes it was to see her in the full glory of her beauty, with the flush of health upon her cheeks, with rosy fingers, her skin cool, soft and perfumed, her eyes bright, her lips smiling, and her magnificent hair in order. But from that moment onward she was always about him, nestling close to him when they were alone, her eyes on his when they walked arm in arm through the streets.

In the morning she bathed in the sea while Wilhelm sat on the shore and watched her. She swam like a fish; he could not swim at all. She pledged her word to make him equally proficient in a few days, but her superiority made him feel small, and he would not accept her offer. For twenty minutes she practiced her art in the water, lay on her back and on her side, turned somersaults, dived, trod the water and finally came out, like Venus newly risen from the waves, and joined Wilhelm, who was waiting for her with her bath-mantle. He enveloped her in its soft folds, she roguishly shook the drops of water off her rosy finger-tips into his face and hurried to her bathing house without a glance for the spectators who had been watching her graceful play in the water, and devoured her with their eyes when she came on dry land.

The rest of the day was filled up by long walks broken by delightful rests under the shade of cornricks on grassy hillslopes beside some purling brook. Then Pilar would sit on the rug or the camp stool, while Wilhelm lay at her feet with his head in her lap caressed by the little hands that played with his hair or wandered softly over his face, resting fondly on his lips for him to kiss. If there were flowers within reach, she would pluck a quantity and strew his head and face with the fresh petals, while he gazed alternately into the blue summer sky and the bright brown eyes above him, or even closed his own for quarters of an hour of delicious dreaming. Then everything outside his immediate surroundings would fade from his mind, and he would be conscious only of what was nearest to him, the faint scent of ylang-ylang that hovered round the beautiful woman, her smooth, caressing fingers, and the low sound of her deep, regular breathing.

"You are so handsome," she whispered in his ear on one such occasion, and bending over him to kiss him; "do you know, I shall draw your portrait."

"Can you draw?" he asked, raising himself on his elbow.

"I hardly know whether I ought to say yes," she returned, with an arch, self-conscious smile that belied the humility of her tone. "But you shall see."

"Very well," said he, "and while you are drawing my portrait I shall draw yours."

"Bravo!" she cried, and wanted to go home at once, so that they might begin.

As was his custom, Wilhelm had all that was needful in his big trunk, and could supply Pilar with materials. The next afternoon they set to work. They established themselves in the middle of a great meadow, committing thereby an extreme act of trespass, and making their way to it over a ditch, a low wall, and through a blackberry hedge. Here no prying eye would annoy them, their sole and most discreet spectator being Fido, and he was generally asleep.

Pilar had a drawing-block and used a pencil, Wilhelm sketched his picture on a page of a large album in colored chalks like a pastel. She kept trying to peep at his work, but he would not allow it, and insisted on their making a compact not to look at one another's work of art till it was finished. Two sittings sufficed, however, and the portraits could be exchanged. Pilar gave a cry of surprise when Wilhelm handed her his picture.

"How strange that we should have had almost the same idea."

She was represented as a Sphinx, after the Greek rather than the Egyptian conception. A voluptuous, soft, round, feline body, graceful, cruel paws, a wonderful bosom as if hewn out of marble, and above it all Pilar's regally poised head with its crown of shimmering gold hair, shrewd eyes, and blood-red vampire lips. Between her forepaws she held a little trembling mouse in which Wilhelm's features were cleverly indicated, and she looked down upon her victim with a smile in which there was something of a foretaste of the joy of tearing a quivering creature to pieces and sucking its warm blood.

Pilar's drawing was a very good likeness of Wilhelm as Apollo in Olympian nudity, handsome, slender and vapid, in its resemblance to school copies of the antique. A charming little cat with Pilar's features was rubbing herself against his leg. The pussy blinked up at the young Greek god with an expression of adoration, half-comic, half-touching, while he bent his head and gazed down at her thoughtfully. Pilar took the sheet from Wilhelm's hand and compared it with hers.

"They are exactly the same," she said at last, "only that they are entirely the opposite of one another. Do you really feel that I am as you have drawn me?"

"Yes," he answered in a low voice.

"How unjust you are to yourself and to me—I a Sphinx and you a frightened mouse! To begin with, the Sphinx-cat did not condescend to mice, but occupied herself with men, and humbled herself before the right one when he came."

"You are decidedly too learned for me," laughed Wilhelm.

"No, no, seriously, it hurts me that you should regard our relations in that light. Am I not at your feet? Am I not your slave, your chattel, your plaything, what you will? Have I not chosen you to be lord and master over me? Am I a riddle to you? My love for you is the solution of any mystery you may find in me. Or do you accuse me of cruelty? That could only be in fun, you bad man."

"You take a mere playful idea too tragically, dearest Pilar. The character of your head suggested it to me, that was all. And then—"

"And then?"

"Well, if you must know it, the fearless, what shall I say, Amazon-like manner in which you seized upon a man and took possession of him, body and soul."

"Did I do that?"

He nodded.

"And you are mine?"

He nodded again.

"Tell me so, dearest, only love—say it."

He did not say it, but he kissed her.

"It is quite true," she remarked after a short pause, "I did take possession of you. That was unwomanly, but I could not help it. You are a cold-blooded German, and different from any man I ever knew before. You did not know how to appreciate the good fortune that befell you when chance set you down at my side in that dreary little hole. You abominable creature, for a whole fortnight you took not the slightest notice of me; you sat there beside me like a block, and never so much as looked at me. For a long time I did not know what to make of you. At first I tried to think you as ridiculous as the other idiots round the table, but I could not, try as I would. Your ugly owlish face had made too great an impression on me. And then I was annoyed by your reserve, and when I used to see you stalk in, looking so haughty, and you bowed so coldly to me and remained so distant, I thought to myself—just wait, monsieur the iceberg, some day you will be at my feet begging for love, and then it will be my turn to be proud, and I shall be triumphant."

"There you see the Sphinx and the mouse."

"Oh, but it all happened quite differently. I spoke first, I made you every sort of advance; and what did you do? You held forth to me on the mortification of the flesh. You ought to be ashamed of yourself. And even when I saw that love was burning in your eyes, you remained stiff-necked and tried to run away from me. If I was set upon happiness, I found I must take it by force. I know you better now. You were capable of never confessing your love to me, of never asking anything of me. Am I right or not, tell me?"

"You are right," he murmured.

"But that would have been a sin—a deadly sin, a capital crime against the High Majesty of Nature. What! Fate takes the trouble to think out the most improbable combinations, sets the most complicated machinery in motion to bring us together; it drags you out of the depths of Germany, and me from Castile, and brings us to a little hotel in a little village in Picardy, the very name of which was unknown to either of us a short time before; we instantly feel that we are made for one another and are certain to be happy together, and yet all these exertions on the part of Fate are to have been in vain? Never! Our paths crossed each other at a single point, for a moment they were united, it depended on us whether they should always remain so. And I was to let you go, never to meet again on this side of eternity? It was not possible, and as you were so clumsy, or so timid, or so self-torturing—"

She finished the sentence with a long kiss, at which he closed his eyes once more, and shut out everything but its flame.

Was it calculation, was it her natural instinct?—suffice it to say that Pilar never by any chance alluded in their conversations to her past. She was fond of talking, and talked a great deal, and her conversation was always startling, original and vivacious; her power of imagination as lively as her sparkling eyes, springing from the nearest object to the furthest, from the ordinary to the sublime, but never one word escaped her which might remind Wilhelm that she had gone through confessed and unconfessed experiences of every kind, and reached the turning-point of her existence without him. Her life, it would appear, had only begun with the moment at which he had risen upon her horizon. What went before that was torn out of the book of memory—one scarcely noticed the gaps where the pages were missing. She did all she could to make him forget that she was a stranger to him, and to strengthen in him the delusion that she belonged to him, that she was one with him, that it had always been so. She took possession of his past, she crept into his ideas and sentiments; she wanted to know everything about him, down to the smallest details. He must tell her about every day, every hour of his existence; she made the acquaintance of his entire circle of friends; she loathed Loulou, she adored Schrotter, she went into raptures over gentle, refined Bhani, she smiled at Paul Haber and his well-dressed Malvine, and her inventive grandmamma; she determined to send good Frau Muller (who had looked after Wilhelm for ten years like a mother) a beautiful Christmas present. She could make personal remarks on all his friends and acquaintances, and her only trouble was that she knew no German. What would she not have given to be able to read the letters he wrote or received, to converse with him in his mother-tongue! She loved and admired the French language, which, although she retained the ineradicable accent of her country, she spoke as fluently as Spanish; but now, for the first time, she felt something akin to hatred against it for being the one remaining barrier—certainly a very slight and scarcely perceptible one—between herself and Wilhelm, which forever drew his attention to the fact that she was not naturally a part of his life, and prevented their absolute union, the growing together of their souls. She therefore determined to learn German as soon as she returned to Paris, and, if need be, to stay for some length of time in Germany in order to master the language quickly and thoroughly.

She thought and spoke much of the future, and in all her dreams, plans, and resolves Wilhelm was always, and as a matter of course, the central figure and sharer of her life. In him her life found its consummation she had him fast, and would never let him go.

Her love was a curious mixture of ardent passion and melting, sentimental tenderness. At one moment the Bacchante, drinking long draughts of love and life from his lips, at another, the innocent girl who sought and found a chaste felicity in the mere rapturous contemplation of the man she adored. The longer she knew him, the deeper she penetrated into his character, the more did the Bacchante recede and yield her place to the Psyche. The allegory of Wilhelm's pastel seemed wrong, her own drawing right. She was no bloodthirsty Sphinx revelling in human victims, but a harmless little cat purring against the side of the young god. She was diffident, eager to learn, slow to contradict. She broke herself of her paradoxes, and concealed her originality. She liked best to listen while he talked. He must explain everything to her, enlarge her experience, correct and improve her judgment. Her favorite words were, give me, show me, tell me! From morning till night he must give, tell, show. The sea washed up a medusa to the shore—give it me! They surprised a crab in the act of shedding his armor—show me! A ride on donkeys to a neighboring village reminded him of a students' picnic at Heidelberg—tell me about it! Such of his peculiarities of temper as she did not understand, she guessed at and felt with her fine womanly instinct. If at Ault she had been extremely simple in her dress, here she was almost exaggeratedly so. She banished the "kohl" with which she had underlined her brilliant eyes, and strewed the violet powder to the four winds, as soon as she discovered that he preferred to stroke her full, firm cheeks when they were guiltless of powder. She dropped her former freedom of speech, gave up the telling of highly-spiced anecdotes, and checked her roving glances and the frolicsome imps—somewhat too deeply versed in Boccaccio—that haunted her lively brain, when she saw that he took umbrage at anything the least risky. Her cigarettes horrified him, so she threw them out of the window, and never smoked again. She even quelled the sensuality of her self-surrender, and veiled it with a show of shame-faced backwardness and the adorable ingenuousness of a schoolgirl on her honeymoon. She strove to obliterate the remembrances of the heathenish abandonment of the first days, with their unrestrained impulses, testifying all too plainly to the fact that she was a woman well versed in all the arts of seduction. At first this was dissimulation, the maneuvers of a shrewd, reader of character, but it soon came to be instinct and second nature; she deceived herself honestly, and returned, in her own mind, to the pristine virginity of her soul and body, finally coming to look upon herself as a simple-minded girl, ignorant of the world and of life, and conscious only of her boundless love for this one glorious man, and to whom the memories of a less harmless past seemed like wicked dreams sent by the Tempter to molest her chastity. This self-deception, or rather retrogression of her instincts, led her into touches of mysticism. The story of little Sonia who had fallen in love with the ten-year-old Wilhelm at first sight, to die shortly afterward with his name upon her lips, made a deep impression on her, and set her dreaming. "When sweet little Sonia died I was born." Now this was not quite accurate, as Pilar must have been at least two or three years old at the time, but mystic raptures take no count of time. "My life is a continuation of hers. Your Spanish love inherited the soul of your little Russian. Thus I have been yours since my birth—and before. I loved you before ever I knew you. I have had a presentiment of you, have felt and expected you from the beginning. Hence my troubled seeking all the time, hence my horror and shuddering when I discovered that I was mistaken, that it was not the one I yearned for whose image I bore secretly in my heart. Now I see why I was so irresistibly drawn to you from the first moment I set eyes on you. The man of my dreams stood in bodily shape before me. Here at last was my heart's dear image in flesh and blood. I had no need to get to know you; I knew you already. My own, my Wilhelm."

  Real tears rolled down her cheeks as she spoke, and Wilhelm was not sufficiently blase to scoff at the doting nonsense of a love-sick woman. Love has enormous power, and at its heat all firmness, all resistance, melts away. Pilar's affection filled Wilhelm with heartfelt emotion and gratitude. He denied himself the right of judging her, suspecting or doubting her, or of discovering dark spots upon her shining orb. As she was forever at his side, and made it her sole care to occupy him entirely, body and soul, his whole world was soon filled by her and her alone. Wherever he looked his eyes fell upon her; she intercepted his view on all sides. Her shadow fell even upon his past, as far back as his childhood. He failed to notice that whole days passed now without his giving a thought to Schrotter or Paul, and he was quite surprised when he discovered that he had left a letter from the former unanswered for a week. His former life began to fade and grow dim, and, compared to the sun-flooded, glowing present, looked like the dark background of a courtyard beside an open space in the full blaze of a summer day.

The whole society of the place was deeply interested in the handsome couple, who took so little trouble to conceal their love. The young people thought it most affecting, the older ones, especially the ladies, turned up their noses, with the remark that even people on their honeymoon might put some restraint upon themselves on the beach, or in the street. Wilhelm and Pilar were quite unconscious of the talk for which they furnished the material. They had no eyes for anybody but each other. They were unconscious of the flight of time. Their lives passed as in a morning dream, or a wondrous fairy-tale, where two lovers wander in a sunny garden among great flowers and singing birds, or rest, surrounded by attendant sprites, who fulfill each wish before it is uttered.

They were disagreeably brought back to the realities of life when one day Anne asked, with her most impassive air, when Madame la Comtesse thought of leaving, for if she were going to stay any longer, they must provide themselves with winter clothing. They had reached the end of September; it rained nearly every day, the streets of the village were impassable, sitting on the shore out of the question, the equinoctial gales howled across the country from the tempestuous sea; all the world had gone home, and Wilhelm and Pilar were the last guests in the desolate hotel, spending most of the day in their room, where an inadequate fire spluttered on the hearth. For a fortnight past Anne had boiled with silent rage, which she sometimes let out on poor, snorting, asthmatic Fido. She had been absent from Paris since the middle of July, and had counted on being back by the beginning of September at the latest, and here was October coming upon them in this God-forsaken little hole, and her mistress showed no signs of returning home.

Anne's question came like a rough hand to shake Pilar out of sleep. Like a drowsy child who does not want to get up, she kept her eyes closed for awhile. Another week! Four days more! Two days more! But then she had to pack, for Anne exaggerated a slight cold, and at short intervals let off a dry cough with the suddenness and force of a pistol-shot, tied her head up in a white shawl, and begged to be allowed to send to Paris for warm underclothing and her fur cloak. In the hotel, too, from which all the servants had been dismissed, and only the landlord, his wife, and a half-grown daughter remained, the neglect became conspicuous. The rooms were not put in order till late in the evening, and even then the landlady would come and grumble that she could not manage so much work, and that was the reason everything was late. A leg of mutton appeared upon the table three days running, till nothing was left but the bone. In short, it was not to be misunderstood that the hotel family wished to be alone.

At last, at the beginning of the second week of October, the return to Paris took place. During the five hours' railway journey Pilar was silent and moody. She felt that an enchanting chapter of her love-story had come to an end, and a fresh one beginning, the unforeseen possibilities of which filled her with alarm. She held fast to Wilhelm, and would not let him go free; but what form was their life together going to take in Paris? Not that she cared for the opinion of the world—far from it; but other difficulties remained which menaced her happiness. At the seaside all the circumstances had combined to aid and befriend them. Surrounded by people to whom she and Wilhelm were alike strangers, they were thrown entirely upon one another, and even his scruples could find nothing to prevent him treating her openly as his wife. In Paris, on the other hand, all the circumstances became disturbing and inimical. Pilar had her circle of friends, and her accustomed way of life, to which Wilhelm would have to adapt himself. Would that occur without opposition on his part? Would not many a tender sentiment be wounded beyond the power of healing in that struggle? But of what avail were all these tormenting questions? She had to look the future in the face, and prepare to engage in a struggle in which he was determined to come off victorious.

From time to time she glanced at Wilhelm, and always found him deep in thought. He was reviewing, with a touch of self-mockery, the latest development of his affairs. Here he was on his way to Paris. He had not chosen this destination. Once again another will than his own had determined his path for him. He resigned himself without a struggle; he allowed himself to be taken along like an obedient child. Was it weakness? Perhaps. Possibly, however, it was not. Possibly he did not think it worth the trouble to call his will into play. Why should he, after all? As long as he might not live in Berlin, what did it matter where he lived? and Paris was as good a place as any other. To have resisted Pilar's persuasions would not have been an evidence of strength, but simply the obstinacy of a conceited fool, who wants to prove to himself that he is capable of setting somebody else at defiance. So that after all he was going to Paris because he wished it, or rather, because he saw no reason for not doing so. But as he spun the web of these thoughts in his mind, he heard all the time a still small voice, which contradicted him, and whispered: "It is not true. You are not your own master; you are going you know not whither; you are doing you know not what. Two beautiful eyes are your guiding star, and in following their magic beckoning your feet may slip at any moment, and you may be hurled into unknown depths."

Pilar must have divined that Wilhelm's thoughts were enemies to her peace, and must be dispersed. They were alone in the carriage, and she could give free rein to her feelings. She took his hand and kissed it, and laying her arm round his neck, she said fondly:

"Don't be so depressed, Wilhelm. Of course it is only natural that one should be afraid of any change after one has been so happy, but you shall have no cause to regret St. Valery. You will see, it will be still nicer in Paris. We remain the same as we were before, and surely my little home is a more fitting frame for our love than the bare room at the hotel!"

Wilhelm started back.

"You surely do not imagine that I am going to live in your house?" he cried.

"But there can be no question about it!" she answered in surprise.

"Never!" Wilhelm declared, with a determination that frightened Pilar, it was so new to her. "How could you think of such a thing?"

"But, Wilhelm," she returned, "what else could we do? I should not like to think that it was your plan we should part at the station and each go our different ways. If I believed that, I would throw myself under the wheels of the train this very instant. We have not been indulging in a little summer romance, entertaining enough at the seaside, but which must die a natural death as soon as we return to Paris. My love is a serious matter to me, and to you too, I hope. You are mine forever, and as long as there is life in this hand, it will hold you fast," and she cast herself passionately upon his breast, and clung to him as if he were going to be torn from her.

"I never said I would leave you," he returned gently, and trying to disengage himself; "but it is quite inconceivable that you should have thought you would simply bring me back with you from the journey and present me to your people."

"My people! You are my all, and nobody else exists for me."

"One says that in the heat of the moment, but you have relations—you told me so yourself. What will they think of us if I calmly settle down in your house?"

"Think?—always what people will think. That is the only fault you have, Wilhelm. How can you do people the honor to take them into consideration when it is a question of my life's happiness? Let them think what they like. They will think you are the master and I am your slave, who only lives in and for you."

Wilhelm only shook his head, for he was unwilling to wound her by saying what he thought of such an unworthy connection. She hung trembling on his looks, and asked, as he still did not answer:

"Well, darling, is it to be my way? We will drive quietly home and pretend we are at St. Valery?"

"No," he answered firmly, "that is impossible. I shall go to an hotel. No, do not try to dissuade me, for it would be useless."

"And you can let me go from you?"

"Only for a few hours. We shall be in the same town, and can see one another as often as we like."

"And you would be satisfied with that?"

"It will have to be so, as the circumstances will not permit of anything else."

She broke into a storm of tears, and sobbed, "You do not love me."

He soothed and comforted her; he kissed her eyes, he pressed her head to his heart, and tried to calm her as he would a child, but it was long before he brought her round. At last she raised her head and asked:

"You are determined to go to an hotel?"

"I must, dear heart."

"Very well; then I shall go too."

He had nothing to say against this and so it was settled.

It was close upon midnight when the train ran into the St. Lazare station. Anne came hurrying from the next carriage.

"You can drive home," said Pilar to her. "Take the large boxes with you. You can leave the small one and the portmanteau with me. I am going with monsieur. I shall come round to-morrow and see if things are in order."

Anne opened her eyes in astonishment, but her face did not betray any further emotion, and she answered calmly:

"Very good, Madame la Comtesse. Auguste is here with a cab. Does madame desire to use it?"

"No, Auguste can get us another. You take his."

Auguste, the man-servant, had come up meanwhile and greeted his mistress. He shot a quick glance at the strange gentleman on whose arm she leaned, but it was more expressive of curiosity than surprise; he then hurried away to carry out the remarkable orders Anne had dryly transmitted to him. Soon after he reappeared, and announced that the other fiacre was there. Fido, released from the captivity of the dog-box, sprang upon the countess with short-breathed barks that soon degenerated into a cough, and wagged his tail and frolicked madly about. When Pilar and Wilhelm entered their cab, Anne and Auguste remaining outside, the dog seemed undecided as to which party he was to follow. Chancing to catch Wilhelm's eye, he made up his mind, jumped into the cab, regardless of Anne's angry call, and licked Wilhelm's hand delightedly, accepting his friendly pat as an invitation to stay.

By Pilar's direction the cab took them to an hotel in the Rue de Rivoli. As they drove along Pilar leaned silently in her corner, only heaving a deep sigh from time to time; and Wilhelm, too, found nothing to say, oppressed as he was by the consciousness of being in an untenable situation, the eventual end of which he could not foresee. Arrived at the hotel, they retired at once to their rooms and to rest, scarcely touching the supper which Pilar had ordered rather for Wilhelm than herself. She lay awake for hours, and it was daybreak before she got any sleep.

It was nearly midday when she opened her eyes. Wilhelm was sitting fully dressed at the window that faced the Tuileries, gazing down upon the dreary autumnal park with its trees half-bare, the paths covered with dead leaves—its marble statues and silent fountains. She stretched out her arms to him, and he hastened over to kiss her fondly. As her eye fell upon her tiny jeweled watch, she gave a cry of dismay.

"Twelve o'clock! Oh, go away—quick—and send the chambermaid to me. I will do my best to be ready soon. Wait for me in the salon. You can read the papers or write letters. But whatever you do, you must not leave the hotel—do you hear?"

An hour later she appeared in the salon to fetch him to lunch, which was served in their room. Pilar was nervous and put out. The chambermaid's assistance had not been all that she could have wished. The slow waiting at lunch vexed her. Whatever trifle she might require she was obliged to go into the untidy bedroom herself and search in her boxes. Her head was full of schemes and plans, to none of which, however, she gave expression. Never had she had such an uncomfortable meal with Wilhelm.

"What are you going to do now?" asked Wilhelm, when the waiter had cleared the table.

"I think we had better go and have a look at our house," answered Pilar, trying hard to assume a perfectly unconcerned tone.

"Of course," said Wilhelm; "and while you go home, I will take a look at the streets of Paris."

"What—you are not coming with me?"

"I think it better you should go by yourself the first time. You have no doubt got a good deal to set in order, and I should only be in the way."

"Wilhelm," she said very gravely, "you are determined to hurt me. Have I deserved that of you?"

"But, dearest Pilar—"

"I want proofs that I am your dearest Pilar. I have given myself to you—body, soul and spirit. If you want my life as well, then say so. I should be overjoyed to give it you. And you? Since yesterday your every word and look tells me plainly that you regard me as a stranger, and want to have nothing more to do with me. Oh, yes, you do it all in a very delicate and considerate manner, that is your way, but there is no need to speak more plainly to me."

"Do not excite yourself Pilar, I assure you that you are entirely wrong."

She shook her head.

"I am not a child. Let us talk it over seriously. I told you yesterday I would not let you go. Of course you understand what I mean by that. I will not keep you if you want to be free. But then be honest, and tell me frankly that you are tired of me, and want to be rid of me. I shall at least know what I have to do. Do not be afraid, I shall not make a scene, I shall not cause you any annoyance, not even reproach you. I shall receive my sentence of death in silence, and kiss the hand that inflicts it on me."

She buried her face in her hands, and tears trickled down between her fingers.

"And all this," said Wilhelm, "because I thought it better not to accompany you to-day. The whole affair is not worth one of your tears."

"Then you will come with me?" she cried excitedly, lifting her face to his.

"I suppose I shall have to, since you talk about death sentences and terrible things of the kind."

She embraced him frantically, rang the bell, threw the things that lay about anyhow into the box, and when the waiter came, ordered a carriage. As they went downstairs she gave a hurried order in the office, and with a beaming and triumphant face, passed through the hall on Wilhelm's arm to the carriage.

Their destination was a small house on the Boulevard Pereire, of two stories, three windows wide, and a balcony in front of the first-floor windows. At Wilhelm's ring the door was opened by Anne, who made him a careless courtesy, but greeted her mistress respectfully. Wilhelm was going to let Pilar precede him, but she said: "No, no; you go first. It is a better omen."

Assembled in the hall they found Auguste, an old woman with a red nose, and a man not in livery, who expressed their satisfaction at their mistress' return, and complimented her on her improved appearance, but were in reality chiefly engaged in taking stock of Wilhelm while they did so. Pilar gave the man some direction in Spanish, and then drew Wilhelm into the salon, which opened into the hall.

"Welcome, a thousand times, to this house," she said, clasping him in her arms; "and may your coming bring happiness to us both. I will take off my things now, and say a word, to my servants, and be with you again directly."

With that she hurried away, and Wilhelm found himself alone. He looked about him. The salon was luxuriously, if, according to Wilhelm's taste, somewhat gaudily furnished. The walls were draped in yellow silk, the portieres, window-curtains, and gilt-backed chairs being of the same brilliant hue, though its monotony was fortunately broken by numerous oil paintings, forming, as it were, dark islands in a sea of sulphur. Opposite to the window hung two life-sized portraits of a lady and an officer. The lady wore a Spanish costume with a mantilla, the gentleman a gorgeously embroidered general's uniform, with a quantity of stars and orders, and the ribbon of the Grand Cross. In another life-sized picture this personage figured in the robes of some unknown military order, and appeared a third time as a bronze bust in a corner, on a black marble pedestal. The chimney-piece was adorned by a strange and wonderful clock, a painfully accurate copy in gilt and colored enamel of the Mihrab of the Mosque in Cordova. Between the windows, on a high buhl cabinet, stood a marble bust of Queen Isabella, a gift, according to an inscription on the base, to her valued Adjutant-General Marquis de Henares. A charming pastel under glass showed Pilar as a very young girl. As Wilhelm gazed at the dewy freshness of this sixteen-year-old budding beauty, the dazzling complexion of milk and roses, the sparkle of the merry, childish eyes, an immense tenderness came over him, and he thought to himself that surely nature had not sufficiently protected all these charms against the desire they must necessarily awaken in the beholder. Such a ravishing creature might well be excused if her heart led her astray. How could she choose aright when her beauty roused men's passion before she had had time to gain experience or judgment enough to defend herself?

There were a thousand other attractions in this room. A picture, or rather a sketch, by Goya, with all the fantastic want of finish, the gorgeous dabs of color that make so many of that master's works like the visions of delirium; on an inlaid table, a little Moorish casket, through the crystal lid of which one saw a collection of old Spanish coins of astounding dimensions; a small cabinet on the wall, containing stars and orders, with their chains, on a white satin ground; a trophy formed of a sword, gold spurs, epaulettes, and a gold-fringed scarf; here and there great Catalonian knives with open blades, daggers in rich sheaths and with engraved handles, and even an open velvet-lined case with a pair of chased ivory pistols. Some photographs on the chimney-piece and on the gold brocade-covered piano arrested Wilhelm's attention. First of all, Pilar in two different positions, then the pictures of three children, a girl and two boys, and finally the full-length portrait of a gentleman in the embroidered dress coat and sword of the diplomatic service, and the handsome, vacuous, carefully groomed head of a fashion plate.

Wilhelm was engaged in studying this face, with its fashionably twirled mustache, when Pilar entered the room.

"You have changed your dress?" cried Wilhelm, surprised; for she had donned an emerald-green velvet tea-gown, with a long train, and her hair was hanging down.

"Yes," said she, as she kissed him fondly, "for we are not going away again just yet. You will stay and dine with me—I have given the necessary orders. You must be quite sick of the monotonous hotel meals. For my part, I simply yearn to eat at my own table with you."

So saying, she took his hat out of his hand, coaxingly relieved him of his greatcoat, then rang and ordered Auguste to take them away. Taking advantage of this distraction of Wilhelm's attention, she rapidly snatched up the photograph he had been examining when she came in, and hid it under the piano-cover. She then opened the piano, seated herself, and gazing passionately over her shoulder at Wilhelm standing behind her, she began playing the Wedding March out of "Midsummer Night's Dream." The melodious sounds rushed from under her fingers like a flight of startled doves, and fluttered about her, joyous and exultant. She went on with immense power and brilliancy till she came to the first repetition of the triumphant opening motif, with its jubilant blare of trumpets, then stopped abruptly, and jumping up and throwing her arms round Wilhelm:

"Isn't it that, my one and only Wilhelm?" she said, with a beaming look.

"My sweetest Pilar," he answered, and clasped her to his breast. His heart was really full to overflowing at that moment She took his arm and proceeded to lead him about the room, showing and explaining the various objects to him. "This is my mamma as she looked twenty-five years ago, when she went to the Feria at Seville. That is a sort of fair at Easter, and one of the most famous popular festivals of Spain. We must go to it some day together. And that is my late father as major-general. Here he is in the robes of a Knight of San Iago, one of our highest military orders. It has existed since the twelfth century, and, strangely enough, one of my ancestors was among its first members. These are my father's decorations and badges of office. Come and look at this clock, it is quite unique. The province of Cordova had it made, and presented it to my father when he gave up his command there. I suppose you recognized this pastel. It is a very good likeness. Do you think it pretty?"

"Pretty! The word is a gross injustice. Say rather exquisitely, ravishingly beautiful."

"Thanks, my Wilhelm. And if you had known me then, you would have loved me and wanted to marry me, would you not?"

"But you would hardly have wanted to marry me, a poor devil of a plebeian, who was badly dressed and did not even know how to dance."

"Do not make fun of me, you sweet, bad creature; if I had had as much sense then as I have now, I should have loved you then as I love you now, and I would have belonged to you, even if it had cost me my father's love." She gazed thoughtfully at the picture in which her innocent past confronted her in so angelic a form, and continued in tones of indescribable tenderness: "Why did I not know you sooner? Is it my fault that you who were made for me should live so far away and wait so long before you came to me? How I should have rejoiced to be able to offer you the pure young creature of this picture! But I can but give you all I have—my first real love, the virginity of my heart—surely that is something?"

Her hazel eyes pleaded for a great deal of compassion, and her full scarlet lips for a great deal of love, and only a heart of cast iron could have refused her either.

Beyond the salon was a roomy dining-room, hung with magnificent Cordova leather, and from this a glass door led into a pretty little garden with an arbor in the corner, and some old trees. High, ivy-clad walls inclosed the square green spot of nature. Up the stairs, on the walls of which hung many valuable pictures, for which there was no place in the rooms, Pilar and Wilhelm mounted to the second floor. They entered first a red salon with windows opening on to the balcony and in which the all-pervading scent of ylang-ylang betrayed that it was the favorite apartment of the lady of the house. She did not keep Wilhelm long in this dainty bower, but drew him into the large bedroom adjoining. The walls were draped with Japanese silk, patterned with strange landscapes, fabulous flowers, gay-colored birds on the wing, and a network of twining creatures, and drawn together at the ceiling like the roof of a tent. Out of the soft folds of the center rosette hung a lamp with golden dragons on its pink globe. There was a wardrobe with looking-glass doors, a toilette table, an immense bed of carved ebony inlaid with scenes from the antique in ivory, and chairs covered with Persian stuffs. Beside all this there was an old oak Gothic priedieu, a small altar draped in rose color and white lace, a mass of flowers, and numerous crucifixes and Madonnas of various sizes in silver, ivory and alabaster.

"Are you so devout? That is news to me," exclaimed Wilhelm, surprised. He little knew that the first thing Pilar had done on entering the house was to hasten to her bedroom, kiss the holy silver Madonna del Pilar with deepest devotion, and kneel for a few moments on her priedieu.

"Oh, no, I am not at all devout. I am just the pagan you have always known. But—que voulez-vouz?—one has old habits. I regard the Blessed Virgin chiefly in the light of Our Lady of Sorrows, whose heart is pierced with seven swords, and Christ as the eternal type of sublimest love. You are a heretic, but I know that pictures and symbols are not as offensive to you as to certain vulgar free-thinkers."

Going up to the bed, she clung still more fondly to Wilhelm, and murmured in coy and halting tones—"Perhaps you have not noticed that everything in this room, except the altar and the priedieu, is new; I had this fresh little nest arranged for us while we were in St. Valery. I hope our rest may be sweet and our dreams happy ones."

He sought nervously for some appropriate answer, but she gave him no time, and opening a door in the wall beside the fireplace, she went on—"And this is your room. Tell me, have I guessed your taste?"

Without even glancing into the cozy, one-windowed room, he said, taking Pilar's hand in his: "Why torture me, Pilar?—you know it cannot be."

"Wilhelm!" her voice was firm, and she looked him full in the eyes, "do you love me?"

"You know it."

"Do we belong to each other?"

"Yes—and no."

"That is not a straightforward answer. We do belong to one another. You know perfectly well that if I were free you would marry me, and then you certainly would have no scruples in coming into this house as its master. Where is the difference?"

"You know where the difference lies."

"It is enough to drive one crazy! Is a paltry prejudice to triumph over our right to be happy? We are both of age. We are accountable to no one on earth for our actions. An insurmountable obstacle, for the moment, prevents us making our relations respectable in the eyes of the butcher, the baker, and the candlestick-maker by paying a few francs to a registry-office and a priest.

Has the mumbling of a priest so much meaning for you? Must you first enjoy the edifying spectacle of a mavre in a fringed scarf before you can feel like my husband? Or do you want any one else's consent? My father is dead, but my mother would adore you and do anything in the world for you, if I told her you made her only child unspeakably happy. What more do you want?"

"I could not reconcile myself to such a position, There is nothing to be said against your arguments. But for me to live on you—"

"For shame!" she cried, and tapped him lightly on the cheek with her forefinger. "Ah, you see I love you better than you love me. If you were very rich and I had not a penny, I would not hesitate for an instant to accept everything from you. I trust my heart is of more value to you than this paltry little house and its sticks of furniture. You have my heart—what is all the rest compared with that?"

He still shook his head unconvinced, but she knelt before him and said imploringly: "Wilhelm, you will not hurt me so. Even if it costs you a great deal, make this sacrifice for my sake. Give it a trial. You will see how soon you will get accustomed to it. And if not, then I am ready to go with you to the ends of the earth—to the Black Forest—wherever you will. Only try it, Wilhelm—have pity on me."

He stooped to lift her up, but reading in his eyes that he was yielding, she sprang to her feet and threw herself, gleeful as a child, upon his breast. Her victory filled her with such joy she could have shouted it out of the windows. She coaxed and fondled Wilhelm, called him by every endearing name, drew him over to the long mirror that he might see how handsome he was, dragged him into his room and then back into the bedroom, and required a considerable time to recover her self-control.

Meanwhile it had grown dark. She did not notice it till now, and rang for Anne to bring lamps.

"Has Don Pablo come back?" she asked of the maid.

"Half an hour ago, madame."

"Then send up the boxes at once."

"You have sent for the luggage already?" was Wilhelm's astonished inquiry when Anne had left the room.

"Naturally, my darling. I was certain, you know, that you would not break your Pilar's heart."

Auguste and the man whom Pilar called Don Pablo now carried up the one small box and two large ones Wilhelm always took about with him. Pilar asked him for the keys, and proceeded to put away his belongings in the various receptacles of the room. She would not suffer him to help her. Only his books she allowed him to pile up in a corner for the present; their orderly arrangement in the bookcase was put off till the daylight.

At dinner Pilar was in the seventh heaven, and more in love than ever before. In her wild spirits she threw all her glasses into the garden, and would only drink out of Wilhelm's. It was a real banquet: costly Spanish wines, red and white, rough and sweet, from her well-stocked cellar, accompanied by choice dishes, and finally champagne, of which Pilar partook—valiantly. After dessert she skipped into the salon, put the champagne glass down on the piano, and between sips and kisses played and sang Spanish love-songs that drove the flames to her cheeks. That evening she was all Bacchante. In the bedroom she tore off her clothes with impatient fingers, and held out her small, high-bred feet for Wilhelm to pull off her silk stockings. He knelt and kissed the little feet, while she gazed down at him with burning misty eyes, and between the blood-red lips slightly parted in a wanton smile gleamed pearly teeth that looked as if they could bite with satisfaction into a quivering heart. It was the Sphinx and the poor trembling mouse in the dust before her to the life.

When Wilhelm awoke next morning, he saw Pilar standing all fresh and ready at the bedside to greet him with a happy smile. With her iron nerves and superabundant animal strength, she required but little sleep, and had at once resumed her old habit of stealing away early to perform the rites of her toilette while he still slept.

He dressed quickly, she being occupied meanwhile in completing the coquettish adornment of his room with knots of ribbon, bouquets of flowers, Japanese fans, pictures and bronzes which she arranged with unerring taste on the walls beside the mirror, over the doors and window, or strewed about the secretaire, the table, or the chest of drawers, in studied negligence. They had breakfast in the red salon, after which she led him to her boudoir, which he had not yet seen, and that looked like a pink silk-lined jewel box. She drew up an armchair beside the crackling wood fire, begged Wilhelm to sit down put a little inlaid rosewood table before him, and out of a cabinet she fetched a large Russia leather pocketbook with a gold lock and laid it on the table.

"Let us settle these details once for all," she said to Wilhelm, who had watched her proceeding with surprise, "so that we need never refer to them again. You are my husband, and must relieve me now of all my business cares. Here—" she opened the pocketbook and spread out some formidable-looking papers, with stamps and seals attached, before him: "This is my check book, here the deposit receipts for my government stock and, bonds."

"What do you mean?" cried Wilhelm. "I understand nothing of such things; I have never had anything to do with them, and I am certainly not going to begin now, and with you." He gathered up the papers impatiently, thrust them back into the pocketbook, which he closed with a snap, and seeing Pilar standing there like a disappointed child balked of a surprise, he added: "However, I am grateful for the suggestion, as it helps me out of a dilemma. I was at a loss in what form to put what I must say to you—you have helped me in the nick of time. Pilar," he drew her on to his knee and kissed her, "at the seaside the matter was very simple, we had only to divide the bill between us. That will not do here. I am not well enough off to defray half the expense of such an establishment as yours."

"Oh, Wilhelm!" she exclaimed, horror-stricken, and attempted to jump down, but he held her fast and continued:

"I know this subject is painful to you, so it is to me; but, as you said yourself, it must be settled once for all. You must allow me to defray my own expenses as I would in a good family pension. I will put the trifling sum in your pocketbook once a month, and you will have a little more for your poor—one cannot have too much for them."

"I am simply petrified," murmured Pilar, "that you can take such a thing into consideration?"

"It is the one condition on which I stay here," returned Wilhelm firmly.

"What a dreadful proud boy you are! You will not accept a thing from me, and I told you yesterday that I would never be too proud to share your possessions with you. And if you had married me, you would no doubt have scorned to touch my dowry, and wanted to pay me for your board too."

"Dear heart, I imagine the question is settled between us, and never to be discussed again. I simply cannot live free of expense in the house of my—"

"Your wife," she broke in hastily.

"Of my—wife."

"Very well," she said, resigning herself, "you must have your own way, I suppose. But explain to me, my Teutonic philosopher, how comes it that so high-bred a body and so noble a mind can contain a corner holding such a tradesman's idea? How can one make these commonplace calculations when one is in love? Are you Germans all like that, or is it an inherited weakness in your family?"

"In my family," he answered simply, and without a trace of bitterness, "as far back as I know of (though that is certainly not anything like as far as your ancestor, the first knight of San Iago), we have always worked for our living, and owed all to our own industry. I am the first who found the table ready spread for him, and who knows if it has been an advantage to me."

"Now you are making fun of my ancestors, you disagreeable man—when did I ever say such a silly thing?"

"I never said you did, but you asked an explanation of the German philosopher, and the German philosopher has done his best to give you one."

She locked her pocketbook in the cabinet again, and there the matter ended between them.

The rest of the household, which seemed to accept the establishing of the new guest without the faintest surprise, consisted, beside Anne, of the man-servant Auguste, a young, knowing-looking southern Frenchman, with a clean-shaven, lackey's face, the old Spanish cook Isabel, a colossal, unwieldly, hippopotamus-like person with a red nose, watery, bloodshot eyes, and a strident voice, and Don Pablo, who seemed to be a mixture of servant, major-domo, and the confidential attendant of the old plays. Pilar esteemed him highly, and always spoke of him in terms of respect. According to her, he came of a good Catalonian family, had served with the Carlists and received titles and orders of distinction from Don Carlos. After the downfall of the cause for which he had fought he had come to Paris like so many of his compatriots and Pilar had rescued him from terrible want. He did not live in the house, but had an attic somewhere in the town. Every morning he appeared at the Boulevard Pereire to receive Pilar's orders, was occupied during the whole day in going on errands and doing shopping of every description, and his work over returned late in the evening to his lodging. He was a tall, thin, middle-aged man with a long leathery face, a long painted nose, long oily hair, and long gray mustache. The entire loose, bony figure looked like a reflection in a concave glass—all distorted into length. Don Pablo had a deeply melancholy air, never smiled and spoke but little. During the few spare hours which the countess' service—in which his legs were chiefly in demand—permitted, he might be seen in a back room on the ground floor, engaged in manufacturing pictures out of gummed hair—an art in which he was a proficient. He had even achieved a portrait of Pilar in blonde, brown, and red hair. It looked like the queen in a pack of cards, but Don Pablo was very proud of the masterpiece, and never forgave Pilar for not hanging it in one of the salons, but in quite another place. It was this accomplishment of his which led Auguste to declare firmly and with conviction that he was nothing more nor less than a common hairdresser. The relations between the two were altogether very strained. Auguste was annoyed by the Spaniard's high-and-mighty airs, and his French instincts of equality revolted against Don Pablo's pretensions to be better than the rest of the servants. They had their meals in common, but Don Pablo occupied the seat of honor and demanded to be waited upon, while Auguste, Anne and Isabel had to be content to wait upon themselves. As ill-luck would have it, Auguste had once got a sight of Don Pablo's uniform and great order; whereupon he instantly cut out a monstrous tin star out of the lid of a sardine box and wore it at meals. Don Pablo was so furious that he spoke seriously of challenging Auguste to a duel to the death, and it required a stern order from the countess to make him give up his bloodthirsty design and Auguste his practical joke.

The sharp-tongued Anne and noisy old Isabel were on a similar warlike footing. The maid was jealous of the cook because she had long, secret confabulations with the countess, who let her do exactly as she pleased, and even forgave her her pronounced liking for her excellent Val de Penas, of which she—Isabel—drank at least a barrel a year to her own account. One day Wilhelm, coming unexpectedly into the boudoir, surprised Pilar and the red-nosed cook together, the latter engaged in telling her mistress' fortune by the cards. This was the secret of Isabel's influence. She hurriedly took herself off with her cards, but Wilhelm shook his head: "I should not have believed it of my clever Pilar."

"What would you have?" she returned, half-laughing, half-ashamed; "we all of us have some little remnant of superstition in some dark corner of our minds. And after all, it is very odd that ever since our return she is continually turning up the knave of hearts." And as Wilhelm was obviously still unenlightened, she explained, "Barbarian, don't you know that that always means a sweetheart?"

Pilar arranged their life as if they were on their honeymoon. Every midday and evening meal was a banquet with flowers, choice dishes, and champagne, till Wilhelm forbade it; every day a drive in an elegant coupe; every evening to some theater in a half-concealed stage box, in which Pilar hid herself in the dim background. Wilhelm did not care for the theater, but Pilar insisted that he should become acquainted with the French stage. She showed him about Paris as if he were a schoolboy allowed to come to town in the holidays as a reward for having passed his examination well. And she was such an interesting, entertaining guide! She was thoroughly acquainted with the history or the anecdotes connected with the various streets and buildings, and on their way from the Column of July to the Opera House, from the Madeleine to the Arc de Triomphe, from the Odeon to the Pantheon, she unrolled a sparkling picture of Paris, past and present, now showing him the seething crowds of the lower classes and their customs and doings in good and bad hours, now describing well-known contemporaries with all that was absurd or commendable in them. Stories, scandals, traits of character, encounters she had had, adventures that had befallen her, all flowed from her lips in a gay, babbling, inexhaustible stream, and initiated her hearer into all the intricacies of Parisian life. She was as familiar with the galleries as with the famous buildings, and in front of the works of art in the one and the facades of the other she fired off a rocket-like shower of original remarks, paradoxes, and brilliant criticism. She knew exactly where to scoff and where to be enthusiastic, jeered with all the ruthless slang of the Paris gamins at the pompously mediocre sights recommended to the tourists' admiration by Baedeker, and gave evidence of deep and true comprehension of all that was really beautiful.

At the very beginning she dragged Wilhelm to a photographer's studio and disclosed to him, when it was too late to beat a retreat, that he was to be photographed. What for? A fancy of hers—she wanted to have his likeness. Half-length, full-length, full-face, profile. Only when the pictures were sent home did he discover, that she did not want them for herself, but to send to her mother. It was high time she should see what the man was like who alone made life worth living for her only child. That she should draw her mother into an affair of the kind of which women do not, as a rule, boast to their families, seemed to him peculiarly bad taste. "What," he cried, "you have told your mother the whole story?"

"My mother is a Spaniard, she will guess what one leaves unsaid."

"And you are not ashamed that she should know?"

"That is why I am sending her your likeness; she will then understand that, on the contrary, I have every reason to be proud."

What she did not consider it necessary to explain to him was, that she had palmed off a complete romance upon the Marquise de Henares, to the effect that Wilhelm had saved her life at Ault while bathing, that he was a celebrated German revolutionist, and the future President of the German Republic, to whom she was affording a refuge in her house because, for the time being, he was obliged to be in hiding from the German secret police, and so forth, and so forth.

The marquise believed every word. In her answer, she certainly reproached her daughter gently for having anything to do with foreign conspirators, but otherwise praised her evidence of gratitude toward her preserver, and frankly expressed her admiration for the handsome person of this interesting German. She even inclosed a note to him, in which she thanked him from her overflowing mother's heart for all he had done for her only child, and adjured him to be very prudent. He could make nothing out of it, and Pilar declared that she was equally in the dark. "I only see this much," she said in an off-hand manner, "that mamma loves you already, and will do still more so when she gets to know you personally. And that is all that matters."

It was on the second Sunday after their arrival in Paris that the children came to visit their mother. Pilar looked forward with some uneasiness to Wilhelm's first meeting with them, and he too felt far from comfortable when Pilar brought a half-grown girl and a ten-year old boy to him, and addressing herself to them said, "Embrace Monsieur le Docteur, and look at him well. He is the best friend your mother has on earth. You must love him very much, for he deserves it."

The girl was fair like her mother. She was already dressed with conspicuous elegance, and her manner betrayed extreme self-consciousness. She glanced at Wilhelm with sly and wanton eyes, in which it was easily to be read that she had a very good idea of the real state of the case. She offered her forehead for his kiss, bestowed a few cold and perfunctory caresses on her mother, and slipped away to Anne, with whom she spent the whole afternoon in eager whispered conversation, till the governess came to take her back to the fashionable boarding school where she was being trained to be a perfect great lady, and to make some enviable man happy in the future by the bestowal of her hand.

The boy, who was accompanied by a priest, and was being educated at a fashionable Jesuit institution, was of a better sort. He gave his hand to Wilhelm shyly but heartily, while his innocent eyes looked frankly and openly into his, and then hung over his mother with a tenderness that had a touch of chivalry in it—half-funny, half-affecting. Wilhelm felt decidedly drawn to the slender, healthy-looking boy.

But in the course of the afternoon another—a third child—appeared upon the scene; a lovely, brown, four-year-old boy, with bold black eyes and long raven curls, whom a maid-servant brought to Pilar that he might kiss his mamma.

Wilhelm was much surprised. "Three? You never told me that," he whispered.

"This is little Manuel, my sweet little Manuelito," she answered in a low voice, and buried her face in the child's black curls that she might not have to look at Wilhelm. She covered little Manuelito with kisses, and then pushed him gently over to Wilhelm, in whom the most conflicting emotions were struggling for the mastery. It was impossible to feel any ill-will toward this captivating mite with the dark Bronzino face, and yet to Wilhelm he seemed to represent a distinct act of treachery. How could she have been so underhand as to hide the fact from him that her connection with the fashion-plate diplomat had not been without results! He made as if to draw away from the boy, who stood staring nervously at him, but the next moment his natural love of children prevailed, and he clasped the sweet little fellow to his breast.

"Such a lovely child!" he said, "and so young, and in need of a mother's care. Why does it not live with you?"

"He lives with a sister of his father," she answered, hardly above her breath.

"And you let it go?"

"The father would not let me keep it. And I could not do anything against it because—it is not registered as my child, and does not bear my name."

The past, to which Wilhelm and Pilar had closed their eyes till now, presented itself that afternoon in incontestably lively form before them. Dispelled was the artificial fabric of their dream of a love that was as old as life itself—dispelled the poetic figment that they were in the honeymoon of a young pure union of the heart! These three children told a tale of Pilar in which Wilhelm bore no part, and the chapters of that story bore different names, as did the children themselves.

Pilar divined easily enough what was passing in Wilhelm's mind at sight of the children. She never let them come to the house again, but henceforth went to see them at their respective homes. He was sure that they liked coming to the Boulevard Pereire, and was sorry that they should miss this pleasure on his account. Pilar begged him, however, not to allude to the subject again—he was dearer to her than her children, and there was nothing she would not do to spare him a moment's unpleasantness.

The first visitor whom Wilhelm saw in Pilar's house was a little tubby gentleman with a clean-shaven face and a rosette in his buttonhole, composed of sixteen different colored ribbons at the very lowest computation. He enjoyed the privilege of coming at any hour of the day, and being instantly admitted to the boudoir. He was introduced to Wilhelm as Don Antonio Gorra, and Pilar explained afterward that Don Antonio was a lawyer, an old friend of her family, and that he conducted her business affairs for her. For a time she had long daily consultations, to which Wilhelm was not invited. As soon as he left, she would come to Wilhelm with a significant and mysterious air, evidently expecting that he would ask what all this putting together of heads might mean. As he did not evince the slightest curiosity, she grew impatient at last, and asked with assumed lightness:

"Are you not at all jealous, you fish-blooded German?"

"Jealous? No, I certainly am not. Besides which, you give me no cause."

"Indeed! and what about my tete-a-tetes with Don Antonio?"

"Oh, Don Antonio!" laughed Wilhelm.

"You are quite right, sweetheart, but it aggravates me that you should not want to know what he and I are brewing. You do not take nearly so much interest in my affairs as you ought."

"But you told me that Don Antonio was your man of business."

"Well, then—no—this time it is not a matter of business. I wanted to prepare a surprise for you." She seated herself on his knee, and laying her cheek to his, she whispered: "I have been trying to have myself naturalized in Belgium, and then, as a Belgian subject, get a divorce from Count Pozaldez. In that way I might have become your wife before the law as well."

He looked at her with a face expressive rather of alarm and astonishment than joy, and she went on with a sigh, "However, Don Antonio has just told me I must give up that pleasant dream—it cannot be realized."

He kissed her lips and brow, and stroked her silky hair. She laid her head on his shoulder, and remained long in silent thought. Presently she rose, walked up and down the room once or twice, and finally seated herself on a footstool at Wilhelm's feet. "But something I must do to bind you to me," she said. "I shall not rest till there is some written bond, something legal between us. I shall alter my will, and give you the place in it you occupy in my life."

"Pilar," exclaimed Wilhelm, "if you love me, and if you wish that we should remain what we are to one another, never say such a word again. If I ever find out that you have mentioned me in your will, all is at end between us." She drooped her head disconsolately, and he continued in a milder tone—"Dorfling's will has not brought me so much luck that I should ever wish to inherit money again."

The idea to which she had given expression did not leave Pilar, however. There should be something in writing—some document with stamps and seals to testify that Wilhelm belonged to her. This wish assumed the proportions of a superstition with her, and she never rested till it was satisfied.

One morning the inmates of the house on the Boulevard Pereire saw the arrival of three carriages, which discharged eight persons at the door. A well-dressed gentleman rang the bell, marshaled his seven companions in the hall, and desired to be shown up to the countess. She was expecting him, and received him in the red salon. After a short conversation, she went downstairs with him to the yellow salon, where Wilhelm, at her request, followed them. The visitor was the Spanish consul in Paris. He produced a casket ornamented with mother-o'-pearl, broke a seal with which it was fastened, unlocked it with a small silver key, and took out a document in a closed envelope, and handed it to Pilar. He then opened the door, and permitted his followers to enter. They came in in single file, and ranged themselves silently along the wall. They were tall, lean men in great circular Spanish cloaks of brown or bottle-green, defective in the matter of footgear, and with shapeless greasy hats in their ungloved hands. Their deportment was as dignified as if they had been the chapter of a religious order, and every face was turned with an air of contemplative solemnity toward the countess. With nervous haste she wrote a few lines at the foot of the document, read it over three or four times and altered a word here and there; she then folded the paper, returned it to the envelope, and handed it back to the consul. She sealed it with her seal and wrote something on it, the seven men then advanced one by one to the table, and with extreme gravity and precision put their signatures on the envelope. The casket was then relocked and resealed, and the company withdrew with a ceremonious bow, not, however, without leaving behind them such a piercing smell of garlic that the yellow salon was still full of it next day.

When Pilar found herself alone with Wilhelm, she asked: "I suppose you would like to know what all this means?"

"Well, yes."

"We have in Spain what we call mysterious wills, the contents of which may be kept secret. A will of that kind is valid if an official person and seven witnesses vouch for it by their signatures on the envelope that it has been written or altered in their presence. To-day I have added something to my secret will."

He made a movement, but she would not give him time to speak.

"Do not be afraid, I have not acted against your wishes nor wounded your pride. On our Vega de Henares in Old Castile, we have a family tomb where my ancestors have been laid to rest since the sixteenth century. It is the Renaissance mausoleum of the picture hanging in your room. The marble tomb stands in the middle of an oak wood, not far from a little brook, and it is cool and still there. I shall lie there some day, wherever I may die, and I have assigned you a place beside me. Promise me, Wilhelm, that you will accept it. Promise me that you, in your turn, will make the necessary arrangements for your remains to be brought at last to our vega. I do not know if I may ever belong to you as your wife in my lifetime, but in death I want to have you forever at my side. Grant me this consolation. Give me your hand upon it."

Great tears welled slowly into the hazel eyes, and it was plainly of such sacred and earnest import to her that Wilhelm had not the heart to smile at her strained and sentimental idea. Moved and touched, he clasped her to his heart in silence.

CHAPTER XII.

TANNHAUSER'S FLIGHT.

"To be as much alone with you in great Paris as if we were on a desert island in the Pacific—in the midst of the crowd, yet having no part with it; spectators of its amusing doings, and yet unnoticed by it. You all my world, and I yours—what a sweet and perfect dream!" Thus Pilar as she went out in fine weather, thickly veiled, on Wilhelm's arm into the crowded streets, and she did her utmost to prolong the charming delusion as far as possible. She paid no visits, invited no one to the house, avoided every familiar face in the street. Through the consul and Don Antonio, however, her more immediate circle got wind by degrees of her return to Paris, and visitors began to call at the little house on the Boulevard Pereire who would not submit to being sent away. With the versatility of mind peculiar to her, Pilar soon adapted herself to the new position of affairs, and tried to make the best of it. Of course it would have been infinitely more agreeable, she said to Wilhelm, to have been able to remain longer in their delicious seclusion, but, sooner or later, social life would have to be resumed, and it was best he should make a beginning now. "Do not be afraid," she added, "that I shall ask you to make the acquaintance of all the asses and parrots that have chattered and gesticulated round me for years. You shall only know a really select few, who are fond of me, and who can offer you friendship and appreciation."

And so the march past of the elect began, most of them being invited either to lunch or dinner. Wilhelm found them very peculiar and uncongenial, and, on the whole, derived but little satisfaction from their acquaintance. Pilar had a small weakness; according to her account, each one of her more intimate friends was a striking and original character, the possessor of the rarest qualities. It was the only touch of snobbishness of which one could have accused her. She announced the arrival of an old Spanish general, "a hero of quite the antique, classic type, one of the most remarkable figures in the history of modern warfare," and there entered to them a little old man, shuffling in with the flurried, dragging gait of a paralytic, unable to lift his feet from the ground, stammering out a few commonplaces, who could not keep his gold eyeglasses on his nose, and who, when he was informed that Wilhelm had fought in the Franco-Prussian War, frankly admitted that, though he had commanded at many a grand review, he had never been in real action.

Another time a Great Thinker was to appear, a profound sage, with whom Wilhelm would be delighted, thoroughly versed in German philosophy, a critic of immense and independent spirit. But what Wilhelm really saw was a slovenly, pock-marked man, with a very arrogant manner, who smoked cigarettes without intermission, and preserved an obstinate silence, behind which one was naturally free to imagine the profoundest thoughts, if one wished it; and who, when Pilar tried to lead him on to air his opinions on German philosophy, answered sententiously: "I do not care for Kant; his was not a republican spirit." A man who was said to be famed for his wit perpetrated such atrocious puns that even Pilar was forced to admit after he left that he had had a surprisingly bad day. An aristocratic member of the Jockey Club, "a truly distinguished being"—when Pilar wished to give any one the highest praise she always alluded to them as "a being"—"and not superficial like the most of his class," talked for two consecutive hours of the coming elections to the Jockey Club, and of the attempt to bring in the wearing of bracelets as a fashion among gentlemen. The only figure in this gallery which made anything like a favorable impression on Wilhelm was a Catalonian, naturalized in France, a professor at a Paris lycee. He had simple, winning manners, spoke and looked like an intelligent person, and met Wilhelm with much friendliness. He was to learn later on that this amiable, frank, unfailingly good-tempered acquaintance had made the most ill-natured, not to say defamatory remarks about him, before Pilar and her whole circle of friends.

One afternoon Anne announced that "the consumptive poet was below, and begged to be allowed to pay his respects to Madame la Comtesse." "Another great man, no doubt," thought Wilhelm, sadly resigned to his fate. To his surprise Pilar turned furiously red, and said angrily:

"I am not at home!"

Anne retired, but came back again immediately.

"He sent to ask," she said, in a tone of studied indifference, which ineffectually concealed her inward satisfaction, "what he had done to deserve madame's displeasure, and why he should be treated like a stranger?"

"Anne," cried Pilar, her voice quivering with rage, "how dare you bring me such a message! If the man does not go instantly, then order Don Pablo and Auguste to see that he does."

The maid withdrew, and Pilar, without waiting for Wilhelm's question, muttered resentfully:

"A man I was kind to out of pity, because he was such a poor wretch, an unknown poet, and bound to die soon—and now he is impudent and intrusive. But that is just what one may expect when one is kind-hearted."

Wilhelm thought no more of this episode, and had almost forgotten that it had ever occurred, when one day soon afterward a friend of Pilar's, the Countess Cuerbo, came to call. She was the wife of a fabulously rich Spanish banker, whose house, racing-stables, picture gallery, carriages, and dinners were among the marvels of Paris. This lady's most striking characteristic was a vulgar boastfulness, such as is seldom met with even among the worst upstarts of the Bourse. It was said that she had originally been a washerwoman or a cigarette maker in Seville, but this was perhaps an exaggeration. So much, however, was certain, that her husband had begun in a very small way, and had received his title at the accession of King Alfonso, in return for financial services which had materially helped toward the re-establishment of the throne. The Countess Cuerbo could now give points as to pride of station to the bluest-blooded grandee. She associated exclusively with persons of title, and strove, in every possible way, to play the "grande dame." She was always bedizened with the most costly diamonds, and so shamelessly rouged that she must have been mobbed had she gone through the Boulevards on foot. She was not actually plain, but so affected that she did not know what to do with herself, and made such frightful grimaces that one was afraid to look at her. Nor could she be called stupid, for she had the inborn natural wit of the Andalusians, and when she spoke Spanish, could give very droll turns to her remarks. Her French was calculated to induce toothache in her hearers, and in the unfamiliar language the wit evaporated and left only the vulgar behind. She was the terror of her female friends, for she considered absolute freedom of speech to be the privilege and badge of nobility, and thought herself every inch an aristocrat when she alluded, without the faintest regard for decency, not only to her own numerous affairs of gallantry, but to those of her friends to their faces. Her tactlessness had been the cause of many a disaster, but she remained incorrigible, in spite of repeated and severe snubbings and even bitter insults.

No sooner had she entered the room than Wilhelm received a sample of her peculiar style. Anne announced the Countess Cuerbo. Wilhelm rose, prepared to leave Pilar alone, but the visitor had followed on the heels of the maid, and rustled into the red salon, exclaiming in her strident voice and horrible Spanish accent as she embraced Pilar:

"This is your German friend, I suppose, about whom I have heard so much. Oh, please don't go away, I am so curious to know you."

Wilhelm was dumfounded. Such calm insolence he had never yet encountered. Pilar shot a glance of fury at the countess, to which she did not pay the slightest attention, but examined Wilhelm insolently through her gold eyeglasses, and went on with a vulgar laugh:

"General Varon told me about you, and described you to me. He thinks you very nice, and I must say I think he is right."

Pilar's patience gave out.

"Madame," she said very dryly, "if Monsieur le Docteur Eynhardt feels himself honored by your astounding familiarities that is his affair. I do not disguise from you that I think them in very bad taste."

"Oh, my dear countess," replied the lady, in no way discomposed by this snub, "don't be so severe upon me. I have no designs upon your friend, and you need not be prudish with me. Surely ladies of our rank have no need to be particular like any little grocer's wife."

That was Pilar's own creed, and before any other audience she would smilingly have agreed with the Countess Cuerbo. But she pictured to herself what an effect this tone would have upon Wilhelm's German, middle-class sense of propriety, which she knew so well, and was indignant at her visitor's cool cynicism.

"Madame," she returned, still more icily, "you force upon me the opinion that there are circumstances under which it would be well to take an example by the grocer's wives whom you despise so much."

This remark, in which the Bourse-countess did not fail to hear the ring of the real aristocrat's disdain, touched her in her tenderest point. She tried to smile, but turned livid under her paint, and determined to return the stab on the spot.

"Don't be angry, dearest countess, I was only joking, and you know as well as anybody that we Andalusians do not weigh our words too carefully. By the bye, your French poet—you know—the one before you went to the seaside—is simply beside himself. You have thrown him over, it seems. He comes to me every day, imploring me to say a good word for him to you. He talks of challenging his fortunate successor, and goodness only knows what nonsense beside."

Pilar turned very white. She sprang to her feet.

"Shall I give a name to what you are doing?" she cried, her voice shaking.

"Don't trouble," returned her visitor, perfectly delighted, and rising as she spoke. "I see, dearest countess, that you have one of your nervous days, so I had better come again another time."

So saying she swept out of the room, throwing an offensively friendly nod at Wilhelm as she passed. To the grinning Anne, who was waiting in the hall to see her to her carriage, she said:

"Well, it looks serious this time—the countess is over head and ears. But it is quite true, he is much better-looking than any of the others."

"Looks are not everything," returned Anne sagely, and her contemptuous shrug conveyed plainly enough that she did not share her mistress' taste.

Upstairs Pilar had rushed over to Wilhelm as soon as the countess disappeared, and hid her face on his breast.

Wilhelm pushed her gently away, and said sadly:

"I have no right to reproach you, or, if I did, it would only be for not having been open with me, although you boast of your extreme truthfulness."

"Wilhelm," she entreated, clasping his hand in both of hers, "do not judge me hastily. I might excuse myself, I might even deny it, but I am not capable of that. When I told you the story of my life, I believed honestly that I had made you a full confession. You shake your head? Is it true—I swear it is! This man had entirely escaped my memory. Why, I never loved him! It was in some part a childish folly, but principally pity and perhaps little caprice on the part of a bored and lonely woman. My heart had not the smallest part in it. He was given up by the doctors, they thought he might die any day—in such a case one gives oneself is one would offer him a cup of tisane—the action of a Good Samaritan."

"Your defense," he said grimly, as he freed himself from her grasp, "is far worse than any reproach I might bring against you. You never loved him? Your heart had no part in this childish folly? That makes it all the uglier—then it becomes unpardonable. Love alone could extenuate such a fault to some degree."

He turned to leave the room, but she threw herself upon him and clung to him.

"You are right—quite right, darling," her voice half-choked with terror and excitement; "but forgive me—forgive me for the sake of my love to you. That story belongs to the past, and the past is buried—buried forever. I cannot believe myself that it is not all a hideous dream—that it should be really true! It was not I—it was another woman, a stranger whom I do not know—with whom I have nothing in common. I was not alive then—I have only lived since you were mine. Oh, why did you come so late?" And her wild, passionate words sank into heartrending sobs.

He could not but be sorry for her. Was it wise, was it fitting to rake up the past? Had he any right to call her to account for faults which were not committed against him? She was good and pure now. She had not broken faith with him—not even in her thoughts—for she had no eyes for anybody in the world but him! He held out his hand to her.

"I will forget what I heard to-day," he said, "and do not let us ever speak again of what has been."

He was quite sincere in saying this, for he really wished to forget. But our memory is not subject to our will. Do what he would, he could not banish the consumptive poet from his mind, nor the diplomat with the silly, handsome face, and other figures more shadowy than these two, but none the less annoying. He learned to know that most torturing form of jealousy— the jealousy of the past—against which it is hopeless to struggle, which will not be dispelled, and which, in its unalterable steadfastness, mocks at the despair of the heart that is forever searching after new grounds for torment, and yet cries aloud when it finds what it sought. His imagination wandered perpetually from the lovely pastel in the yellow salon to the new ebony bed, with its inlaid ivory scenes in the bedroom, and saw or guessed things between these two points that made him shudder.

Thus, New Year's night found him in a very gloomy frame of mind, and the letter he wrote to Schrotter expressed a still deeper dejection than that of the year before. Since recounting the conversation about the donkey in Ault, he had never again mentioned Pilar to his friend, nor betrayed by a single word the circumstances in which he had lived since the middle of August. Such disclosures would have necessitated a moral effort on his part, for which even his friendship for Schrotter could not supply him with sufficient force. He knew that Schrotter's views on morality were neither narrow nor pharisaical, that to him virtue did not consist in the outward observance of social rules, but in self-forgetful, brotherly love and a strict adherence to duty. It would have afforded him unspeakable relief to have been able to pour out his heart to his friend, to give him an insight into his turbid love-story and the conflict in his soul. But a sense of shame—the outcome, no doubt, of his own disgust at the unsavory accessories of his love—had withheld him from making these confidences. He made none now, complained only in a general way of the emptiness of his life, to which neither desire nor hope bound him any more; especially that he had no future, and looked forward to each new day with horror and shrinking.

Schrotter's answer was, as usual, full of faithful affection and wise encouragement. He chid him gently for his want of spirit, and then went on to say:

"You have no future! I am amazed at such a remark in the mouth of a man of thought. Which one of us can say he has a future? To say we have a future is simply to say that we wish for something, strive after something, set some aim before us. That which we call a man's future does not lie outside of him, but in himself. I would have you observe that events rarely or never happen as we expect, and that the plans which we have worked out most zealously are scarcely ever carried out. And yet we firmly believe, all the time, that we have a future. Nature permits us no outlook into Time. A wall rises before our eyes to hide what is coming. But the cheerless nakedness of that wall being unbearable to us, we paint it over with landscapes of our own devising. And that is what the unthinking mind calls the future. Any one can paint these pictures on the wall, and to complain of its bareness is to acknowledge the poverty of one's own imagination wishing for something,— never mind what. The higher, the more unattainable, the better. Only desire earnestly, and you will feel yourself alive again. Your misfortune, my friend, is that you have not to work for your daily bread. A settled income is only a blessing to those to whom the attainment of the trifling and external pleasures of life seems worth the trouble of an effort. You are wise enough to set no value on what the world can give you. You are neither vain nor ambitious. Therefore you do not exercise your capacities in wrestling for position, recognition, honors, or fame. On the other hand, you have no need to trouble yourself about the bare necessities of life, and are thereby deprived of another occasion for bringing your strength into play. Now, you are provided with organic forces, and it is the circumstance that these forces are lying fallow that affects you like a malady. It is in work alone that you can hope to find a cure, or at least an improvement. Accordingly, if you have not sufficient strength of will to set yourself some task, my will shall come to your aid. I suggest, nay, I insist, that you proceed manfully with your 'History of Human Ignorance,' about which I have heard nothing for months, and that you show me at least the first volume ready for the press by the end of this time next year."

  Wilhelm caught desperately at this advice, offered to him by his friend in the paradoxical form of a command. He got out his books and papers again, and began devoting his mornings to work. Pilar was delighted. She was far too wise not to know that honeymoons do not last forever, and although she was persuaded that she, for her part, would never desire anything better than to be always at Wilhelm's side, passing the time in interminable conversations about herself and himself, in kissing and fondling, she quite understood that that was not enough to satisfy a man accustomed to a wider range of pursuits. She had looked forward with anxiety to the moment when mere love-making would pall upon him, and he would begin to be bored, and wish for a change. She had kept a sharp lookout for the approach of this ticklish moment that her ingenious mind might have some fresh interest ready for him. This trouble had been spared her. He himself took thought for a suitable occupation to fill up his time. So much the better. He had adapted himself to the circumstances, after all. He no longer looked upon it as a passing liaison, but had settled down permanently and finally to lead his accustomed life with her.

It took a weight off her mind, and gave her a sense of peace and security such as she had not known since the return to Paris. She too began to come out of her shell, and to resume her former mode of life. She fulfilled her social duties, and paid and received calls, which Wilhelm was allowed to shirk. At the end of January the first ball of the Spanish embassy took place. Pilar's whole set was invited, and she could not well absent herself without exciting remark. She therefore made the necessary preparations for the festivity. A diadem of brilliants was sent to be reset, a sensational gown composed, after repeated conferences with a great ladies' tailor, a pattern in seed pearls chosen for the embroidery of the long gloves. Don Pablo galloped about like a post-horse from morning till night; gorgeous vans, with liveried attendants, from the fashionable shops stopped constantly at the door to deliver parcels; there was an unceasing stream of messengers, shop people, and needlewomen. But Wilhelm was oblivious of it all; Pilar did not trouble him with such frivolous matters. It was not till the very day of the ball that she handed him the card of invitation she had procured for him at the embassy, and asked, as a precaution:

"You have all you require, have you not?"

Wilhelm glanced at the pink, glazed card.

"But, Pilar, do you know me so little?"

"I know that you do not care for these stupid entertainments," she answered coaxingly, "but I thought you would go to please me."

"So you are going?" he asked.

"I must," she replied. "They know that I am in Paris, and I wish to avoid the remark that would be made if I stayed away."

"You are quite right," said Wilhelm, "but you will have to go without me."

"Don't be a bear!" she urged. "It will interest you to see this side of Parisian life. I don't say that I would ask you to do it often, but you might—just this once. Beside, you have been more than three months in Paris, and you do not know one real Parisian. Now, here is an opportunity of meeting artists, authors, academicians, senators—and there are some remarkable men among them, well worth talking to."

"I am sincerely grateful," he returned, and kissed her hand. "Please do not trouble about it. I am quite sure that there are many people in Paris I should like to meet, but they are scarcely likely to be present at an embassy ball. And even if they were, a mere introduction, an interchange of society platitudes, would not bring me any further. No; go you to your ball, and leave me at home."

Pilar sighed, and gave up the struggle, and then received the jeweler, who had brought the newly-set ornament for the hair, a miracle of taste, delicate workmanship, and splendor.

In the afternoon Monsieur Martin, the prince of Paris hairdressers, arrived, to compose her a coiffure for the ball. He was a little man, with a clean-shaven upper lip, and the mutton-chop whiskers of a solicitor. He wore a long black coat, of severe cut, buttoned up to the top, and a ribbon in his buttonhole. In his very pale cravat was a breastpin with a magnificent cat's eye. Patent leather boots and kid gloves completed the faultless attire of this gentleman, whom one would sooner have taken for a minister than a hairdresser. A liveried servant followed him, carrying a silver-bound morocco box, which he took from him at the door of the boudoir, and placed with his own hands on the rosewood table.

After an extremely ceremonious greeting, he drew off his gloves, seated himself in an armchair by the fire, and made the countess describe what she was going to wear. He listened with almost tragic attention, his forehead in his hand, his eyes closed. After some reflection, he exclaimed:

"Where is the diadem?"

Pilar placed it on the table in front of him.

He contemplated it earnestly, and then murmured:

"Good, very good. But now I must see the robe."

"Monsieur Martin," Pilar returned reproachfully, "don't you know that my tailor respects himself far too much to send home one of his creations before the last moment?"

"It is always the same story," he complained mournfully; "I am to arrange a coiffure for Madame la Comtesse, the coiffure is to harmonize with the whole, and I am not permitted to see the robe."

"But I have given you the general idea of it."

"General idea! general idea! Does Madame la Comtesse think that that will suffice?"

"For an artist like you, Monsieur Martin—"

"Oh, of course—for an artist like me! I can answer for myself, but how do I know if the tailor has caught madame's style correctly? I am perfectly competent to compose a coiffure which shall agree entirely with the type of

Madame la Comtesse, but what if the tailor has been mistaken—what if the robe turns out a disguise rather than an enhancement? In that case, adieu to the harmony."

Pilar reassured the sorely-tried master, and exchanged glances of amusement with Wilhelm. She had described him to Wilhelm beforehand as a Parisian oddity, and invited him to be present during the visit. While Anne enveloped her mistress in the white dressing-mantle, Monsieur Martin laid out the battery of combs, brushes, and tortoise-shell hair-pins provided by the maid, added, out of his own box, two hand-glasses, and a box of gold-powder, and began to loosen the countess' abundant tresses. As the golden waves flowed over the back of the chair to the ground, he murmured, drawing his fingers repeatedly through the silken mass:

"What a fleece, Madame la Comtesse! It takes a Spaniard to have such hair."

He now began rapidly and skillfully to comb, brush, coil, and fasten, to smooth away here, loosen there, shook the gold dust over it, touched the locks upon the forehead, placed the diadem, and fell back a step to review his work. A groan burst from him.

"That is not it! that is not it!" he wailed, and shook his head dolefully from side to side. "I am not permitted to see the costume of Madame la Comtesse, I am not to use pads or curling-irons, and yet all is to be in the grand style—only a diadem—not a flower, not a feather! No, it will not do." He glared at her for a moment, and then cried suddenly, "No, it positively will not do!" And before Pilar could prevent him, he had rapidly pulled out all the hairpins, removed the diadem, and disarranged with nervous fingers the whole artistic edifice.

"A coiffure that bears my signature must not be allowed to leave my hands like that," he said. "And yet the ground is burning beneath my feet. It is three o'clock, and I have not yet lunched."

"Poor Monsieur Martin!" cried Pilar. "Will you have something to eat at once? They shall serve it to you downstairs."

"Madame la Comtesse is very good, but I have no time to sit down comfortably at a table. I have all that is necessary in my carriage, and shall take some slight refreshment there, on my way to my next client."

"Have you much to do to-day?"

Monsieur Martin drew out a little notebook, with ivory tablets, and a silver monogram, and held it up before Pilar's eyes.

"Eleven heads after that of Madame la Comtesse."

"All for the embassy ball?"

"No, madame; I have another dance to-night in the Faubourg, and a betrothal party in the American colony."

While speaking he had not remained idle. The coiffure was being built up on a different plan, and this time Monsieur Martin appeared to be satisfied with his creation. He walked all round the smiling countess, begged her to walk slowly up and down the room once or twice, touched up the front locks a little, and then the back, and finally ejaculated:

"Charming! Ravishing! Our head will have a great success!"

He departed, after a ceremonious leave-taking. At the door of the boudoir his servant again relieved him of his box, and carried it after him downstairs, and a few minutes later they heard his carriage drive away.

"You have not anything like that in Berlin yet," said Pilar, laughing, when the solemn and important artist had left.

"I think not," Wilhelm replied; "at least, not in the circles with which I am acquainted. But I do not laugh at him—on the contrary, I envy him. He takes himself so seriously, and combs with his whole soul. Happy man!"

It was about half-past ten when Pilar entered the red salon, in full ball dress. Wilhelm was sitting by the fire reading. She came up to him:

"How do you like me?" she asked.

She had on a salmon-colored broche velvet dress, with ostrich feather trimmings, and a long train. Shoulders and bust rose as out of pink foam from the scarf-like folds of some very airy material; brilliants flashed at her breast and on her arms, the diadem was in her hair, two solitaires in the delicate little ears, a double row of pearls round her neck, and an ostrich feather fan, with enameled gold mounts, in her hand. A superb figure!

"How beautiful!" he said, and stroked her chin fondly. He dared not touch her cheeks, for fear of disturbing the pearl powder. "But you look just as regal without the brilliants."

"Flatterer! Would you not like to come, after all? Make haste and dress."

He only shook his head, smiling.

"But are you not a little bit jealous, when you see me go off by myself to a ball? I shall talk to the men, and take their arm and dance with them; the people will look at me and pay me attention—does it not make any difference to you?"

"No, dear heart, for I hope it will make none to you either."

"Ah, yes—you need have no fear on that score. But still—in your place—you men, you love differently from us. And not so well," she added with a sigh, as Anne appeared with her fur-lined cloak, and announced that the carriage was waiting.

Some hours later Wilhelm was startled out of a deep sleep by burning kisses. He opened his dazed eyes, and, blinking in the lamplight, saw Pilar standing by the bed as if in a cloud. She held her great bouquet in one hand, and with the other was plucking the roses and gardenias to pieces, and strewing the petals over his head and face, as she did in the sunny afternoons at St. Valery. She must have been engaged in this pastime for a considerable time, for the pillows and quilt were covered with flowers, and his hair was full of them. As neither Pilar's entry with the lamp nor the shower of blossoms had succeeded in wakening him, she had leaned over him and roused him with a kiss.

"Oh, sleepy head!" she cried, and continued to rain flowers on his dazzled, blinking eyes. "At least you have been dreaming of me?"

"To tell the truth," he returned, "I have not dreamed at all."

"And I have never left off thinking about you all the time, and have longed so for you. Look here!"

She took a lamp off the chimney-piece, and held up her ball programme before his eyes. The blank places were filled up with pencil-writing, which looked as if it might be lines of poetry: which in truth it was—Spanish improvisations breathing burning love and passionate longing. He would have understood or guessed their meaning even if Pilar had not translated them with kisses and caresses.

"Now, you see, you bad boy," she went on, "those were my thoughts while I was away from you. I had not thought it would be so difficult to enjoy myself without you. It was impossible. It is only three, but I could not stand it any longer. I escaped before the cotillion. If you only knew how hollow and stupid it all seemed to me! How dull I thought the men's conversation, how ludicrous the affectations of the women! What are all these people compared to you! No, I will never go out again without you. Come, Wilhelm, and help me to undress. I will not have Anne about me now—nobody—only you."

Had she been drinking champagne at the ball? Had the lights, the music, the dancing, the perfumes, her own verses gone to her head? Whatever was the cause, her nerves were certainly very highly strung, and only calmed down when the morning was well advanced, and she had exhausted herself in a thousand fond extravagances.

During the next few days Wilhelm noticed something odd in Pilar's manner which he failed to understand. She seemed strangely absent and thoughtful, by turns unnaturally silent and feverishly talkative, would sit for hours beside him glancing mysteriously at him from time to time, as if she knew something very wonderful, and were debating in her own mind whether to tell it or keep it to herself. She blushed if he looked at her inquiringly, and rushed away and locked herself into her boudoir.

He watched these peculiar proceedings patiently for about a week, and then asked one day, not without a secret misgiving:

"Pilar, what is the matter with you lately?"

Probably she had only waited for this. She cast herself upon his breast, drew his head down, and whispered something in his ear. He straightened himself up with a jerk.

"Are you certain?" he asked, with an unsteady voice.

"Almost, I think; yes, Wilhelm, it must be so," she stammered, hiding her face on his shoulder.

It was well she did not look at him at that moment. Unskilled as he was in the art of dissembling, his face expressed no pleasure at all, but only painful surprise. For weeks, but more especially since his gloomy broodings on New-Year's night, the anxious thought lay heavy on him, "What if our connection should have results?" The situation would then become so complicated that he saw no prospect of ever putting it straight again. The idea had only hitherto been an indefinite cause of anxiety—now it resolved itself into a fact which appalled him. At the same time he could not but see how happy Pilar was at the prospect, and it seemed to him unkind, even brutal, to let her have an inkling of what he felt at her news. He kissed her in silence, and pressed her hand long and warmly.

"You have not said yet that you are glad," she said, and raised her eyes to his in fond reproach.

"Must one put everything into words?" he returned, with an uneasy smile.

"It is true," she answered; "I ought to be accustomed to your German ways by this time. But your reserve is quite uncanny to us Southerners. You are silent where our hearts simply overflow with words quite of themselves. You are content to think where we shout for joy."

With these words Pilar depicted her own state. She felt in truth that she could shout for joy, and the happy words flowed of themselves from her lips. Now at last the future stood clearly and definitely outlined before her eyes.

Now indeed she was bound to Wilhelm, as was her burning desire, and that far faster than by any documents with solemn signatures and official seals. Her heart was so light, she felt as if her feet no longer touched the ground and that she must float away into the blue ether like the ecstatic saints in the church pictures of her own country. She talked incessantly of the coming being, and thought of nothing else waking or sleeping. She had not the slightest doubt that it would be a boy. Isabel had to lay the cards a dozen times, and the knave of spades came to the top nearly every time, an infallible promise of a boy. And how beautiful he would be, the son of such a handsome father, the fruit of such transcendent love! She consulted with Wilhelm what name he should receive, and wanted a definite statement or a suggestion, or at least some slight conjecture as to the profession his father would choose for him. And should he be educated in Paris? Would it not be too great a strain upon the little brain to have to learn French, Spanish, and German at the same time? What anxieties, what responsibilities, but at the same time what bliss! She did not even let Wilhelm see the whole depth of her feelings, knowing that he would not follow her in these extravagant raptures. She did not let him see her kneel two or three times a day at the altar or on her priedieu, and cover the silver Madonna del Pilar with ecstatic kisses. He knew nothing of her having sent for the priest of the diocese and ordered a number of masses. She did not take him with her when—her impatience leading her far ahead of events—she rushed from shop to shop looking for a cradle, and only put off buying one because she could find none in all Paris that was sumptuous and costly enough.

This went on for about a fortnight, till one day she tottered into Wilhelm's room, all dissolved in tears, sank sobbing at his feet, and hid her face on his knee.

"Pilar, what has happened?" he cried in alarm.

"Oh, Wilhelm, Wilhelm," was all the answer he could get from her; and only after long and loving persuasion did she murmur in such low and broken tones that she had to repeat her words before he could understand her, "My happiness was premature, I was mistaken."

She was inconsolable at the destruction of her airy castle, and was ill for days, the first time since Wilhelm had known her. He sympathized deeply with her in her grief, but he did not conceal from himself that he was infinitely relieved at the turn affairs had taken. With such a morbidly analytical and yet profoundly moral nature as his, no rapture of the senses could possibly last for six months and more. The passion in which reason plays no part was past and over long ago, and during the last few weeks he had reflected upon the situation with ever-increasing clearness and deliberation. At first he had not been quite sure of his feelings, but earnest self-examination by degrees made everything plain to him. What he was most distinctly conscious of was a sense of profound disgust at his present manner of life. Things could not remain as they were. Sooner or later it must inevitably come to the knowledge of his friends. What would they think of him for leading such a life at Pilar's side, in her house? She had children who would some day sit in judgment upon her conduct and his. And how did he stand in the eyes of the servants and the visitors whose acquaintance Pilar had forced upon him? If at least she would give up her outside circle of friends! But that she either could not or would not do, and so brought ill-natured witnesses of their relations to the house, and Wilhelm must needs accommodate himself to an intercourse with second-rate people who inevitably form the set of a woman whose domestic circumstances are not clearly, or rather all too clearly defined. And before these people, who appeared to him greatly inferior to himself, both morally and intellectually, he was forced to cast down his eyes. Reflect as he might upon the situation, the result was always the same—it must be put to an end to. But how?

There remained always the possibility that her husband might die and she be thus free to marry him. Strange, he always hurried over this solution of the difficulty. In his inner consciousness he was apparently not desirous of making the connection a lifelong one, even if sanctioned by lawful formalities. Leave her. He shuddered at the thought. It would be criminal to cause her so great a grief, for he was assured that she loved him passionately, and he was deeply and fondly grateful to her for doing so. She might some day grow tired of him. He hoped for this, but the hope was so faint, so secret, so hidden, that he hardly dared confess it to himself, knowing well that it was a deadly and altogether undeserved insult to her love. And even this faint hope vanished when she whispered the news of her prospective motherhood in his ear; now there was no possibility of a dissolution of their connection. If a human creature was indebted to him for its life, he must give himself up to it, and to this sacred duty he must sacrifice freedom, happiness, even self-respect. But his heart contracted with a bitter pang at the thought. It was as if a black curtain had been drawn in front of him, or a window walled up which permitted a view over the open country from a dark room.

However, he had been spared this crowning addition to the burden of his discomfort, and he breathed more freely. But the episode had served to rend the last remaining veil that hung before his moral eye. That the situation should seem so unbearable, that he was so sensitive to the opinion of others, that his blood had run cold at Pilar's news, that he had felt the disappointment of her hopes as a relief, that the idea that the danger might recur should fill him with terror—this all pointed to one fact, the realization of which forced itself upon him with inexorable persistency; he did not love Pilar, or at any rate he did not love her sufficiently—not enough to take her finally into his life, and, possessing her, to forget himself and all the world beside.

In the midst of his torturing efforts to come to some conclusion he noticed that Auguste, who had come to his room with a letter, lingered about in an undecided manner, as if he had something to say but did not know exactly how to say it.

"What is it?" asked Wilhelm, coming to his assistance.

He liked Auguste, for he was always civil and attentive to him, whereas the hostility of the rest of the servants was easily discerned in spite of their forced show of servility.

"Monsieur le Docteur must excuse me," said the man, "but I really can't listen to it any longer and keep quiet. The lady's maid never stops saying the most scandalous things about monsieur. She says it is not true that monsieur is a celebrated doctor and a member of Parliament, and that they are not going to make him President of the German Republic."

"Who has been trying to impose upon you with such stories?"

"But Madamela Comtess tells everybody so, and all the world knows it. I have long wanted to ask monsieur for something against the rheumatism in my left shoulder, but did not like to because madame says monsieur may not practice here."

What object could Pilar have in inventing these fables?

As he remained silent Auguste resumed:

"Monsieur may trust me, I am discreet, and I always defend him against Anne, who is spiteful as a cat. She says monsieur is a Prussian spy and a fortune-hunter, and is simply preying upon madame. And she calls monsieur something still worse, which I would not like to repeat. It is a shame, for monsieur has never done her any harm, and it would not be quite so bad if she only let out her vile temper before us, but she slanders monsieur to outsiders and gives him a dreadfully bad name."

"I am sorry that you should retail such gossip to me," said Wilhelm, making a great effort to appear unmoved.

"I considered it my duty, as an honest man. I am not saying more than the truth about the maid, and am perfectly ready to repeat it all to her face. Madame la Comtesse is really wrong in keeping the viper. There are plenty of respectable and handy young women who would think themselves lucky to be taken into madame's service. I have a cousin, for instance, who has been in the best houses—Anne couldn't hold a candle to her; if monsieur would recommend her to Madame la Comtesse—"

"I can do nothing in the matter," said Wilhelm brusquely.

He turned his back upon the man and absorbed himself pointedly in his books. Auguste stood a moment, but seeing that Wilhelm would take no further notice of him, shrugged his shoulders and left the room.

Wilhelm was surprised himself at the impression the man's information had made upon him. Dismay, anger, and shame struggled for the mastery in his breast. What a suffocating air he breathed in this house! How vile and underhand and insincere were the people by whom he was surrounded! But was this true that Auguste told him? Did he not lie and slander like the rest? Was he not doing the servant far too great an honor by letting his mind dwell on the low gossip of the servants' hall? He felt a kind of dim revolt against his own excitement which he felt to be unworthy of him, and, under other circumstances, he really would have been too proud to allow such tale-bearing to exert the slightest influence upon his thoughts or actions. But, in his present state of mind, Auguste's words sounded to him like a brutal translation of his own thoughts, condemning him for his cowardice in submitting to his humiliating position, and he recognized more clearly than ever that he must fight his way out of this degradation.

It was not easy to carry out this resolve. When Pilar came to his room and took his arm to lead him down to lunch, she was as bewitching and fond as ever. At table she chattered brightly about an exhibition of pictures in the Cercle des Mirlitons, which she wanted to see with him that afternoon, asked him about the work he had done to-day, and if he had given a thought to her now and then between his crusty old books, and altogether gave evidence of such childlike and implicit confidence in his love and faith, such utter absence of suspicion as to possible rocks ahead, that that which he had it in his mind to do seemed almost like a stab in the dark. His mental suffering was so poignant as to be visibly reflected in his countenance, and Pilar interrupted her lively flow of talk to ask anxiously:

"What is the matter with you to-day, darling? Don't you feel well?"

He took his courage in both hands, and answered with another question:

"Tell me, Pilar, did you really trump up a story about me? That I was a celebrated doctor and member of Parliament, and the future President of the German Republic?"

She flashed, but tried to laugh off her embarrassment. "Oh, it was only a harmless little romance to amuse myself. You could be all that if you liked, I am sure, you are ever so much cleverer than these puppets—" She stopped short in the middle of the sentence as she caught sight of the menacing frown upon his face, drew her chair with a rapid movement close to his, and said, in her most humble and insinuating tones, "Dearest, are you vexed with me?"

"Yes, for it is a humiliating, and beside which, a totally unnecessary invention, and lays me open to the worst construction."

"And who has taken upon themselves to retail it to you? That Cuerbo, I suppose?"

"It was not the Countess Cuerbo—not that it matters if the actual fact is true."

"Forgive me, Wilhelm," she pleaded, "I thought to act for the best. The whole story was chiefly for my mother's benefit. I wanted her to love you and be grateful to you. I wanted her to take you to her heart like a son. I do not care a bit about the other people. I only told them the story to keep myself in practice. And beside, you know what the world is. A man's personal worth goes for nothing, it only cares for the outward signs of success, and that is why I said you were a celebrated man and had a great future before you. That is no invention, for I believe it firmly. And I told them that you had saved my life, because it is true, for life was a burden to me till I knew you, and you have made it worth living."

"But do you not see into what a degrading position you force me?"

"I hoped you would never hear about it. My intentions were so good. Our relations to one another must be explained in some way. I wanted to shield your reputation from these people and shut their mouths."

"You see, my poor Pilar," said Wilhelm sadly, "your excuse is the bitterest criticism upon our relations. You yourself feel how ugly the naked truth would look, and try to dress it up before the eyes of the world. That kind of life cannot go on. We are doomed to destruction in such an atmosphere of lies. We must return somehow to truth and order." At his last words she let go of him and turned very pale.

"Ah, then it is only a pretext," she cried; "you want to get up a quarrel with me as an excuse for breaking with me. That is unmanly of you, that is cowardly. Be frank, tell me straight out what you want. I have a right to demand absolute candor of you."

Her words stabbed him like a knife. There was some truth in her accusation. It was neither honest nor manly to make so much of her fibs when he had something very different in his mind. She appealed to his candor—she should not do so in vain.

"It was not a pretext," he said, and forced himself to look into her face that seemed turning to stone, "but a prompting cause. You ask for the truth, and you shall have it, for I owe it you. Well then, things cannot remain as they are. I cannot go on living as a hanger-on in this house. I—"

He sought painfully for words, but could find none.

Pilar breathed hard. "Well—in short—" The words came out as if she were being strangled.

"In short, Pilar—I must—we shall have—"

"I will not help you. Finish—you shall say the word."

"We shall have to part, Pilar."

"Wretch!" The cry wrenched itself from her breast.

Wilhelm rose and prepared to leave the room. But at the same instant she had rushed to him, and clinging wildly to him, she cried, beside herself with anguish:

"Don't go, Wilhelm, don't be angry with me. You don't know what I feel—you are torturing me to death."

Her sobs were so violent that she could not keep upon her feet, and sank on the floor in front of him. He lifted her up and set her on a chair, and his own eyes were wet as he said:

"I am not suffering less than you, Pilar, but the cup of bitterness must be drunk."

"You do not love me," she moaned. "You have never loved me."

"Do not say that, Pilar. I have loved you, but it is our ill-luck—"

"You have loved me, you say. So you do not love me now? Wilhelm, speak—do you not love me any more?"

He tried to evade the question. "You know, from the first, I did not want to come here. My weak compliance is revenging itself upon me now. You yourself only spoke of it as a trial; if I could not accustom myself to it you would not insist on my remaining."

"You do not love me any more! So that is your boasted German constancy of which you are so proud! These are your vows which I took for gospel truth!"

"I have no recollection of having made any vows," he retorted. He was sorry for it the moment the words had left his mouth.

"That is true," she answered bitterly; "you never promised anything. You left me to do all the vowing. It is unpardonable of me to reproach you, I have no claim upon you. I forced myself upon you—why don't you tell me so? Shout it in my ears! Despise me, kick me—I deserve no better. I have been guilty of the deadly sin of loving you madly, and forgetting everything else in the world for that. You are quite right to punish me for it. And see how low I have sunk! see what my love has brought me to! You may curse me, you may ill-treat me; I love you all the same, Wilhelm—do what you will, I love you all the same."

She was so distraught that she could not stay in the dining room. With a sudden violent movement she grasped his arm and dragged him away with her upstairs to the bedroom, where she threw herself exhausted on the sofa. Wilhelm stood before her, looking thoroughly crestfallen, and wishing devoutly that he had the dread hour behind him. The silence frightened Pilar. She raised her head, and said in a weak, changed voice:

"It is all over, is it not? Tell me that it was only a bad dream—tell me that you will not frighten me like that again."

"Pilar," he returned miserably, "I wish you would listen to me quietly. You are generally so reasonable."

"No, no," she cried; "I am not reasonable—I will not be reasonable. I love you out of all reason. I shall repeat it a thousand times, till you give up talking to me of reason."

"And yet it is impossible for me to stay in this house."

She straightened herself up, looked at him for a moment, and then said with unnatural calmness, as she wiped the tears from her eyes:

"Very well; but if you go I shall go with you."

"What! you would leave your home, your friends, your beloved Paris—give up all you have been accustomed to, and follow me to Germany?"

"To Germany—to the Inferno—wherever you like."

"You do not mean it seriously."

"I do mean it, very seriously. I cannot live without you."

"But you have duties, you have your children—"

"I have no children, I have only you. And if my children were a barrier between you and me, I would strangle them with my own hands."

She spoke with such savage determination that he shuddered. But the battle must be fought out. He must not yield now.

"There is nothing for it," he said after a pause, during which he stood with downcast eyes, fumbling nervously with the buttons of his morning coat. "Our position would be equally wretched wherever we were. Fate is stronger than we are. I do not see how we are to escape it. Wherever we went, we should have to hide the truth, and surround ourselves with a tissue of lies, and that I cannot stand. I would rather die."

"Die?" she exclaimed, and her eyes flamed up weirdly—"I am quite ready. That is a way out of the difficulty. Die—whenever you like; but live without you? No, I will cling to you; no power on earth shall tear me from you. If you want to shake me off, you will have to kill me first." "And yet you said you would not try to hold me back if I wished to leave you."

"And you remembered those foolish words! While my heart was overflowing, you listened coolly and took note of everything, so that you might use it against me afterward. I really did not think you were so noble, so generous minded, as that."

"You see that you were mistaken in me. I am narrow-minded, mean-spirited, a thorough Philistine; you have said so repeatedly. What do you see in me to care for? Let me go."

"Oh, how you fix on every word and then turn it against me! I am not equal to you; you are stronger than I, because you do not love me and I love you. What do I care if you are narrow-minded—a Philistine? If you were a highway robber I would not let you go."

She stretched out her arms to him and drew him to her, and pressed him so tightly to her bosom that he could hardly breathe. Then she burst into tears, and wept so bitterly, so inconsolably, from the bottom of her heart, like a child who has been very deeply hurt. In order to value woman's tears aright, one must have often seen them flow. Wilhelm was a novice in this respect. He imagined that Pilar's tears were the outcome of the same amount of pain as he must have felt to weep like that, and every drop fell like molten lead upon his heart. His resolutions melted like ice before the fire; he had not the courage to wound this clinging, loving, sobbing creature. He rocked her gently in his arms till, exhausted by her frightful excitement, she fell asleep.

The storm was averted for this time, but her confidence, her joyous sense of security, was gone forever. The scene left her with a nervous restlessness which gradually increased to morbid fear. She was haunted by the idea, that Wilhelm had some plan for deserting her. She could not get rid of the thought—it assumed the aspect of a possession. She changed color as she did regularly two or three times in the course of the morning—she opened the door of his room unexpectedly and did not see him at the writing table, because, maybe, he had gone out on to the balcony for a moment, to rest from his work and cool his heated brow. Then she would search the house distractedly till she found him, and breathed again. In the night, she would start up, and feel about her hurriedly, to make sure that Wilhelm was there. She would not let him go a step out of the house without her. She even accompanied him to the National Library, and while he read or made notes, she sat beside him apparently occupied with a book, but in reality never taking her eye off him. She made no more visits except to the houses where she could take Wilhelm with her. She had curious jealous fancies, examining, for instance, with great care every letter that came for him, lest the address should be in a feminine hand. Her desire to be forever proving to herself that he was there, that he still belonged to her, took the form of an insatiable craving for love, admitting, so to speak, of no pauses for digestion. She was a beautiful, greedy werewolf, knowing neither consideration nor restraint, her vampire mouth forever draining the warm life-blood.

"She is crazy," said Anne to one of Queen Isabella's ladies who had been calling on Pilar, and remarked afterward to the maid that she found the countess strangely altered. Isabel, the cook with the red nose and alcoholic, watery eyes, passed whole mornings with her mistress laying the cards, till she forgot all about lunch. The father confessor, too, became an ever more frequent guest in the house of his fashionable parishioner, and received in exchange for his mild and discreet exhortations, donations for his church, gifts for his poor, and requests for masses and prayers. But in none of these distractions did Pilar find the peace she sought, and in her terror of heart she telegraphed one day to her mother to come at once to Paris and stay with her for a time. Don Pablo had taken the message to the office, and talked about it afterward downstairs. Auguste hurried to retail the news to Wilhelm, who had no difficulty in understanding the motive. In the first moment he thought he was glad of the approaching arrival of the Marquise de Henares. For, distasteful as the idea might be that the mother should become a witness of the daughter's questionable relations, he hoped that her presence would have a quieting effect on Pilar, and help to bring her to reason. But, on second thoughts, he was seized with afresh anxiety. He knew that Pilar's was the stronger spirit of the two, that she had a great influence over her mother, and could induce her to adopt any opinion or feelings she might choose. What if the marquise ranged herself on her daughter's side? Then, instead of one, he would have two women against him, and his struggle for freedom, in which he had already succumbed to one of them, would be utterly hopeless.

The Marquise de Henares did not come. She wrote that she was out of health, and was beside detained in Madrid by a thousand social duties; but in the spring or summer she would be very pleased to come and spend a few weeks with her only child and her grandchildren.

Wilhelm maintained an outward show of calm. He did not renew his attempt at revolt, made no resistance against the fact that Pilar took entire possession of his existence, and clung to him like his shadow; he only grew paler, and quieter, and more despondent than before. But he pondered day and night upon some way of unraveling the knot, and was in despair at finding none. Should he cut it? He could not. He lived over again the scene in the dining room; he pictured to himself how Pilar would sob, and fling herself on the floor, and clasp his knees, and tear her hair, and saw himself, after a useless repetition of his torture, disarmed anew. For one moment he thought of giving a cry for help, of calling Schrotter to his aid, but he was ashamed of his want of manliness, and put the idea from him. There was nothing for it but to resign himself. He did so with a gloomy, desperate relinquishment of all his principles, his sense of morality, his ideals of life. He was the victim of a malign fate, and there was no use fighting against it. He must accept it as he would sickness or death. He was untrue to himself, was a dissembler before himself and others: it lay in the inexorable logic of things that he must suffer for it. But what a shipwreck! After a pure and dignified life, wholly filled up by duty and a striving after knowledge, entirely devoted to warring against the animal element in man, and to educating himself up to an ideal standard of freedom from ignoble instincts, thus shamefully to choke and drown in the muddy lees of a love-potion!

Pilar, who fancied him reconciled to the situation, grew easier in her mind, and by degrees lost much of her distrust. About a month later, toward the middle of March, she had so far regained her equanimity as to allow herself, after a steady resistance, to be persuaded by a friend to attend her house-warming ball—"pendre la cremaillere," as they call it in Paris. The friend was quite as superstitious as Pilar herself, and had vowed a hundred times over that she would have no luck in her new house if Pilar were absent from the opening ball.

It was not till ten o'clock in the evening that she finally made up her mind. She waited till Wilhelm had gone to bed, and then sent for Isabel, and shut herself up with her in the boudoir. After Isabel had turned up the knave of hearts eight times running, and she had seen that Wilhelm was in bed, reading the newspaper, she gave Anne and Don Pablo a few orders, dressed hurriedly, and went off, after many kisses and embraces, and with the promise of not staying long.

Wilhelm read his paper to the end, blew out the light, and turned himself to the wall. But sleep forsook him, and he stared with wide-open eyes into the darkness. Suddenly an odd suggestion flashed across his mind—was rejected—returned again obstinately, grew stronger, and finally was so imperative that Wilhelm sat up in bed excitedly and relit the candles. Don Pablo had gone home, Anne had accompanied Pilar, Isabel was in the back premises, engaged upon the Val de Penas, two fresh casks of which had lately arrived, and Auguste was probably in his bedroom asleep. He was as good as alone in the house. Now or never!

He sprang out of bed, and began to dress with a beating heart. Had it come to this with him? He was on the point of committing an act of cowardice—yes, but no greater, perhaps even less so, than smouldering away in slavery and degradation. It was an ugly breach of trust. Not really so, for he had expressed, himself plainly to Pilar, and she must know how matters stood between them. Moreover, if you fall into the mire, you cannot expect to get out of it again without besmirching yourself. But—what will poor Pilar's feelings be when she comes home and finds him gone? At the picture he faltered, and very near returned to bed. But no—he put it forcibly from him.

He rapidly finished dressing, and went into his room to collect such things as were absolutely necessary. The two large trunks had been removed, and would in any case have been out of the question at this juncture. The portmanteau lay behind a wardrobe. Into it he stuffed some linen and clothes, a few books and his manuscript, cast one look round the rooms in which he had encountered such heavy storms of the heart, extinguished the lights, and walked resolutely downstairs.

The gas was burning in the hall, the front door stood half open, and on the doorstep was Auguste, talking to a maid-servant from the next house. She flitted away as the man turned round, and, to his astonishment, perceived Wilhelm with a portmanteau in his hand. He stepped quickly indoors.

"Ah," he said in a muffled tones, "Monsieur le Docteur! I understand—I understand. I would have done it long ago. It really couldn't go on like that any longer. But monsieur might have said a word to me; for as to me—I am dumb!"

Wilhelm was crushed to the earth. So he was not to be spared one humiliation, not even the patronizing familiarity of this lackey! But it could not be helped now. Regardless of his opposition, Auguste took the portmanteau out of his hand, and asked with eager civility where he should carry it.

"Only to a fiacre," Wilhelm answered.

They went out together into the Boulevard Pereire, and as they walked along beside the deep cutting of the circle railway, Auguste inquired:

"Monsieur is leaving Paris, no doubt?"

Wilhelm made no reply.

"Has Monsieur le Docteur left any address?" he continued urgently.

"No," answered Wilhelm.

"But it would be better if he did so, in case any letters might come. And it will surely interest monsieur to know how things go on in the house. Monsieur need only confide it to me. I would not tell it to a single soul, not even if le bon Dieu himself came down with all his saints."

Wilhelm was weak enough to form a fresh link between himself and Pilar, when he had just severed the old one. He wrote Schrotter's address on a leaf of his pocketbook and gave it to Auguste, saying:

"Anything will reach me safely under that address."

They reached the cab stand in the Avenue de Villiers; Wilhelm got into one, took the portmanteau inside, and pressed a sovereign into Auguste's hand, who thanked him and asked where the cabman was to drive to.

"First of all, just along the avenue," answered Wilhelm.

Auguste grinned as he repeated this order to the driver, and was just closing the door, when there was a yelp of pain.

"Infamous beast!" cried Auguste, and gave Fido, who had followed them unperceived, a kick. The poor animal had always been accustomed to going with them when Wilhelm and Pilar drove out, and now was preparing to jump into the vehicle, when he just escaped being crushed in the door. Wilhelm stooped to give the puffing, affectionate creature a farewell pat.

"Monsieur should take him as a souvenir," said Auguste, with thinly-veiled sarcasm. "Nobody will take any notice of him now, in any case."

"You are quite right," said Wilhelm, and let the dog come in. The fiacre moved off, and Auguste looked after it for a long time, as he whistled the latest popular air.

CHAPTER XIII.

CONSUMMATION.

It wanted but little to midday when Wilhelm came out of a hotel on the Neuer Jungfernstieg in Hamburg, and made his way toward the Alster, Fido trotting behind him, whose coat, for want of its accustomed daily washing and brushing, looked sadly neglected.

The sky was thickly overcast, the air unusually mild, on account of the prevailing west wind, and the pavement of the Jungfernstieg damp and muddy. A thin veil of yellow fog lay over the Binnen Alster, giving the objects far and near the indefinite, wavering appearance of a mirage. Above the dark masses of houses to the right rose four sharp spires, from the points of which, smoke-wreaths seemed to rise and trail away. Far away in front the Lombardsbrucke was just distinguishable, its three arches apparently hung with gray draperies. Swans glided lazily in groups or singly over the muddy-looking surface of the water, or came under the open windows of the Alster Pavilion, through which late breakfasting guests threw them crumbs.

The small, green-painted Uhlenhorst steamer lay alongside of the second landing-place. Wilhelm stepped on board, and remained on deck, staring absently into the fog or at the dim outlines of the houses on the shore. On the night of his escape from the Boulevard Pereire he had driven to the Gare du Nord, and taken a midnight train, which brought him at about six the next evening to Cologne. He was dead with fatigue when he got there, stayed the night, and went on the following afternoon to Hamburg. He had been there two days now, but had not been able till to-day to gather sufficient courage to go and see Paul. Solitude had been an absolute necessity to him; he fancied that he who ran might read upon his brow the story of how he had lived and of what he had been guilty. His thoughts were incessantly in Paris. During the journey, in Cologne, since his arrival in Hamburg, he saw nothing but Pilar's room, her return from the ball, and her passionate exhibition of grief during the hours and days that followed. He only lived in these imaginings. There seemed as yet no immediate connection between his natural surroundings and his mental life. He felt as if a few steps would bring him again to Pilar's side, and more than once the desire came over him to return to her, and lay himself at her feet, there to vegetate luxuriously henceforth, without a will or thought, to the end. He resisted this impulse, but he was powerless against the tyranny of his imagination, which ceased not to call up before him the scenes that were being enacted in the house in Paris.

After a minute or two the boat started. The shores receded and spread apart, and the lines of houses came and went like dissolving views upon a white wall. The boat shot under the dark and clammy arch of the bridge, where the echo increased the splashing of the steamer waves and the thump of the machinery to a roar. The noise subsided suddenly, as when a damper is laid over a resounding instrument; the steamer had passed the bridge, and floated out on to the broad waters of the Aussen Alster, which widened apparently into a great bay, the mist having wiped out the boundary lines between its oily surface and the flat shores which barely rose above it. The boat described bold curves from side to side, touching at the different landing-places, and presently—dimly at first and then more distinctly—the square tower and ponderous, castle-like structure of the Fahrhaus Hotel came in sight. The steamer had reached the furthest point of its journey.

Wilhelm found himself once more at the familiar spot which had so often been the goal of his short walks with Willy. Scarcely ten months had elapsed since he had looked at it for the last time, but his morbid mental vision prolonged that time to an eternity. He felt like the sultan of the Eastern legend, who fancied he had lived an entire lifetime, while, in reality, he sank for one moment into his bath in sight of his whole court. He overcame a strange attack of shyness, and rang at the door in the Carlstrasse. The liveried servant opened it, gave an exclamation of surprise, and hurried before him to the smoking room. Wilhelm followed closely on his heels, and only left him time to open the door and call loudly into the room:

"Herr Dr. Eyuhardt!"

"What! Is it you or your ghost? Well, I must say—" cried Paul, overjoyed, receiving him with open arms.

The first tempestuous greetings over, he pressed him, down upon the sofa, seated himself beside him, and rained down a torrent of questions upon him—Where had he come from? How had he fared all this time? What were his plans? And, above all things, where was his luggage?

"At the hotel," Wilhelm answered, a little nervously.

"At the hotel? Are you in your right senses? There is only one hotel for you in Hamburg, and that is the hotel Haber. Were you so uncomfortable there before that you have withdrawn your custom from it?"

"Don't try to persuade me, my good Paul. Believe me, it is best so. Your hospitality oppresses me."

"Is that the remark of a friend?" grumbled Paul.

"It is a fault in me, I know, but I do beg of you to let me have my own way."

"Just wait till I send Malvine to you—you will have to lay down your arms before her."

"No, Paul, I really cannot live in your house again. I will come and see you—so often that you will get tired of me—"

"Never!"

"But let me live here as I am accustomed to in Berlin, especially as it will probably be for a long time."

"Then you are going to stay in Hamburg? That is splendid!"

"For the present at least. I see nothing else to be done."

"But in the summer you will surely come and spend some weeks at Friesenmoor?"

"That is more likely."

The door opened and Malvine hurried in, and ran up to Wilhelm as he rose to meet her.

"To think of you falling from the clouds like this!" she cried, and shook both his hands warmly. "Not a letter, not a telegram, nothing! Well, you knew, at any rate, that you would always be welcome."

Again he had to make a determined stand against having their hospitality forced upon him, and kind, persistent Malvine would not give up the struggle as easily as Paul. As Wilhelm, however, was equally persistent in his refusal, and would not even divulge the name of his hotel till they had sworn to leave him his independence, they finally gave up the fight.

"And now tell us all that has happened to you," said Paul, patting him on the shoulder. "You must have had a very good time, for you either did not write at all or only in a flash—like this: 'Dear friend, am quite well—how are you all? Best love—always yours.' Well, I don't think any the worse of you. In gay Paris one has something better to do than to think of dull old fogies on the Uhlenhorst."

"You don't think that seriously," answered Wilhelm, pressing his hand.

"I should rather be inclined to think that the doctor had been ill," said Malvine, whose woman's eye had instantly remarked the pallor and weariness of Wilhelm's thin face.

"Really—have you been ill?" cried Paul, concerned.

"No, no, there is nothing the matter with me," Wilhelm hastened to answer, with a forced smile.

The awakened anxiety of his friends would not be dispelled, however, till he had repeated his assurance many times, and reinforced it by additions and enlargements.

Paul then returned to his question as to Wilhelm's adventures, the latter doing his best to get out of it by a few vague remarks on the uneventful character of his life during the last few months, and then hurried to descant on Paris, describing the town to them with the volubility of a guide-book. On his inquiring in return about their affairs, Paul and Malvine vied with one another in the redundancy of their account. All was well, so far. At the last distribution of Orders Paul had received the Order of the Red Eagle, and beside that, during the course of the winter, two new foreign decorations. There were all sorts of innovations on the estate, which he described in detail. At present he was hard at work on an entirely new scheme: the founding of a colony on the moor, composed of discharged prisoners, tramps, and such like ne'er-do-wells; where, by supplying them with agricultural labor, they might be brought back to a decent and remunerative way of life.

Malvine had much to tell of the autumn and winter festivities, both at her own and other houses, and also, that of the three heiresses whom she had picked out for Wilhelm, one was married, another engaged, and there remained only the third, the one with the curly hair, who still asked after him from time to time.

Meanwhile the news of Wilhelm's arrival had penetrated as far as Willy, who now came rushing in.

"Onkelchen, Onkelchen! have you come back?" he shouted, long before he reached Wilhelm, and stretched out his little arms to him. He had not grown much, but was plump and rosy as a ripe apple. Wilhelm kissed him, and stroked the soft, fair curls that felt so much like Pilar's silky hair.

"Have you been a good boy all this time?" he asked.

"Oh, yes, very good—haven't I, father?" the boy cried eagerly. "And I can read now—everything—the newspaper too. I got a beautiful big box of bricks for it at Christmas."

Wilhelm had taken him on his knee, but the lively child would not keep quiet for long. He jumped down and hopped about in front of his godfather and chattered away.

"I say, Onkelchen, you have just come in time for my birthday, haven't you?"

Wilhelm had not thought of it.

"When is your birthday, my boy?" he asked, rather crestfallen.

"Why, don't you know? It is the day after to-morrow. And what have you brought me?"

He did not wait for an answer, having caught sight, at that moment, of Fido, who, shy as all dogs are in a strange place and among strange people, had crept away under a table, and sat there very still with his eyes firmly fixed on Wilhelm.

"A dog! A spitz!" Willy shrieked with joy. "Is he for me, Onkelchen?"

He rushed at Fido, took hold of him by the paw, and dragged him out.

Malvine cried anxiously:

"Let him go, Willy!"

But Wilhelm reassured her.

"He won't hurt him, he is quite gentle."

Fido allowed himself to be dragged without much resistance into the middle of the room, only turning his head away nervously and eying the child askance, as if doubtful as to his intentions. But when Willy began to pat and stroke him kindly, and set him on his hind legs in the first position for begging, Fido realized that no harm was going to befall him, and attached himself instantly to the new friend with that easy confidence which was this sociable creature's great fault of character. He fell to wagging his bushy tail in a highly expressive manner, tried to lick Willy's rosy face, and was altogether so overcome by pleasing emotions that he got a severe attack of coughing, sneezing, and snorting, and Willy exclaimed:

"My Spitz has caught a cold on the journey. We must give him some black-currant tea, mother!"

The boy took a great delight in the dog, playing with him the whole time of Wilhelm's visit, feeding him at dinner, and even wanted to make him drink beer, which Fido steadfastly refused to do, and was much disappointed when, at leaving, Wilhelm prepared to take the dog with him.

"Didn't you bring him for me?" he asked with a pout.

Wilhelm consoled him by promising that he should see Fido every day, and solemnly transferred to him all legal rights to the animal. On these conditions Willy was content that Fido should go on living with Wilhelm, and that he should come frequently on a starring tour, as it were, to the Carlstrasse.

Wilhelm's first visit to his friends on the Uhlenhorst did not tend to lighten his spirit. In their home he breathed a pure and wholesome atmosphere, which, it seemed to him, he must contaminate by the heavy, noxious perfume which still clung to him, and which he could not get rid of. Their life was as transparent as crystal, every moment would bear the scrutiny of the severest eye. He, on the other hand, had much to conceal. His memory recalled many a scene; he saw himself again in various situations, and thought—what would they say if they knew? Paul and Malvine told him cheerfully of all that had occurred to them during the last eight months; he was condemned to lock away his experiences in the depths of his heart. His open and confiding nature was little used to keeping a secret. It rose to his lips as often as he found himself alone with his friend, and his longing to unburden himself was all the more intense that he had himself formed no certain judgment on his course of action, and yearned to hear from the mouth of an unprejudiced person of sound moral tone and worldly experience, that he had done no great harm. He carried in his own breast an accusing voice which called him faithless and mean-spirited, and showed him Pilar as the victim of his treachery; and he had need of an advocate, seeing that he was himself unable to refute these accusations with any sort of confidence.

He was to receive the support he longed for. Soon after his arrival in Hamburg he had written to Schrotter, telling him of his change of residence, and expressing, at the same time, his intense desire to see him again after their long separation, also, if it would not be asking too much, to propose that he, Schrotter, should make a short journey, say to Wittenberg, where they might meet and spend a few days together, if it were possible for Schrotter to get away from Berlin for a short time.

Schrotter answered by return of post. He was delighted to find that Wilhelm was so near, and promised to take advantage of the first fine days of April to make his little excursion to Hamburg. He would arrange it so that he could at least spend a week with Wilhelm. It was not impossible that he might bring Bhani with him.

Only a fortnight had passed since Wilhelm received this letter, when, on his return one afternoon from the Uhlenhorst, the hotel porter informed him that a gentleman had arrived from Berlin, and had asked for him; that he was expecting him in his room, the number of which he mentioned. With joyful foreboding Wilhelm hurried upstairs so fast that Fido could not follow, and knocked at the door. A familiar voice answered. "Come in!" and the next moment he was in Schrotter's arms.

The first greetings over, Schrotter gave his young friend a long and penetrating look from under the half-closed lids, and remarked

"I suppose you are surprised that I did not wait till April, but dropped down upon you unawares like this?"

"I am too delighted to be surprised," answered Wilhelm, and pressed Schrotter's large, strong hand.

He had scarcely altered at all in the year and a quarter, and with his herculean shoulders and powerful head, his fair hair, blushed into a great tuft above his forehead, only just beginning to turn gray, he was still the very type and picture of ripe manhood and strength.

"But I had a reason for changing my original plan," Schrotter went on. "Unwittingly I have committed a breach of good manners against you, for which I must personally ask you to forgive me." He drew a letter out of his breast-pocket and handed it to Wilhelm. "This letter came yesterday. Seeing the address, I took it for granted that it was for me, and so I read it, and discovered then that it was for you."

Wilhelm turned pale as Schrotter handed him the letter. It bore the Paris postmark, and Schrotter's name and address in a large, clumsy hand. Nothing on the outside to betray that it was for Wilhelm. Auguste—Wilhelm divined at once that he was the writer of the letter—had not thought of putting it in a second envelope directed to Wilhelm, or of adding his name to the original address.

Wilhelm's hand shook as he unfolded the letter, and a veil fell before his eyes. For one moment he had the idea to put the letter in his pocket, and say he would read it later on, for it was torture to him that Schrotter should be a witness of the emotion he knew he must feel on reading it. But of what use was it to dissemble? Schrotter would have to know. He glanced over Auguste's stiff characters.

The man wrote in his ill-bred tone, with spelling to match:

"PARIS, March 26, 1880.

"MONSIEUR LE DOCTEUR: It is a week now since you left, and time that you should know what has been going on during that time. It was as good as a play! But you shall hear.

"When Madame la Comtesse came home, and I opened the door to her, I said nothing, but I thought to myself—what a row there will be presently. And sure enough, she had hardly set foot in her rooms when we heard an awful scream. It didn't scare me, because I knew all about it; but Isabel came tumbling out, and howled in French and Spanish mixed: 'Is it a fire? Are there thieves in the house?' It was enough to make you die of laughing.

"I was called upstairs and questioned by Anne—the countess had not the strength. She was kneeling in her ball-dress beside the bed, her face buried in the pillows that still showed the pressure of your head, and crying as if her heart would break. I know that madame cries very easily—she has always been that way as long as I have known her—but I really should not have thought, to look at her, that she could hold such a quantity of tears. Anne cross-examined me like a magistrate, but of course I made an innocent face, and knew nothing at all. I saw plainly that she did not really care a bit, the viper, for while she was cross-questioning me she gave me a look once or twice that told me quite enough. But Madame la Comtesse is very sharp. She saw at once that I knew more than I had a mind to tell. She turned a face to me, as white as a cheese, and looked at me with such eyes, that I might well have been frightened if I had not—I may say it without boasting—been born in Carpentras. At first she tried it with kindness, and then she threatened to turn me out of the house that minute, and then she wanted to bribe me by all sorts of promises—ma foi! it was not a very easy moment, but I stood firm, and madame threw herself back on the bed, and the tap was turned on full again. Would you believe it, that that Anne had the face to say to madame she had better look in the bureau to see if her money and jewels were safe. 'Silence, wretch!' cried Madame la Comtesse, so that the windows rattled, and gave the person a look that made her double up like a penknife. She does not come from Carpentras. To make a long story short, none of us went to bed that night. Madame took it into her head you might have gone for a little walk in the middle of the night, and would come back. Good idea, wasn't it? But when the morning came, she saw that the bird had really flown, and that changed the whole affair. She took to her bed, and stayed there for five days with the room all darkened, ate nothing, drank nothing, was delirious, had four doctors called in each at fifty francs the visit, beside priests and nuns, and Madame la Marquise, her mamma, got three telegrams, one longer than the other, and arrived here the day before yesterday, and now they are trying which can cry the most. But the daughter has the best of it. Since she had her mamma with her, madame seems calmer. She got up yesterday for the first time, and—not to keep back anything from you—I have great hopes that in a fortnight or three weeks' time we shall see her going to balls again. That will do her a world of good.

"She had your things taken up to the box-room, so that she might not see them any more, and Madame la Marquise has your room, but Madame la Comtesse never sets foot in it. The artist in hair says that there is talk of renting a new house, or even of going to Spain. I should be very sorry to leave Madame la Comtesse, but to Spain I would not go.

"I should be glad to know from Monsieur le Docteur whether, after madame has consoled herself a little, I may give her monsieur's address, that his things may be forwarded. I hope you are well, and that you will write me a line. You need not be anxious about madame, she will soon be all right again. You were not the first, and, let us hope, you will not have been the last.

"I salute Monsieur le Docteur, "Your very obedient servant,

"AUGUSTE.

"POSTSCRIPT.—In spite of her desperation, madame had the presence of mind to try and persuade Anne you very probably had to fly from your political enemies, or had even been carried off and murdered by Prussian agents. Anne said, 'Yes; such things have happened.' The viper! You did well to take yourself out of this."

Wilhelm was unaware that he read the letter twice or three times over without a pause between. When he was beginning for the fourth time, he suddenly remembered that he was not alone, and that Schrotter was sitting there watching him. He folded the letter in confusion. He had not the courage to say anything, or even to look at his friend, but dropped his hands and his head, and cast down his miserable eyes.

Schrotter was the first to break the silence.

"I must beg you once more to forgive me for opening the letter. Of course, I could not have an idea—"

"No," said Wilhelm in a low voice, "it is for me to ask your forgiveness for not having been open with you. But I had every intention of making good my fault. It was for that I asked you to meet me at Wittenberg."

"Spare yourself the telling of anything that might be painful to you," said Schrotter, with kindly forethought. "I can guess the drift of it, and now understand your last letter. I thought you would probably be in a frame of mind to need a friend near you, and so I came without delay."

"I will not leave you to guess anything," Wilhelm returned, and pressed Schrotter's hand. "I will tell you all; it is an absolute necessity to me, and will, at the same time, be a kind of atonement."

And he began his confession in a low, dull voice, and with downcast eyes, like a sinner acknowledging a shameful deed, and Schrotter listened to him gravely and in silence, like a priest before whom some poor oppressed soul is casting down its burden of guilt. Wilhelm kept nothing back, neither the mad intoxication of the first weeks, nor the bitter humiliation of the last. He disclosed Pilar's passion and his own weakness, the pagan sensuality and the artifices of the woman's insatiable love, and the unworthy part he had played in her house before the servants and strangers. He spoke of his tormenting doubts as to the justice of his actions, and concluded: "And now, tell me, shall I answer this letter?"

"What are you thinking of?" cried Schrotter, when Wilhelm stopped speaking, and looked at him in anxious expectation. "Your only plan now is to keep dark. If, notwithstanding your silence, they write to you again, I would advise you to burn the letters unread. That will demand a certain amount of fortitude, no doubt, but as the letters will come to my address, I will do it for you, if you authorize me."

Wilhelm tried hard to make up his mind.

"No, do not burn them unread," he said, after a pause; "open the letters, and then judge for yourself, in each case, whether you will let me know the whole or part of the contents."

"Always the same want of will power!" returned Schrotter. "First you free yourself, and then have not the courage to burn your ships behind you. Believe me, it is best that you should have no further news from Paris, and after some months you can send for your things through a third person. Have you anybody in Paris who could arrange that for you?"

"No."

"Then I will do it. And even if you were to let the things go, it would be no great loss. Above all things, no renewing of old fetters. This lackey takes a healthy enough view of the matter, for all his cynicisms. You must not take it too tragically. You have passed through your heart crisis—it comes to most of us—only with you it has happened late, and under unpropitious circumstances. That has tended to make it more severe than is usually the case. But now, let it be past and over, though naturally it will take some little time for your mind to regain its normal balance. What I regret most in the affair is, that it precludes the idea of marriage for you for some time to come, and I had wished that so much for you. As long as the fascinations of this siren are fresh in your memory, no respectable German girl will have any attraction for you, and the love she is able to offer you will seem flat and insipid."

"You only speak of me," Wilhelm ventured to remark, "but that is not the worst side of the story; what weighs most heavily on my mind is, that I have broken my faith with her."

"Do not let that worry you," Schrotter replied. "You were in such a position as to be forced to act in self-defense. It would have been inexcusable in you to have stayed any longer where you were. For a liaison of that kind is only conceivable when the man loves the woman very deeply. You, my friend, did not love the lady at all. If you have any doubts about it in your own mind, you may take my word for it—had you loved her, you would not have parted from her. You would, if necessary, have carried her off from Paris, and continued to live with her in some world-forgotten spot, as you did at St. Valery. Or you would have gone off to the Philippines, and fought her husband to the death, in order to gain free possession of her or die in the attempt. That is how love acts when it is of that elemental force which alone can justify such relations before the higher natural tribunal of morality. But if your love is not strong enough to prompt you to do these things, then it is immoral, and must be shaken off."

Wilhelm was still unconvinced.

"I surely owe her gratitude for having loved me? That imposes certain duties upon me; I have no right to break a heart which gave itself wholly to me."

"Your idea has a specious air of generosity," answered Schrotter firmly, "but in reality it is morbid and weak. Love accepts no alms. One gives oneself wholly or not at all. Do you imagine that any woman of spirit would be satisfied if you said to her: 'I do not love you, I should like to leave you, but I will stay on with you because I do not wish to give you pain, or from pity—soft-heartedness.' Why, she would thrust you from her, and rather, a thousand times, die than live on your bounty. On the other hand, the woman who would still hold fast to a man after such a declaration, must be of so poor a stuff that I do not consider her capable of feeling any violent pain. Woman, in general, has a far truer and more natural judgment in this question. Where she does not love she has no scruples about want of consideration, and the knowledge that it will hurt the man's feelings has rarely restrained her from rejecting an unwelcome suitor. There is such a thing as necessary cruelty, my friend—the physician knows that better than anybody."

Wilhelm shook his head thoughtfully.

"Your cruelties are not for your own advantage, but for that of your patient. I have no such excuse to offer."

"Yes, you have," cried Schrotter. "You cure the countess of a morbid and hysterical sentiment. This Auguste is right—she will console herself."

"And if does not?"

"If not—why, what can I say?—we must simply wait and see. But it would surprise me very much. The worst is over. In such cases, if women mean to commit some act of madness, they do it in the first moment. The countess has her mother with her, she has three children, she has, from all I hear, an extremely buoyant nature, her despair will soon calm down. If not, it is always open to you to return in a year's time and do the prodigal son, and have the fatted calf killed for you."

As Wilhelm looked at him with suppressed reproach, Schrotter laid his hand on the young man's shoulder.

"You no doubt think me a hard-hearted old fogey—you miss the ring of romance in what I say. That is quite natural. The language of reason always sounds flat to the ear of passion—and not to passion only, but to sentimentality and feebleness. Let us finish. You know my advice. Give no sign of life, and so give time a chance to do its work. Try to forgot the past, and help the lady to do likewise, and do not remind her of it again by letters, or any other kind of communication. And now let us talk of something else. What are your plans?"

"I have none," answered Wilhelm, with a dispirited gesture. "I have not forgotten what you wrote to me at New Year. If our wishes make up our future, I have no future before me, for I have no wish."

"Not even to be near me again?" asked Schrotter.

"Ah, yes," answered Wilhelm quickly, and looked him affectionately in the deep-set blue eyes.

"You see now. This wandering life is no good for you. You must see about getting back to Berlin."

"Yes, but you know—"

"Of course I know. But something must be done. You must apply to the authorities to withdraw your sentence of banishment."

"And you advise me to do this?"

"Unwillingly, as you may well suppose. But I see nothing else for you."

"And how should I word such a petition? I could neither acknowledge a transgression in the past, nor promise amendment in the future."

"No, it would be of no use going into details. It would have to be a bald petition for pardon." And seeing Wilhelm recoil involuntarily, he added: "It does not do to be too proud in such a case. In the preposterously unequal struggle between the individual and the organized power of the State, it is no disgrace to declare yourself beaten and ask for quarter."

"A petition without any gush or protestations of loyalty, in which I would simply say: 'Please allow me to come back to Berlin, because I prefer it to any other place of residence,' would certainly be ineffectual, and I should only have humiliated myself for nothing."

"We must get somebody to take up your cause. I shall do all in my power to make the Oberburgermeister put in a good word for you."

"Would you yourself do what you are advising me to do?"

Schrotter was silent for a moment.

"I am not in the same case. If Berlin were as much a necessity to me as it is to you I would do it—most certainly."

Wilhelm looked as if he were swallowing a bitter draught. But Schrotter's strong hand lay tenderly on the dark head.

"Yes, friend Eynhardt," he said; "you will send in the petition, and it will, I hope, have the desired result. Do it for my sake. Yes, look at me; I have need of you. I miss you. I am getting to be an old man. At sixty years of age one does not make new friendships. All the more carefully does one keep those one has. Berlin has seemed to me a desert—almost unbearable, without you. You do not know how impossible things have become there. They are misusing, without one pang of conscience, the most touching and lovable characteristic of our people—its sense of gratitude, which it exaggerates to the point of weakness. They are doing all they can to bind Germany hand and foot, to gag her and drag her back into absolutism before her sentimentality will allow her to put herself on the defensive. They are pandering to the lowest instincts of the people, and enervating their manhood by every artifice in their power. Thus they have successfully achieved the introduction into Germany of that most degraded form of self-worship—Chauvinism. They poison her morality by wisely organizing that every conscience, every conviction, should have its price. They debase her ideals by decreeing that henceforth the officer is to be the national patron saint to whom the people are to offer up their devotion and worship. The press, literature, art, lecturing-room—all preach the same gospel, that the highest product of humanity is the officer, and that "soldierly discipline and smartness"—in other words, slavish submission, self-conceit, arrogance, and the upholding of mere brute force—are the noblest qualities of a man and a patriot. The army is taught to forget that it is the armed population of the country, and is trained to be a band of body servants. And even when the soldiers return to private life, the idea of servitude is carefully kept up, and he finds again in the military 'Verein' the beloved barrack life, with all its servile submissiveness and abnegation of free will. Whichever way I look, I am filled with horror. Everything is ground down, everything laid waste, the governing spirit has not left one stone standing upon another. Even our youth, with whom lies our hope for the future, is rotten in part. In many student circles I see a want of principle, a low cringing to success, a cowardly worship of animal strength, that is without its parallel in our history. Instinctively, this corrupt youth sides, in every question, with the strong against the weak, with the pursuer against the pursued, and that at the age when my generation exerted itself passionately, without a question as to right or wrong, for everyone oppressed against every oppressor. Of course we were simpletons, we of '48, and the golden youth of to-day scoffs superciliously at our naive ideals. In the present order of things everything has become a curse—even the parliamentary system. For that gives the people no means of making its will known, and has simply become a vehicle for general corruption at the elections. Our officials, on whose independence of spirit we used to pride ourselves so much, have sunk into mere electioneering agents, and unless they pursue, oppress, and grind the opponents of the government, have no chance of promotion. It is a Police State such as we have never known, not even before '48. For at least every man got his rights in those days, scanty as those rights may have been, and the official was not the enemy of the citizen, but his somewhat despotic guardian and protector. Shall I say all? The most consoling class to me in Germany to-day are the Social Democrats. They have independence of spirit, self-denial, character, and idealism. Their ideals are not my ideals—far from it—but what does that matter? It is relief enough to find people who have any ideals at all, and who are ready to suffer and die for them. I fear that not till this generation has passed away will the German people become once more the upright, true-hearted, incorruptible idealists they were, who, at every turning-point of their history, were ready to bleed to death for freedom of opinion, and other purely spiritual advantages. I take a very black view of things perhaps. If only the harm done is not permanent, if only Germany retains sufficient virile strength to throw off the poison instilled into her veins and recover her former health!"

In his excitement he had risen, and was pacing the room like an angry lion in a cage. Wilhelm did not like to interrupt the stream of words, which seemed to be forced from him by some powerful inward pressure. Now he said:

"I can well understand your point of view. You emigrated in '48, and kept your democratic ideas fresh in your heart. Twenty years of absence, and an intense longing for your home, glorified the Fatherland in your eyes. You come back and find a country whose historical development has taken a totally different turn in the meantime, and the plain reality in nowise corresponds to the poetical picture you had painted for yourself. Naturally you are painfully disappointed. I know that of old from my own father. But may I venture to remark that your criticism is hard, and perhaps not altogether well founded? A system of government passes—the people remain. In its inner depths it is untouched by official corruption, and you yourself acknowledge that the aggressive boasters only formed a small part of our youth. I am not uneasy for the future of my country."

"You may be right," returned Schrotter, grown calmer meanwhile, and standing still in front of Wilhelm. "But the present is gloomy, that is very certain. But enough of this. I came to cheer you, and have instead lightened my own heart. It was overflowing, and I have no one in Berlin to whom I can unburden myself. You see, I must have you near me. So write your petition, and if it is not accepted, why then—then we will go together to Switzerland or America, and love our country from afar, and without any admixture of bitterness, just as I did in India."

In face of this deep and unselfish concern over the condition of the commonalty which trembled in Schrotter's voice and spoke from his gloomy blue eyes, Wilhelm felt half ashamed of having made so much of his own small troubles. He declared himself willing to send in the petition, and for the first time for weeks he was able to think of something else than Pilar and his dealings with regard to her.

Schrotter stayed for a few days, which he passed almost exclusively with Wilhelm and Paul. All three felt themselves younger by ten years in this renewal of their intimacy, and Paul said more than once, "Would it not be splendid, Herr Doctor, if you two would buy some property near me? Then, in the summer months at any rate, we could all live together, so to speak. I am quite convinced that that would be a sure way of keeping ourselves young forever." Schrotter smiled at this proposal. All he wanted was to have Wilhelm near him once more. In the meantime, Bhani, his patients, his poor, recalled him to Berlin, and he left in hope that Wilhelm might be able to follow him ere long.

Schrotter lost no time. He did his utmost to persuade influential people to exert themselves on Wilhelm's behalf, but the difficulties were greater than he had imagined. Wilhelm was in very bad odor with the police authorities, who would not believe that he was not a Socialist, and that he did not afford that party valuable support in the shape of money.

Some three weeks after Schrotter's visit to Hamburg another letter came from Auguste. He was surprised, he said, that Monsieur le Docteur had not answered, and proceeded to inform him of a new turn in the affair. They had discovered that Madame la Comtesse injected herself secretly with morphine, pricked herself, Auguste said, and two Sisters of Mercy had to watch her day and night to prevent it. Schrotter judged it unnecessary to inform Wilhelm of the contents of this letter.

Schrotter's visit had had an extremely salutary effect on Wilhelm. His self-torture grew less poignant, the memory of Paris receded into the background, and in proportion as it paled the red returned to his cheeks and the light to his dull eyes. He still held aloof from the busy turmoil of the world, and was still dominated by a profound consciousness of the aimlessness of his life, and yet, for the first time for years, perhaps since he took his degree, he entertained a desire, a hope, that he might be permitted to return to Berlin.

On the last Sunday in April Wilhelm was spending the afternoon at the Uhlenhorst. The family were preparing to remove shortly to Friesenmoor, and Paul had gone over to the estate to make some arrangements. He was expected back in the evening, when they were all to go for a row on the Alster.

Spring was unusually early that year; the trees showed gay sprigs of green already, the air was wonderfully mild and balmy, and in the exhilarating blue of the sky feathery white cloudlets were floating, whose course one was fain to follow with sweet dreams and fancies. It was a sin to stay indoors on such a lovely afternoon, Malvine declared, and so proposed that they should go out to the terrace overlooking the water and sit there till Paul came home.

The terrace belonged to the villa in the Carlstrasse, laying on the path round the shore which bears with perfect right the name "An der schonen Aussicht"—the beautiful view—and was built out in a square into the Alster. A low stone parapet surrounded it on three sides, the fourth—that toward the pathway—being formed by an iron paling with a locked gate in it. One corner of the terrace, which was otherwise paved with asphalt, was laid out in a round flower bed, in which the primroses and violets were just beginning to come up. Near the balustrade at the waterside, under a large tentlike umbrella, stood a garden table and a few chairs. Here Malvine and Wilhelm seated themselves, while Willy played about with Fido. To the right of the terrace was a narrow little bay where the shallow boat was fastened in which they were to make their pleasure trip later on. The boat was tied to a wooden landing-place, which inclosed the little bay on the side away from the terrace, and from which a few mossy steps led down to the water. The Alster was swollen with melting snow and spring rains, and almost washed the foot of the terrace; only one of the steps of the landing appeared above the surface of the water. Willy, finding it rather dull on the terrace, elected to play on the pier, and began jumping in and out of the boat, into which Fido refused to follow him, as he was afraid of the water.

The view was enchanting. The opposite shore gleamed silvery blue in the delicate white light of a northern spring day. In the distance, the masses of houses and the spires of Hamburg hung upon the horizon like a faintly tinted, half-washed out transparency. A light breeze ruffled the broad bosom of the Alster, and the red and green steamboats plowed dark furrows in its brightness, which remained there long after the boats had passed, and faded away finally in many a serpentine curve. Numbers of little rowing and sailing-boats floated upon the slow current, peopled by couples and parties in their Sunday clothes, their talk and merry laughter sounding across the water to the shore. A sailing-boat passed quite close to the terrace on its way to the Fahrhaus. A young boatman handled the sails, a little boy was steering, and in the stern sat a young man and a pretty rosy girl, their arms affectionately intertwined, softly singing, "Life let us cherish." Malvine smiled as she caught sight of the little idyll, and turning to Wilhelm, who was gazing dreamily into the quiet sunny beauty of the surrounding scene: "Can you imagine any more delightful occupation on a spring day like this," she said, "than to go love-making like those two little people over there?"

A shadow passed over Wilhelm's face. He saw himself lying in the high grass under a wide-spreading tree in St. Valery, and over him there hovered a white hand that strewed him with fresh blossoms.

At that instant they heard a little frightened cry, followed immediately by a second one, and then a gurgle. Both sprang to their feet, and Malvine uttered a piercing shriek of terror. Right in front of them, not more than a step from the terrace, they saw Willy in the midst of a whirl of foam which he had churned up round him with his desperate, struggling little limbs. His arms were tossing wildly above the water, but the head with its floating golden curls dipped under from time to time, and the little distorted mouth opened for an agonized breath and scream, only to be stopped by the inrushing water. The boat rocking violently close by explained with sufficient clearness how the accident had happened. The boy had clambered on to the edge of the boat to rock himself, had overbalanced and fallen into the water, and in his struggles had already drifted some paces from the shore. Fido stood barking and gasping on the step and dipping his paws into the water only to draw them out again.

Malvine stretched out her arms to the child, but her feet refused their office, she stood rooted to the spot, unable to do anything but utter terrible inarticulate screams. Only a few seconds elapsed—just long enough to realize what had happened—when Wilhelm sprang with lightning rapidity on to his chair, and from thence, with one bound, over the parapet into the water. He disappeared below the surface, but rose again at once just beside the child, who clung to him with all his remaining strength. How he managed it he did not know, but, although he could not swim, he managed to push the boy in front of him toward the terrace, crying anxiously, "Catch hold of him! Catch hold of him!" Life returned to Malvine's limbs, she leaned over the parapet and stretched out her arms. Wilhelm made a supreme effort and lifted the boy so far out of the water that she could grasp him, put her arms round him, and drag him up, and with him apparently Wilhelm, for his head and shoulders rose for a moment above the water. With a jerk she dragged the fainting boy over the parapet and held him in her arms, while she continued to scream for help. People came running from the shore the Carlstrasse, the Fahrhaus, and in an instant the terrace was crowded. They relieved the still half-demented mother of the dripping child to carry him across to the house. She was pushing her way through the closely packed groups and tottering after them when a cry reached her. "There is another one in the water!" Only then did she remember Wilhelm. Terrified to death, she turned and flew back to the edge of the terrace. A crowd stood there gesticulating wildly, all talking at once, and obstructing the view. A gap opened when two or three men with more presence of mind than the rest rushed down to the landing, jumped into the boat, untied it, and pushed off from the shore. And now, to her unspeakable horror, she saw that Wilhelm had disappeared, and the thick muddy waters gave no clew to the spot where he had gone down. This was too much, and she altogether lost consciousness. When she came to herself she was lying on the sofa in her husband's smoking room, her dress in disorder, and the maids busy about her. She first looked round her startled, then her memory returned with a flash, and she cried with quivering lips: "How is Willy—and Dr. Eynhardt?"

"Master Willy has quite come round, and they are putting him to bed," the servants hastened to answer.

"But Dr. Eynhardt?"

To that they had no reply.

Malvine jumped up and would have rushed out.

"Gnadige Frau!" cried the girls, horrified, "you can't go out like that!"

They held her back; Malvine struggled to free herself, but at that moment there was a sound of heavy footsteps and a confused murmur of voices in the hall, some one flung open the door, the man-servant put in his head, but started back at sight of his mistress and closed the door abruptly. Then he went on, and the footsteps and murmuring voices followed him.

"They are bringing him in!" shrieked Malvine, and they could hold her back no longer. A moment later and she knew that she was right. On the billiard-table, in the room to the right of the hall, lay Wilhelm's motionless form, while the people who had carried him in stood round. Water flowed from his clothes and made little pools on the green cloth and trickled into the leather pockets of the billiard-table. His breast did not move, and death stared from the glazed, half-open eyes.

A doctor was soon on the spot, the curious were turned out of the house, and they began the work of resuscitation. They had labored uninterruptedly for nearly an hour when Paul burst in, crying in a choking voice: "Doctor—doctor, is he alive?" The servants had told him all in flying haste outside.

The doctor shook his head. "There is nothing more to be done."

But Paul would not believe it. He would not suffer them to cease their efforts. The rubbing, the movements, the artificial respiration had to be kept up for another full hour. But death held his prey fast, and would not let them force it out of his clutches.

Two days later, on a gray rainy day, they buried him. Schrotter came over from Berlin for the funeral. He looked quite broken down, and grief had aged his leonine features to an appalling extent. Malvine and Willy were lying ill in bed, so that Paul and Schrotter followed their friend alone to his last resting-place. When the coffin was carried out and lifted into the hearse, and Paul came out of his house, he saw through the veil of tears that obscured his vision that several hundred men were standing in orderly array on the opposite side of the Carlstrasse. They were young for the most part, but there was a sprinkling of older men among them; all were poorly, but cleanly and decently dressed, and every man had a red everlasting in his buttonhole. They stood as motionless as a troop under arms, and apparently followed the orders of a gray-bearded man who paced authoritatively up and down the silent line.

Paul was surprised, and asked the undertaker, who was waiting for him beside the hearse, who these people were. He had not invited anybody, and did not expect there would be a crowd of any kind, although the Hamburg papers had devoted whole columns to the accident.

The undertaker went over and addressed himself to the man who was evidently the leader of the party. He informed Paul on his return: "They are workingmen's societies from Hamburg and Altona. Their leader says the deceased was not one of them, but they wanted to show him this last mark of respect because he had been kind to them during his lifetime."

CHAPTER XIV.

UDEN HORIZO.

On the first of May of the following year, which happened to fall on a Sunday, a long procession of carriages drove along the road from Harburg to Friesenmoor. They stopped at the entrance to the estate. Before them rose a triumphal arch composed of branches of fir garlanded with flowers, and adorned with flags and ribbons, and a gold inscription on a blue ground, which ran as follows:

**"A gracious Sovereign's due Reward
To fruitful Labour, honest Work."**

A "Verein" with its banner was posted beside the arch. There was a roar of cannon, the banner waved, the Verein gave three "Hochs!" and its chief, or spokesman, stepped up to the first carriage, in which sat a youngish gentleman with spectacles, and an officer in the gorgeous uniform of a Landwehr dragoon, his breast covered with stars and crosses. The spectacled gentleman was the Landrath of the circuit, and the cavalry officer was no other than Paul Haber, now Herr Paul von Haber. For he had been raised to the nobility, and celebrated his auspicious event to-day in the midst of his retainers and a host of invited guests, whom he had fetched in a dozen carriages from the station at Harburg, supported by his distinguished young pupils.

The spokesman of the Verein, a man of some fifty years of age, with a grizzled beard, addressed the proprietor in a glowing speech, in which, among other things, he assured him—the man of thirty-seven—that "We all look upon you as our father, and honor and love you as if we were your children." Paul smiled, and returned thanks in a few warm words, then renewed "Hochs!" more waving of banners and firing of cannon, and the procession set itself in motion again.

At the entrance to Kaiser Wilhelm's Dorf there ensued a second and more elaborate welcome. Here too there was a triumphal arch and cannons, and instead of one there were three Vereins with flags and banners, also the schoolchildren, headed by the pastor and the schoolmaster, and the whole female portion of the community lining the roadway on either side, or massed round the base of the arch. The pastor made a speech, a fair-haired schoolgirl recited a long piece of poetry composed by the master in the sweat of his brow, the Choral Verein sang, the Young Men's Verein—who were given to instrumental music—piped and blew a chorale, and not till the all-prevading joy and enthusiasm had found sufficient vent in the firing of cannon, in speeches, poetry, and music, did the carriages move on, and finally reach the steps of Friesenmoor House, where the guests were received by Frau von Haber, assisted by Frau Brohl and Frau Marker. At the moment of leaving the carriages three flags were run up the flagstaff on the tower—the black, white, and red flag of the empire, then the white and black Prussian one, and finally a green, white, and red banner with a large coat-of-arms in the center. This third flag, somewhat enigmatical to the guests, was the new family banner of the House of von Haber, with the coat-of-arms of that noble race, now displayed for the first time to the admiring gaze of the beholders.

The designing of a coat-of-arms had been no light task to Paul. From the moment—now five months ago—that he knew his promotion to the nobility was a settled affair, he had devoted the best part of his thoughts to this weighty question. He hesitated long between medieval simplicity and modern symbolism. An illustrative crest that should be a play upon his name was out of the question; for of course it was only another of Mayboom, the farce-writer's, jokes—he had taken him into his confidence on one of his visits to Berlin—to suggest a sack of oats, gules on a field, vert. After devising a dozen crests, each of which he thought charming, only to reject it a day or two afterward as inappropriate, he finally fixed on the one which now adorned his proud banner. It displayed on a field, vert, three waving transverse bars argent, and in a free quarter-purpure-dexter a medal of the Franco-Prussian War in natural colors. The waving bars were in allusion to the drainage canals on his marsh estate, and the medal to his career in the war. He did not forget that he owed the realization of his life's scheme to his wife's marriage-portion, and wished to show his appreciation of the fact in a delicate manner by crossing the transverse bars with a marshmallow in natural colors. However, he abandoned this design when they pointed out to him at the Herald's office that the crest would be rather overladen thereby, and at the same time would betray too plainly the "newly-baked" aristocrat. Paul left nothing undone. He provided himself with a motto. The incorrigible Maybloom recommended, "The Moor has done his duty." Paul decided on "Meinem Konige treu"—True to my king. Somebody at the Herald's office suggested putting it "Minem Kunege treu," but he had not the courage.

But though his promotion had occupied him almost exclusively during the last few months, necessitating frequent journeys to Berlin, he did not cease to think of poor Wilhelm. For a whole year he, as well as Malvine and Willy, wore deep mourning for the friend who had sacrificed himself for them, and Paul erected a magnificent monument over him in the St. Georg Cemetery in Hamburg, on which neither marble nor gilt nor verses were spared. The monument is one of the sights of the churchyard, and pointed out to visitors with great pride by the sexton. Old Frau Brohl, too, kept green the memory of the departed friend. Her speciality now was the manufacturing of flags and banners since Paul had founded quite a number of Vereins among the settlers on his estate—latterly a Military Verein, and one for Conservative electors. She was hard at work from morning till night on these objects of art, which she constructed out of heavy silk, and covered so thickly with symbolical devices, and embroidered mottoes and inscriptions, that they were as stiff as boards, and would neither flutter nor roll up. But when Wilhelm's funeral monument was to be dedicated, she put aside Paul's banner and coat-of-arms, upon which she was engaged, and wove a wreath of wire and black and white and lilac beads, a yard and a half in diameter, on which, between laurel leaves, were Wilhelm's name and the date of his death, and the words: "Eternal gratitude." Nothing the least like it had ever been seen in Hamburg before, and it was much admired on the occasion of the ceremony.

Paul showed himself throughout as a man of feeling and character. When his patent of nobility was signed, and he came to Berlin to be admitted to the emperor, to thank him for the honor accorded to him, he went to Schrotter, and begged him, as a personal favor, to accept his invitation to the festivity which should take place on his estate on the first of May. "I look upon you as Wilhelm's substitute here on earth," he said, "and our friend must not be absent from my side on this joyful occasion. I owe everything to him. He laid the foundation of my prosperity, and preserved my heir to me, for whom alone I am working and striving. If Wilhelm were with us now, he would not refuse my request, and with that thought before you, Herr Doctor, you will not pain me by refusing." The words came from Paul's heart, and showed that he felt keenly the desire to do homage, in his way, to Wilhelm's memory. Schrotter could not but accept.

To all outward appearances he had recovered from the terrible shock of his friend's death, in reality, however, he was all the less likely to have got over his loss, owing to the circumstance that he was often busied with the management of Wilhelm's affairs, and thus the wound was inevitably kept open.

Wilhelm left no will. After much inquiry, it was discovered that he had a very distant relative living at Lowenhagen, near Konigsberg, married to a poor village smith, and lavishly endowed with children. The house in the Kochstrasse went to her—a very windfall, for which the honest wife and mother was too thankful to be able to simulate grief at the death of the relative she had never known. She generously handed over all Wilhelm's papers to Schrotter, after having assured herself by inquiries in various quarters that they would only fetch the value of their weight. Schrotter gave them to the young man whom he and Wilhelm had supported in his studies out of the Dorfling legacy. The recipient was clever and shrewd, and justified the confidences his patrons had placed in his future. He found that the first volume of the "History of Human Ignorance," testing of the early ideas of mankind and their psychological reasons, was completely ready for the press; and all the notes and literary sources for the two following volumes only needed putting together to bring the work up to the end of the eighteenth century, and the experiments of Lavoisier, from which the indestructibility of matter was deduced.

The first volume appeared in the autumn. On the title page he gave his own name as the author, but did not omit, as a man of honor, to mention in the preface that in compiling the work he had availed himself of "the preparatory notes of the late Dr. Wilhelm Eynhardt, an eminent scholar, lost all too early to the scientific word by a tragic death." In the ensuing editions which followed rapidly upon the first, the book meeting with great success, this preface was omitted as unnecessary. The second volume appeared in the following year; the third—very prudently—not till two years later. There were no more. In the two last volumes there was no more mention of Eynhardt. After the publication of the first volume, the young man whose name adorned the title-page received a call to a public school, of which he now forms one of the chief ornaments. To various inquiries with regard to a concluding volume which should treat of the nineteenth century, he replied by pointing out the doubtful wisdom of a history or criticism of hypotheses and opinions which were as yet incomplete and still under discussion, and put them off with vague promises for the future. Schrotter only shrugged his shoulders. He knew Wilhelm's views on the subject of posthumous fame, and the immortality of the individual, and considered it inexpedient to punish the clever young professor for being a man like the rest.

About three months after Wilhelm's death Schrotter received one more letter from Auguste. He observed curtly and dryly that Monsieur le Docteur evidently did not wish to have anything more to do with him; he wrote, however, once more, and for the last time, in order to give him his new address in case he might desire to answer. He had been obliged to look for another place, the game was up at the Boulevard Pereire. In spite of all their watchfulness, madame had managed to obtain morphine, and one night in July, when the sister who shared her room was asleep, she had given herself so many "pricks" that they had been unable to bring her round again. Anne declared that it was on the anniversary of the day on which Madame la Comtesse had made the acquaintance of monsieur. At the breaking up of the household, Monsieur le Docteur's things had been handed over to him, Auguste, and he held them at monsieur's disposal. Schrotter wrote in answer that he might keep them, and sent him a small sum of money as a bequest from Wilhelm.

Pilar's suicide made somewhat of an impression on him. So there were women, after all, who could die of love, and that not in the first moments of a mad and passionate grief, but after months, when the nerves have had time to cool down. "She was hysterical," Schrotter said to himself, endeavoring thereby to dispel various uncomfortable suggestions. He did not wholly succeed.

As Paul begged him so earnestly to come to his festival, he accepted the invitation, and found himself, on the first of May, among the guests whom Malvine received on the steps of Friesenmoor House.

In the great oak-paneled dining room, with its windows looking to the west, a banquet was laid for twenty-four guests. Following the country custom, they sat down to table at twelve o'clock. Malvine, handsomely dressed and richly adorned, sat enthroned in the middle of the long side of the table, and had Chamberlain von Swerte (of the House of Hellebrand) and the Landrath, to right and left of her. Paul, who sat opposite, insisted against all the rules of etiquette on having Schrotter beside him as his left-hand neighbor. On his right, Frau Brohl, in rustling silk, sat in rapt silence. The ever-modest Frau Marker was content to take a lower place.

The pastor said grace before the dinner began, which seemed to surprise the Landrath, but the Chamberlain was much edified. The Young Men's Verein played dance-music and marches in front of the open windows. Paul proposed the health of the emperor, whereupon the Landrath, in a carefully worded speech, drank to the host and the ladies. They all clinked glasses with an enthusiasm which was in no way feigned, but perfectly accountable after so splendid a dinner and such well-assorted wines. In the midst of the gayety and noise, and while the clarionets and trumpets blared away outside, Paul turned to his neighbor, and tapping the foot of his glass against the edge of Schrotter's, he whispered to him, unheard by the others: "To HIS memory!" He turned his head away abruptly, bent over his glass, and was busily engaged in furtively passing his table-napkin across his face and eyes. Schrotter put his lips to his glass and closed his eyes. One could positively trace upon his broad brow how a thought passed over it like a shadow.

The dinner lasted fully two hours, and brought Malvine in many a fiery compliment, especially from the chamberlain, which she could accept with a good conscience, knowing well how much she would have to pay to the great Hamburg pastry-cook who had provided it. At dessert the heir was handed round. Willy, who was really beginning to grow a little, was unquestionably a well-bred child. He went with much dignity and propriety from guest to guest, closely followed by Fido, who had grown far too stout, offered his cheek politely to each one, shook hands prettily, and was permitted to withdraw, accompanied by his short-winded dog, after they had all sufficiently admired him.

After dinner the guests amused themselves according to their several tastes. Some went to enjoy Paul's excellent cigars in the smoking room, others went down to the village to look on at the rural festival arranged by the master for his people, and where, between singing, music, dancing, and drinking, the fun ran high; others again took a walk through the fields of the estate where the young crops were just coming up, spreading a green haze over the yellow coating of sand. It was altogether a radiant picture of joy and prosperity; and the happiest of all, whether of the guests flushed with the good dinner or the villagers stamping on the green, seemed to be the master of the house. He was rich, respected, full of health and spirits, his family life unclouded; he had a high position, possessed numberless decorations, was a captain of the Landwehr, had been promoted to the cavalry, and now was even raised to the nobility. What more could he desire?

Well then, if he seemed happy appearances were deceptive. A worm gnawed at his heart. He had hoped to be created Freiherr—baron—and here he was a simple "Herr von." How rarely is happiness perfect here below.

Pleading important business next morning in Berlin, Schrotter left soon after four o'clock. He would not hear of Paul's deserting his guests to accompany him to the station, as he was most anxious to do, but drove alone to Harburg, and took the train that left at five o'clock, bringing him to Berlin by way of Uelzen.

It was nearly two in the morning when he reached home. He stole on tiptoe into his room, but Bhani, whose sleep was light and restless when he was not there, heard him directly. She stretched out her arms to him with a low exclamation of joy, pressed him to her bosom while he kissed her on the brow, and was for jumping up and attending to his wants. He would not suffer it, and declared that he wanted nothing. So she remained where she was, only following him with her eyes while he unpacked his bag and put everything in order. He then went into his study adjoining and locked the door behind him. Bhani heard him walking up and down for awhile, and then caught the sound of a creaking as of a drawer being opened. She knew what that meant and heaved a deep sigh. He was taking out the great leather book with metal-bound corners; his diary, which had become his sole confidant now that Wilhelm was dead. Guided by the delicate tact of the Oriental, the poor simple creature divined easily enough that her sahib had cares which she could not understand and sorrows which she might not share, and yet how happy she would be if he would but deign to enlighten her ignorance, to explain it all to her and disclose his heart to her fully. But, proud and reserved, he scorned to acknowledge his troubles to any but himself, and it was only in his diary that he unburdened himself of all that weighed upon his heart and mind.

And now he sat at his study table and wrote in the big book.

"My poor Eynhardt! Only a year since he departed, and already it is as if he had never been. What remains of him? A book that bears a stranger's name upon the title-page; a little dog that is perhaps happier now than when it belonged to him; a child like a dozen others, who will presumably grow up to be a man like a dozen other men; and a memory in my heart which will cease with the day, not far hence, when this heart shall cease to beat. Now if Haber were to die to-day, a flourishing tract of land and a hundred people whose existence he has improved would testify aloud that his term on earth had not been in vain.

"And for all that, Eynhardt was a rare and noble character, and Haber the personification of all that is commonplace and work-a-day. Eynhardt's gaze was on the stars, Haber's eyes fixed on the ground at his feet. Wilhelm plucked that supremest fruit of the Tree of Knowledge, the consciousness of our ignorance; Paul has the conceit to think himself a discoverer, to have solved enigmas. But the noble, soaring spirit leaves no trace behind, and the dull, mediocre person plows his name in deep and enduring characters in the soil of his native land. What was wanting in Eynhardt to make him not only a harmonious but a useful being? Obviously only the will. But was this want an organic one? I do not think so, for his lofty moral beauty was perfect in proportion and balance, and this noble nature could not possibly have been born incomplete, impossible that in a being so perfectly formed in all other respects such an important organ as the will should be missing. His absence of volition was but the result of his perception of the vanity of all earthly ambitions, and his absence of desire the outcome of his contempt for all that was worthless and transitory, his aversion to the ways of the world a tragic foregoing of the hope of ever getting behind it, and reaching the eternal root and significance of the thing itself.

"Why was this German Buddhist not endowed with Haber's cheerful activity? What an ideal and crowning flower of manhood would he not have been if he had not only thought but acted! But am I not desiring the impossible? Does not the one nature preclude the other? I fear so. In order to attack unconcernedly that which lies nearest to us, we must be unable to see beyond, like the bull charging at the red cloak. He would not do it, if behind the red rag, he saw the man with the sword, and behind the man with the sword the thousand spectators who will not leave the arena till the sharp steel has pierced his heart. He who sees or divines behind the nearest objects their distant causes, paralyzed by the vision of the endless chain of cause and effect, loses the courage to act. And inversely, to retain that courage, to strive with pleasure and zeal after earthly things, one must make use of the world and its ordinances, must move the pieces on the chess-board of life with patience, and, according to its puerile rules, attach importance to much that is narrow and paltry, and that is what, in his superior wisdom, the sage will not stoop to do.

"I always come back to this thought. If the world consisted entirely of Habers the earth would flourish and blossom, there would be abundance of food and money, but our life would be like that of the beasts of the field that graze and are happy when they chew the cud. If, on the other hand, there were only Eynhardts, our existence would be passed in wandering delightfully, our souls full of perfect peace, through the gardens of the Academos in company with Plato; but the world would starve and die out with this wise and lofty-minded race; unless, indeed, the sun took pity on them, and brought forth grains and fruits without their assistance, and unless a few flighty little women, particularly inaccessible to the higher philosophy, should surprise these transcendental and passionless thinkers in an unguarded moment, and beguile them into committing some slight act of folly.

"To combine in one intelligence Haber's circumscribed vision, naive self confidence, and enterprising activity with Enyhardt's sublime idealism and knowledge of good and evil is outside the range of possibility. And which of the two is of the greater benefit to the world? Which of them raises mankind to a higher level of development? Which of them best fulfills his purpose as a human being? Whose point of view of the world and of life is the more correct? Which of the two would I set up as a model before the child whom Eynhardt snatched from death at the price of his own body, and in whom his life as it were finds its continuation? My old friend Pyrrhon, thou who hearkened, two thousand two hundred years before my day, to the profound wisdom of the Brahmins, I can but answer in thy words, 'Uden horizo,'—I do not decide."

THE END.

CPSIA information can be obtained
at www.ICGtesting.com
Printed in the USA
LVHW100314101222
734929LV00004B/223